Luck of the Draw

A Chance of A Lifetime

Kate Clayborn

LYRICAL PRESS
Kensington Publishing Corp.
www.kensingtonbooks.com

First Electronic Edition: April 2018
eISBN-13: 978-1-5161-0512-0
eISBN-10: 1-5161-0512-5

First Print Edition: April 2018
ISBN-13: 978-1-5161-0513-7
ISBN-10: 1-5161-0513-3

Printed in the United States of America

Buying a lotto ticket with her two best friends didn't change Zoe's life. Only following her heart would do that . . .

Sure, winning the lottery allows Zoe Ferris to quit her job as a cutthroat corporate attorney, but no amount of cash will clear her conscience about the way her firm treated the O'Leary family in a wrongful death case. So she sets out to make things right, only to find gruff, grieving Aiden O'Leary doesn't need—or want—her apology. He does, however, need something else from her. Something Zoe is more than willing to give, if only to ease the pain in her heart, a sorrow she sees mirrored in his eyes . . .

Aiden doesn't know what possesses him to ask his family's enemy to be his fake fiancée. But he needs a bride if he hopes to be the winning bid on the campground he wants to purchase as part of his beloved brother's legacy. Skilled in the art of deception, the cool beauty certainly fits the bill. Only Aiden didn't expect all the humor and heart Zoe brings to their partnership—or the desire that runs deep between them. Now he's struggling with his own dark truth—that he's falling for the very woman he vowed never to forgive.

Visit us at www.kensingtonbooks.com

Books by Kate Clayborn

A Chance of A Lifetime
Beginner's Luck
Luck of the Draw

Published by Kensington Publishing Corporation

Prologue

Zoe

Like most of my dumb ideas, this one came from the internet.

Okay, the internet and insomnia.

Fine. The internet, insomnia, and wine.

I'd been lonely that night, stuck inside in deference to the miserable end-of-August heat and humidity, almost every day culminating in rolling thunder, heat lightning, flashes of pouring rain that did nothing to cool the air. My two best friends, Kit and Greer, were both unavailable for my proposed let's-get-drunk-and-do-a-puzzle night—Kit was with her boyfriend Ben, newly reunited and too cute by half, and Greer had just left for a week-long Hawthorne family vacation. And I was still unwilling, over eight months since I'd quit in a blaze of jackpot-winning glory, to call up any of my friends from my former firm. Or maybe I was realizing, finally, that they hadn't really been friends at all.

Lonely, a little drunk, and only a laptop for company? Truly, it was a recipe for disaster—or I guess for watching pornography—but instead I'd decided to try, once again, to get something going with my long-promised lottery-win project. *An adventure,* I'd told my friends on that night we'd bought the ticket, staking my claim for what I'd do with the cash. I'd imagined an around-the-world trip, something to take me away from everything familiar, something that would be different enough that I'd come out a whole new Zoe—more perspective, more peace, more *something.* But every time I'd tried to make a decision, every time I said to myself, *Today, you plan your trip*, I'd been paralyzed.

"I don't know what's wrong with me," I'd said to Greer one night as we'd strolled through the travel section of the bookstore, a place—along with the gym, the park nearest my house, and my friend Betty's restaurant—where I'd spent an embarrassing number of hours since leaving my job. "You're in school. Kit's bought the house. You're doing it, doing what you said you'd do, and I'm—stuck." Utterly and completely *stuck*.

"It's a big change," Greer had said. "Your whole life was your work. It takes time to recalibrate, right?" She'd paused, narrowed her eyes at the shelf in front of her. "'Recalibrate'? I think I've been having dreams about Kit's microscope. Let's just buy a bunch of these books and see if we get any ideas."

But the books hadn't helped. Greer's gentle encouragement hadn't helped. Kit and Betty sticking labels to the dartboard at the bar with various place-names on it hadn't helped, especially because I have superb aim. I was in a rut. I'd only ever felt like this once before in my life, and back then I'd dealt with it by doing something so insane and reckless that I knew I had to tread carefully this time, not fuck up my life—or someone else's—again.

Maybe I'd been approaching it wrong, I told myself as I opened my laptop, smooshing myself into the corner of the couch, a lame, furniture-assisted cuddle that was the best I could get in my single state. Maybe I needed to stop thinking about a schedule, a set-in-stone path for this trip, and think about—inspiration. Pictures of places I wanted to see. Travel *vibes*, not travel *plans*.

So I'd navigated to some feel-good lifestyle site, the kind that shows you a bunch of food you should be cooking and crafts you should be doing to make your life fuller and happier and also more suitable for display on your Instagram. Never mind that my cooking is rudimentary and my last craft project was a noodle-jewelry box I made in third grade; never mind that I don't even have an Instagram. Something about the *possibility* of such a lifestyle soothed me that night, and so there I was, clicking through a bunch of filter-heavy photos of artisanal kale and handwoven hammocks and fingerless-glove-clad hands wrapped around huge, latte-filled mugs, clever heart shapes foaming on top, forgetting, once again, all about my longed-for travel vibes.

Looking back, I wonder if I'd not only been drunk, but also perhaps stunned into some kind of nectarous, curated-lifestyle coma, because why in God's name would I, Zoe No-Time-for-Bullshit Ferris, click on a picture of a "gratitude jar"? But there it was: a rustic-looking Ball jar, weathered pastel slips of paper with rough-hewn edges folded and tucked inside, and, so far as I could tell, several strands of completely unserviceable pieces of jute twine wound around the outside. Each day, the idea was, you record a good memory on a small slip of paper, fold it up, and put it in the jar. Then, when you're feeling low, you extract one of those little shabby-chic scraps of joy from your jam jar and get on with feeling grateful about what life has handed to you.

Well. I certainly had well over a million reasons to be grateful, didn't I? So why didn't I feel any joy? Why couldn't I just *get on*? *Maybe,* drunk-lonely Zoe had thought, *I need the* jar.

Of course, I didn't have a jar, or twine, or antique-looking paper. I had a Baccarat Tornado vase and a stack of Smythson stationery. And somewhere between me cutting my cardstock into squares (not rough-hewn; are you kidding, I wasn't that drunk) and actually putting pen to paper, the real idea—the *dumb* idea—had hit me.

What I need is a guilt jar.

It seemed so clear. It was the guilt that was keeping me from doing the trip, or from doing anything, really, since I'd taken home my share of the winnings. It was the guilt that was always there, ever since I was nineteen years old, piling on year after year, but now that I wasn't working seventy hours a week, now that I wasn't scheduling my free time down to the second, now that I'd been the beneficiary of the kind of luck I knew I didn't deserve, I actually had time to really wallow in it. Sure, the wine wasn't helping, but that night, I was brutally honest with myself: *You've done wrong. And you need to fix it to move on.*

After that, it'd been easy. On those little scraps of cardstock, I'd recorded my failures, starting with the comparatively minute. *The time I made Dan cry at work. When I snapped at the Starbucks barista for not knowing my regular order. When I parked in one of those* For New Moms Only *spots at the grocery because I had menstrual cramps and it felt close enough. Forgetting my assistant's birthday (2x). Avoiding eye contact with the homeless man who always sits outside Betty's, even when I give him money.* On and on, until it'd gotten trickier, until I'd had to get to the truly painful, did-you-even-drink-that-wine sobering ones. The ones I confined to names: first, names from the cases I was having such trouble forgetting. Then, names I wouldn't ever forget:

Dad.

Mom.

Christopher.

At first I wasn't exactly sure how the guilt jar would work. The gratitude jar was for contemplation's sake, but the problem with my guilt was that I contemplated it pretty much every fucking night of my life, and so if I was going to get any joy out of this thing, I was going to have to do something other than simply *look* at my recordings. I was going to have to fix what I'd broken, or at least I was going to have to try.

Thanks to the lottery, I had means.

Thanks to my unemployment, I had time.

And that jar, it was going to give me the *will*.

Chapter 1

Zoe

I choose a Wednesday morning to draw my first guilt slip.

That's far enough away from the night I came up with the idea to give me perspective, but not so far that I seem like I'm avoiding it. I try not to be weird about it, but the slip-drawing does take on this ritualistic quality, even though I'm wearing monkey pajamas and an antiaging face mask. The worst thing about leaving my job since the lottery win has been what's happened to my days—or, I guess, what's *not* happened to them. Before, when I was working, my days were so regimented that they were almost comical; once I asked my assistant to set a timer every time I went to pee to see how many minutes my bladder was costing me (too many minutes, so I cut back on coffee). Now I spend a lot of time drifting around, wondering what to make of my time, wondering whether I'll ever go back to some kind of work, wondering how I managed to become the kind of person who isn't working at all, who hasn't worked in well over half a year.

But the guilt jar, much as it contains my most painful flaws, is giving me a sense of purpose I haven't felt in a while, and so I put it in the center of my dining room table and take a seat, setting my mug of tea in front of me. There's a familiarity to this setup, sort of like the Sunday mornings I'd get up early and work on briefs before meeting Kit and Greer, and I try to let that familiarity blanket the contrasting feeling of unease. The steam rising out of my mug isn't helping, though—the vase is starting to take on magic cauldron-like qualities. Maybe one of those slips is going to fly out and hit me in the face.

I take a deep breath, cut the bullshit, and reach in.

And...well. Not that a lottery winner is going to get a lot of sympathy here, but rotten luck that I couldn't have drawn the Starbucks barista first. Instead, I've drawn a name—or, rather, two names: *Robert and Kathleen O'Leary.*

Damn.

I saw a lot of unhappy people in conference room four, but I don't think I'll ever forget Robert and Kathleen O'Leary. Their settlement mediation was the last I'd sat in on, and I like to believe that even if I hadn't won the jackpot that night, it still would've been my last day at Willis-Hanawalt. That I would have said to myself, *Enough is enough*, and never gone back again. They'd been gray haired and slight, Mrs. O'Leary barely over five feet, her husband only a couple of inches taller—though between the two of them, he'd been the more diminished, the more fragile. Mrs. O'Leary's eyes had been puffy and red, but focused; she tracked the conversation with a sad, knowing acuity—well aware her lawyer was outmatched, well aware that whatever money she walked away with, she'd never get what she really wanted.

An admission of guilt.

But Mr. O'Leary—he'd barely been more than a bodily presence. At one point, I'd wondered if he'd had a stroke, or some other kind of catastrophic medical event that kept him from moving or speaking. I still don't know if he had. But I do know that he cried: silent tears that tracked down his cheeks and dripped off his jawline onto the conference table.

"What a performance," my boss had muttered, when the O'Learys had finally gone.

I swallow thickly, rubbing the slip of paper between my fingers. It's so uncomfortable thinking about those days when we were doing the settlements, thinking about how clear I'd been that something was off, thinking about how many opportunities I'd had to say something. And yet I think about those days a lot, too much, when—as my guilt jar is reminding me—I should be *doing* something.

And so I do: I grab my laptop, spend a few minutes getting the information I need. I take off the mask, I shower, I dress carefully. When I walk out to my car, I'm doing so with purpose. When I drive, I keep the radio off, so I can focus, so I can keep that little slip of paper in my mind.

The O'Leary house is a small, brick rambler, tidy at first glance, but there are signs of neglect—the two clay pots on the front porch are full of leafless, tangled twigs, the bushes that line the bed underneath the shutters are shaggy, a few aggressive limbs of growth reaching up past the windows.

The left side of the iron railing leading up to the front porch is listing to the side, two newspapers still in their bags beneath it.

I think, briefly and nonsensically, about whether I'll pick up those papers when I knock on the door, whether I'll have to start by saying, *Oh, I just picked up these papers that were here*, and it's this stray, silly thought that finally gives me pause, pause that I should have had about ten thousand times before I got here: if they aren't picking up their papers, maybe they aren't around, or maybe they don't open the door for anyone; maybe they don't want to be bothered.

They *wouldn't* want to be bothered, not by me of all people. Even if they don't remember me, I'll have to explain in order to apologize. I'll either be poking at a festering wound or reopening one that can only be, even under the best of circumstances, barely healed. I grip my steering wheel, so hard that it hurts my fingers, in plain, simple frustration at myself. The real me—the smart, sharp, ambitious me, the me who proofreads everything six times, reading both forward and backward, the me who practiced presentations until notes were a distraction rather than an aid—that me would've thought of this. Instead, I've come over here thinking only of my own guilt, my stupid internet jar, and my stupid, lazy sense of purposelessness driving me.

If I really mean to make up to people, I have to do better than ambush apologies that they may not even want to hear.

My hand is back on the key, ready to turn, ready to back out and go home where I can rethink this.

But then the front door opens.

It's not Mr. or Mrs. O'Leary there, that's for damn sure, because this is about six feet two of muscled, fully alert dude, his thick, dark brown hair messy, his square jaw stubbled.

And he definitely does not look happy to see me, though I suppose he'd have that in common with the O'Learys.

It's still possible to turn the key, wave an apology like I've found myself at the wrong house or something. But there's something that stops me—something about the way this man stands so still, watching me, and something about that heavy fatigue I feel, all the time, pulling at my shoulders. Maybe this man knows something about the O'Learys. Maybe he can help me get some of this fucking *weight* off.

So I take my keys from the ignition, *inhale, exhale*—even doing the noisy puff of breath that my yoga teacher is always suggesting—and get out of the car. My heel wobbles a bit on the cracked pavement, and I steady myself on the top of the car door before shutting it behind me, smoothing the front of my dress, which is another terrible choice I made this morning. It's a gray herringbone, sleek and tailored, a jewel neckline, and sharply cut cap sleeves. It's a dress I'd wear to work, a dress that makes me look as cool and detached as I probably did on that day. It appalls me how little I thought this through, what a massive, selfish mistake I made this morning. I think of making a new slip, later: *Bothered a man at his home, because of my narcissism.*

"Hello," I manage, surprised that my voice sounds very much like it always does when I meet new people, which is to say: it sounds detached and professional, when I came here to be anything but that. When I came here to show them that I do, in fact, have a heart.

A heart that is beating so fast that I suspect this man can see it pulsing in my neck.

"What can I do for you?" he asks, and however harmless the question is, however polite seeming, it is clear he does not mean it to seem so. His voice is gruff, clipped. He stands, feet slightly apart, arms crossed over his chest, like he's here working security.

"I was looking for Robert and Kathleen O'Leary," I begin. "But I believe I've—"

Before I can finish that, before I can say, *I believe I've made a mistake,* he cuts me off. "They moved."

It's him that's made the mistake now, because I've lain awake so many nights wondering about what has happened to the O'Learys, to other families I ran mediation for, that I am now desperate to know more. Did they take the money, buy a home somewhere beautiful, somewhere away from the place that must remind them of terrible grief? Do they live a better life? Have they been able to move on, at all? That little shred of information—*they moved*—makes me curious enough to keep pressing.

"Do you happen to know where they went?"

"I do." It seems like—I don't know what. It seems like he has made himself bigger somehow. He is looking at me like I am something unpleasant he stepped in.

"I guess I'll have to be more specific with my questions," I say, annoyed now. My concern is for the O'Learys, and this man is becoming an unnecessary roadblock.

"Guess so," he grinds out, but then he shifts slightly, his hands tightening around where they are crossed, at the join of his elbows. And then he says, "I know who you are. And believe me, they would not want you to find them."

I swallow, once, then again, suddenly feeling hot and sick. I should've had something to eat before I came, something light that would settle my nervous stomach. My eyes lower automatically, an old habit that I'd fully eradicated in my adult life, when I made my living off being completely unflappable. I am torn between wanting to ask how he knows who I am and wanting to turn back and get in my car, to pretend this morning never happened.

"I'm their son," he says, and my eyes snap up, taking him in with renewed interest. My first thought is automatic, innocuous: *How can this—this giant—be the son of the short, ruddy-skinned couple from conference room four?* My second is more painful: *their* surviving *son.*

"I apologize for bothering you," I say.

"You didn't," he says, firmly. The sentiment is so clear: I am not worth him being bothered.

I offer a small nod, turn my back to return to my car, to put this entire mistake behind me. *A guilt jar.* What a fucking joke. What a perfect encapsulation of the worthless person I've become. I feel so strangely unwell; it's hot out here, the still-muggy heat of a southern September.

When I have my shaking hand on the car door, he speaks again. "If you have business with them, you need to take it up with me. I don't want you trying to contact them. They've been through enough."

And haven't you? He was your brother, after all, I think, surprising myself.

I turn back to face him, my spine straightening, even though I am desperate to fold myself back into the safety of my car. "I came to apologize. That's it. I can see it was..." I have to pause, take a deep breath in response to his forbidding expression. "I can see that was a mistake."

"Can't imagine your firm would like that."

"I don't work for them anymore," I answer, as though this might magically change his opinion of me.

"I know. I heard you came into some money."

If it was possible for me to feel sicker, I didn't know until now. Kit, Greer, and I had all agreed on privacy when our numbers came up. The state required a public disclosure of identification, but the jackpot had been comparatively small, the most interesting part of the win being the grainy security video of the three of us buying the ticket, which I'd buried as best I could with some threatening legalese. Greer and I had helped shield Kit—who'd had bigger reasons for keeping it quiet—by doing the small, state-lottery-required press conference, which didn't even make the news, and other than a brief clipping in the local paper, which had identified us by first initial and last name only, we'd flown under the radar. He would've had to go looking.

"Listen, I came to apologize to your family," I say, the effort to keep my voice steady almost Herculean. "That apology extends to you. I can see you're not interested, and I'm sorry for that too. I'll leave you alone. I would appreciate the same courtesy." It's a warning. If this guy has been sniffing around my private life, he'll find out there are limits to my guilty conscience. I don't deserve to be stalked, for God's sake.

He makes a derisive noise, a half snarl. "Believe me, I don't care to know anything more about you than I have to. Your former secretary told me. Without prompting."

Ugh, Janet. Probably because I forgot her birthday (*2x*, per my guilt jar). And made her time my bathroom breaks. Still, my brow furrows in curiosity, wondering what dealings he's had with my former firm. He'd certainly never been involved with the Aaron O'Leary settlement before. But I stifle this curiosity; it seems my sense of what's appropriate has picked this moment to return. Would that it had a better sense of timing.

"Well," I say. "Again. I am sorry for bothering you."

"Are you on some kind of apology tour?"

Good God, this man cuts like a knife, doesn't he? Or am I really that transparent?

"Something like that," I manage.

"For your next stop, I'd say show up in something other than a Mercedes."

I am torn, at this moment, between two instincts. The first is to fight back against this man's ire, to cut him down to size, to push back against his scorn. That Mercedes is four years old, after all, bought not with lottery winnings but with my own salary, the salary I earned for billing the most hours in the entire firm in my first year on the job.

But the second? The second is to stand there and take it. To invite more of it, in fact, because—because in some sick, dark corner of me, it feels good to have his scorn. It feels like I earned it as much as I earned that Mercedes. Maybe more, because, after all, I question every single billable hour I worked for Willis-Hanawalt. It wouldn't feel easy. But it would feel like what I deserve.

There's a long pause while I stand, frozen, caught between these two instincts, while he stares right through me, pinning me to the car with that gaze. In another context, I would find this man so sexy as to make me weak in the knees. But right now, I'm just…weirdly, uncomfortably weak in the knees, fuzzy headed and still overly warm. I have a distant memory, suddenly, of the senior partner at Willis-Hanawalt coaching me the first time I went before a judge. "Whatever you do, don't stand there with your knees locked," she'd said. "You'll faint dead away from the nerves."

I think I set a hand to my forehead. I think I hear this man say, "Are you all right?"; I think he moves closer to me.

But then, everything goes gray around the edges.

And then, it all goes blissfully, forgivingly dark.

* * * *

When I come to, my first sight is of lace curtains, yellowed but beautiful, delicate and fluttering before an open window. I jerk up, instinctively, and hear the man's voice, lower now, no trace of anger. "You're all right," he says.

I'm inside the rambler, sitting in a dusty rose velveteen chair that is both hideously ugly and incredibly comfortable. "Oh God," I mumble. "Was I out for long?"

"Maybe two minutes." He's kneeling in front of me, a black duffel next to him. "My name is Aiden. I'm a paramedic. Do you know where you are?" I stare down at him, bewildered at this new information. *Aiden. Paramedic. Probably carried me in here.* But I realize I need to answer, if I don't want things to get more awkward.

"Ah—I'm assuming I'm in your house?"

He nods, sets his hand gently on my wrist. "Good. Do you know what day it is?"

I tell him, respond to his question about the year, the approximate time. He looks so different now, his face placid, his body curled into a protective posture at my feet, though he only touches me in that one spot, one warm hand on my wrist, two fingers touching the soft inside of it. *Taking my pulse,* I realize, but he presses on with his questions.

"Do you know how you got here?"

I can't help but smirk. "Well. It started with this jar," I say, but my mouth flattens when he looks up at me, quick and concerned. "No—no, I mean, sorry. That was a joke. I got here because I was making an inadequate, ill-considered apology in your driveway. And I guess I fainted."

"All right. Is it okay with you if I check you over a bit?"

"I think I'm fine," I say, scooting forward a bit in the chair. "I didn't eat today, and I—I think I was a bit nervous."

If he weren't sitting so close, I don't think I'd catch the slight crinkle of tension in the corners of his eyes, maybe something like remorse. But that's ridiculous; it's not him who has to feel remorseful. "I'm sure you're fine," he says, and *God.* I bet he is really good at his job—calm and careful, no sense of panicked urgency. "But I really do need to check you over."

I offer a weak nod, and he quietly sets to work. First, he takes my blood pressure, reads it off to me, tells me it looks good. When he removes a stethoscope from the bag, I stiffen, thinking there'll be a moment where he has to try to get into my dress somehow, but he seems to know. "Just going to listen over your clothes, all right?" he says, and I nod again. I watch him from beneath my lashes as he does it, his eyes lowered, his face serious. After a minute, he tips his chin down, says, "Sounds good." Then he takes out a small, flat, egg-shaped device, a digital screen on the front. "I'm going to prick your finger. A little pinch. It's going to tell me what your blood sugar is."

I don't like needles, of any kind, and it probably shows, because where he's taken my hand, he squeezes gently and says, "Look only at me." That would probably work in normal circumstances, because he's so good looking, and so calm, so *good* at this. But this isn't normal; ten minutes ago he looked like he'd buy tickets to my public humiliation.

It's a little pinch, like he says, but he frowns down at the screen. "Fifty. Tell me when you ate last?"

"Last night, at dinner. Around seven p.m."

"Can you remember what you had?"

"Um—a small salad. A piece of chocolate for dessert."

"You don't eat breakfast?" His voice has changed now, not quite hostile, but not quite the soothing, softened offerings of before.

"I do eat breakfast. Usually. But—it's like I said. I was a little nervous. I drank a cup of tea. I should've had something. I realize that."

He stands, turns his back toward me, and walks down the hall, to where I can see glimpses of a kitchen—a line of oak cabinets, an almond-colored refrigerator. I can hear him moving around in there, and while he does, I scan the room, which is similar in aesthetic to this pink chair, and those lace curtains—feminine, old fashioned, and very, very lived in. I wonder whether Aiden actually lives here, or if he's only staying here. If Mr. and Mrs. O'Leary have moved, maybe he's checking in on the place, or—

He comes back in, a glass in one hand and a small glass bowl in the other. He crouches back in front of me, hands me the water. "Are you sick to your stomach?"

I shake my head. "No, I think maybe I was, but because of the heat out there. I feel okay now."

"Have a few sips of this, but go slow." While I drink, he pulls a plastic honey bear bottle from his back pocket, squeezes a bit into the glass bowl, and then takes a small spoon from his other pocket.

"Those aren't part of your regular supplies, I take it?" I ask, between sips of the cool water. Already I feel better, physically. It's only the incredibly awkward emotions I need to be treated for now.

"No," he says. "Got this from the kitchen. I'd like you to take a spoonful or two of this honey. I know it's sweet, but it'll help the immediate issue with your blood sugar."

"I really am okay." I set my hands on the armrest, readying myself to leave.

His voice is forceful, gruff again when he replies. "This is bare minimum what you're going to do for me before you go. Or I'll call the squad."

I take the honey.

He backs away from me for this, leans against the jamb of the open front door, arms crossed again, and watches me closely. The honey makes my teeth ache, and I have to set a hand over my mouth so I can discreetly lick at my lower lip, sticky with it. But within seconds I feel oddly restored, not quite normal but almost so. "I think I'll go," I say, standing slowly, expecting a head rush that doesn't come. "Obviously I am very grateful for your help. And very sorry to have inconvenienced you more."

"It'll be more of an inconvenience if you walk out of here and faint again, and then I get sued for not ensuring you got standard of care."

I know, of course, what he means—Willis-Hanawalt does medical malpractice too, and a paramedic could get sued for negligence. He's made contact with me, a patient, and I did not deny treatment, and technically, he should have to turn over care to a person of equal or higher qualification. But I want out of here so bad that my mind is ahead of these rules. I spot a phone on the coffee table and gesture to it. "Is this yours?"

He nods, and I pick it up, walking it over to him and holding it out. "Turn on your video camera." When he makes no move to take it, I swipe a finger across the screen, see the menu of apps. "You should have a password on this," I mumble, opening the camera and flipping the screen so it points at me. I back up, extending my arm so my face fills it, happy enough that I at least seem to have color in my cheeks. I use my thumb to press Record.

"I, Zoe Ferris, assert that I fainted outside the property at 631 Old Crescent Road in Barden, Virginia. I was treated at the scene by paramedic Aiden O'Leary. I was informed of my condition. I understand that there are possible medical consequences for not seeking additional medical treatment. At this time I am refusing further medical advice and/or transport to a medical facility by the aforementioned paramedic." I hit the Record button again, stopping the video, then open the file and make sure the time and date were saved before handing it back to him. "Okay?" I say.

Something has shifted in the way he looks at me, something speculative and interested. Less like I'm a pile of dog shit, and more like I'm some odd, nonthreatening species of insect he's never seen before. "Why did you really come?" he asks.

I take a deep breath, look out the door to where my car sits in the driveway. "I'm sure you have no reason to believe me. But I had intended to leave my job even before I—well. Before I came into the money you mentioned. That doesn't excuse how long I stayed. It doesn't excuse anything, really. Your family went through something terrible."

He lowers his head at this, adjusts his booted feet on the carpeted floors. "My parents moved to Florida. I still don't want you to contact them. But that's where they are."

"Are they happy there?"

He looks up at me, and I'm on the bottom of his shoe again. I hear everything he's thinking in that look. Of course they're not fucking happy. Their son is dead.

"I'm sorry," I say again, uselessly. "I realize there is nothing I can say. Nothing I can do." I look at him one last time, offer a brief, placating downward tip of my chin before setting my fingers on the screen's door handle.

"There is nothing you can say." Blunt and honest. I almost admire him for making sure he sticks it to me, in the end. For not making it easy on me. "But there may be something you can do."

My hand stills and my head bows, almost like I'm waiting for a benediction. I *want* him to tell me what to do, and I am not—maybe strangely, maybe naively—afraid at all. Aiden is angry, but he's not cruel, or at least this what I tell myself. All the possibility of that damn vase feels like it's in this room with us, and I think maybe, *maybe* it wasn't such a terrible idea after all.

"Marry me," he says, and it's a wonder I don't faint all over again.

Chapter 2

Aiden

In my thirty-one years of life, I have said and done a lot of stupid shit, but not one single thing so stupid as saying the words *Marry me* to Zoe Ferris.

I don't mean it, of course, but I don't rush to clarify, mostly because it takes me a few seconds to get my mouth and brain reconnected. Long seconds where Zoe stays still, where I watch her profile and make sure that she's steady and that she still has good color in her face. This is the first time I notice that she is beautiful. When I saw her first, in a small, professionally taken headshot on her former firm's website, I did not think beyond what my intention had been: to imagine what my parents had seen that day when Aaron's life was weighed and measured, counted out in dollars. When I saw her again, standing in my driveway, I did not think beyond getting her off my property. And when I saw her close up, having caught her right before she hit the pavement, I did not think beyond treating her.

But now. Now I notice that she's beautiful, her blond hair straight and cut blunt past her shoulders, her eyelashes long and dark, her top lip almost as fully plump as her bottom.

When she turns to face me, I clear my throat and speak again. "Not a real marriage. Obviously."

"Whatever *that* is," she says, an unsubtle thread of sarcasm in her voice. "Explain."

If I hadn't seen it myself, I wouldn't believe that this woman had, minutes ago, turned the whitest shade of pale and crumpled in my front yard. Her cheeks are pink and her posture is ramrod straight; her voice is sharp, crystal clear, every word she says articulated fully.

But I *did* see it myself, and at least my ridiculous proposal has provided me an opportunity for some professional peace of mind. "It's a long story," I say. "How about you come on in and sit down, and I'll tell you."

She cocks her head at me, amber eyes flashing with recognition. "I released you from all your obligations to me. I told you; I feel absolutely fine."

"You also asked if there was anything you could do for me, and I told you there was. Was that just you blowing smoke up my ass?" Jesus, my attitude. My mother would bean me—hard—if she heard me talk to a guest like this, even if that guest is a sworn enemy of our family.

"No," she says, and takes her hand from the door handle.

Success. I guide her back inside, snag her water from the coffee table, and walk her through to the kitchen, pulling out a chair for her at the small table in the corner. When she sits, it's prim and proper control: back straight against the chair, legs crossed, hands folded in her lap.

"I'll make you a sandwich," I say, setting the water down in front of her.

"I don't want a sandwich."

"It'll be peanut butter and jelly," I say, ignoring her and pulling down a loaf of bread from off the top of the fridge.

"I said I don't want one."

"Are you allergic to peanut butter, jelly, or bread?"

"No."

"Okay. Then I'm going to make you this damn sandwich." It's like I can feel my mother's anger and embarrassment all the way from Florida. "You can eat it or not, but it'll make me feel better to make it. All right?"

There's a beat of silence, and I wonder what expression she must be leveling at my back right now. "All right." I think there may be a thread of amusement in there, something slightly lighter than what I've heard in her voice up to now.

I pull the peanut butter and jelly from the fridge, grab a knife from the drawer. Now that she's in here—now that I actually have to say out loud the insane idea that had popped into my head when she'd been preparing to walk out, I don't know where to begin. *You haven't said anything yet, dumbass,* I think. *You can still take this back.* But something—some*one,* I guess, stops me. This idea, crazy as it is, may do some good for Aaron. *For the memory of Aaron,* I correct myself.

"The money my family got from the settlement," I begin, keeping my back turned to her while I spread the peanut butter, thin on each slice of bread, then jelly in between. "I've been left in charge of that."

"Has something happened to your parents?" From behind me, her voice is higher, concerned.

"Other than them not wanting to deal with a payoff for my brother's life? No." She says nothing to this—fair enough—and I slice her sandwich in half, set it on a plate, and turn back to her. "This is a good sandwich," I say, ridiculously. It has three fucking ingredients, and I'm acting like there's something to sell.

I think her lips might purse in suppressed amusement. "I'll try it. Do you have a napkin?"

A napkin? For Christ's sake, this woman. It's peanut butter and jelly, not lobster. I tear off a paper towel from the roll beside the sink and hand it to her. When she smooths it across her lap, I have to press the heels of my hands in my eyes, just to process the insanity of this entire situation.

"Anyways," I say, leaning back against the counter and crossing my arms, "I'm in charge of the money. I'm looking to buy a large piece of land with it, a campground in Stanton Valley, about two hours from here."

She takes a bite of the sandwich, small and precise, then lifts the paper towel to the corner of her mouth. I have a weird hope that some of the jelly blobs onto her chin, or dress, or something. Something so she doesn't look so *perfect* sitting there. "Continue," she says, once she's swallowed.

"The current owners are..." I have to pause, to think about how to phrase this to get her on board. "They're—a very traditional couple about certain things."

"Fair Housing Act applies. They can't choose a buyer based on religious beliefs."

"I didn't say it was religious beliefs," I say, curt, frustrated more at myself than at her. The truth is, Paul and Lorraine are religious, had always incorporated a bit of their faith into the running of the camp. But it wasn't what the camp was *about.* "They—they're hoping to see the camp continue with similar traditions. They want a family-owned operation. They haven't fully committed to a sale yet, but they know there are a few people like me who are interested. People who know the camp well."

"This was a camp you went to?"

I nod. To say I *went* there feels like an understatement. I lived a good portion of my childhood summers there. Almost all my best memories of Aaron, of me and Aaron together, are at that camp. I swallow down an inconvenient wave of fresh grief.

She makes a small hum of assent. "Is this jelly homemade?" she asks, taking another bite.

"Yes," I say, involuntarily glad on my mother's behalf that she's noticed. And that she's eaten an entire half. Her color looks even better. "The Dillards have invited some of the interested parties to spend six weekends in Stanton Valley, starting next week. To see what people imagine for the future of the camp. To..." I pause, recalling Lorraine's exact words. "To feel that they are making the choice God wants, if they decide to sell."

She makes an unladylike snort, a sound that, weirdly, sends a shot of heat through me. When the tip of her tongue snakes out for a fraction of a second to catch a crumb in the corner of her mouth, I have to lower my eyes to stop my thoughts from going where they're going. "And you think you have a better shot at this if you're married?"

"I'm the only person going who doesn't have a family."

I can see from her thoughtful expression that she knows this would matter, my outlier status.

"What do you want to do with the campground?"

I think of the small bedroom at the back of the house, the one I've turned into my office. The drawer of files I've kept, meticulously. The whiteboard I hung on the wall to keep track of my ideas. The bookmark folders on my browser, each full with websites related to different aspects of my plan. It is months, hours upon hours of work, work I do in between my shifts, work that is challenging and sometimes goddamn painful too.

I don't want to tell her any of this.

"That doesn't have to be your business," I say, and at this, I see something true in Zoe Ferris, something beneath the placid demeanor she's worn like a piece of clothing since she got out of that car. I see a fire in her—an eyebrow arch, sharp and eviscerating, a tightening at the corners of her mouth, tiny parentheses enclosing everything she's not saying. If I could set a hand on her, I think, I'd feel that all her muscles have gone tight.

But it's gone in a flash. She's collected herself, distant again. "I'm assuming they're not stupid?"

I cock my head at her, a wordless inquisition.

"Because if you know these people, even casually, they'll wonder why you're showing up with a wife they've never heard of. Better if I'm a fiancée. It might be helpful, actually. Lots of—I don't know. Promise for the future, or something." She calmly takes another bite of the sandwich, then sets it down on the plate and wipes her mouth again, folding the paper towel and setting it on the table before clasping her hands again and looking back up at me. Everything she does is careful and exact. I am standing, looking down at her, using her guilt to get something I want. But somehow nothing about this interaction suggests I'm in control.

"That makes sense," I say.

"It doesn't bother you that you'll be lying? Lying to good people?"

Yeah. Yeah, it *does* bother me. But this idea—it has so much potential, so much opportunity to do good, to make that money feel less like it's coated in my brother's blood. And I have to believe that Lorraine and Paul will see this, once they get to know the idea. I just need a way *in*. "Did it ever bother you?" I ask, and watch her face transform, mask-like and frozen. I expect her to say that she never lied. That she did her job within the law, that her particular role had nothing to do with whatever deceptions the makers of Opryxa had perpetrated.

"It did," she says, simply. She's looked right at me to say it, and there's something about it—that fire in her eyes set against that flat tone in her voice—that thuds right into my chest, makes me vibrate, for a split second, with a curiosity I haven't felt about anything in months and months.

I look down at my feet, break the connection, clear my throat. "I want in the door. I want an opportunity to show them what I can do with the camp. Once they hear me—once they agree to sell to me—we move on from this. We have an amicable breakup, whatever. It doesn't have to be dramatic."

"You're that confident in your idea?"

"I am." This is maybe half-true. I'm confident as hell in the idea. I'm less confident in my personal abilities to pull it off.

"Why me?" she asks.

What I want to say is, *I have no fucking idea.* I want to say that this morning has gone in an entirely unexpected direction and that I'm sure I will spend the rest of the day kicking my own ass over it. But now that we've come this far, now that we've actually talked about it, I can *see* her there. Not, obviously, in the dress and heels. But I can see—despite the fainting, which really does seem like a one-off—how she'd be composed and unflappable in such odd circumstances. Hell, I can see how she'd be better at it than I'll be.

She's waiting for my answer. She's hardly moved in that chair, not even a fidget or toss of her hair. "Because you're here, and because you said you'd do anything to make up for what happened. And because you seem like you'd do well at deception."

Somewhere inside, I feel the answering pang at saying this—I said it for no other reason than to hurt her. It's small, petty, cruel. I want to believe that's not who I am, but who am I except for the shit that I say and do? I'm surprised, all over again, by how angry I still am and how much I still let it show. If she says no now, I don't have anyone to blame but myself.

She stands from her chair. This close, the short length of the kitchen separating us, I notice how tall she is. In her heels, she's only a few inches shorter than me, and the way she holds herself—she owns every bit of that height. I think she's about to give me the dressing-down of my life, even worse than whatever my mother would say to me about the way I've acted.

But instead she says, "Fine. I'll do it." I open my mouth to respond, to give her details, but she holds up a hand and stops me. "You need to know that when I leave here, I'm going to call the investigator from my former firm and have him run a background check on you. If that's a problem, tell me now, and we don't do this."

"It's not a problem," I tell her, honestly. She's thinking of shit I should've thought of, if I hadn't come up with this idea in literally a half second.

"I'll leave you with my cell phone, address and my email, but I'd prefer we correspond by email for the time being. You can send me details about the camp, including where exactly it is located, and what exact time we'll be leaving and returning. You'll need to give me your contact information too, because I'll be sharing that with—with people who know me."

"Fine."

"And you can tell me—you can write to me about who you want me to be for this."

"Who I want—"

She speaks over me, again, not acknowledging the way I struggle to keep up with her. "Obviously you know this family, and I don't. If you feel that there are characteristics I should have in their presence, you can tell me about that, and I'll do my best. I would say, in general, that while I've traveled a lot, I'm not much of a camping person, so you may want to bear that in mind. I probably can be charming enough as a fish out of water."

"Jesus Christ," I say. "Have you done this before?"

She gives me another one of those looks, one of the ones that could slice me right in half, and says nothing. I turn and open a drawer, pull out a notepad and pen, and extend it to her. I look away when she bends over the table to write; somehow I know it would be colossally stupid for me to see that view. I listen while the pen scratches across the page, and I have a strange thought: I've seen her handwriting before. I know she writes the *Z* of her name so that it looks like a number three. I've seen her signature on countless documents, all related to my brother's death.

But then it's done—she leaves the notepad and pen on the table and turns to look at me, and for a minute we're quiet, probably the shock of what we've agreed to. It's no conference room. But I have the sense, somehow, that like my parents before me, I've just finalized a contract with Zoe Ferris.

* * * *

"It's fucking insane, is what it is!" Ahmed shouts this from across the table, his mouth half-full of a turkey and cheddar sub, the only order he ever places at Dicky's, our usual takeout run when we've got long enough for breaks. It's Thursday night, and we're in the kitchenette of the squad's living quarters, shoving food in our faces as fast as it will go, knowing that we'll probably start getting calls any minute—the college crowd tends to get rowdy on Thursday nights—and I have just made my second major mistake of the week, telling Ahmed about Zoe Ferris.

"Quiet, man," I say back, jerking a thumb over my shoulder toward the next room, where two cots, a worn-out sofa, and a tube TV on stacked milk crates are set up. "Charlie's sleeping."

"I don't fucking care! Charlie!" he shouts, spraying a few breadcrumbs in his haste. "Get in here and hear what this bag of hammers has done."

I reach a fist out and punch him hard in the shoulder, but he barely flinches. I'm a big guy, but Ahmed is massive, a relic he's kept from the two years he played semipro as a linebacker.

Charlie—the third member of our crew, the driver—stumbles in, tying her hair back into a ponytail while glaring daggers at Ahmed. "This better be good, asshole. I was having a dream about Lucy Liu."

"Got you a sub, Charlie," I say, nodding toward the fridge, and she squeezes my shoulder in appreciation on her way to get it.

"Like a sex dream?" Ahmed says, forgetting about me and my personal crisis for a moment.

Charlie rolls her eyes my way, commiserating. I joined this crew six months ago, right after I'd moved back home—only a few weeks before my parents decamped to Florida, and that was on purpose too, another way for me to hide from the worst of their grief and another way for me to hide my own. I'd been with my last crew in Colorado for almost five years, and we'd had the kind of shorthand forged only through time and the stress of constant emergencies. I'd expected to come here, do a job, keep as much of my focus as possible on my side project with the camp, and entirely avoid emotional interactions of any kind, since all my insides still, over a year after Aaron's death, felt like shards of glass. But Charlie and Ahmed are hard to ignore, big personalities who seem wholly unconcerned with whatever sharp replies or brushoffs I've handed out, and already we've worked out a preliminary shorthand of our own, Charlie and me the straight-faced, secretly amused maturity to Ahmed's mostly-sixteen-year-old sensibilities.

"No," Charlie says, settling into her chair and unwrapping her sub. "We were solving crimes together."

Ahmed stares. "Is that a metaphor?"

"Oh my God. No. What did you wake me up for?"

At this, Ahmed gets his feet back. "Aiden's asked some woman to be his fake fiancée for this camp thing."

The fact that Ahmed refers to the biggest project of my adult life as *this camp thing* is further evidence of the limits to our bond. If it'd been possible, I wouldn't have told Charlie or Ahmed about Stanton Valley, but since I'm relying on their help with coverage for the next month and a half, they had to know something, and for now I've settled for telling them about the real estate, not my plans for it. Charlie hadn't been keen to let that lie, either—she grew up on a farm not far from Stanton Valley, knows land out there doesn't come cheap—and so I'd also fessed up to the bare minimum about the money: my brother had died, and my family had received wrongful death and survival damages from the pharmaceutical company responsible.

That had been awkward enough to keep them from asking much more. Until, of course, I'd mentioned Zoe.

Charlie swallows, sets down her sub. "This does sound dumb," she says, grudgingly, and Ahmed smiles in satisfaction.

"It's not how it sounds," I say, my neck hot. But of course, it is exactly how it sounds, and they don't even know the half of it. I tell Charlie about the Dillards, tell her about the disadvantage I'm at, up against three other families.

"Man, Aid. When you go all in..."

"It's important," I say.

"How'd you meet this woman?"

"She's a friend of the family," I say, an appalling, offensive lie. One morning and maybe she's rubbed off on me; maybe by the end of this thing I'll be as deceitful as she is.

"It's not the worst idea I've ever heard," says Charlie, and Ahmed groans, slapping a hand to his forehead.

"Aww, Charlie. Don't encourage this."

She picks up her sub again, takes a bite, and chews. Charlie's a thinker, a problem solver, and dear God I wish Ahmed hadn't called her in here. I wish I hadn't mentioned any damn thing about Zoe. "What's she like?"

Confusing, I want to say. *Weak enough to faint in one moment, strong enough to stand up to me the next. Scary enough for me to want her to leave, intriguing enough for me to ask her to stay. Cold, hot.*

"Convenient," I say. "Available. Willing."

Ahmed snorts, and Charlie narrows her eyes. "You're going to have to do better than that if you want to convince anyone of this thing. You've got a look on your face like indigestion's coming on."

"Maybe the sub," I say.

"I'm serious," she says. "You want people to think you're engaged to her, you're probably going to have to break your three-words-or-less-per-sentence rule and actually *talk*."

"I'll work it out."

"That was four words," says Ahmed.

"If she's a friend of your family, you've got to know something more about her. What about your parents, are they close to her?"

Fuck, fuck, fuck. "Not really," I say, and Ahmed holds up two fingers.

The truth is, I'd only really thought of how this thing would work in terms of my parents *after* Zoe had driven off. They know about the camp, know about how I'll be spending time out there, making my case to the Dillards. But there's no way I can tell them this, and so I'm going to be a liar twice over, at least. I tell myself it won't matter; they've pretty much cocooned themselves down there in Florida, my dad not really fit for keeping in touch with friends back home, and my mom preoccupied with him and with the ten thousand hobbies she's buried herself in to get over Aaron. I doubt they'd ever find out, but just to be safe, I'll think of something. I'll tell them it'll make it easier for me to stay on message, present a coherent package to Paul and Lorraine, if they stay well out of it.

"Do you see what I mean, Charlie?" Ahmed says, balling up his wrapper and tossing it into the trash. "He can't pull something like this off."

I keep my head down and concentrate on finishing off my food, feeling both of them stare at me, waiting for me to protest. But I'm not going to. They're both right—it isn't the worst idea, nor is it something I'm likely to pull off.

When I stand from my seat, clearing my trash and theirs, I catch Charlie nudging Ahmed's elbow. No doubt they're doing their own silent commiseration now—I'm the odd one out, again, as it should be. As much as Charlie and Ahmed rag on each other, there's genuine affection there, the kind where they know details about each other's families and occasionally hang out outside of work, and that's the kind of shit I am still, and probably forever, avoiding. It's clear that I'm rattled by what happened with Zoe, or else I never would've opened my fucking mouth in the first place, a thoughtless response to Ahmed's endless questions about the camp, about whether I was ready for next weekend.

"I'm going to check the rig," I say, not looking back at them as I head into the bay. There's nothing to check, not really—when we came on duty we did all our procedures—but I need some space. I climb into the back of the ambulance, pull the eTablet down from its tray, and open up inventory lists—the kind of mindless task that seems good for me right now. I'm counting syringes, pads of gauze, bags of saline, whatever, losing myself in the work. But I'm not as lost as I want to be, not so distracted that I'm not still thinking of her, and everything that's brought her into my life. *Your family went through something terrible,* she'd said, and I'd felt a new wave of frustration at that. As one of the lawyers who'd worked on behalf of Opryxa, she knows it all, the whole terrible story: my brother, an opioid addict since he was twenty, not long after he got prescribed prescription painkillers after a minor car crash. My brother, in and out of rehab since he was twenty-three, long, expensive stays that had bankrupted my parents twice, had prevented me from ever getting to more than a thousand bucks in savings. My brother, prescribed another drug, one that would help him kick the habit.

A drug that killed him at the age of twenty-nine.

I'd read every single correspondence from Willis-Hanawalt. I knew what they'd argued about my brother. I knew the carefully phrased liabilities they'd acknowledged when proposing settlements. I knew the ugly digging they'd done about his past, the way they'd made it seem like Aaron was likely to die anyway, was always an unlikely candidate for success in pharmaceutical treatment of addiction. I knew now how hard they'd worked to settle individual cases, to prevent class action suits. To bury the extent of Opryxa's risk factors. I knew that my parents had agreed, once they took the settlement, to release them of all liability.

I'd seen her name on all that correspondence, and it gives her a strange, uncomfortable power over me, all she knows about my family. I don't know whether she's made the worst, most painful connection between Aaron and me, and I don't know whether I want to know. But it's Aaron I have to keep in my mind here, Aaron who's at the front. Aaron who I'm doing all this for, and I'll do anything. It's the attitude I should've had when he was still alive, and it's the attitude that'll make it possible for me to do what I have to do with Zoe Ferris, to pretend to be in love with her.

And there it is, the alarm letting us know we've got a call in, and I can already hear Charlie and Ahmed hustling out to the bay.

I try not to take it as an omen.

Chapter 3

Zoe

At 7:00 a.m. the next Saturday morning, I'm waiting outside my building, my backpack at my feet and a bag of breakfast goodies in one hand, purchased from the same Starbucks where I dished out early-morning abuse as a snippy, work-obsessed caffeine hound. I'm still getting the side-eye from the regular morning barista, a college kid I now know is named Joseph, but ever since I showed up a few days ago, waited patiently in line, and apologized for giving everyone so much hell, it seems like a thaw is in the offing. I don't even worry that someone's spitting in my espresso as vengeance.

Now if only I could stop worrying about what I'm waiting out here for. I've dressed in what I have determined is camp-appropriate clothing, though I imagine that somewhere in my combination of hiking boots, jeans, and long-sleeved knit top, I've managed to get something wrong. No doubt the first of many things I'll screw up on this initial outing, but judging by Aiden's brief email—*Go ahead and be yourself. Let's not make this harder*—he wouldn't expect anything else.

My phone pings with a text from Greer, sent to both Kit and me, part of a long strand of a group text we keep constantly going to check in with each other. *Are you nervous?* she asks. I think about sending a bunch of those emoji faces with the clenched teeth, because I *am* nervous, but good thing I don't, because Kit's reply comes before mine, all caps: *YOU SHOULD CALL THIS OFF.* When I'd finally worked up the courage to tell them about this, the Sunday after I'd gone to see Aiden, Kit had nearly exploded with shock. "You can't go out into the wilderness with some guy who basically *hates* you,*"* she'd said, her voice rising with each word. "This is a ridiculous idea! This isn't adventure, Zoe. It's self-immolation."

"Kit," I'd said, calmly, trying to keep the volume down. "You are really ratcheting up the drama."

"I think she means," Greer had said, "that we thought you might do something a little more—of your own choosing?"

"I do a lot of things of my own choosing," I'd said. "Maybe that's the problem."

I hadn't told my friends about my late-night guilt jar making, hadn't told them that my lottery-night wish for adventure wasn't really my heart's desire. But everyone knows you can't buy forgiveness. Everyone knows you have to work for it, and this thing I'm doing with Aiden? This is working for it.

All this week, I've been preparing. I got a camping wardrobe, sure, but I'd mostly been mentally preparing. Aiden may have told me to be myself, but I think the trick is I need to be a better version of myself. Friendlier. More flexible. Warm and polite. I almost tailed Greer to her classes to see how she manages it, but I figured that'd be crossing a line. The bag o' breakfast stuff is a good start, a peace offering for Aiden, but I also need to remember to smile more, to lay off the snark. Also it would be good if I stay upright this time around.

I close my eyes, thinking again of that awful attempted apology, the moment I'd fainted, and the unfamiliar, shuddery feeling I got when he looked right at me. I think of him walking to my car, after we'd settled the details, the way he'd watched every step I took, and the way he'd scanned my face before I drove off. He made me feel like I was transparent, like he could see straight through every one of my finely polished pretenses. At least this first weekend is a short one, Saturday morning to Sunday noon; after this we'll be heading to Stanton Valley on Fridays.

My phone pings again, Kit a second time. *Why aren't you answering?!* I smile down at the phone, appreciating her concern, however neurotic. *I'm fine,* I type out. *Remember, he checked out. You have all the contact numbers.* Once I'd gotten Aiden's number, and the numbers associated with the camp, I'd given them all to both Greer and Kit. And it was true that Aiden had checked out, though that was probably an understatement—my investigator turned up a squeaky clean record, but he'd also been two grades ahead of Aiden in school, and knew him and the family, had said everyone knew Aiden O'Leary as a stand-up guy, one of the best. There'd only been a few short pages to the report, showing that Aiden had been a licensed paramedic for eight years, that he had one speeding ticket, that he'd lived in Wisconsin, and then Colorado, before moving back here a little over six months ago.

I take a deep breath, send another text. *I'll be okay. Not nervous.* I add a thumbs-up emoji, which is probably suspicious; I don't think I've ever used a thumbs-up emoji, but oh well.

Right then, an older-model, dark green SUV pulls up alongside the curb. I tuck my phone into my back pocket and reach down for my bag, hearing a door slam. *Here goes,* I think, and arrange what I hope is a smile on my face when I look up at him. He is…not returning the gesture, instead wearing that same forbidding, stern expression he had before. "Why don't you let me take that," he says, gesturing to my bag, not really a question, and I've got to remind myself: *Try to get along. Six weekends will be six thousand times worse if this guy quietly hates you the whole time.*

"Sure, thanks," I say, handing it over.

Once we're both strapped in, pulling away from the curb, it becomes painfully clear that we've not managed to say any additional words to each other. Aiden is staring straight ahead, way too much focus given the fact that there are very few cars out and about, and as for me—well, I'm pressed so far against the passenger door that I sort of feel like I should offer to buy it dinner. I inhale quietly, gathering courage, and shift so that I'm less awkwardly arranged, then reach down to where I put the white paper bag.

"I brought a couple of donuts," I say, my voice sounding unnaturally loud in the quiet car. "But I didn't know if you'd like those, so I brought a muffin, too. And a bagel."

"I already ate."

Warm and polite, I think, like a mantra. "Well, maybe you'll want some later," I say. "Take it from me, right? You don't want to get woozy on the road."

No response.

I set the bag down by my feet, ridiculously disappointed. Both because I wanted that to work, and also I sort of wanted a donut. My stomach, traitorously, growls.

"You can eat," he says.

"Maybe in a bit."

I think he might—I don't know what. Grunt? This drive is going to take *forever.*

"So," I venture again, "your email mentioned that I should—you know. Be myself?" I hate the way I've done that, the way I've hitched my voice up into a question. I used to counsel first years at my firm about that—*Be declarative. It projects confidence.* I clear my throat, make another attempt.

"But it may be easier if myself—well, if myself knows yourself a little better. For the purposes of this thing we're doing."

If myself knows yourself? Less a projection of confidence than of complete idiocy.

"You had your background check done?" he asks.

"Yes, but—"

"Then you know the basics."

Well!

"But if this is going to be convincing, we should know some things that couples know. Favorite foods, TV shows, that kind of thing."

He adjusts his hand on the steering wheel, grips it a little tighter before loosening his fingers again. "I don't think we'll get around to talking about stuff like that. We'll be busy."

"Okay, but if we show up and it's this awkward—"

"Fine. You can tell me your basics. Where you're from, that kind of thing. You know more about me than I know about you."

That's a painful truth between us—I not only know what I know from the background check, but I also know too much about what has to be the worst tragedy of his life.

"I'm originally from Pasadena," I say, trying to keep my voice light. "My mother still lives there." *Stick to the basics,* I remind myself. "I went to USC for undergrad. UVA for law school, and moved here right after. I worked at Willis-Hanawalt until—well, you know. But probably you don't want to mention anything about where I worked. You can say—I guess you can just say I'm a lawyer, if it comes up."

"But you're not a lawyer now."

"I'm still a lawyer. I'm just not practicing," I say, surprisingly defensive. Aside from a little informal work I've done for Greer over the past few months, I *haven't* really thought of myself as a lawyer, not since I quit the firm. But once, being a lawyer was so much of my identity that I had hardly any room for anything else.

"What do you do all day, anyway?"

There it is again, the most incisive question he could have asked. I entirely ignore it.

"The two most important people in my life are my best friends, Kit and Greer. I met them when I first moved here and they're like my family. They both have your number. Kit's a research scientist, and Greer's recently gone back to college. I'm missing six of our weekly Sunday brunches for this," I add, uselessly. It's not because I'm trying to complain, though I realize now that's how it sounds. It's struck me, suddenly—I miss them already. They're my anchors, more so now than before the jackpot, and I feel more than a little at sea driving away from them.

"What a shame," he deadpans. "Missing *brunch*."

I fold my hands tightly in my lap, clamp my mouth shut and feel my molars grind together. I can't imagine the next two hours like this, let alone the next six weeks.

After a while, I get up the courage not to initiate conversation but at least to manage the crushing silence. "Should we put on some music?"

"Doesn't matter," he says, and just because he is being so recalcitrant, so sullen and walled off when that is entirely counterproductive to our mission, I feel a streak of belligerence. I feel the opposite of warm and friendly. I lean over and turn the knob, tune to the most irritating station I know, the one with the guffawing morning show hosts and the same ten pop songs in constant rotation.

"Oh, listen to this," I say, dramatically, when the electronic beat fills the car. "This is a song, I believe, about a young man who doesn't mind a woman with small breasts, so long as she has a larger than average posterior. What a delight! Already I feel so encouraged by this song, which is obviously a femin—"

He leans over and shuts it off.

I pause, letting the moment stretch. "Is it because you do not share a fondness for a large—"

"Zoe," he says, and I clamp my mouth shut. That is definitely the first time he has said my name. It sounds like a different name the way he says it—a gruff exhalation. "Is this you being yourself?" For a flash, nothing more than a second or two, he slides his eyes my way, then snaps them back to the road. "Because I remember you being a little more—reserved."

I shrug, reaching over to turn on the radio again, though not quite as loud this time. "I'm a woman of many contradictions, Aiden," I say, trying for levity. "Much like our friend the pop star here."

He doesn't even blink in reaction.

It's going to be a long six weeks.

* * * *

For the rest of the drive, we're mostly quiet. I offer something from the goody bag again when I finally give in and go for a donut, and Aiden takes the other. This alone feels like an Olympic-size victory, like maybe it'll crack open some reservoir of conversation, but nope. The next time Aiden speaks, it's to point out to me that we're in a small town called Coleville, only about fifteen minutes outside Stanton Valley.

"There's a drugstore and a small grocery," he says. "You need to stop for anything before we head on?"

I do kind of want to stop—Coleville looks lovely, a half-mile main street dotted with small, quaint shops, the sidewalk liberally dotted with elaborate planters full of blooming chrysanthemums and trailing ivy. It'd be a nice place to stroll around, get some small town flavor. But since my companion doesn't much seem like a stroller, I pass.

And then it's straight on to Stanton Valley, the road becoming more wooded, more narrow as we approach. When we're about two miles away, I notice the signs—old, painted wood with *Stanton Valley Campground* carved into them, arrows pointing the way. When we reach a tall, wide wooden arch, *Welcome Home* carved across the top, I brace myself, thinking we'll pull in and be there, but it's another mile of bumpy terrain, dust and gravel kicking up all around us. Aiden, if it's possible, seems even more tense than before, the kind of tense that you can *feel* radiating off a person. I sneak a look over at him, notice the clench of his jaw, the corded muscle of his forearm as he again tightens then loosens his grip on the wheel.

We pull into a dusty lot where there's only two other cars, both pickup trucks. Through the windshield, I can see a large, two-story lodge, paneled with rounded, honey-colored wood, like the whole thing has been built with perfectly halved tree trunks. There's a porch running the length of it, the railings bulky and rustic, including those that line the big stone stairway rising up to the lodge's front door.

"This is really—" I begin, ducking a little for a better look, but I'm startled by Aiden's arm reaching over to pop open the glove box in front of me. I shift, so there's more room between my knees and the panel, and he grumbles out an apology before reaching in and grabbing something he encloses in his fist, popping the door closed again with the side of it.

He clears his throat and sets his hand down on the bench seat between us. When he lifts it, there's a small box there, old, faded blue velvet.

A ring box.

Oh, no, I think, my stomach turning over. This is too much. There is not one single thing that would make me want to bolt more than this moment.

"It's not a diamond or anything," he says. "But you should have a ring for this."

"Right," I say, perfectly calm. I wipe my hands on my jeans, steadying them, before reaching one over to pick up the box. He cannot know how awful a moment like this would be for me, and he never will, so I keep my face as placid as I can as I open it.

It's a thin, yellow gold band, a plain setting for a small, ivory pearl. It's beautifully simple, nothing fussy about it. I want to ask him where he got it, why he didn't spring for some cheap CZ at the department store. This looks like an heirloom, far too personal for what we're doing here. "Thank you," is all I manage, and he waits quietly while I take it out and slide it onto my finger, an almost perfect fit. I feel as if I've been collared. Brought to heel.

His head snaps up when he hears voices, and he takes the box from my lap, his fingertips briefly touching my thigh, before shoving it under the seat between us. "You're ready?" he asks, looking out to where an older couple approaches us, waving and smiling broadly.

"Absolutely," I say, because it seems like offering the exact opposite answer from how I feel is the right way to go here. *Warm and polite,* I tell myself, again, as I get out of the car. Aiden comes around to my side, and there's a tense moment where I wonder if he's going to do something weird, like put an arm around me or try to hold my hand, but he only comes to stand by me, surely closer than he would otherwise, but definitely not in a *Hi, old friends, this is my fiancée* type way. "These are the Dillards," he says, low into my ear, so I guess he's warning me that it's *really* showtime.

"Oh, it's you! It's you!" says the woman, clasping her hands together as she approaches. She's short, compact, her dark, curly hair cropped close to her scalp, her boots and khakis and green thermal all about function. Beside her, in an almost identical outfit, is a tall, lanky man, his pale skin a contrast to hers, his eyes kind behind wire-rimmed glasses.

The woman stretches out her arms for a hug, first from Aiden, and then, surprisingly, from me. "I can't *believe* he waited so long to tell us he'd be bringing you," she says, pulling back and holding me at arm's length, smiling widely.

"Lorraine," the man says, setting a hand on her back. "Let's give her a minute to get introduced."

Beside me, Aiden shifts, maybe moves a fraction closer. "Paul, Lorraine—this is Zoe. Zoe, this is Paul and Lorraine Dillard, who—uh. Who I've told you about."

Barely, I think, but I keep my smile pasted on, reaching out a hand to Paul, and then to Lorraine, who merely gives me another hug. "Can you believe he left us a *message* saying he'd gotten engaged?"

"Oh. Um, sure. I can believe that," I say. "Sort of a—strong and silent type, this one."

She laughs, steps back to pat his arm. "You sure are right!" I like the drawl in her voice, more pronounced than what I usually hear in the city. "He's always been a little like that. Wait until I show you the pictures I have of him, from every year he came. You'll love that—"

"Did you have a cabin picked out for us?" Aiden says, interrupting her, and I stiffen with the awkwardness of it, with the taken-aback expression on Lorraine's face. He's being rude to this woman who is so obviously happy to see him, and who is one-half of the couple he needs to impress to buy his precious campground.

"Oh, goodness," I say, playfully slapping his arm, a gesture I hope I pull off. "That's my fault, Mrs. Dillard. The whole way up here all I could talk about was seeing one of these cabins! I've never been to a camp like this—I'm so excited!" That right there is more exclamations than I've ever used in polite company.

She smiles, points a finger at me. "No Mrs. Dillard stuff. I'm Lorraine to everyone who comes here, even the kids, and I'll be Lorraine to you too."

"Yes, of course," I say, happy that I seem to have defused the situation. Paul tells us we must be tired from the trip up, that most of the other guests won't be here for another hour or so, and so we might as well go on up to our cabin, settle in a bit before lunch at 12:30.

"We can catch up then, and you can account for being so out of touch, young man." Lorraine pats Aiden's arm again. She takes a lanyard from around her neck and disentangles a key, passing it to him. "Now I set you up in your old cabin, and I hope that's all right. I realize it might be a little strange for you, but you'll have lovely Zoe here to keep you company. And we've prayed on this, Aiden, Paul and me, and we think it's right for you to stay in that cabin."

I look up to catch Aiden's throat move with a tense swallow as he takes the key, offering a brief nod. "It'll be all right," he says quietly. A fiancée, I think, would know what that pained look in his eyes is. A fiancée would reach out, take his hand, or maybe lean into him in comfort.

I do neither. Next to him, I am so acutely aware of the stance I've taken, all business: back straight, shoulders square, my hands clasped loosely in front of me. *I'm blowing it,* I think, even as Lorraine turns to me, smiling widely.

"If you've never been to a camp like this one, I should warn you that the accommodations are spartan. But that's as it should be. Keeps our campers in the great outdoors as much as possible. And I think you'll find you've got everything you need, though it can take a bit to get used to at first."

Lorraine is so welcoming, such a contrast to the last two hours in the truck that I kind of want to ask her if she'll take me in, let me stay in that nice lodge with her and Paul. But Aiden and this spartan cabin are part of my penance, I guess, so I return her smile and say, "I'm sure I'll be fine. I'm pretty mentally tough."

Beside me, Aiden makes an unfamiliar noise.

I think it might've been a laugh.

* * * *

It was cool when we'd set off this morning, but as we make our way to our cabin—a not-insignificant hike through narrow, wooded trails, it heats up quick—the sun peeks through the cracks in the trees, starting to turn for the autumn season. By the time we reach a clearing, my back is damp with sweat where my pack has pressed against it, my shoulders are sore from its weight. No surprise that before last week I'd never owned a backpack of this size, and I suspect the woman at the outdoor sports store was trolling me when she sold me this one.

"Right up ahead," Aiden says as we trudge on, and a small cul-de-sac of four cabins comes into view, a wooden sign announcing them as the *Good News 1* cabins.

"Good News?" I ask, trying to make my stride look natural as I rush to keep up with him. I'm tall, but Aiden's legs eat up this ground like tractor wheels.

"Gospels. There's four cabin sites like this, each with four cabins."

"You're sure it's okay with Lorraine and Paul that we're staying together in here? With us not being married and all?"

He shrugs. "They don't tend to fuss over things that don't matter." I pause a half step, thinking of that. Things that don't matter? Maybe I was way off base and unfair, but Aiden's talk of the Dillards being "traditional"—not to mention cabins named after Gospels—had me expecting something a lot different here, something a little less…flexible? I want to ask him about that, but he's forged ahead, head down, making his way up to the second cabin on our right.

When I catch up, he's paused in front of the door, his body still. Then he turns back toward me, snags a water from the side pocket of his bag, and holds it out. "You look hot," he says, pushing the bottle at my hand. There's no kindness in the gesture; it's like I've insulted him by being too warm.

"Mr. O'Leary, how you flatter me," I snipe back, taking the bottle and twisting the cap off with a satisfying crack. He watches as I take a few sips, and I lower the bottle. "Are we going to stand here all day, or...?"

If I weren't watching him so closely, I'd miss the way his shoulders raise slightly from the deep breath he's taking in through his nose. He turns his back to me again, fumbles the key in the door, a quick flick of his wrist to open it.

As soon as I cross the threshold, I drop my pack on the floor, taking another long drink of water to keep myself from letting out the groan of relief I feel at having it off. I'd like to sit down right where I stand, start unlacing the boots that feel too new, too tight, but I'm too curious to check out the cabin and see what manner of domestic lunacy I'm supposed to endure while I'm here.

And it is, in fact, domestic lunacy. I'm standing in a long room, cheap tile floors underneath my feet, two sinks bolted to the wall on my left. Past them, two putty-colored stalls, same as you'd find in a public restroom. And past that? A pale blue, very thin curtain hanging from a square of steel rods, a utilitarian showerhead visible above.

"Nope," I say, and turn back toward the door.

I hear Aiden's derisive snort behind me. "This is that mental toughness you mentioned?"

I stop, turn back to face him. He's leaning in the doorway that leads to the part of the cabin I haven't yet seen, his arms crossed over his chest, his gaze assessing. But there's this quirk at the edge of his mouth, not a smile, but the beginnings of one. *I'd like to make him smile for real,* I think, surprising myself. It's the way he holds it back, that's the thing. It makes me want to chase a smile right onto his face.

I take a deep breath, look again at the sinks, the stalls, the shower. "Here's the deal. You leave this cabin when I have to—when I use the facilities, or shower. You can wait outside on the front stoop, and I'll knock when I'm done."

"Fine."

"Fine," I repeat back, brushing past him to see the rest of the cabin.

It's clear that everything here is designed for functionality, for summers of kids and teenagers. Commercial-grade carpet, a seen-better-days pine dresser with a drawer missing, and two sets of bunk beds, the kind of plastic mattresses I had in my college dorm room, each with a set of sheets and a thick navy blanket folded on top. There's a desk pushed underneath the cabin's one window, a compact wood chair to match, and no way is Aiden ever going to be able to sit in that thing, let alone get his legs underneath the desk. Come to think of it, he's not going to fit easily in one of the bunk beds, either, so at least I'm not the only one who doesn't quite belong here.

"Top or bottom?" he says, hefting my pack from where I dropped it and bringing it over to me.

"Uh. Bottom?" I say, pointing to the bunk that's closest to the far wall. He sets his own pack on the bottom bunk that sits a few feet away, and I don't like this, the thought of us sleeping next to each other, even with a few feet of floor between us. "Top," I correct.

"Harder to make the bed up there."

"That's okay. I've never slept in a bunk bed. Might as well get the full experience."

"Suit yourself."

For a while we unpack in silence, Aiden making up his bed first, me pulling out my few items of clothing and placing them in a single drawer. It's a strange sort of quiet, none of the faint mechanical noise I'm used to hearing in my condo—the HVAC kicking on or shutting off, the hum of my appliances, the tinny noise of the television even when it's switched off. On the drive, at least we had the noise from the car engine, and, when the music had given way to static, the sonorous tones of the NPR station Aiden had found to get us through the rest of the way. So maybe it's this particular quiet that makes me extra aware of the way he moves, sharp and forceful as he tucks the sheets, as he arranges his bag at the foot of his bed. When even those noises have faded, I turn toward him, and find him standing there beside his pack, one hand clenched around the metal bed frame, his eyes focused on the top bunk.

"I need to go out," he says suddenly, releasing the bed and heading for the entryway.

"Wait—what?"

He takes a quick look at his watch. "I'll be back in an hour so we can walk over to the lodge for lunch."

"Wait—" I repeat, more forcefully this time, but he talks right over me.

"I'll be on the west trail," he says, which means absolutely nothing to me. I have no idea why he'd even say it.

"Aiden." He pauses, turning his profile toward me. He really is handsome, carved planes for cheekbones, his nose bold—on a smaller man, it would be prominent, the first thing you'd notice. But on Aiden it's perfectly fitted. "You can't leave me here."

But he *can* leave me here. He's got no reason not to. There are no witnesses to this; there's no one here to fake it for. I'm not an idiot—based on what Lorraine said down at the lodge, and based on that hollow look in Aiden's eyes, this cabin is full of painful memories for him. If we were friends—if he were even willing to *try* to be friends, I could ask him, maybe, if he's okay. If he'd like to go for a walk. Or, hell, help me make my top bunk, which I can see now is clearly going to be complicated. At the very least that ought to give him the pleasure of mocking me further.

"One hour," he says, and then he's gone.

Chapter 4

Aiden

She's on the front stoop when I get back, her elbows propped on her knees, chin resting on her upturned hands, looking almost—amused? When I approach, hands stuffed in my pockets, she looks up at me. Her eyes are fall colors, the burnished gold of an early sugar maple turning for the season, so well suited to this place that it's startling.

"This is going *real* well so far, am I right?" she says.

"It'll get easier," I say, telling her what I've spent the last hour telling myself, walking through the woods, burning off all the frantic, angry energy that had been building up all morning, almost bursting forth after a few minutes in that cabin. Damn if I didn't see my brother everywhere in there, the way I'd wake up in the morning to half his arm, hanging down from the top bunk. The way the bones of his spine would show through his green camp t-shirt; he was always too thin. This little cough he'd get when he'd lie in bed at night, a bad ragweed allergy I never got. His insistence on flushing both toilets every time I took a shower, how he'd shake his skinny arms over his head in victory while I shouted my frustration. The time I got food poisoning from eating a bad hot dog and he sat up with me all night, helping me change my clothes twice, as gentle and quiet as he always was.

It's fucking *hard*. It's harder than I imagined.

"I'm going to guess that was about your brother."

Oh, she has a lot of fucking nerve, reading my mind like that. "We don't talk about my brother," I say, forcefully. "You need to understand that. You and me, we don't *ever* talk about my brother."

She stands, uses her hands to brush at the backside of her jeans. "If that's how you want it."

"That's how I want it."

She shrugs, then heads back down the path, like she's not bothered at all, and this is so annoying to me that I have to grind my teeth together. It's been this way since she got in my car this morning, her strange blend of sarcasm and sweet that sets me right on edge. She's got this way about her, this woman. She comes to apologize and I'm the one feeling sorry. She crosses a line and I'm the one who comes off looking like a hothead. I give her a ring and she looks like I've slapped her.

"Probably I am going to need help making that bed," she says, still walking ahead of me. "I think I pulled a muscle attempting the fitted sheet."

"Fine."

She stops on the trail. I stop too, right behind her. A strand of her hair blows back toward me, and I breathe through my mouth.

"Listen," she says, not turning to look at me. "I get it that you hate me—"

"I don't," I say, but she holds up a hand before I get it all the way out.

"But I'm nervous too. I'm doing the best I can with zero information, and I just saw a bug in that cabin big enough to lift free weights, and I'm pretty sure this lunch is going to have things that make me uncomfortable, like out-loud prayers or singing or food served from a Crock-Pot, and you are really terrible at small talk so I'm assuming I'll be doing the heavy lifting down there. So it would be great if you could—you know. Cut me some fucking *slack*."

Then she's off again, head held high, and it's a beat before I can get my feet moving again after her.

When we come to trailhead that leads us out to the lodge, I have to pause again, take a deep breath. What I know about the next six weeks is more than what Zoe knows, but it's limited too. I know there's three other potential buyers. I know we're each going to give a presentation at some point over the next six weekends, but I don't know when. Mostly I don't know how I'm going to handle being here, doing things I've done dozens of times before but without my brother by my side. I turn to look at Zoe, who's stopped to wait beside me, her eyes downcast toward her boots. They look new, stiff, the kind you've got to break in. I'll bet her feet are feeling it.

"It won't be food out of a Crock-Pot," I say. "Camp's always had better food than you'd expect. Lorraine's a good cook, and I'm guessing she'll have done the meal for a group as small as ours."

"Okay."

"Can't say for sure about the praying or the singing. And I'll kill that bug later, if it's still there."

"Thanks." It's almost funny how we both inhale at the same time—the same steeling, deep breath to get ready for this.

But neither of us laugh.

When we step onto the lodge's porch a few minutes later, I can hear the clamor inside, the excited voices of reunion. Beside me, Zoe smooths her hair, straightens her shoulders, and when I open the door for her, she—I don't know. She *arranges* her face, I guess, a slight cock of her head and a wide smile, her eyes bright and searching, as if she's genuinely excited to meet a roomful of people she'll be lying to for the next six weeks.

In-fucking-credible, I think, simultaneously disgusted and impressed.

The main floor of the lodge looks exactly the same—a large, wide-open space with long tables and benches set around the thick, dark-stained wooden posts that we all used to dream of climbing to reach the high, timbered ceilings. All the walls are painted cream, except for the one facing east, which is made up of floor-to-ceiling windows, giving a full view of the lodge's heavily treed backyard. During predawn breakfasts, you'd see the best, most kaleidoscopic sunrises of your life through those trees. Upstairs, in Lorraine and Paul's apartment, it's the same wall of windows, like living in a treehouse. I'd like a few minutes to take it in, to adjust to the wave of nostalgia and pain that had hit me in the cabin too, but there's nowhere for me to run here. It's only seconds before we're enveloped into the group, a flurry of introductions.

I know two of the three families here, or at least I know one member of each, former campers who had been here around the same time as me. There's Hammond Dwyer, who's now married to a former Redskins cheerleader named Val; they have three little girls who look like they walked out of a Gap ad. Hammond's all right, I guess, but he did hang Aaron's stuffed monkey from his bunk one time, so I don't have 100 percent positive feelings. Sheree Talbot—Sheree Hamilton now that she's married—was a camper three years behind me and Aaron; she's a school principal and her husband Tom is a minister who works with low-income kids in the city, and their little boy is wearing a bow tie. Then there's the new-to-me competitors, Walt and Rachel Coburg; they own a farm nearby and have left their five kids home with grandparents, and the only thing I can think is whether all the kids have the same carrot-colored hair as the parents.

It's a lot, meeting and re-meeting all these people, the kids running around, me trying to stay close to Zoe so I can keep one ear on whatever she says, making sure we don't have any mishaps with our stories. But it's too chaotic for much real conversation, or maybe it's that Zoe seems to know how to direct the chaos where she wants it to go—*Oh, I love your top,* she says to Val. *What part of the city do you do most of your work in?* she asks Tom. *I'm obsessed with baby goats; there's a whole YouTube channel!* she exclaims to Rachel, when conversation turns to animals on the Coburg farm. By the time we sit down for the meal Lorraine and Paul and a few camp staffers are bringing in, I realize with a start that I've barely said anything at all. I'm dead weight, a dark contrast to this light, open friendliness she's put on, unlike anything I saw from her on that first day.

I clear my throat, shift slightly on the bench—but I don't get any more comfortable because I've brushed my leg against Zoe's and she jerks, instinctively, away from me.

I think Lorraine notices.

"Let's join hands and give thanks for our meal," Paul says, and Zoe's eyes slide toward mine, a trace of a smile there. *Out-loud prayers.* It's barely a second, but it's a second where we've got something between the two of us, a shared secret no one in this room knows. Of course, Lorraine doesn't notice *that*—she's got her head bowed and has joined hands with Paul on one side, Sheree on the other. When Zoe's hand fits into mine, her skin cool and soft, I don't even notice who's on my other side. I don't notice what Paul says.

I only try to make this look natural.

* * * *

"What we don't want is a competitive environment," Lorraine says. We've finished lunch and have moved to the campground's outdoor classroom, a set of rough-hewn benches set in a circle and an inexpertly carved tree stump serving as a podium. The weather is perfect—warm and sunny, a clear blue sky above and the scent of turning leaves in the air—but it's not putting me in a better mood. I botched that lunch, could barely string a sentence together the whole time. Zoe floated the conversation, keeping the focus on everyone else with questions and deflections. My only contribution had been to make one of the Dwyer girls cry because of my—as she had put it—"mean face." That had gotten a big laugh.

Up at the podium, Lorraine and Paul are giving us a rundown of the weekends ahead, the presentations they want us to do, the time they hope we'll all spend together.

"This camp has been our life's work," Lorraine says, "and when we think about leaving it behind, of course what matters most to us is that it stay in our family. And you, of course—our campers—you are our family, and we hope over the next six weeks you'll treat each other like family."

"*Awww*," says Val, sticky sweet, while one of her kids—the one who didn't like my face—pokes the other two with a twig. Hammond isn't paying attention, and I'm pretty sure that's because he's ogling Zoe, same as he did through most of lunch, so now I'm at 0 percent positive feelings toward him.

Paul passes around thick packets for each of us, our six-weekend detailed itinerary. Paul and Lorraine run a tight ship—the first day of camp always involved each of us getting special booklets for the summer, brightly colored and tabbed with sections for our chores, our daily schedules, our meal plans. I turn immediately to the second page, feel a strange comfort that they still use the same cartoon map of the campground—trees that look like green clouds, our cabins tiny and sharp cornered.

"We go last," Zoe whispers to me, already pages ahead.

"What?"

"Our presentation. We're week five, just before the farewell weekend. That's good, right?"

I shrug. What does she mean, *we* go? *I* go last. It's my presentation. She's flipping through the pages with a new purpose, and I can picture her, all those years of fancy-ass education. Probably a front-row sitter, this one.

"We can see what everyone else does first," she whispers.

Definitely a front-row sitter.

"Now, Lorraine, we're going to have to skip the night hike," Tom says, pointing to tonight's scheduled activity. "Little Tommy here doesn't like the dark."

"Bet he doesn't like being called 'Little Tommy,' either," says Hammond under his breath.

"Oh, Tom," says Sheree, patting her husband's knee affectionately. "Let's not blame our son for your fear of the dark. We'll do the night hike! I'll put Tommy in the hiking carrier we brought." Sheree is like I remember her: cheerful, unflappable, always the first volunteer for anything—kitchen duty, babysitting for the youngest campers, spot checks of the cabins for cleanliness. I'll bet Sheree is my top competition, no matter what Lorraine's said.

"This brings up a good point, though," says Paul, returning to Lorraine's side. "What you see in this packet isn't mandatory. We've designed these events so that we're spending time together, and so that all of you—even those of you who aren't familiar with the camp—really get to know it well. But you're not campers here now, of course, and while we hope you'll take advantage of this time to be a part of this family, you can certainly make your own choices here."

"Damn," Zoe whispers, "Paul does a good guilt trip. I should record this for my mother." I can see what she's doing with this shit, this running commentary she's offering me, this sense that we're somehow a team. What I can't figure out is how I almost want to lean into it.

"Lorraine," Hammond says, raising a hand, "How'd Val and I get put on the schedule first for presentations? Because it seems like—"

"Quiet, Hammond," Val snaps, finally rescuing her two younger kids from the sullen one with the weaponized twig. "We don't mind going first."

"I think that the people with kids—"

I can almost hear Zoe's eye roll at Hammond's obvious slight on us, the only two here without kids in tow or kids left at home.

"We'll go first, if you want," Walt says, but Lorraine shakes her head. Hammond must've forgotten. When Lorraine makes a schedule, everyone sticks to it.

"Now one thing we do want to draw your attention to, Walt and Rachel," Paul says. "We'll have you do your presentation on Sunday morning of the fourth week, instead of Saturday. We've closed down the camp's usual activities for this time we're here together, but that particular Friday we do have a former counselor's wedding scheduled here, and so you all can come Saturday morning."

"I *love* weddings," says Val. "Hammond and I married at the Crestwood Hotel, in the city? Do you know it?" Val's obviously the type to ask questions but not care about the answers, because she goes right on. "I wore this Venetian lace—"

"Baby, I don't think they want to hear," says Hammond, and Zoe snorts. "Of *course* he calls her *baby*," she whispers to me. She's got to stop that, the whispering. Her breath on my neck makes me feel ten thousand kinds of confused. I lean forward on the bench, rest my elbows on my knees, so I'm farther away from her.

"Oh, maybe Zoe wants to hear!" says Sheree, gesturing toward us, and I pretty much want to dig a hole and hide in it. "Have y'all started planning yet?"

"Oh my God, if you haven't, I have *so* many ideas," says Val.

I feel my neck prickle, the onset of nervous sweat. So far I have not even managed to sit next to Zoe comfortably; with everyone looking at us now, this has to be apparent, and all I want is for the spotlight to go elsewhere.

"I think we'll do something small," says Zoe, quickly. "Aiden's shy."

"George is shy too," says Lorraine. "That's the groom. Well, one of the grooms! His fiancé wanted something big, though, and so he's done most of the planning—"

"Wait," says Rachel. "It's a *gay* wedding?" Oh, man. Points off for the Coburgs, if I know Paul and Lorraine.

"It's a wedding," says Lorraine, her voice like ice. I look over at Rachel, who's wearing an expression of mild displeasure, and catch Zoe's eye. She's looking back and forth between Lorraine and Rachel, her brow furrowed, same as it was earlier today, when I'd told her about us sleeping in the same cabin. I fucked up, back when I met her, saying the Dillards were "traditional." She'd obviously gotten an idea in her mind about what that meant, and I'm guessing her version sounded more like Walt and Rachel.

"Zoe, I could bring my wedding scrapbook next weekend, if you want to see it," says Val.

"Oh," she says, a single syllable of disinterest before she corrects. "Yeah, of course. I love scrapbooks. They're so…you know. Creative! Helpful, really. I'm always looking at…things like that. Wedding ideas, that sounds great." I press my lips together, suddenly fighting the urge to smile. I get the sense Zoe's never looked at a scrapbook in her life.

"I think it's pretty bold, what you two are doing," says Hammond, something in his voice I recognize. Something I don't like.

"What's that?" I say, and even I can hear the edge in my response. Noncompetitive environment, my ass.

Hammond shrugs, the picture of casual nonchalance. "Looking to take on a business like this now. I'll bet any one of us here could tell you how tough that first year of marriage is, whew! Adding a business to the mix? Don't think Val and I could've done it."

"You're *so* right, baby," Val says, and Zoe coughs. "It's a real adjustment, even if you've been living together first. Do you live together?"

"No," Zoe says, at the same time I blurt, inexplicably, "Yes."

"Well, *basically* we live together," Zoe corrects. "But I have my own place." When I look at her, her cheeks are pink. Does she know how to fake *blushing*? Jesus Christ, she's good.

"I think what matters is the foundation you've got," says Tom. "A couple can get through anything with a strong foundation."

I stand from the bench. "Lorraine, I think I'll take Zoe back to our cabin for a while, if that's all right."

"Oh, sure," Lorraine says. "But we do have a group tour scheduled…"

"She needs to rest. She faints easy," I say.

"I do *not*," she snaps. That one's not a fake blush, I'm pretty sure. It's a bit…splotchier. Angrier.

"Oooh, Zoe," says Val, clasping her hands together. "Maybe I need to bring one of my *other* scrapbooks for you, hmmm?" She looks meaningfully toward her kids.

Shit, even I'm not dumb enough to miss that. "She has low blood sugar," I say. "Nothing else. She doesn't have anything else."

"Anything else like a baby?" says Rachel. I like her least of all.

"I don't have a baby. Or low blood sugar," Zoe says. "Lorraine, your food was delicious."

"Thank you, honey," Lorraine says, but she's watching us with a look that says she knows every single thing. It's the same look she gave Aaron and me and our bunkmates when we thought we were being secretive about our toilet-papering plans for the lodge when we were thirteen.

"Maybe they want some alone time?" says Sheree, raising her eyebrows. "That's how it is before you've got kids to distract you!"

"We can go on the tour," says Zoe, her voice flat. "I've never felt less like fainting in my life."

"It's a long tour," I say.

She turns to look at me, and there's a too-long pause for this audience, something crackling in the air between us that's definitely not the need for alone time. But still—there it is again, inconvenient—me noticing how beautiful she is. In this light her eyes look all gold, the dark brown around the edges shined right out.

"Well," she says, one of her eyebrows arched up. "It's a good thing I like walking."

* * * *

By seven that night, I can't do it anymore.

All through the camp tour, Zoe smiled, laughed, asked questions, chatted with everyone. When we'd stopped to rest by the swimming hole, she'd braided one of the Dwyer girls' hair. Later she'd taken out her phone and shown Rachel and Walt the baby goat YouTube channel. She'd asked Tom all about his work out in Shaftesbury Park, had found out all about

Sheree's night-school master's program, the one she finished before she became a principal. When Paul and Lorraine stopped to point out parts of the camp—the line of blackberry bushes planted alongside the camp's storage warehouse, the small zip line that's suspended amid a thick canopy of trees, the various clusters of bunkhouses—Zoe listened, or at least I think she did. She's got this thing she does, when she's listening: she sets one arm across her stomach, palm facing up, then rests her other elbow there, setting the tips of her fingers on her full lower lip. Sometimes she taps, a little, on that lip.

It is fucking irritating.

At dinner, it'd been the same, except for one notable exception: when Lorraine had turned to Zoe and asked whether I'd yet told her much about Aaron.

For a few seconds, all of Zoe's easy charm had flickered, like a brownout—the corners of her mouth turning down, her cheeks paling, her gaze falling immediately to her plate.

"Let's not get into that here," I'd said, my only attempt, this whole miserable day, at rescuing her from something unpleasant. And my reward had been a sharp look from Lorraine, sad eyes from Paul, and a projectile pizza crust sent over by Little Tommy. I'm a hit with the kids, I guess.

We're supposed to be making a quick change for the night hike, more layers for the chillier evening weather, but the minute we cross the threshold into the cabin, I tell her.

"I think you ought to stay here tonight."

From where she stands at the sink, washing her hands, she turns her head toward me. "I feel fine. I don't know how many times you want to hear it. The fainting was a one-off."

"It's not that," I say, staying near the door. "I need a break."

"Twelve hours engaged and you're already looking for the escape hatch?"

"Not looking for an escape hatch. It's like I said. I need a break. I'm not used to putting on a performance like that."

"And it shows," she snaps, shaking her wet hands over the sink, *one, two, three* flicks of her fingers, sharp and precise. Here, she's the Zoe I met that first day. She's not the friend-to-everyone charmer she's been since lunch.

"What's that supposed to mean?"

"It means that I've spent the day engaged to Groot."

What the fuck is Groot, I'm thinking, but before I have a chance to ask, she says, "Surprise, you never go to the movies, either. Jeez, I expected to do most of the talking, but this…"

I've tried to keep my temper all day, but right here, right now, I've had it. Had it with being around her, had it with how much better she's doing at this than I am, this thing that's on me, that's so important to me and my family. "Hard to get a word in edgewise," I say, and she straightens, crossing her arms over her chest.

"Don't do that." In her voice is something like a warning, something I heard once before, back in my driveway. "That wasn't easy for me."

"I told you to be yourself, not Miss America, for fuck's sake."

"Keep up, Aiden. Val is Miss America. *I'm* the suck-up trying to cover for her asshole fiancé."

"I'm not trying to be an asshole."

I'm not trying, but I'm succeeding. I can feel it coming off me like a bad smell. I've tried to sound placating, apologetic, but I know it hasn't come out that way. This is why I need to get out of here. This is why I need a break. If Ahmed and Charlie could see me now, they'd know all their suspicions about this idea have been confirmed. It was a mistake. I'm not up to it.

"If I'm doing something wrong, you need to—"

"I need to go," I say. "I'll be back in a couple of hours. All right?" I ask it like a question, like I want her permission, but in the end I turn and leave without waiting, closing the door behind me, the second time today. In the fading light I walk to the trailhead on the western side of the camp, for the first time realizing I've forgotten to put on any extra layers, have forgotten my flashlight. I could go back—there's still plenty of time—but I don't want to risk another confrontation with Zoe. I'm an asshole, a chickenshit, a liar, every terrible thing, and if it feels this bad now, I won't make it another five weekends. I'm going to tell her when I get back: this is off. I'll tell the others we had a fight. It won't be a stretch for anyone to buy it, the way she and I have been acting.

"You're early," says Lorraine, startling me. She's leaning against the wooden post that marks the trailhead, her lantern resting at her feet. "You're not dressed right, either. You know better."

Damn. I'm here to make a bid on her business, but Lorraine obviously still thinks of me as the eight-year-old she first met me as. "Where's Paul?"

"He and Tom and Val are staying back with the kids at the lodge tonight. I'm not saying it's about Tom's fear of the dark, but I'm not *not* saying it, either. Where's Zoe?"

"She decided to turn in early," I lie.

"Does that have something to do with you?"

"Yes." Because I can't tell one more tonight, especially not to Lorraine.

She's quiet for a minute, tipping her head back to the sky, where the moon's just starting to shine. "I've been married to Paul a long time," she says. "That's what a fight looks like between us too, though usually it's the other way around. I'm too quiet, and he tries to compensate."

"You know me, Lorraine," I say, rubbing a hand over my hair. "I've never been much of a talker."

"You were never sullen or difficult, either."

"Lorraine, I—"

"I felt sorry for that woman today, Aiden. You may think this is about the camp, but she was looking for *your* approval today, God knows why. You ought to be ashamed of yourself. "

I am, I want to say. But also want to say: *You don't know who she is. What she's done.* She *ought to be ashamed.* But even as I think it, I know: she *is* ashamed. That's the worst part.

I settle for a lame, "It's complicated."

"Maybe it's not a good time for you to be here, then. You know, I was so happy to know you'd be bringing someone, someone who'd be your partner in this," she says, sweeping an arm out, her *this* meant to encompass the whole camp, everything that means something to her. "We take this seriously, Paul and me. This is our place, Aiden. It's difficult for us, considering the sale, and we want it to go to a family who's in it together."

I look down at her, and for the first time since I pulled up here I really feel the weight of years between us. I remember Lorraine as the surrogate mom I had for six weeks every summer, the woman who hugged me close every time it was time to say goodbye until the next year, and not as the woman who holds my future in her hands. She still looks young, her face mostly unlined, her cheeks full and her eyes bright. But her hair is more gray, her shoulders a bit more stooped. At Aaron's funeral, Lorraine had cried silent tears and held Paul's hand tightly as they moved through the receiving line. She'd brought a small box of photographs she'd had of him from camp. She gave that box to me, not my parents.

It reminds me what I owe her, and what I owe to this place. "I take it seriously too. I'm sorry about today, and—I'll fix things with Zoe. It's my fault, the way it was with us. I—" I break off, look down at where Lorraine's lantern rests on the path. "*We* really want to do this. It's something we've worked on a lot." I know now, I won't call it off with Zoe. I can't. If I want this, it has to work with Zoe for these next few weeks. I've got to remember that she's nothing to me. She's a means to an end.

"She certainly seemed enthusiastic," Lorraine says, softening immediately like always. *Two weeks bathroom duty,* I remember her saying to me, stern and disappointed, when I was nine and had been caught out after curfew. But then she'd walked me back to the cabin and bent down to give me a hug when she'd seen my quivering chin. "I liked her. She's probably too good for you."

"Probably," I say, automatically, and I realize with a hitch of discomfort in my shoulders that I'm not lying. I don't like her, don't want her, but that doesn't mean I can't see that she's way out of my league.

"How did you meet?" Of course she asks—of course it seems like the perfect moment to her for this conversation, now that we've got a minute alone. And of course I'm wildly unprepared.

"Oh. Just—around town." Suddenly it is painfully apparent to me what a mistake it was to leave Zoe behind. I think of her, back in the cabin. About now she's probably figuring out how you've got to steer well clear of that curtain when you're in the shower, or else it'll stick right to you, no matter how many times you peel it away from yourself. And I hope that bug she mentioned didn't come back and spook her. I hope she managed with her bed.

"Was it one of those websites?" Lorraine asks. "You can tell me, you know. Don't be embarrassed. I hear that's what most people do these days."

"It wasn't a website," I say, but I don't have a better answer. I'm saved by the sound of Hammond's loud voice, Sheree's softer one, the leaves rustling underneath their feet as they approach. Walt and Rachel are no doubt on the way. Lorraine nods at me, straightens from the post, and pats my arm. "We'll talk more soon, all right? But when you get back to your cabin, Aiden, you either apologize to that woman, or you'll be sleeping alone for the foreseeable future."

Either way, I think. *Either way, I'm sleeping alone.*

Chapter 5

Zoe

"I'm telling you. He tried to kill me."

"I don't know how you can say that about Kenneth," Greer answers, appalled. "He's the sweetest cat who ever lived."

"Greer," Kit says, taking another fry from our shared plate. "He tried to sleep on my face. He was trying to kill me or trying to suck out my soul. Take your pick."

We're on minute eight of this argument, Kit's catalog of Kenneth's sins while Greer was on vacation, followed by Greer's gentle defensiveness, and honestly I think they're both keeping it up for my benefit. Of the three of us, I'm generally the talker, but since I got back on Sunday I've been feeling pretty introverted—jarred and unexpectedly exhausted from what was, all told, only a few hours of deception. Maybe I should've been grateful to Aiden for leaving me out like he did, but instead all it'd done was make me more unsure about the weekends to come, about how it'd even be possible to keep this up. No matter how much I keep telling myself that it's Aiden who's making things difficult, I can't shake the feeling that I'm responsible for what happens in Stanton Valley, that I've got to make sure Aiden has what he wants.

Despite my ruminating, I don't miss the beat of silence, the hope I might finally chime in, so I oblige. "Maybe I should watch Kenneth next time. It's up in the air as to whether I have a soul, so it's possible having a feline around will reveal the truth."

Hmm. Went too dark, I think, because Greer purses her lips and Kit says, "Honey. Stop that."

"Sorry." And I am. I don't want to be a spoiler, especially not tonight, since Ben's gone back to Texas for another week, tying up loose ends at his job before he moves here full-time. Kit keeps busy, as independent as she's ever been, but I know she misses him. "How many more weeks of the back-and-forth?" I ask her.

"About three and a half." A wide smile spreads across her face. "His dad and I are planning a welcome back party for him," she says, proudly. "Obviously you guys will come, and I think…"

I lose track of what she's saying when I spot a familiar form duck through the bar's front door—so tall, so broad shouldered, that distinctive way he carries himself, alert and slightly tense. He's wearing a uniform—heavy black boots, dark navy cargoes, a dark navy t-shirt fitted to his body, the white EMS seal of his crew over his right pectoral.

Aiden.

"Oh, fuck," I say, instinctively turning back to the bar, my face hot and my palms sweaty. What is he *doing* here? Despite my low mood, I'm out tonight to be with my friends, to be with people who don't look at me with barely concealed disdain. I dressed up a little too—a short, bohemian-style dress under a denim jacket and low-heeled suede boots, feathered earrings dancing at my earlobes. It was all just for the fun of it, a little pick-me-up to help me feel more like myself. I don't want him to see me like this. I get enough of his disapproval when I'm actually trying to please him.

"Are you okay?" says Greer, touching my arm gently. She and Kit have both tucked in, each on one side of me, immediately protective.

"Uh—that guy who just came in. That's him. That's Aiden."

Neither of them are apparently protective enough to keep from twisting dramatically on their stools to gape in his direction.

"Oh my *God*," I say, in embarrassment, at the same time Greer says it, in a decidedly different tone.

"He's like—" she begins, then breaks off, before finishing lamely, "tall."

"Holy moly, *that's* the guy you're faking an engagement for?" Kit whispers loudly. "He's gorgeous!"

"He's with a woman," Greer says, and my head snaps up and around, back to where I saw him come in.

And sure enough, Aiden's with a woman—petite, curvy, brown haired, and wearing the same uniform as his, which she manages to make look cute as all get out. Her hair is pulled into a messy topknot, her face tanned and smiling. My stomach plummets, maybe to somewhere around the area of my knees. And then Aiden looks up, catches me watching, and my stomach probably slides out from beneath my feet.

"Just—you know," I say, my teeth gritted. "Act normal."

"Uh, right," says Kit. "We'll follow your lead, huh?" I catch her tossing a sidelong glance to Greer, who offers a sympathetic wince in my direction.

"It's fine," I say, raising a hand in halfhearted greeting. "We're not together, obviously." *But why didn't he ask* her *to be the fake fiancée?* I think, the voice in my head whinier than anything I'd ever actually verbalize. Aiden nods back, leans down to say something to his companion, who smiles widely in my direction. Of course, she has fucking dimples! She saves lives *and* has dimples. She probably bakes and does crafts, like with all that antique-looking paper I didn't have for my guilt jar. "Maybe I should go to the bathroom," I say, watching as Dimples makes her way over, tugging a reluctant Aiden by his forearm.

"God hates a coward, Z," says Greer.

"You're supposed to be the *nice* one," I snap, but my eyes don't leave Aiden's. I don't know him well, but I feel like I see something there—embarrassment or apology—and this gives me what I need to straighten my spine, to tip my chin up. I don't have to be Miss America here.

"Hi, I'm Charlie," says Dimples, and I hold my beer a little tighter, right around its sweaty neck. "And you're Aiden's fiancée!"

I look toward him, panicked, unsure of what to do now. Is this not a person he's with? Do people outside of Stanton Valley think this engagement is real? Am I supposed to do something fiancée appropriate here, to keep the ruse going? I slide from my stool and stand, about to go to him, but he says, "She knows," before I can humiliate myself, I guess, by trying to greet him affectionately.

"Right." I stick out my hand, all business, and she shakes it vigorously.

"You must be some kind of *saint*," she says, still shaking. I'm trying not to stare, or gape, or reveal anything on my face that suggests how profoundly confused I am about why any woman would date a man who is faking an engagement for the next month and a half.

"Oh, I—well. I am not." But Charlie's moved on, shaking hands with Kit and Greer before turning back to Aiden and saying, "Budweiser?"

She knows his beer! I'm indignant for no sane reason whatsoever.

"Doesn't even look like this place *serves* regular beer," he grumbles.

"Hey," I say, defensive. "This is a good place."

"He's in a bad mood," Charlie says. "Our last run was a repeat caller."

"Charlie, stop." Aiden's voice is low and serious, but Charlie rolls her eyes, and I envy that too, the shorthand they seem to have together, the kind Aiden wanted no part of with me.

"Let's just say someone's got a big crush on their friendly local paramedic. She was wearing a new nightgown, Aiden. Did you notice?" Charlie's eyes are full of mischief, and I am less ashamed than I should be for hating her so much just from this tiny glimpse of her closeness with Aiden.

Aiden stares at the ground, shaking his head wordlessly.

"Aiden," I say, and he looks up immediately, right into my eyes, setting off a shower of sparks in my middle that I try to tamp down, since I'm pretty sure I'm standing next to his actual girlfriend. "These are my friends that I told you about, Kit and Greer."

"Hey," he says, shaking their hands, giving them a dose of that eye contact that half stuns me, and even though I know Kit is as loyal as it comes, I'm pretty sure she bats her eyelashes at him, and Greer's mouth is open a little. Traitors, both of them. If they expect to get more conversation out of him, they're going to be disappointed, because as far as I know Aiden is about as talkative as Kenneth.

I can't take the way Kit and Greer are staring at him, probably devising a list of ten to fifteen questions they have about him personally and about our ridiculous arrangement, so I decide to take control of the situation. Unfortunately, the conversational control I have around Aiden is like a two on a scale of one to one million. "This is, um," I say, awkwardly, "a place we come to. A lot. You probably don't, right? Because we would have seen you, I'm sure. We come here a lot."

"You said," he answers, and I'm not sure—I'll probably have to consult with Dimples Charlie on this—but is Aiden maybe...*teasing* me a little?

The moment is interrupted by the arrival of a man even bigger than Aiden, also in uniform, who slaps Aiden on the back and says, "Sorry, stopped and got food."

"We came here to *eat*," says Aiden, his voice disbelieving.

"There's a good taco stand around the corner." He shrugs, then looks at me and smiles, white teeth beneath his black beard, his eyes crinkling genially. "Hi," he says, sticking out a hand. "I'm Ahmed."

"This is Zoe," Aiden snaps, before I can say anything.

"No shit?" Ahmed pumps my hand in his. "You're beautiful."

Aiden lowers his head again, says something sharp I don't catch, but Ahmed clearly does, straightening away from me and exchanging friendly introductions with Kit and Greer, who seem to be enjoying themselves far more than is appropriate, given that I have the kind of flop sweat that should be documented for science.

"It's Charlie's birthday tomorrow," Aiden says to me. "She wanted to come here."

"Yeah, sure. I mean, you don't have to explain. I don't own the place."

Charlie returns, holding two bottles and handing one to Aiden. "Sorry, Med," she says to the new member of this strange, cobbled-together group. "You'll have to get your own. The bartender here is gorgeous." She tips her chin to where Betty pulls a Guinness.

"You're a married woman, Charlie," says Ahmed before heading toward Betty, and my shoulders slouch briefly in relief, but not so briefly that Aiden doesn't see it, his lips quirking at the corners.

Charlie heaves out a sigh. "I'm noticing for you, jerk," she calls after him before turning back to us. "But it has been a whole month since I've seen my wife."

"Oh, are you doing long distance too?" Kit asks, patting the stool beside her, and Charlie settles in, Kit completely ignoring the death-ray look that I am sending, which is meant to say, *Stop this please; we need to separate from these people and get the fuck out of this bar.*

"Charlie's wife is in med school up in D.C.," Aiden says. "They don't see each other much lately." Like me, he seems to be trying to telegraph a message of his own, but Charlie is oblivious, dimpling all over Kit and Greer, and I know for a fact Kit has a weakness for dimples. Pretty soon the three of them are laughing like old friends, while Aiden and I stand awkwardly apart.

"So. Someone's got a crush on you?" I try, knowing that at least Charlie got a reaction out of Aiden with this topic.

"She's eighty." He shrugs, looking down at the floor, a little embarrassed, I'd bet. "Just lonely, I think."

"Ah." And that's the sum total of all my conversation ideas. I don't know who to be around Aiden when I'm not playing the roles he's cast me in: as a villain in the story surrounding his brother's death, or as his too-enthusiastic, "Miss America" fake fiancée.

"Boss says no tables for a while," Ahmed says when he returns, hooking a thumb over his shoulder toward Betty.

"You could probably have our stools." I'm eager to get out of here, but Kit's been listening enough to say, "We *just* got here." I'm starting to wonder whether Kenneth did, in fact, suck out her soul.

"It's all right," Aiden offers. "Med, let's go play a game of darts."

"I play darts," I say, without thinking. It was awkward before; now I've made it excruciating, because Aiden seems to stiffen, clearly expecting the darts idea to be his way out of being around me.

Somehow, though, his rising discomfort emboldens me. I'm suddenly indignant that I have to feel out of place in my favorite bar, with my best friends, all because of this weekend-only farce I'm enduring for Aiden. I flick my hair over my shoulder, feel my feathered earrings tickle the sides of my neck.

"301 up?" I say, and head to the dartboard, ignoring the way Ahmed's eyebrows have raised in surprise, and the way Aiden's have lowered in what I can only assume is annoyance. On my way, I toss a look back where my friends sit at the bar, and Greer gives me an encouraging thumbs-up.

I may have to eat humble pie at camp with this guy, but here, I'm in charge.

* * * *

Ahmed sucks at darts, mostly because he's too talkative, unfocused and easily distracted. He asks me what my favorite item on the menu is, how long I've lived here, if I think lawyer jokes are funny. Aiden, though—he's decent, surprising because I generally think players as tall as him are at a disadvantage. Betty takes darts pretty seriously, and the board she has up is exactly regulation, the bullseye 5'8" off the ground. When I'm wearing a couple inches of heel, like I am tonight, I'm 5'11", nearly eye level with the board from where I stand at the oche. Aiden, when he aims, has to curve down slightly to accommodate his height, and while he's by no means a natural—his movements too forceful to be an outstanding player—he's got all the focus and determination Ahmed lacks. When our game is interrupted by the arrival of several plates of food that Charlie ordered from the bar, Ahmed happily quits, but Aiden waves the food away.

He's at 167, and if he were better he could end this on the next turn—t20, t19, bull. But he's not that good—at this point, he's more likely to bust. Me, though? I'm sitting pretty, a nice 160, and I can check out in my next turn, no problem. I expect, given how intense his focus has been, that Aiden won't like losing, but when he picks the darts from the board and brings them to me, he looks at me and says, "Don't be holding out on me, now," like he relishes the opportunity to get beat by a good player. That slight drawl in his voice—I've heard it from a hundred different guys, living around here, but it's never made me weak in the knees like when it comes from Aiden.

"I wouldn't do that to you." And I don't. My next three darts hit their targets: t20, t20, d20, and that's the game, which I signal with a *whoop* of victory and a cocky smile sent in Aiden's direction. He tips his beer to me, not quite smiling but not his usual barely maintained tolerance. Over the course of the game, our friends had wandered over, settling in at the nearest table that opened up during our game, and they offer loud applause, Charlie ribbing Aiden for getting beat by a girl, Kit and Greer standing to clap while I take a bow.

"Where'd you learn to play like that?" Aiden asks, staying put rather than heading toward the table.

I feel myself blanch a little at the question—simple, but with a complicated answer. That summer, the one I lost my way, the one where I'd met a bar owner named Christopher who taught me to waste time with beer and a dartboard. "Oh, you know. Around."

"If only this camp thing came down to darts," he says, deadpan.

"Was that—not a joke, exactly, but *almost* a joke?" I'm teasing, a little hopeful.

But Aiden just shrugs.

"Wishful thinking, I guess."

"I'm sorry I don't have your sparkling personality."

"At this point, I'd settle for *a* personality," I snipe back, before I can think better of it. What am I *doing*? I've got half a weekend in this thing and I'm not making it any easier on either of us. "Hey, I'm—" I begin, ready to apologize, but Aiden speaks at the same time: "You want to get something to eat with me?"

I feel about as surprised as I did when Aiden dropped his *Marry me* bomb. I'm pretty sure I look briefly over my shoulder to see if he's talking to someone else. But Aiden's looking right at me, hands in his pockets, as big and as forbidding as always. "Uh. Okay." Points to me, obviously, for being consistently inarticulate tonight.

Aiden offers a short nod and turns away from me, walking over to the table where our friends sit. Once I figure out how to engage the muscles of my jaw enough to close my gaping mouth, I head over to gather the darts from the board, taking my time. Kit's at my back when I turn around. "Do you want to stay here with him?" She looks as serious as a heart attack, and I love her for this, for the way she looks out for me. "Because Greer and I will stay. We can help—I don't know." She wrinkles her nose, obviously still displeased that I've agreed to this arrangement. "Smooth the way."

I offer a weak smile, squeeze her forearm in thanks. "No, no. I think maybe this is his attempt to call a truce. Make it easier on the weekends."

She looks over at him, her face somehow both suspicious and contemplative. "He's a little—um. Remote."

"That's kind."

Kit leans in, lowers her voice. "Charlie says this is the first time he's ever agreed to come out with them after a shift. She says she thought he only spoke in monosyllables for an entire month when he joined their crew."

"That sounds right." But when I look over, he's talking to both Ahmed and Charlie. Judging by the tightness around his jaw, the way his brows slash over his eyes, he's talking about me, about how he's going to suffer for the greater good by actual sharing a meal with the harridan he's stuck himself with for the next few weeks. "I'll be fine, Kit," I say, even though I don't feel fine. I feel like my face is going to get stuck this way, in this perma-everything's-great-fake-smile. Kit leans in, hugging me hard, and says in my ear, "You're doing enough for him, Zoe. You know that, right?"

"Sure." I pull back and widen my smile, just in time for Aiden to return to my side.

It's a good ten minutes of goodbyes, nice-to-meet-yous, where'd-you-park-the-cars before everyone's on their way and Aiden and I are settled in a back booth, both of us switching to water while he looks over the menu and I wait, hands folded, for him to decide. When Betty comes by to take our orders—I don't miss that she's not serving this section, so I assume Greer's insisted she check up on me—Aiden gets a BLT, and since I've already had a good many of those fries from earlier, sitting heavy in my stomach with nerves, I opt for a cup of Betty's tomato soup.

"So you're always a light eater," he says, once Betty has winked and shimmied away.

"Are you going to be in charge of what I eat too?"

He clears his throat, shifts in his seat. "No. Sorry. We—ah—we have trouble talking to each other, I guess."

"You *guess*?"

He leans forward, sets his elbows on the table, and clasps his big hands loosely together.

"Last weekend, on the ride out, you said we should try getting to know each other a little before—before this whole thing began." He looks down at his hands, runs one thumb across the other. "You were right."

My chin lifts automatically, even though I know I should be gracious here. Before I can think of something to say to convey such graciousness, Aiden speaks again. "Last weekend wasn't good, in terms of believability. I think people buy that you're my fiancée, but I don't think they believe you're real happy about it."

"Oh, so it's my fault?"

"That came out wrong."

"You're absolutely right it did. You barely *looked* at me. You hardly spoke. We didn't even manage a single gesture of affection."

His lips flatten into a line, his eyes looking at the door, around the room, anywhere but at me.

"Maybe I should get my food to go," I say.

"Don't. I'm sorry. I *am* trying."

When he looks at me, his face grave and his eyes sad, all the fight goes out of me, and I'm back there in his parents' living room, feeling like I'd do anything to give him, his family, just a little resolution. "I know you are," I say, my voice quiet. "It's not an easy situation."

"Let's just—try having a meal together. Talk like adults. You can tell me about all the people you've hustled playing darts."

"I've never hustled anyone. I'm completely up front about my skills. It's not my fault if most guys don't take my word for it."

There's an awkward lull, two people not used to talking with each other pleasantly. "So, uh. You said you went to USC?"

"Yes." My voice is still too clipped, too unthawed. "And you went to Wisconsin? That's pretty far from home," I say, hoping that shifting the focus off me will help warm me up.

He swallows, looks over my shoulder and back down at the table before he answers. "I had a football scholarship there, but got injured pretty early on."

"That's too bad." I sound casual, but inside I feel disproportionately thrilled that he's speaking to me at all. It's not comfortable, but it's something.

"Thought about dropping out, but stayed on, worked with the team on training and rehab stuff."

"Is that how you got into being a paramedic?"

He gives a noncommittal shrug. "We had an EMT course at school, so I was running with crews even before graduation. Then after I worked for my paramedic certification."

"And then Colorado," I say.

He pauses, his jaw tight with tension. "It's sort of weird, you knowing all this. Hard to feel like we're getting to know each other in the regular way."

"I don't think it's ever going to feel regular with us."

Betty comes with our food, sets both plates down, and levels me with an even stare. "You're okay?" she asks, as if Aiden isn't even there.

"I'm good, thanks." I give her a reassuring smile. I don't miss the way she turns toward Aiden, giving him a look like she's got every reason to be suspicious.

"You've got nice friends," he says, once she's gone. There's a slight tone of surprise to it, him trying to make sense of a puzzle piece that doesn't quite fit for him.

"The nicest." We eat in silence for a while, maybe our first real détente. The quiet between us is easier here than it is in the cabin, where I'm so out of sorts and unsure of myself. Still, I wish we were better at this. I wish it came more naturally.

"I'm working on being better friends with Ahmed and Charlie," he says suddenly, surprising me. "Haven't been very social since I came back."

"Was it for the camp? Is that why you came back?"

He chews his sandwich, takes a drink of his water before answering. "Sort of. My parents were thinking of selling the house, and—that was hard for me, I guess. The house we grew up in and all." He pauses, leans back in his seat and takes another drink. He looks a little shell shocked, as if he forgot for a minute that he shouldn't say anything personal to me. I heard it, that *we*. I know he means him and his brother. "But I'd had this project in mind for a while, with the camp. If it wasn't Stanton Valley, I would've found someplace else around here."

"You know, you're going to have to tell me about it. About your plans for the campground." It's ridiculous that he hasn't yet, a liability for what we're doing that we can't let go on for another week. Maybe he was waiting, figuring out if he could stand me long enough to get through even the first weekend, but even he's got to know that it's risky to keep me in the dark.

He takes a deep breath, head lowered, and passes a hand over his hair, back to front, before looking up at me. "You know how my brother died," he says, his voice quieter now, so I have to lean forward in the booth to hear him. I do, of course, know how Aaron died: a fatal overdose of Opryxa, the very drug that promised him eventual sobriety. I know he'd had three seizures. That his heart stopped beating after the third one.

"Yes," I answer, though he wasn't asking.

"In Colorado, there's a camp—well, there's more of them now, one in New Mexico, one in California, one in Maine. It's a Wilderness/Wellness program, for addicts. It's live-in, with individual and group therapy. Equine therapy. Outdoor excursions, work programs. Relapse prevention. They have a fifteen percent higher success rate for opioid addiction than other live-in programs. I want to bring one here."

Now I get a puzzle-piece feeling too, some information about Aiden that changes my perspective of who he is. Like me, Aiden's got a burden of his own, but he's doing something *real* about it, something that could make a difference. "That's—wow," I stammer. "That's wonderful."

"Obviously the settlement money is only for the land. And obviously I'm not an addiction specialist. But I'd be the owner of the land, leasing it to someone who does the start-up and runs things."

I swallow, my soup all but forgotten. I don't want to move. I'm afraid anything I do or say will stop him talking, and every single thing he's said I want to hear more about it. It hurts, but I want that. I want to keep feeling every single thing.

"I tried to get Aaron to come to Colorado. I prepaid for a three-month stay for him. But it was always hard for him, me having moved away, and uh—you know. He was really sick. Colorado seemed far away to him."

"Sure," I say, as if I understand even a fraction of how it must've felt to be Aaron, twice in the thrall of drugs doctors prescribed him.

"I know you noticed that—well, I know that Lorraine and Paul are maybe not as traditional as I let on. But turning their camp into a rehab facility—it'd be a real different version of the camp's future. I don't want them to see me as the lone wolf, screwed up and grieving. I want them to see me as stable. Happy."

"Aiden, this is—" I begin, but he stops me.

"That's all I want to say about it, for now." He goes right back to eating his sandwich, finishing it off in a few bites while I basically alternate between staring at him and staring at my bowl. What he's said—it's everything he should've told me before. But there's no "should've" when it comes to me and him. There's too much between us. I know how big a revelation all this is; I know that what he hates the most about our situation is my professional proximity to his personal crisis. We'll never be friends, that's for sure, not with what he knows about me. But him telling me this, it's *something*.

"I haven't worked since I left the firm," I rush out, and he looks up at me. "You asked me what I do all day. The truth is, right now, I don't do anything. I go to the gym. I read a lot. I spend time with my friends. I was supposed to be planning a trip but I haven't." I clear my throat and look away, out over the crowded dining room. He's watching me, I know he is, but I can't look back for this part. "Mostly I think a lot about people like your brother."

From the corner of my eye I see him shift in his seat. I watch Betty deliver a tray of beers to a table across the way, watch her trademark wink, familiar and comforting, everything to me Aiden is not. I look back at him then, right into his hazel eyes. "I'll do whatever I can to help you. I'll be a lot better this weekend. I promise you that."

"No," he says, and for a second I think he's going to say, *No, this is over; you're as useless to me as you are to everyone else.* But instead he says, "You were great. This weekend, I'll be better."

And with that, Aiden and I make a fragile peace.

Chapter 6

Aiden

At Betty's, I'd thought Zoe and I had called some kind of truce, but damn if she doesn't get in my car on Friday afternoon and annoy me first thing.

"Look at this t-shirt," she says, once she's settled her bag in the backseat. She unzips her jacket and points at her chest, and it's a good three seconds—too many seconds—of me looking without understanding that I'm supposed to be reading. *Stanton Valley Campground,* it says, in a retro, nineteen-eighties-style font, a cartoon squirrel's face underneath, goofy and smiling. The t-shirt is gray, everything on it faded. It looks soft, thin. I can see the faint ridges of the cups of her bra.

"Uh," I say, and I'll bet if I got out of the car right now my knuckles would drag on the road.

She doesn't seem to notice. "I got this at Goodwill. They had a lot! I guess your campground was pretty popular, huh? Anyways, I thought Lorraine would get a kick out of it."

She turns to put on her seat belt, and I turn to look out the windshield.

Here's the problem: I don't feel the right things around Zoe. She's supposed to be an enemy I'm keeping close, a tool I need to get something I want. But I don't feel what she's supposed to be to me; I haven't since that first day. And since Wednesday—hell, if I'm honest, since last weekend—it's more than me noticing, in some semidetached way, that I find her attractive. Sure, she's got an edge to her, one she seems to delight in sharpening on me. But she's also whip-crack smart in a way that's terrifying and exhilarating to be around, a way that keeps you hanging on for whatever too-true thing she's going to say next. And seeing her at the bar—with her friends and with Ahmed and Charlie—I can see now that she wasn't really faking it last weekend. She's damned likable, that's the thing. She's got a smile that can go all the way up to her eyes, she kicks ass at darts, and when you talk to her, she listens to every single word.

"Oh, wait," she says, undoing her seat belt and swiveling so her knees are on the seat. She reaches into the backseat, rustles around in her bag, her ass right next to my face. *Not what I meant by truce.*

"We need to get going," I say, my voice gruff.

When she turns back, a Tupperware container in her hand, she levels me with a long look. It's a look that says, *I thought we were going to try this another way.* But I say nothing, just wait for her to put on her seat belt, and when she does, I pull away from the curb. She's set the Tupperware on the floor between her feet, and I'm as curious about what's in there as I am about what's underneath that t-shirt.

Which is a lot. A lot curious.

I clear my throat, try to start this thing over. "How'd the rest of your week go?"

"Fine," she sniffs.

The silence stretches, and finally I decide to get out of my own way for once. "What's in the container?"

Out of my peripheral vision I see her turn toward me briefly, and then she reaches down again, picks up the Tupperware. "It's kind of a long story."

"Kind of a long drive."

"Well, I guess it's not that long. I took a cooking class. It's actually something I did with my former assistant from the firm." There's a pause, like she's waiting for me to give some signal that I'm not okay with her talking about her old job. When I don't say anything, she continues, her index finger tracing along the lip of the container. "I kind of—I used to give Janet a pretty hard time, made her work a lot."

"After that she wanted to take a cooking class with you?" I ask, regretting it immediately when I see her expression turn stricken, her eyes widening.

"Oh, shit. Do you think she felt obligated? Because it was her idea. I took her out for lunch, and actually we got along pretty well, but maybe—"

I rush out a correction. "I'm sure she didn't feel obligated. You don't work there anymore, right?"

"Right," she says, but she's still got her lips pulled slightly to the side in concern, or maybe worry. This is what comes of my efforts at conversation. "Anyways," she says. "We made cookies. Want one?"

Obviously I have to eat one. I'll look like an asshole if I don't. "Sure."

The cookie is disgusting, I mean really disgusting. It tastes like there's soy sauce in it. But I say, "Good job," and eat the whole thing. My eyes might be watering.

"You want another one?" she asks, hopeful.

"Better not." I'm close to saying a prayer of thanks when she relents and puts the lid back on. But it's helped—she's not so stiff over there anymore. Still, two polite questions and I've reached my limit, I guess. I don't know what to say to her now. So I reach my hand down to the panel along my door and pull out my ace in the hole, my guarantee that she'll see I was serious about letting her in.

"Brought this for you." I pass the binder over to her.

She takes it, looking over at me, but I keep my eyes ahead, focus on the heavy Friday traffic. I'm nervous to have her see it—I've got no problem admitting that to myself. Zoe went to the best schools, did a tough job with a lot of smart people, and I had to work my ass off for a C average in both high school and college. The effort contained in that binder is more than I want her to know about, no matter what we'd talked about on Wednesday. The spreadsheets especially, fuck. I'd almost crushed the computer with my bare hands doing those, I swear to Christ. My hands tense around the steering wheel at the memory, and at the fact that she's opening it up.

"This is your—is this a proposal for the camp?"

I manage a grunt of assent, look over to see her rolling those eyes. Amber in this light, with that dark ring around the edges. They're gorgeous, frankly—with her blond hair and tan skin she reminds me of a bar of gold.

I try to concentrate on the aftertaste of the cookies.

"You must be terrible on road trips. Like it's just all heavy silence and hands at ten and two. No license plate games for you, I'll bet."

"Just look at the damned binder," I say, but this time, there's something else to the way we talk. Something lighter.

She resettles herself, folds her long legs up underneath her, crisscross-style, and puts the binder in her lap. One of her knees is resting against my thigh. *Ten and two,* I think.

"Turn on the radio," she says.

I sigh. "I like the quiet."

"Well, I want to read this and not focus on your breathing and your loud thoughts about how unpleasant I am."

"You're not unpleasant," I say, but I wait until I've turned on the radio, so maybe she doesn't hear.

She's quiet for a long time, almost a full hour, studying each page carefully. This is my copy, but I've got a plan to have two more made for Paul and Lorraine once we get to the presentation. It still needs some work—it's not just the spreadsheets that look dull as hell in there. I've incorporated stuff from a lot of the other Wilderness/Wellness camps, brochures and photographs, but a lot of it is numbers, budgets for necessary renovations, stables, that kind of thing. But I've also got a long—maybe too-long—section on the opioid addiction stats in this part of the country, which is about as sad as it gets. And there's not much of me in there, not much that'd make Paul and Lorraine feel like it's a trusted friend who'd be buying up their property.

"This is good," she says, finally, and I don't think I'd realized the way I'd tensed up my shoulders. "I mean I hate the spreadsheets, obviously." She shifts and turns down the radio. Her knee is no longer touching my thigh.

"Obviously?"

"Spreadsheets are awful, God. Those equations up top when you're trying to do them? Who even understands those? No one, that's who. Okay, well. Other people, I guess. You seemed to do all right."

"I almost Hulk-smashed my laptop over those spreadsheets," I say, and she laughs, this quick, loud, *Ha!*, like a checkmark next to my joke. *This one passes.* I bite the inside of my cheek to keep from smiling.

"Not that I'm saying you should take them out. They're good for your budget stuff." There's a catch on the end of that, almost like she's getting ready for a *but*, but she says nothing.

"Tell me." *Two words,* Ahmed would say.

Zoe doesn't miss a beat—she knows what I want. "Do you have a plan for distributing this? Because if you just hand them each a binder—that's going to be a lot to take in. This is a lot to take in," she says, smoothing her hand down the cover.

I think about lying, saying, *Yeah, I have a plan.* But there's not much good that would do, except maybe saving what little pride I have left with this; Zoe already knows how shit I am with people. "I guess I thought I'd walk them through it." She's already shaking her head no.

"Boring. That's the worst, when you're in a presentation and someone's reading you handouts that you've got right in front of your face. You can't do that."

How this blunt, forceful statement can be so much less annoying than the squirrel t-shirt is beyond me. But I'm getting used to her, I guess, getting used to the way she cuts through the bullshit, says what she means.

She makes this little humming noise, taps her fingernail on the front of the binder. "I'm going to think," she says, but instead she undoes her seat belt again, swivels to the her-ass-in-my-face position, and rummages around back there. When she comes back, she's got a small notebook and a pen. She reopens the binder and opens her notebook, and then she's off, making notes. She writes like she speaks—firm, quick, and I can hear the pen scratch along the paper. At one point she gets out a cookie from her Tupperware, takes a single bite, and says, "This is gross. Why didn't you say something?" But she's not really interested in my answer. She goes back to writing even before I formulate a response about not wanting to hurt her feelings. She stops to look up once we get to Coleville, and I think I catch something wistful, wanting in her expression.

"Need to stop?" She looks over at me, almost like she's forgotten I'm there.

"I'm okay," she says, getting back to her notes. I keep trying to sneak glances over there, but I can't see much of what she's doing without taking my eyes off the road for too long. I'm curious, and—well, this is fucking weird, but I'm kind of lonely, too. I wish she'd start talking to me again, even if we're just insulting each other.

"We need to make this more accessible," she says, as though she can hear what I'm thinking. "We need to tell a story. That's what all good arguments are, really. Stories."

"Sure," I say, but the problem is, I can't think of a story right now, not with her sitting so close. The problem is that t-shirt. And her ass in those jeans. Her knee on my thigh. Everything about her that is annoying.

"I mean, it may not be your usual style," she says, right as I turn into the drive to the campground. "But I think you just have to decide how bad you want it."

My only response? Another knuckle-dragging grunt.

* * * *

By the time we get to Saturday evening, I've got a new word to describe Zoe.

Game.

Last weekend, Zoe's exposure was at a minimum—easier because it was a shorter weekend, but also because I kept acting like a dick and leaving her behind, obviously. But whether it's because of our dinner on Wednesday or her look at the binder, or maybe the comfort that comes with being here a second time, Zoe's got a new determination about her. Learning how to run the Hobart in the lodge's kitchen? Game. Early Saturday morning hike with the Coburgs and the five kids they brought this time? Game. Spray-painting a set of tires for the obstacle course on the western edge of the camp? Game.

Having me in the cabin while she showers, though?

Not game.

I shift on the decking of the stoop, hard and crooked beneath me, and wait for her to knock. It'd made me nervous, most of today, being apart from her, but Paul had rounded up me and Hammond to help do some tree clearing over by Good News 4, a sweaty and satisfying job that had taken nearly all day. *What if we get our stories crossed,* I'd thought, *what if Lorraine's asking her about all the shit I haven't wanted to make up, what if Zoe tells her we met on a website?* But when I'd met up with her back here, I'd asked her about it, an agitated edge to my voice that I'd hated. "People who know how to have conversations know how to steer them," she'd said. "Anyways, the kids were a good distraction. Who can talk when you've got someone screaming or crying or holding their privates all the time? Now get out, so I can shower."

See? Game.

So even though my shoulders feel heavy with tension, thinking about what's coming in Hammond and Val's presentation tonight, I'm looking forward to it too, only because I'll be watching it with her.

A knock comes from behind me, and I stand, brushing off my jeans and taking the deep breath I need to stop thinking about her in the shower.

Inside the cabin it's humid, steam fogging up the two mirrors, the scent of her shampoo thick in the air. She's dressed, but she's dragging a comb through her wet hair, the color of dried wheat when it's like this, leaving little droplets on the red-and-black flannel she's got on.

"God," she says, not even looking at me. "Showers aren't even relaxing when you're mostly checking for ticks all the time, I swear. I thought I found one in my hair but it was just a peanut from the Coburgs' trail mix. I'm telling you, I think my heart stopped for a minute, thinking I'd found a peanut-sized tick."

She turns her head and looks at me, her brows furrowing. "Don't have that look on your face. Ticks are not a joke."

Whatever look I had on my face, I suspect it's not gotten any more serious, because she sets down her comb a little aggressively and rolls her eyes, then crosses into the bunk room where she starts pulling on a pair of socks.

"Ticks are not a joke," I repeat back to her. "I had one once, right behind my knee. It got in there good."

"*What?*" she says, freezing with her left sock halfway on. "Did you get a *disease?*" She has this look on her face like I am the actual tick. This is a woman who I've basically blackmailed into being my fiancée and right now she looks like this is the most offensive thing I've ever said to her.

"No." I'm wearing out that spot on my cheek that I keep biting to stop me smiling. "I just got—"

"Oh my God, *don't*. Don't tell me anything! Was it bigger than a peanut? No, wait, don't even tell me. God!" She pulls on the rest of her sock, stands, and does this...I don't know what. A clumsy, ridiculous, full-body *shake*, like no other way I've ever seen her move. "Let's stop talking about it," she says, crossing the room to pull on her boots. "Did you find out anything from Hammond today?"

"Find out anything about what?"

She looks up at me from where she's lacing her boots, does the eye roll that's becoming increasingly familiar to me. "About tonight. About their presentation."

"Oh. No?"

"You were with him all *day*. It would've been good to gather some intel."

"We were using chain saws. It's not good for conversation."

"You had the whole ride over there and back. And I'm guessing you didn't turn on the chain saws at minute zero and then run them for four hours straight. You never took a water break?"

Jesus, this woman. She was probably a really good lawyer. I do the equivalent of pleading the fifth, which in this situation involves me shrugging, a movement she answers with a gusty sigh. "Val skipped the hike this morning to stay in their cabin. I'll bet she was prepping for the presentation. I'm telling you, she's the brains of that operation."

I snort. "No surprise there." I may not have had a lot conversation with Hammond, but it doesn't take much to realize his bulb runs about as dim as it did when we were kids. On the ride back he'd asked me if I'd ever had to treat one of those "four-hour erections" he was always hearing about on commercials.

"But that's brains enough." She stands and grabs her jacket from the hook by the door. "She runs that household. I'm pretty sure Hammond's real estate career is a daily gift from his father, and you know Val came from this little coal-mining town in West Virginia and got a full ride to Georgetown? She knows her shit. That wedding scrapbook she brought me looks like a professional did it."

"It's a wedding scrapbook, not a business plan."

"Don't be dumb," she says, bluntly. "These days wedding plans are business plans. I'm telling you, she's smart. We need to watch out for her tonight."

When we get out onto the stoop, she pulls her still-damp hair back from her shoulders, gathers it into a messy twist that she clips with something she's pulled from her jacket pocket. "We're not supposed to be competitive," I say, even though it's the exact opposite of what I believe. I'm just being contrary, and I realize it's because there's something oddly familiar about being contrary with her.

"Whatever you say, Boy Scout," she says, and sets off down the path.

"You think ticks like the smell of that shampoo you use?" I call after her. She stops still where she's standing—maybe she's trying to suppress another one of those shudders. But when she turns back to look over her shoulder, she's smiling.

"Don't know," she says, "but I'm pretty sure you do."

* * * *

You wouldn't think a presentation about a campground business plan would be considered a romantic event, but you also wouldn't know otherwise by being in this goddamn room right now.

Val and Hammond have turned the lights down low for their presentation; they're at the front, setting up a laptop and murmuring quietly to each other, *baby* this and *baby* that. So far as I know, all the kids are up in Paul and Lorraine's apartment with two of the camp staff members, though I can't imagine that's going well since the Coburgs said no TV or movies. It seems the relative dark and the lack of children is putting everyone in an affectionate mood, because Tom's got an arm draped over Sheree's shoulder, his fingertips stroking up and down her skin, and Rachel's standing behind Walt, giving him a shoulder massage, which frankly seems unnecessary since Walt didn't spend four hours clearing trees today, and also I've never seen him carry any one of those five kids. Paul and Lorraine sit closest to the front, side by side, their hands joined. Both of them seem nervous, and I'm guessing that the first presentation is bringing the reality of the sale home.

Either way, Zoe and I look like we're on the most awkward first date ever, a slice of space always between us, her arms crossed tightly over her chest, my hands clasped loosely between my knees. When Paul looks over his shoulder at us and waves, Zoe waves back, and I do something completely insane.

I put my arm around her.

All right, it's not around *her*, it's basically my arm across the back of her chair, but a line of my forearm is grazing her back, and Zoe—because Zoe is fucking *game*—scoots her chair closer to mine, and sets a hand on my knee.

I feel that hand like it's a thousand pounds, a new weight I'm going to carry while I'm here: the addition of physical affection with her. When Val claps her hands together and Hammond moves off to the side, the presentation beginning, I can barely think for the first minute, so attuned am I to the heat of her palm, the way her index finger taps a little as she listens, as if my leg is the natural replacement for her bottom lip. She wears her ring—*my* ring, the one I bought for her the day before I picked her up the first time—on the same hand that's touching me.

Up at the front, Val flashes a picture on the screen, a group shot from the early days of the camp, most of the campers in short white shorts, tube socks pulled up, green t-shirts. Before I've got the chance to process much, she flashes another, from the next year, and the next, again and again until she reaches a group shot that looks recent, Paul and Lorraine a little grayer, the campers all wearing green t-shirts again, but the more relaxed uniform requirements in clear evidence. I'm in some of those pictures, I'm sure I am, and so is Aaron, but mercifully Val's cycled through them so quickly I don't have much time to look for our faces, and when she finally pulls up a slide with the first and last photos side by side, I'm glad that they either predate or postdate me.

"If we take a look at these photos," Val says, "we can see how much Stanton Valley Campground has changed over time, and I'm not just talking about the tube socks. When I look at the history of this campground, I notice something different."

"More girls," Zoe whispers, and I look over at her, then back up the screen—and, yeah, in the first picture, there's maybe a dozen girls, all in the front row. In the second, it's closer to even but not quite.

"Historically, sleepaway camps catered primarily to boys and young men, stemming from the nineteenth-century focus on male self-reliance. Sleepaway camps were an opportunity to foster independence, strong bonds between men, a separation from the domestic influence..."

Zoe taps my kneecap harder, looks up at me, and raises her eyebrows. *Told you so,* she's telling me silently, and fuck, she is right as all hell, because this presentation is really, really good.

Val starts with statistics about how many girls across the country attend sleepaway camps, about how coed camps consistently see lower enrollments from girls, while single-sex camps for girls thrive. Then she's got quotes from psychologists on why single-sex campground environments can be more empowering for girls and young women, particularly camps that allow them to explore fields that are historically targeted at young men in schools—science, math, physical activity. She's got examples of single-sex campgrounds all across the country, graphs that show their profitability and their success rates in aiding the mental and physical health of campers. She's got a design plan that looks professionally done, a link to a website that she tells us has gone live today so we can learn more, and maybe the most effective thing of all: Hammond doesn't say one goddamn word.

"Hammond and I are raising three girls," she says, and here I recognize the way her voice changes—a higher pitch, maybe a slight drawl added in, closer to that voice she used when she *aww*-ed at me and Zoe last weekend. She's got one hand over her heart, and uses the other one to gesture to Hammond, a small wave of her hand that he answers by moving to the back of the room. "And my"—she begins again, clearing her throat—"*our* goal is to make sure they can be whatever they want."

"A ballerina!" comes a small voice from the back, and all of us turn in our seats to see the oldest in a black leotard, pink tights, her blond hair in a tight bun.

"A pilot!" comes another, and there's the youngest, dressed in what looks like a miniature Amelia Earhart costume.

"The president!" says the last, wearing a business suit and a flag pin, and it seems like everyone is clapping and chuckling, Val's final words on how a campground like hers could make this possible getting lost in the shuffle.

On my leg, Zoe's hand is squeezing. "Damn," she breathes, and finally I answer one of her asides.

"Yeah." That presentation was so good that for a second *I* even think the all-girls campground would be the best idea, and if Lorraine's face is any indication, she does too; she's rushed over to hug the Dwyer girls and is praising their performances. I don't miss the self-satisfied look on Hammond's face, like he wants a fucking cookie for marrying so far out of his league. Maybe Zoe can give him one of those soy sauce ones.

Up at the front, Val is waving off praise from Paul, shutting the cover of her laptop, and looking pleased. Right now I'd like to get a look at that wedding scrapbook, see if I could get some of her magic by osmosis.

"We need to get up," Zoe says, still sounding as stunned as I feel, and she's the one who wasn't dumb enough to underestimate Val. When she takes her hand from my knee and stands, I feel the loss of contact everywhere—my shoulders, my stomach, my legs. It's strange, this feeling. All weekend I've known there was some new closeness between Zoe and me, some sense that we'd really shown up to do this thing together. But that small, innocent point of contact—my arm around her chair, her hand on my knee—while we watched this thing unfold? Somehow, it's the first time I've really felt we're on the same team.

It's a jumble of polite congratulations and questions in the room, most everyone circling around Val and the girls, who at first cling to their mother in thrilled pride and, I'm guessing, a good deal of giddiness at being up late. Zoe handles the praise for us both, and is kneeling down to compliment the ballerina on her twirling style when the youngest of the Dwyer girls moves away from her mom and looks up at me.

"Hello," she says, reaching out a hand for me to shake in a gesture so mature that I imagine she's practiced it with her parents. I take her small hand and shake it once. "Did you like our presentation?" she asks.

"Yes," I say, keeping my voice serious to match her grave expression. It's not too hard since I still feel punched in the face by Val's star turn up there. "I like your costume."

"It's not a costume. It's my *uniform*." Her little-kid voice is so proudly assertive.

Beside me, Zoe rises from her crouch, laughing softly.

"Right, that's what I meant to say," I add. "I like your uni—"

"Miss Lorraine said you got a sister like mine," she says, cutting me off. I smile down at her in confusion. "Oh, no. I don't have a sister."

She shakes her head, strokes her small hand over the white scarf she's wearing. "Miss Lorraine said you were in your mom's tummy with your brother, like me and my sister."

Nothing's changed in here; everyone's still talking. There's still the sounds of chairs being dragged back into place, of the other kids running downstairs now that the evening's over. But it feels like a full minute where I hear nothing at all, where I'm just looking down at this little girl's face. I'd thought she was the youngest of the three, but that's not right. She's a twin, like me and Aaron were twins, not identical. Like her, Aaron was always smaller; my dad used to joke that I took up all the real estate so he couldn't get any bigger, a joke that used to make me laugh but later made me sick with guilt. I was taller, broader, sturdier, healthier.

I lived; he died.

I watch the little girl's eyes track to her twin. "That's Olivia," she says to me. "She's going to be the president."

I think it's Zoe who says something to her, who coaxes her away to turn back to where Val and Hammond are standing with the other girls. And I think Walt asks me what I think of an all-girls camp, but I don't bother answering. I'm halfway to the door before Zoe catches up, grabs my hand in hers, and I don't give a fuck if it's for show or not, I hang on to it. *Just for a second,* I tell myself. *Until you've cleared the door.*

Once we get outside, I drop her hand.

Zoe says one word: "Twins?"

"Yeah," I say. And it's all I say, for the rest of the night.

Chapter 7

Zoe

If this were a regular Sunday, I'd likely be sitting in one of four restaurants. Maybe The Outcast Diner, Kit's favorite, even though I think the tables can be a tad sticky. Maybe Lula's, also a diner, but with a bit less character and a lot more polish, catering to an upscale, professional crowd. It could also be this tiny bakery on Third, Greer's pick, which serves the best Belgian waffles in town, but we always have to eat fast because there are barely any seats and people really start working their stink-eyes on you if you linger over your coffee. If it were a regular Sunday but we were feeling fancy, maybe we'd go to the Crestwood; we'd drink mimosas and eat too many of the sweet biscuits they bring, the ones that have a powdered-sugar *C* on top.

If it were a regular Sunday, I wouldn't have a small serving of scrambled eggs and toast sitting in my stomach like lead. I wouldn't be listening to Rachel pelt Val with questions about her presentation, every single one of them a master class in subtle antifeminism. (*But do you worry about whether these girls would then have a hard time adjusting to the competition they'd face in their schools?*) I wouldn't be working so determinedly to keep from looking over my shoulder every two minutes to see whether Aiden will show up, wouldn't be worrying about whether Lorraine can see the tense set of my shoulders, the circles under my eyes from a mostly sleepless night, me lying awake in my bunk, the ceiling two feet from my face, waiting up to see if Aiden might say something.

He didn't.

If it were a regular Sunday, I'd be unloading to Kit and Greer. *Twins,* I'd say. *How could I miss it?* I'd once known the Aaron O'Leary file so well. I'd known his birthdate. And I'd seen Aiden's a couple of weeks ago on the background check. *You should have seen his face,* I'd tell them, remembering the way Aiden looked down at that little girl, his shoulders actually recoiling, a little, in shock.

But no—if it were a regular Sunday, I wouldn't be talking about Aiden at all. I wouldn't *know* Aiden at all. I'd be doing what I've been doing for every brunch I've had since I quit my job. I'd be deflecting, talking to Kit about her house, or asking Greer about classes, or making a joke about my endless dating dry spell, even though I'm pretty sure all three of us know I've cast that particular spell myself. I straighten in my seat, drag myself back to attention. I have to be here. I have to be doing this, for Aiden and for myself.

"Well, I homeschool my girls," Rachel is saying. "And they don't seem naturally inclined to—"

Please don't say math or science, I'm thinking, but when Val laughs I realize I've said it out loud. "Sorry," I blurt. "I was—conversation interrupting. Ignore me."

"No, no," says Lorraine. "I'm glad you did. We shouldn't be talking about this, not now. Let's just enjoy each other's company!"

There's a beat of awkward silence, probably all of us understanding the truth of this moment, which is that right now we don't have all that much in common except for this camp. Hammond and Walt have taken the kids outside the lodge to play, to burn off energy before their drives home, and Sheree and Tom left early this morning, Little Tommy crying and tugging on his left ear, his nose runny. Paul gave the kitchen staff the morning off, so he's been doing the cooking. As for Aiden? He'd said he'd be right behind me, but there's been no sign of him yet.

"Zoe, I *am* sorry about last night," says Val, that saccharine quality back in her voice this morning, and it's disappointing, really, because I'd liked the badass, take-no-prisoners Val who went up to the front of this very room and talked about girl power. "I caught the tail end of what Hannah said to Aiden. You know how kids are. I'm sure you have nieces and nephews."

I ignore that, because I see Hammond and Val are still exploiting Aiden's and my outsider status on this point as part of their strategy. "Oh, there's nothing to be sorry for," I say, but it comes out a little sharper than I intend. How come I can't get my voice to do that thing Val's does? Maybe if I suck on one of these sugar packets.

"I hope I didn't make a mistake in telling Hannah and Olivia about Aiden," says Lorraine, pulling our empty plates toward her and stacking them. "I know Aiden is still in a lot of pain about Aaron," she says. Val shakes her head and does this tongue-clucking thing, sympathy straight out of central casting, and Rachel nods along with her. It's clear that our quick exit last night was a topic of conversation, and I feel a spike of desperation. *Stable and happy,* Aiden had said, back at Betty's. This is exactly what he doesn't want, everyone thinking about his grief and how messed up he still is over it.

"He is in a lot of pain," I say, because it'd be ridiculous to try to account for last night—that *look* on his face—by saying something else. I take a sip of my coffee and steel myself, because I'm about to lie half my own face right off. "But I think he needed some time with me, to—you know. Get centered again. Aiden and I—we sort of bonded early on about..." I have to pause here, swallow a lump in my throat. "About loss. We support each other." As soon as I say it, I realize the half lie is as painful as the truth. What would it have been like, all those years ago, to have had someone who understood loss, someone I could lean on and build up, all at the same time? I'd looked for it, thought I'd found it once, but of course it'd been a mistake, a huge mistake that had made everything worse. By the time I'd found Kit and Greer, the kind of friends that keep caring about you even when you're a total mess, I'd buried it all. I'd made myself strong enough, became my own support.

"Did you lose a sibling too?" asks Lorraine, her voice gentle.

"No. I lost my dad. But he was—we were really close," I manage, wishing now I hadn't gone down this path, wishing I hadn't given up something of myself to help Aiden, who can't even be bothered to show up to this fucking thing, who's never going to get this camp unless he starts doing better. Beside me, Rachel takes a noisy sip of her orange juice, and I think about asking whether table manners are a part of that homeschooling syllabus.

"I'm so sorry to hear that," says Lorraine. "It's good that you have Aiden, and that Aiden has you. Has he told you much about Aaron?"

"Oh—well. Yes, sure. Of course." Because saying it three different ways is maximum convincing, obviously. But now that I've brought up my dad, I feel nervous, halfway to panic. I can recite twenty different facts about Aaron O'Leary, but they're all the wrong ones. They don't have anything to do with why Aiden looked at that little girl like he did.

I'm saved by the sound of delighted, giggling shrieks from outside. Val stands, her hands going immediately to her hips. "If Hammond gave them candy bars, I'm going to be *furious.*"

"Our kids don't eat sugar," says Rachel.

"Yes, you've *mentioned* that," snaps Val, and Lorraine and I exchange a look—a friendly commiseration that makes me feel as close to her as I've been since I've met her.

We all head to the lodge's door, file out onto the porch to see what the commotion is, and wouldn't you know it, Aiden's shown up after all. He's pushing Hannah and Olivia in a swing made from one of the tires I'd spray-painted yesterday—I've still got bright yellow paint underneath my fingernails as a reminder. The younger Coburg kids are restless around him, waiting for their turn, and when he looks up and notices us all watching, he offers a sheepish nod in our direction.

"He must've dragged that all the way from the obstacle course," Lorraine says.

"I hope neither of them throws up," says Val.

I'm hot in the face, at least three too many emotions to deal with all at once: I'm relieved to be out of that dining hall, out of that conversation. I'm grateful he's shown up. I'm a little proud, too, not that I have any right to be, and not that he'd ever talk to me again if I actually said that. Frankly I'm also really appreciating the way he looks in that thermal and those worn jeans, though I don't know if that's a feeling I should be contemplating in the presence of small children.

He turns and motions to Hammond, who helps the girls off the tire swing so that a couple of the Coburg kids can hop on, and Walt takes over the pushing. We meet in the middle, me and Aiden, slightly apart from the group. I don't want to make too much of it, but I'm suddenly afraid something about that conversation I just had will blow up in my face if I don't keep Aiden in the loop. We can't afford to get our stories crossed. "Nice job," I say, nodding toward the tire swing and sliding my arm around his waist and looking up at him. When he picks me up for these weekends, his jaw is clean shaven; by Sunday it's shadowed with dark hair. I like it better this way, not that I'm entitled to have a preference. I offer up a quiet cough, a clearing of my throat, and he takes the hint and drapes an arm across my shoulders. This fake affection—it's so new. Strangely electric and familiar, all at the same time. My hand on his knee last night had felt like the first time I held a boy's hand.

From here, I can push up slightly on my tiptoes, get close to his ear. He smells like Irish Spring, the bar of soap he has in our cabin shower next to my bottle of body wash. If he stiffens a little at my nearness, I try not to let it hurt my feelings. "Just so you know," I say, trying to keep my voice light, level. "I told Lorraine and Val and Rachel that you and I—well. I told

them my father died. That you and I have something in common, I meant."
Around my shoulders, his arm tightens a fraction. If I weren't so aware of
him, I might not even notice. "I know it's not the same, obviously," I add,
quickly. "But everyone was sort of making a thing about how we left last
night, and I was trying to…"

"Is that true?" Standing this close to him I can *feel* that low voice rumble
against me. I feel it all the way to my toes, and that's saying something,
because I'm pretty sure these boots are a half size too small.

"You said you didn't want everyone focusing on your grief," I say, a
deliberate dodge. I know what he's thinking, but I don't *want* to know. I
don't want to confront this again, this distrust he has for me. It'd seemed,
over the last day, that things were getting better. That he saw me differently.

But he says it anyway. "I mean about your father. Is that true?"

There's a nasty part of me that wants to confirm all his worst suspicions.
No, it's not true. I just have no shame, no shame at all. But, of course,
I *do* have shame, shame and guilt and all the rest of it, and I'd never lie
about this. "Yes," I say.

He looks down at me, a moment that feels as if it stretches forever. I'd
like to say there's some sympathy in the hard planes of his face. But mostly
it's a look I'm well accustomed to from Aiden, though not so up close. It's
half assessment, half *how-the-fuck-did-I-wind-up-with-her.*

I shrug—an answer to that unspoken question, and a rejection of that
arm around me. "Anyways," I say. "Problem solved."

* * * *

The thing about keeping your guilt jar—or your guilt vase, whatever—
right there in the center of your dining room table is that you don't give
yourself all that much time to forget about it. When I get home from
the campground on Sunday, it's the first thing my eyes land on, and I'm
tempted to pick the thing up and throw it right in the trash. So what if I've
made friends with Janet, if I made terrible cookies with her one awkward
weeknight? So what if I've got a meeting with Dan—the crying paralegal—
to help him with his law school application on Tuesday evening? So what
if I'm customer of the week at Starbucks; so what if I park way in the back
row of the parking lot of the grocery store now?

I shouldn't have brought up my dad, that's the thing. So much went
wrong after my dad died. So many of my mistakes seem to be Hydra heads
from that one crushing event, and mentioning it to Aiden—and the tense

moment of confrontation and confirmation that followed—seemed to set off a fresh wave of rumination. The whole drive home I was quiet and sullen, a role reversal that might have delighted me if I could have appreciated the way Aiden had become increasingly restless, uncomfortable with my silence. He'd even put on the radio. "It's that song you like," he'd said, when the obnoxious electronic beat filled the interior. "I *don't* like it," I'd snapped back, guaranteeing that he'd back off for the rest of the drive.

I let my pack thunk onto the floor of the foyer. Probably I should take it straight to the bedroom, start on my laundry right away, check for ticks in every seam. Instead I tug off my boots and head to the table, slumping into one of the chairs. I reach my hand into the vase, pull out my stiff slips of paper until I find the one I'm looking for.

It's not like my dad is in the guilt jar because I'm responsible for his death. No, that honor goes to the massive heart attack he had at home, while he was brushing his teeth one Tuesday night. Sudden, of course, but it shouldn't have been entirely unexpected. He was seventy-one years old, after all, had lived a lot of his first fifty years—before he met a pretty, twenty-five-year-old blonde and settled down—fast and unhealthy, drinking gin and smoking fat cigars and working eighty-hour weeks at his firm in L.A.

And he's not in the guilt jar because I'd disappointed him or been cruel to him when he was alive. At his funeral, dumbstruck and wobbly in a pair of my mother's heels, I'd tried to think of something, *anything*, unpleasant that had happened between us. Had we never had a fight? Had he never said something casually unkind, something dismissive or flippant about my childhood interests? Had I never talked back to him, given him normal teenage grief about rules or curfews? If I could only think of *something*, I'd told myself, the whole thing would hurt less. I'd cling to that unpleasantness, use it as a bandage for the great, sucking hole that seemed to live in my stomach since my mother had called me, my cell phone trilling loud in my quiet dorm room, barely fifteen miles from home, to tell me he was already gone.

But there hadn't been anything like that, no cruelty or fighting or petty annoyances. From the beginning, he'd been my hero, and I'd been his miracle kid, coming into his life well after he'd resolved to be a lifelong bachelor. When I was six he retired; he picked me up from school every day, took me to tennis lessons at our country club, helped me with my homework. Before I went to bed at night he'd give me an article he'd cut out from that day's paper—usually an editorial, something about politics or foreign policy—and then in the morning, while we ate breakfast he had made, he'd pepper me with questions about it, about how I'd answer this point or that. He'd laugh at my precocious answers. He'd tell my mom, who was hardly ever paying attention: *Look at us, having breakfast with one of the greatest legal minds in this country!*

Dad's in the guilt jar because I did everything wrong after he died. I barely managed to finish out the spring at USC, pulled Cs only because there'd been four weeks left in the semester and I'd done so well prior. I spent the summer in bars all over L.A., drunk and reckless, until I'd met Christopher, and after that I'd been sober, but still reckless. I was cruel to my mother—I hated her for barely shedding a tear, told her she'd always been jealous of me and Dad, that everyone knew she'd married him for his money. It wasn't that those things were entirely untrue. She *was* jealous. She *had* married him, at least in part, for his money, or at least she hadn't married him for better or for worse. As he got older, his hair getting thinner and his middle getting thicker, I'd sometimes catch her looking at him with a slight sneer of disgust. At the club, her affair with one of the golf pros was an open secret.

But my dad had loved her, I think, or had at least wanted to take care of her. He would've hated the way I treated her, how petty and small I became, how angry and stupid. He would have hated the way I fell apart. He would have been so *disappointed*. Sure, I'd cleaned up my act, ended it with Christopher after only a few months, a costly disentanglement that had seemed to sever any chance at reconciliation my mother and I might have had.

I'd gone back to USC, finished with honors. I'd even gotten that law degree, had moved all the way across the country just so I could go to his alma mater. I'd tried, like I'm trying now, to correct my mistakes.

But I still don't think I've done right by him. Don't think I'm the person he would've wanted me to be. For one thing, he wouldn't have wanted me to be the kind of person to have enough sins to make an actual receptacle for them. He wouldn't have wanted me to win the lottery, either—he'd come from nothing, a broken home and college on the GI Bill, a legendary work ethic that kept him doing pro bono cases even after he retired. *Work, he used to say to me, is what gives our lives meaning.* When I was still at the firm, when I'd come home from the office at ten o'clock at night, barely awake enough to kick off my stilettos and flop backward onto my bed, I'd sometimes just lie there, staring at the ceiling, an ache in my middle that I'd known was the particular, lingering feeling of grief. *Is this what my life is supposed to mean, Dad?* I'd think. *Is it like this, money and contracts and arranging words in precisely the right way?*

I use the tip of my index finger to push the square of paper aimlessly across the table, suddenly so lonely that I feel my eyes well up. It's a funny thing about the campground: I haven't felt lonely there, not really. Even in the cabin at night, when Aiden and I choreograph our strange nighttime routine—him out on that stoop until I say, me turning onto my side to face the wall when he changes for bed—I feel some thread of connection to him, a mutual awkwardness I know we're both thinking about in that musty cabin. I should call Kit and Greer. Kit especially would get a kick out of my recounting Rachel's math-and-science bit.

I hear the muffled ring of my phone from my pack, and I smile in spite of myself. It's one of them—I'm sure of it. This is how it works with us, a connection that's only grown stronger in the months since our lives changed so drastically, since that damned lucky ticket rewrote our stories for us.

But when I pull my phone from the side pocket, it's not either of their names on the display.

It's Aiden's.

"Hello?" I answer, my voice tentative. I worry there's a sound of tears in my voice, but it's not like he'd notice. It's not like he'd *care*.

"Hey." On the phone, his voice sounds even deeper, too close to my ear. I can hear the scratch of his stubble across the phone's speaker, as if he's adjusting it against his face. I've never seen him use his cell phone—I'm not even sure he carries it with him all the time, a strange quirk these days that makes it seem as if he's from a different time.

"How are you?" I say, because he doesn't make another volley after his *hey*, and someone here has to follow adult rules of communication.

"About the same as I was fifteen minutes ago."

"You called me," I say, annoyed, but at least I don't feel like crying anymore. "Don't keep me. I have to go look at all my clothes and make sure there aren't bloodsucking bugs making a home in them."

I think the sound he makes is a chuckle, but I long to see it in person. He's so *stern*, Aiden. Every time I get even a whisper of amusement out of him, I feel weirdly self-satisfied.

"Wanted to call and say something." It's so quick that some of the words run together.

"If it's about how Hammond called Val *babykins* after breakfast, let's leave it. I think one of my teeth fell out when I heard it."

"I wanted to say I'm sorry about your dad."

"Oh," I manage. No chance of verbal sparring after this. My throat feels closed and tense, my eyes scratchy with unshed tears.

"Didn't say anything before, which was a dick move. So I'm sorry. That it happened, and that I didn't say anything."

"It's fine."

Another stretch of silence, a car door slamming. I tamp down a ridiculous sense of disappointment. Of course we're not going to *talk* about it. He's just doing the right thing; Aiden's the kind of guy who does the right thing. But he isn't the kind of guy who wants to know more than he has to, at least when it comes to me. At Betty's, he'd said he was trying to be better friends with Ahmed and Charlie, and I wonder what that'd be like, Aiden as a friend. I don't suppose he'd ever be like me, too chatty by half, too loud sometimes, overeager to get a laugh. Relentless.

"It is awful how he called her that," Aiden finally says. "Hammond, I mean. I'm pretty sure they're insulting each other with those names."

I feel a smile hook at the corners of my lips, a smile that felt impossible when I first walked into this room, not even a half hour ago. "They *totally* are." I keep the snark in my voice, not overselling it. I'll bet this is what Aiden's like, as a friend, or at least for a second I let myself believe it. Quiet, but he tries. Doesn't leave you hanging, not when it really matters.

"Well. I'd better get going. Got a shift tonight."

"Okay." Then I add, without thinking, "Be careful."

A hot flush spreads up my neck, underneath my ears. I've said that as though he's my fiancé for real, as though I have something to do with his life outside the weekends in Stanton Valley. I'm so embarrassed that I move the phone away from my ear to hang up.

But not before I catch him say, maybe more gently than usual, "Sure. Thanks."

I look down at where my pack rests by my feet, see the hard shape of Aiden's binder pressing against its back side. In my hand, my phone pings with a text, an expected one this time, in our long-running group message. *Back yet?* Kit's written, and I type out a quick reply: *All in one piece.*

She'll want more—she and Greer both will. Right now, though, I don't so much feel like giving it up. I feel like having Aiden's voice as the last in my ear. I type out another quick text to my friends, my friends who so clearly disapprove of what I've chosen to do with my weekends. *I'll call you guys later. Need to shower and start laundry.*

But instead I bend down, unzip my pack and slide out the binder, take it over to the dining room table, and open it again. It's hard, looking at this and thinking about how to make it work—this story of addiction, lives lost and ruined or never really the same, even if they come out the other side—after seeing Val's smiling, healthy girls, all that potential for them in Paul and Lorraine's campground.

It's hard seeing Dad's slip lying there on the table beside the vase.

It's hard—but it's what I deserve.

Chapter 8

Aiden

Thursday night, and I've been on duty since 6:00 a.m., another seven hours to go of the double I'm cramming in before we head back up to camp tomorrow. We're back from a call at Sunset Terrace, a nursing home that's barely five minutes away, where we spend lots of time, easy calls, usually, since the nursing staff there has almost always taken care of the basics, and we're just doing transport. It's fall break at the university, a long weekend that started yesterday, so students are thin on the ground, and I'm hoping it's a quiet night.

"Charlie, you can't be saying that this team deserves to be ranked fourth right now," says Ahmed, overloud. He's stuffed himself into the old, faded recliner—a community donation, like all the furniture in the squad quarters—and is eating microwave popcorn, the bag looking a little charred on the bottom.

"It's about strength of schedule," says Charlie, flopping down beside me on the couch, setting her heavy black uniform boots on the coffee table. "You always overlook strength of schedule."

"You always overlook how they barely squeak out wins," he says, into it now. They love arguing about college football, I've learned, even when neither of them really cares about the teams that are playing. "They're always—"

"You guys," I say, turning up the volume a couple of notches. "Let's just watch the damn game."

"Grouchy," says Charlie.

"I'm not grouchy." But the way I've said it sure as fuck sounds grouchy.

"That camp thing going bad, man?" Ahmed says, and I can tell by the way Charlie grabs the remote from me and returns the television to a lower volume that they've been waiting to bring it up. *We'll get him when he's tired,* I imagine them saying. *We'll distract him first with our bickering.*

"It's going all right."

It should be Val's presentation that's getting to me. All week I'd been turning it over in my mind, replaying it from start to finish, or at least replaying it from the part I'd started paying attention. Val's presentation had what Zoe said mine needed—there was a *story* there—that's how she'd made her argument. Plus she'd used her kids as props, which even I can admit was effective. I'm not creative enough to think of something like that for my own presentation, and bringing in recovered addicts seems like a risky game. There was no darkness in what she'd said. She'd made it entirely hopeful, entirely upbeat.

But that's not really what's getting to me. Zoe is getting to me, that hitch in her voice when I'd called her on Sunday. That vacancy in her eyes when I'd asked her if what she'd told me about her father was true. I'd fucked that up—I knew it as soon as I'd said it. We'd gotten into a good rhythm, last weekend. Started making it look real.

"Aiden, come *on,*" Charlie says, stretching out that last syllable. "Give us something, will you?" She's curious, sure, but she's pissed, too—the frustration of her continued efforts to get to know me better, to make some kind of real friendship between the three of us.

I clear my throat, push my back farther into the cushions until I can feel the hard frame of the sofa across my shoulder blades. "It's—she's different than what I expected," I say, mentally kicking myself for not taking it in another direction. Why didn't I talk about my competitors? Hell, why didn't I tell them about my doubts about my presentation?

"She fucked you right up on that dartboard," says Ahmed. "That was unexpected."

I press my lips together, remembering how she'd lined up. How one of her eyes would narrow a fraction before she'd throw.

"Oh, shit," says Charlie, lifting a boot from the coffee table so she can nudge my shin with it. "You *like* her."

"Jesus, Charlie," I say. "I'm not fifteen fucking years old. We're doing a job together."

"What's that got to do with it? I met Autumn on the job." Autumn is Charlie's wife, the med student up in D.C. who started out as an EMT. From the scraps I overheard when I first joined this squad, it was pretty much love at first sight for the two of them. Autumn quit to go to another crew two days after Charlie was hired, knowing there'd be too much conflict if they worked together.

I open my mouth to reply, to say something about how it's different with me and Zoe, but something about the way Charlie has settled back into her seat and crossed her arms over her chest stops me. I look over at Ahmed, who's shaking his head in what looks like annoyance, digging his fist in the bag for more popcorn. Under his breath he mutters something—I catch a huffy *call her* in the mix.

Right now is my cue to get up and think of some chore to do—scrub the bay floor, check the maintenance schedule on the rig. I'd even get up and clean the bathroom if it'd get me out of this moment, because when I look back over at Charlie, I think her chin might be quivering a little.

Fuck.

It's pretty clear Ahmed isn't going to say shit, and even though I've got my list of avoidance chores queued up, I feel stuck to this couch. For the first time in what feels like forever it doesn't seem right to take the easy option. "All right, Charlie?" I ask.

She swipes hastily at her face, then tucks her arms even tighter toward her. "It's fine. Autumn was supposed to come this weekend, but she's not now. She's got an infectious disease test on Monday."

"That's too bad," I say.

"She's *always* got a test, you know?"

"Yeah, sure. They say med school is like that." Like I know anyone in med school. Basically I'm just trying not to fuck this thing up too.

"I knew it would be hard, being apart," she says, her voice wobbly. "But we're basically newlyweds, you know? And everything was great, and we had this whole schedule and plan for when we would see each other, and it's—it is *not* working out like we'd planned, you know?"

I've never noticed it, this verbal tic of Charlie's—*you know?*—maybe because I've never seen her really upset. But when I hear it now, I take it for what it is. She's looking for someone to say, *Yeah, I get it. I'm with you. I hear you.*

"Charlie, I told you, you're being too hard on her. You should give her—" begins Ahmed, and I cut him a look. Even I know Charlie's not looking for two dumbass single dudes to tell her what to do. She's just looking to *talk.*

"I'm sorry," I tell her, and she nods in appreciation, wiping underneath her eyes again.

"When I met Autumn I thought I'd found my other half. And we barely had a full year together before she moved up there, started this whole new life. *Without* me."

Something about this last thing she's said—it startles me in a place I don't access except by accident, a long-buried fight I'd had with Aaron my first Christmas back from Wisconsin. Before his accident, before he'd gotten hooked on pills—but already he was different, hanging around with a crowd of Ultimate Frisbee guys and seemingly uninterested in his classes. By my third day home I'd only seen him twice, had jokingly bitched at him about it when he came home for dinner. "You forget about your big brother?" I'd said, nudging him playfully, like I did with guys on my team. I was younger, technically, by seven and a half minutes, but he'd never once been bigger, and before he'd always laughed at my teasing about it. "Fuck off, Aiden," he'd said. "*You* do everything without *me*."

"That's rough," I tell Charlie. "Trying to find a place for yourself in someone's new situation. I've been there."

She rolls her head toward me, her eyes wet, but I see the surprise in them. It's not so much for *what* I've said, but for the fact I've said anything at all. Anything that's not *I'd better go do inventory* or *Maybe we should get some shut-eye.* "You have?"

I shrug, overly casual. "Not with a woman. But growing apart from people I was close to."

"Yeah," she says. "It *sucks.*" But she's stopped crying, and when Ahmed suggests that she think about going up to D.C. this weekend, keeping it low key, no expectations, Charlie's more receptive. Barely a half hour later and Ahmed and Charlie are both asleep where they sit, Ahmed clinging to the popcorn bag like it's a favorite childhood blanket, Charlie snoring softly with her phone in her lap. I'm staring at the TV, unseeing, feeling all right about how that conversation went but still stuck in the shit of the memories it'd brought up.

Two months after Aaron died, when I was still half-blind with rage and grief, working any shift I could get even when it broke the scheduling rules, my crew picked up a recent knee-down double amputee who'd called 911 screaming in pain, so out of her mind with it the dispatcher could barely hear her. We'd found her in bad shape, infected sores on her both her stumps. But all she'd said, over and over, was *Please, my feet, my feet hurt so bad.*

"Phantom limb," my partner had muttered as we got to work, but even though I'd known about this from years of training, had seen it time and time again, I'd felt those two words like a punch to my face. *That's what I have,* I'd thought. *I have a phantom limb.*

I'd obsessed over the idea at first, clinging to it as an explanation for the literal, physical, pain I'd felt since Aaron died, an aching in my joints that never seemed to leave me. But after a while, it wasn't enough of an explanation. I didn't have a phantom limb, after all. I had a phantom *self*. I was half myself without Aaron; I always would be. When I'd looked down at that little girl last weekend, I'd had about fifteen different feelings all at once, more feelings than I'm used to having in a single day, and the worst one, the worst one of all, was jealousy. I was fucking jealous of her, the way she'd looked over at her twin. I could remember the way that felt, to find Aaron in a room. Like the ground underneath me got more stable.

I should be annoyed, maybe, at what Charlie's said. Married to Autumn for a year and saying she's her other half? Six months ago, I would've been so bothered that I would've had to leave the room. *You don't understand,* I would've thought. *You could never understand.* But I don't feel annoyed, not even a little. If Charlie feels even a quarter of what I felt over my brother, I hope something turns around for her, and soon. I hope she goes up there this weekend and they work it out. The same way I woke up on Sunday and hoped I hadn't hurt that little girl's feelings.

I shut off the TV, listening to the slight crackle of the dispatch radio in the other room. I don't want to think too hard about why I feel different now than I did six months ago. It feels a little like betrayal, like having that fight with Aaron all over again: You *do everything without* me. Here I am, in our hometown, at my job, with people who I get closer to calling friends every day. It's just time, I guess—that fucker keeps moving forward, no matter how you try to stay perfectly still in your anger. It's time that's changing me, that's all.

But hell if I don't think, just for a second, about a pair of gold-brown eyes staring up at me. Hell if I don't think of her, laying something else on the line about herself, so she can save my ass again.

* * * *

Those gold-brown eyes are lowered—shy, even—when we get to the cabin on Friday afternoon and Zoe pulls my binder out of her pack, holding it out to me.

"I made some suggestions," she says, when I take it. There are bright pink tabs sticking out the sides, a couple of them with her handwriting squeezed on. "You don't have to use any of them, obviously," she says, turning away to tuck a few items of clothing into her drawer. We've got a system now: she takes the three drawers on the left, and I take the two on the right. She always uses the bathroom stall closest to the door, and prefers if I never use that one. She gets in bed first, turns over, and then I change after. She likes to leave the light on at night in the entryway, which I almost always forget until she says, "Light on, *please*," in this snippy voice that I find weirdly hot, especially right before I get in bed. In the mornings, I get up first, pull on pants and a sweatshirt, and go out to the stoop and wait. Twice I've had to piss so bad that I've had to walk out into the woods and relieve myself.

"Thanks," I tell her. "You want to—" I'm about to ask her if she wants to go over them together, but she grabs her phone and a pair of headphones from the side pocket of her pack.

"I missed my workout today so I'm going to head out for a walk," she says.

The weird thing is, I can tell she's lying. At first, of course, I thought Zoe was lying all the time. But it's this small, harmless fib—her not wanting to be around me while I look at her notes—that gives me a glimpse of what she looks like when she's really lying, or at least when she's lying to me: she blinks twice, rapidly, and I can tell she's caught the inside of her cheek with her teeth.

"Which trail?" I ask her.

"What?"

"Tell me which trail. So I know where you've gone." She rolls her eyes, but I'm not budging on this. It's broad daylight and the safest place I know in the world, but I follow the rules around here, and one of them is to always tell someone where you've gone.

"The one headed toward the swimming hole."

"Fine, east trail. Stay on it, all right?"

"God. Do you need to see my permission slip too?"

"Do you have one to show me?" I don't know why, but it sounds a little dirty, the way I've said it. Damn, I must need a nap. I take the binder over to my bunk, flop down, and rest it on my chest, close my eyes. "See you in an hour."

"I didn't say I'd be back in an hour."

I crack open my eyes and look over to where she stands, her hands on her hips. "An hour, or I'll come looking for you. Keep your phone on."

She slams the door behind her, and I'm smiling, a hot rush of something like gratitude that we're still this way, still rough and tumble, still back and forth.

I tell myself I'll rest my eyes for a minute or two, then get to work. I don't want her coming back here thinking I don't care about the work she's done. But I must doze off, because the next thing I hear is the thud of footsteps out on the stoop, the door opening and then quickly slamming shut, Zoe's heavy breathing and a muttered curse.

I'm off the bed as quick as I can be without knocking my head into something, the binder falling to the floor while I rush into the entryway. "What happened?" I say, taking in her flushed cheeks, the twig she's got stuck in her hair. I have a brief, thudding moment of panic—is this not the safest place I know in the world? Holy fuck, could something have happened to her out there?

"Jesus, Aiden!" she shouts, interrupting my thoughts. "It's like—I don't know what! It's Cocktoberfest out there! At the swimming hole, I mean! Just—just—a whole lot of naked dudes!"

I blink, taking a second to process what she's said—*Cocktoberfest?*—and then I nearly double over with laughter, not only at her crass language but at her wide-eyed expression, the pink flags of color high on her cheekbones. "Stop laughing at me! Why did you let me go out there?"

"I didn't know anyone would be out there," I say, between breaths of continued laughter.

"I saw Paul do a cannonball! In the *nude!*"

"Wow," I say, rubbing a hand over my hair, down my face, schooling my expression. "It's always the quiet ones, though."

"Oh my *God*," she says, fanning her face. "I haven't been this traumatized since I saw Simon Callow's penis in *A Room with a View*."

"Is that porn or something?"

"Porn?!" she shouts, shocked. "It's Merchant Ivory, you heathen!"

I don't know what Merchant Ivory is; maybe it's upscale porn or something, but I add it to the mental list of things Zoe says that I'll have to Google later. She's at the sink, washing her hands vigorously, mumbling to herself.

"You didn't get a handful of anything, did you?" I nod toward her busy hands, trying to keep down the smile that's threatening to break my face wide open.

"A handful…? What! No." She looks down at her hands bemusedly, shuts off the water, and shakes them over the sink. "I don't know what I'm doing. I'm in shock!"

"I should've warned you. It's kind of an old tradition around here, jumping naked into the swimming hole before it gets too cold. Paul and some of the staff and a few of his buddies from the area usually do it."

"Well, I guess!" She's turned to face me, crossing her arms over her chest, and I realize something—it's the first time, between me and Zoe, that things feel comfortable, that there isn't something a little ugly between us, the lie we're both telling sitting heavily on both our shoulders. This moment—this funny shock she's had, it could have happened to anyone, to someone I was really with, someone who was here by choice and not because of guilt. And now that she's settled, she's smiling too, leaning back against the sink and shaking her head in disbelief.

"I'm pretty sure they saw me too," she says, and then she laughs, bold and expansive, same as the way she speaks. "I think I gave this—like, squeak? Sort of a *meep!* noise?"

Oh, man. She fucking *does* the noise, the *meep!* she describes, and damn, it's cute, and the ribbon of laughter she lets out after sends a shot of heat straight to my dick.

"Didn't count you for a prude, Zo," I say, not even thinking about it, and her laughing eyes snap to mine, widening for just a second at the nickname. The implication of it. That we're friends, that we're close.

It feels like I've removed an article of her clothing.

I wait, holding my breath, for her to correct me.

But she doesn't. She smiles and says, "I'm really, *really* not. But I met my penis threshold. A couple of them, all right, but more than seven and I go nonverbal."

"Maybe it was Paul's. Paul's dick is your threshold."

"Don't *talk* about it!" she exclaims, but then she's laughing again, her hands coming up to cover her face.

And I don't know what it is, when she lowers her hands. I don't know if it's the fatigue or the shock of adrenaline I got, waking up to the sound of her coming back in, fast and breathless, or maybe it's the fact that I now know what Zoe's laugh—her real, spontaneous laugh—sounds like, but before I can think of what I'm doing, I'm taking a step toward her, reaching out a hand. I'm trailing my fingers across the blush that's settled high on her cheekbones, running them across that soft swoop of skin to tuck a length of hair behind her ear.

And—oh, *fuck*. I've touched her before, but not so many times that I still can't count them—a count I've actually made, one sleepless night last week. But I've never reached out to touch her like this, just for my own benefit, just to feel her skin against mine. It's the work of a second, maybe two or three, to make that journey across her face, to feel the tickling strands of her hair between my fingers, but it's enough to make her breath hitch and her flush deepen.

I don't linger. Because I know if I do, I'm going to let that hand trace down her neck, down to that vee of skin that's showing between the two open buttons of her flannel shirt.

I step back, my smile fading along with Zoe's. She clears her throat and straightens up from the sink. "Did you look at my notes?"

It's possible I'm working up a flush of my own—my neck feels hot underneath my collar—and I turn toward the main room. "Was just now getting to it." She doesn't respond, and when I look back at her, she's still by the sink, looking toward the door.

"I should probably go back out, take a different trail."

"Chicken," I mutter, smiling to myself about this old insult I've drudged up, straight out of a file of immature shit I used to say when I was an actual camper here.

"What?"

"You heard me," I say, picking up the binder from the floor, sitting back on my bunk. "You don't want to be around while I look at this."

"I don't care when you look at it," she snaps, but even she's got to know how childish she sounds. She comes in behind me, sits on the bunk beneath her own, so we're facing each other. When I look across at her, I have to fight another smile. She's trying to keep up that stiff posture, but she's too tall for it with the top bunk in her way, so she scoots forward, crossing one leg over the other, folding her hands in her lap, like that first day she sat in my kitchen. "Anyways, they're just suggestions," she says, when I open the front cover.

She doesn't move while I read over the list she's tucked into the front pocket, a summary of the changes she's made, small arrows instead of bullet points, her tidy script in sharp, black ink. "You sit in the front row a lot at school?" I ask her, recalling that first meeting we had in the outdoor classroom.

"I sat wherever I wanted to, Boy Scout," she says, smirking at me when I meet her eyes. Damn, I'll bet. I'll bet she's the smartest person in any room she's in. There's that hot feeling, right around my collar, and I look back down at the binder in my lap, grateful for something else to focus on.

Zoe's copied my schematic for the Wilderness/Wellness site onto one of those clear sheets my elementary school teachers used to use on the overhead projectors and mapped it onto Lorraine and Paul's cartoonish map of the campground, a numbered x by all the major components. Then she's written out a plan for a tour of it, pieces of my original presentation in the binder tabbed to the various "stops" she's planned.

"It's not that the spreadsheets are gone," she says. "But they're supplements now. And if you do this right, Lorraine and Paul will be interested enough to look at supplementary materials."

"Right," I say, in plain, stupid shock at all she's done. "It's a—so it's a tour?"

She shrugs. "After Val, I figure everyone else is going to follow the leader. Don't be surprised if Tom and Sheree bring some of the kids from his program in Shaftesbury Park for tomorrow. It'll be in the lodge, the projector, the PowerPoint, the whole thing. Val set the tone, I'm telling you. If we go last and do that, we look like we're falling in line. We've got to do something more memorable. Paul and Lorraine have lived their whole lives on this land. We show them your vision for it, while we're actually out on it, and they'll remember."

"It's a good idea," I say.

"It's a great idea. Ideal if the weather is perfect, but even if it's not—Paul and Lorraine won't care, and I'm guessing you won't, either. It'll work."

I'm blinking down at the binder, at everything she's managed to do in less than a week, stunned and grateful and a little embarrassed. Even on the page I'm looking at, I can see a mistake, where I typed *Widlerness* instead of *Wilderness*. She must think I'm an idiot.

"I don't have the story, though," she says, interrupting my thoughts. "Everything you have in there is important. You're going to have to find a way to say it all. But I don't have the story for this. That's down to you. You've got to be able to tell them why this matters."

I reach up one hand, rub it up the back of my neck, where my muscles are tight with fatigue. She doesn't have to say it. I know what she's talking about. I know *who* she's talking about. Lorraine and Paul knew Aaron, and they loved him. They'll want to hear that I'm doing this for him. *Help me tell it,* I'm thinking, deep down inside myself, but I don't know who I'm thinking it *to*. To her? Because that's ridiculous. No matter how I feel about her now—*Cocktoberfest* and her laugh and the feel of her skin—there's still this thing between us, this thing about Aaron that brought us together in the first place. This obligation she's fulfilling to me and my family.

As if she's heard what I'm thinking, she smooths her hands down her thighs, stands from where she sits on the bunk. When she speaks, her voice is cool again, no trace of that big laugh. You'd never imagine this is a woman who'd make a noise like *meep!* in embarrassed shock. "There's only so much of this debt I can work off, Aiden."

There's no reason why it *should* hurt, what she's said. It's only exactly what I was thinking. It's only exactly what this thing we're doing is all about. There's no reason why it should, but it does.

Chapter 9

Zoe

There's nothing quite like a long day of camp and a fading bonfire to make you double down on your commitment to fake affection, I guess.

It's Saturday night, an hour since Tom and Sheree finished their presentation, and I've spent the better part of the last thirty minutes—ever since I licked the remnants of my last gooey s'more off my fingertips—tucked against Aiden's side, his back leaning against one of the thick tree trunks that surround the fire pit, my body fitting right into the space his arm makes. Every single place where we touch I'm warm, and I wish I could say it was just the fire.

We'd been woken at dawn this morning, the thunk of a fist against our cabin door. Aiden had leapt from the bed, every inch of the chest and torso I'd avoided looking at on full display in the dim light from the window. While he'd pawed at the bunk above him for his shirt, I'd watched his muscles move, the golden-brown skin on his corded forearms pebbling with the chill of the early morning. When he'd finally pulled on his thermal and marched to the door, a grumbled *hang on* in his dark, scratchy morning voice, I'd turned my head to press my face against the pillow, to press my knees together in shocked, frustrated longing. It's not that I hadn't *known* I was attracted to him. But in the early-morning fog of sleep, I hadn't yet remembered why I shouldn't be.

It'd been Hammond at the door, announcing that Paul had a surprise, which I could only hope had nothing to do with the swimming hole. Barely twenty minutes later and Aiden and I had hiked, groggy and cold and silent—still a little bruised, maybe, from yesterday's awkward exchange over the tour plan—out past the storage warehouse, a satisfying crackle of leaves on the trail beneath our feet.

Zip-lining, that had been the surprise, and from the beginning almost everything about it seemed designed to break the tension lingering between Aiden and me. When it was my turn up on the deck, Aiden having already gone across, Paul had helped me into a harness and I'd basically done gymnastics with my eyeballs to avoid looking anywhere near his face or his crotch, and even though Aiden had been five hundred feet away, I could feel his smile. I could almost hear that low laugh from yesterday, the one that had lit me up from the inside. And once I'd kicked away from the decking? I'd laughed in delight, seeing everything Lorraine promised—early-morning light winking through the changing colors of the canopy, leaves shiny and pronounced with morning dew. When I'd landed on the opposite side, Aiden waiting there, I'd looked up at him and he'd smiled down at me with the same look he'd given me yesterday in the cabin, just before he'd touched me.

It looked something like affection. Something like desire.

Afterward Lorraine had revealed thermoses of coffee and fresh-made muffins. For the first time, I suspected I'd had something close to the experience of being an actual camper here. Sure, we're all competing for something, but out there in the early morning, zip-lining through the trees, we were all on the same side.

It had lasted, of course, only up until Tom and Sheree's presentation, when the tense edge of rivalry had again fallen over the lodge's dining room, despite Tom and Sheree's constant positivity. It was as I'd thought—similar to Val's, with assists by four teenagers from Tom's program in Shaftesbury Park. Their vision for the camp wasn't as original—modeled on what Stanton Valley already is, but with a focus on programs for kids growing up in the city, far away from what Sheree called *the pleasures of nature*. They hadn't worked out much of the business side of things, some of their slides a bit muddled on details. But details or not, original or not, Tom and Sheree presenting together was its own magic—comfortable and spontaneous, joking and laughing, teasing Tommy where he sat wriggling on Lorraine's lap. Aiden and I had watched—a frozen tableau exactly like we'd been last week, his arm across my back and my hand on his knee—and I think both of us had seen the strength Tom and Sheree brought to the table. They looked like a family. They looked like *love*.

So maybe that's why, once the after-presentation bonfire got under way, Aiden stayed close. A hand on my shoulder while I stuck my marshmallow-topped skewer into the fire. A few fingers to push the hair away from my mouth when I'd first bitten into the s'more. His thigh pressed close to mine while we sat side by side. *Obviously,* I'd thought, with surprisingly grim disappointment, *this is only for show.*

"Aiden," Sheree says, from where she sits on the other side of the fire, passing Little Tommy another unroasted marshmallow, which he stuffs in his face with chubby, sticky hands. "Do you remember when Kenny Templeton sat in the bonfire back when you were a counselor?"

I inadvertently stiffen at this, Sheree's casual invocation of the past, a topic Aiden seems to avoid with everyone, not just with me. Usually that's a comfort, but right now I feel it like a string pulled tight at the back of my neck. I don't want things getting spoiled again. But beside me, Aiden offers a lighthearted groan, and when I look over at him, his lips are turned up at the corners. "You were a counselor here?" I ask.

"Yeah. My last two years." He looks across the fire at Sheree. "The smell." Sheree puts her head in her hands. "I never forgot that!" she exclaims.

"Did someone push him?" I say, my voice weirdly high pitched in concern for young Kenny Templeton, whoever he is. I think I've scooted a centimeter away from the fire, a centimeter further into that space between Aiden and me.

Lorraine laughs. "Kenny was experimenting. With the flammability of his—"

"Of his *farts*," says Hammond, like he's so pleased to have found an opportunity to say a word that any self-respecting adult avoids in mixed company.

"You're *disgusting*," says Val, pushing at his shoulder.

"Aiden was a hero," says Sheree, and though she's talking to the group, I get the sense this is directed only at me. "All the other counselors scattered to the wind! I think Paulie Kilroy left to throw up, even. Aiden was the only one who knew first aid protocol."

Aiden shrugs beside me, and I can't be sure—the light of the fire is too indistinct—but I think the skin beneath his jaw is a little pink. "I'd taken some classes," he says. "For—you know. So I'd be able to handle things, at camp."

"Well," Lorraine says, "and of course, for Aaron."

Lorraine. Come on, I'm thinking, angry on Aiden's behalf. I don't know what she means by this remark, but I find I don't really *want* to know. From the beginning, it seems Lorraine's been on a Good Samaritan mission to get Aiden to open up, to talk more freely about his brother, and whatever I think about that in the abstract, in practice I'd like her to back off, since Aiden clearly doesn't want to talk about it. I open my mouth to say something, but close it again when I feel Aiden's big hand come up from where it's been resting on the ground behind me, settling around my waist. One of his fingers grazes my bare skin, where my flannel shirt has ridden up, and my breath hitches.

"Aaron was—he had asthma," he says, low, just for me. "Lots of allergies. Had to keep an eye on him."

"Oh," I say, but he probably doesn't even hear, because Hammond's talking loudly about the cutoff sweatpants Kenny had to wear to accommodate his bandages. Walt and Rachel, hovering on the edge of our circle, look annoyed and a bit resentful whenever old, shared memories of the camp come up. Val, for her part, only lasts for a few sentences of Hammond's juvenile memories, then clucks her tongue and stands, calling to where her girls have been playing. "We need to get them to bed, baby," she says, her voice tense. I catch Lorraine's eyes darting between Val and Hammond, her lips pursed. Hammond and Val suffer so completely in comparison to Tom and Sheree that I feel a little sorry for Val.

After this, the party breaks up quickly, Tom and Sheree anticipating a sugar crash for Tommy, Walt and Rachel appearing relieved to not have to stick around. Paul yawns, patting Lorraine's knee, and she rises from her spot, gathering the last of the s'mores trash.

Beside me, Aiden hasn't moved. His hand at my waist hasn't, either.

"I'll put it out, Lorraine," he says, nodding toward the fire. "Our cabin's closest, and I've got a lantern."

"You're sure?" she asks, looking back and forth between us. Part of me wants to say, *Lorraine, don't leave. Things are weird and what if they get weirder?* But she's not giving a look like Betty or Kit or Greer would give me, not an *Are you all right with things* look. It's more of a *What a nice night for a young couple* look, and so the other part of me focuses on that, on how convincing Aiden and I must've been today.

She and Paul say their goodnights; when Paul stands from his place on the log I have to feign interest in my shoelace on account of the cannonball thing. Aiden snickers, and I lean into him with my shoulder, a light body check that he contains by pulling me closer. He smells so good, like this bonfire and like the trees and like *him*.

We listen to the fading footfalls of the group, watch their lantern lights dim as they go their separate ways, and then, suddenly, we're alone.

"I'll just—" I say, scooting away from him, closing my eyes at the awkwardness of it, afraid to see his reaction. *Which would be worse,* I think: *relief, or disappointment?*

"So is it because of Aaron you became a paramedic?" I have to tuck my hands underneath my thighs to keep myself from slapping them over my mouth in embarrassment.

Beside me, he's quiet. Out of the corner of my eye, I see him take a deep breath, and I expect he's counting to ten so he doesn't call me a bunch of names or remind me of the deal: *You and me, we don't talk about my brother.* But instead he says, "I guess that's part of it. Spent a lot of time around doctors with him, back when we were young, and I suppose—I was good in a crisis, when it came to him." He pauses and then adds, "Not all types of crisis, I guess."

Well. That lands like a lead balloon, an awful sadness that I don't know how to recover from. I am an *idiot* for bringing it up, for saying his name. I'm as bad as Lorraine.

"Why'd you become a lawyer?" he asks, and I slump against the log behind me in relief.

"My dad was a lawyer."

Aiden nods, like he fully understands this as an explanation. "You think you'll ever go back to it? I know you won that money, but..."

"I didn't win enough money to never work again." I'd been so embarrassed, initially, that he'd known, but now it's almost comforting, not to have to keep it a secret from him. "I thought I'd—I don't know. Take time off? Figure out what I really want, I guess. My first job..." I trail off, thinking of the sleek, glass-walled offices at Willis-Hanawalt. My two-thousand-dollar ergonomic chair. The Tiffany desk clock I got after my second year of service. "I had my eye on the wrong thing. I went to a top law school. I thought that meant I should go to a top firm, same as my dad did. I went through the motions."

"It'd be a shame to give it up altogether. You're smart as fuck."

I look over at him, my smile immediate and spontaneous in a way it's usually not around him. I'm probably blushing all the way down to my boot-cramped toes. "Drives me crazy," he adds.

I know by something in his voice that he doesn't mean an annoyed kind of crazy. He means the same crazy that I felt this morning, in my bunk. The same crazy I felt when he smiled at me on the zip line. The same crazy I felt with his hand on my skin. His eyes slide to mine, one hot second of contact before he stands and reaches behind the log he's leaning against, hefting a large metal pail I didn't even realize was there. He moves to stand between me and the fire, his back to me, and dumps the bucket on top, the fire hissing and popping. It's not all the way out yet, but Aiden grabs a stick that's leaning up against a nearby tree and begins stirring the pit, extinguishing more and more of the flame.

"Might want to switch on that lantern," he says.

But I don't. In the fading light, I watch the muscles underneath his shirt move, watch when he leans forward a little, the muscles in his legs and ass pulling tight. *What would it matter,* I'm thinking. *What would it matter, if we just* did *this, if we did* something *with this attraction other than sniping at each other?* Aiden's the first man I've wanted like this in a long, long time—and if I press hard on that thought, I'll bet I come to the conclusion that I've never wanted a man like this, wanted a man enough that the fact that we barely get along is something I'm willing to overlook. Since Christopher, I pick men who are easy. Men who won't fight with me. Men who won't get in the way of my work. Men who won't ask why I never want to stay over. Men who won't ask anything of me at all.

"That night at Betty's," I say, softly, and he stops stirring. "At first, I thought you were with Charlie."

"No," he says.

"Right, I know. But—I hated that. For some reason." This is as far as I'm willing to go with it without something, *anything,* in return.

"You know the reason." My blood feels as if it turns warmer, thicker at the roughness in his voice. "Same reason I hate the way Hammond stares at you, sometimes. Same reason I've been thinking about getting my hands on your skin since yesterday. Since before yesterday."

"Oh," is all I say, because that was definitely more than *something.* He turns around so he's facing me, looking down to where I'm sitting, knees tucked up against my chest, my arms wrapped around them.

"We do this, and it can't have anything to do with debt. With anything else but you and me."

I stand from my spot on the ground, take a step toward him. "I shouldn't have said that yesterday," I say, but he's shaking his head before I'm even through.

"Doesn't matter about that. I'm talking about this. You and me, and what we want from each other."

It's full dark now, the fire all the way out, smoke and ash heavy in the air. I barely notice. I only notice him coming closer to me, tilting his head down. Not to kiss me—to get close, to put his ear that much nearer to my lips, so he can hear me say it back to him. "You and me," I whisper, an agreement as sure as the one I made with him a month ago, and I am suddenly *desperate* for this, for him to put his hands on my hips and tug me right against him. To work off this tension. We're so well matched, me and Aiden—I can feel it, how good we'll be together. But he doesn't make a move. He's standing close enough that I can hear him breathe, and I reach a hand out, wrap my fingers around his wrist, same as he did to me, on that first day.

I feel his pulse beat, hard, against my fingertips.

We stand like that until the smoke begins to thin, until Aiden's pulse evens out again. Slowly, he pulls his wrist away from me, moves past me and leans down to pick up the lantern, placing it my hand. "On," he says, a dark command, and I flick the switch, watch him crouch down in the column of light to place his palm against the ring that had contained the fire. He moves around it methodically, making sure it's cool all over. It looks as if he's done this a hundred times, as if he belongs in a place like this—out in the woods, building and putting out fires and just like, leaving his testosterone all over the place. My skin flushes with heat, anticipation.

When he stands again, he looks right at me, light from the lantern casting the hard planes of his face in shadow. "Let's go," he says, and nudges me toward the trail.

* * * *

Neither of us says a word on the walk back.

Aiden stays close behind me, close enough that any change in my pace or gait—slowing to push a branch out of the way, turning sideways to step over a log—puts his body against mine. Brief, hot touches that make me impatient to get in the door.

But when we get there, he sets a hand at my waist and turns me away from where I'm unlocking the door, his palm pressing against the side of my stomach until I'm backed against the wood. "We start here," he says, leaning down to press his nose against my throat, just above the notch of my collarbone. "Jesus," he breathes. "What do you smell like?"

I blink into the darkness, realize I've used my free hand, the one not holding the lantern, to grab his forearm. I'm clutching it like it's the only thing keeping me upright. "I don't know," I murmur, shuddering at the way his breath tickles me there. "Probably marshmallows and smoke. And pheromones."

"No," he says, and traces his nose up, his bottom lip dragging against my neck. "You smell like something. I don't know what. You smell so fucking good; it drives me crazy."

"Like how smart I am?" I whisper. He's pressing a line of kisses from where my earlobe meets my jaw across to where my lips wait, ready for him.

"Every single thing about you," he says, right against my mouth, and just like that, we're kissing.

We've skipped the preliminaries—that much is clear. Every kiss I've ever had at my door, after a date, started gentle, a little searching—*Is this okay? Do you think you want more?*—but Aiden and I settled that out by the smoldering fire, and this kiss says so. His mouth is hot against mine, his tongue licking into my open mouth. It feels like it goes on forever, this kiss, long enough that Aiden's brought himself closer and closer, long enough that we've managed to arrange our bodies so that the hardness beneath his jeans meets the space I've made between my legs, long enough that I feel wet and empty. My hand left his forearm as soon as our lips met—I've reached up to tangle it in all that gorgeous, dark hair, one of the first things I'd noticed about him, and I'm tugging at it, telling him, the only way I can, that we need to *get inside.*

At first I don't notice that my other hand is suddenly free to join in the fun, until I realize that the place where Aiden had been touching me—right at my rib cage, frustratingly short of the underside of my breast—is absent of the delicious pressure he'd put there. "I'm going to need to take this," he says, pulling away, the lantern in his hand now. He's breathing hard, but he takes another step back. There's no place now where our bodies are touching, and I bite my lip to keep from whimpering in frustration.

"What?"

"I've got to go—" he begins, and I really do let out that whimper.

"Aiden. I'll kill you if you leave me here right now. I'll kill you, bring you back to life, and then kill you again."

He grins, a particular smile I've never seen on him. Had I thought he was good looking before? Because that was the understatement of my *life.* "I need supplies."

I look down at the bulge in his jeans. "Your supplies seem fine."

"Condoms."

I thud my head against the door, closing my eyes. I have to take a deep breath to settle myself, to manage the ache between my legs. "What man your age doesn't carry condoms? I'm so mad I don't even want to do it anymore."

He says nothing, and when I open my eyes, he's looking at me, his brow furrowed.

"Oh, please," I say, rolling my eyes. "I still want to do it." I grab the front of his shirt, pull him toward me, and kiss him again. "Hurry." He allows himself one nip of my lower lip, a quick pass of his tongue to soothe it.

"I'll hurry."

Once he's gone and I'm in the cabin, though, I'm nervous, impatient. If he's driving all the way to Coleville, it'll be forty minutes until he's back, and by then he'll probably remember what a terrible idea this is, what a terrible idea *I* am, the woman who sat across from his devastated parents at a conference table and negotiated the kind of deal that makes people hate lawyers. Even if he doesn't remember that, he'll probably think of all the ways I annoy him, or all the ways sleeping together could fuck up his plans to get this camp. I go to the sink, look at myself in the mirror. My cheeks are flushed, my lips swollen. My hair looks like I teased it in back. I reach up a hand to smooth it, catching the winking light of that thin gold band, the small pearl that looks far too sweet for me.

What am I doing? I tug the ring off, setting it gently on the small metal ledge underneath the mirror. It doesn't matter if that ring's just a placeholder. That ring is everything I do not do. That ring is complication. That ring is strings-attached sex. I should know that better than anyone.

But it's hard to keep that train of thought when my lips feel warm and bruised from Aiden's firm kiss, when I can still feel the echo of his hands on me. When the cabin door bangs open, Aiden standing there with a strip of condoms in his hand and a hard, determined expression on his face, I feel a gust of relief, or maybe it's just the cold air from outside. Either way, I'm so *glad* he's back. "That didn't take long."

"I broke into the infirmary," he says, a little out of breath. "Picked the lock."

"They keep condoms in there?"

He shrugs, tucking them into his back pocket. "Safety first." He looks at me, eyes moving up and down my body, and I don't know if I imagine the way his glance stutters, for the briefest of seconds, on my left hand. He steps toward me, and same as yesterday afternoon, Aiden's hand reaches up to stroke the skin of my cheek. This time, he doesn't trail off—he tucks his fingers into my hair, lets his palm cup the side of my face, a touch so gentle and so unlike the way the two of us are together that I drop my eyes in embarrassment. "Zo. It's all right if you've changed your mind."

"No," I say, and then, more firmly, "No. But this"—I reach out, tuck the tips of my fingers into the waistband of his jeans, tugging him closer—"we only do this here. Only for the rest of our deal. This is sex, nothing else." Even as I say it, I feel a pang of regret. But it's necessary. I'm not stupid—I'm *smart as fuck*, in fact—and I know this thing between us can't work in reality, not with all the baggage between us.

"Good," he says, maybe a little too quick for my liking, but it doesn't really matter, because half a second later we're kissing again, my tailbone pressed against the sink, trapped by the press of Aiden's hips against mine. My hands roam under his shirt, feeling every inch of warm skin that I can, smooth and taut over all the muscles I saw this morning. His body is deliciously unfamiliar to me—I can feel, in the way his trim waist gives way to broad, ridged planes across his back, in the way his biceps stack right up against the bunched, firm muscles of his shoulders, that this body is made for *work*, lifting and carrying and hurrying, everything about it efficient.

He runs his hands down my sides, around to my lower back to pull me forward, and then he's cupping my ass, the backs of my thighs, and with barely an effort he lifts me, my legs around his waist while he turns to walk us into the bunk room. Our kisses are messy, frantic, our teeth clicking together a little as he moves us toward his bunk. Even when it's the moment for him to set me down, or for me to climb off and get on the bed myself, we stay like that—wrapped up in each other and kissing, our tongues tangling together in a way that almost feels like fighting, my arms tight around his neck, his big hands kneading the flesh at the backs of my legs—hard, electrifying pressure that may well bruise later. I tighten the muscles of my abdomen and curl my pelvis closer to him, a move he answers with a hot, impatient grunt of frustration.

"I've never had sex in a twin bed," I murmur against his lips, and it *works*, because he ducks down, lays me on his bed, the smell of his sheets all around me, his body following mine like we've done this a hundred times.

"Not even in college?" he asks, pressing his face against my neck, and when I don't answer right away, he nips the skin at my collarbone, a move that makes my skin flush anew with pleasure.

"Nuh-uh." I didn't fool around in college, not until I'd met Christopher, and then it'd been—*Stop thinking about him, about that fucking ring,* I scold myself, gripping Aiden's shoulders and pulling him up toward me, so I can get my mouth on his again.

"Doesn't allow for..." He pauses, sucks in a breath when he feels my hands tuck beneath his waistband to grab his ass and pull him closer. "Much movement," he finishes, and his voice sounds like it did this morning. Gruff and a little angry and *oh, God,* I want him to say everything to me in that voice.

"We'll manage," I whisper. He pushes himself up on one hand, careful not to hit his head on the bunk above, and uses his other hand to work at the buttons of my flannel, his eyes on the skin he's revealing, little by little. I don't think I've ever seen a man so focused on a task like this, so intent on just this scrap of skin, when it's damn near guaranteed he's about to see the whole package.

When he spreads the sides of it, revealing my bra—nude, no frills, because I'm at *camp*, for God's sake—he takes a deep breath, reaches out his hand, and traces the line of soft skin above the cups, watching in rapt fascination as my nipples peak underneath the fabric. Never have I so acutely wanted a man to touch me, lick me, suck me there. There's an actual, physical ache. "Jesus Christ," he says. "You make me feel like a teenager."

"That's—nice?"

"It's not nice if I don't settle down." He bends his head, licks across the skin he just touched, and I arch my back in frustrated desire. "Remember that old t-shirt?" he asks, against my skin, and it's taking me a second to do any kind of verbal processing when all I can think about is getting both of us naked. "The one you got at Goodwill?"

Right, the old camp t-shirt. I open my mouth to answer, but all that comes out is a low moan when Aiden lets his tongue dip, just a little, beneath the fabric of my bra.

"I got so fucking pissed at you about that shirt. It was almost see-through."

"Let me guess," I say, my voice thin, my breaths coming so fast from just this little bit of foreplay. "It drove you crazy."

He lifts his head, pushes himself up so he can kiss me again. "It's like that with you," he says. "Half the time I don't know if I want to yell at you or fuck you."

I raise my head to kiss him, to lick across his bottom lip, to tug on it gently with my teeth—a move he answers with a thrust of his hips that's hot, impatient, involuntary. I forget about every single complication this might introduce. I forget about everything but that hardness between his legs, the wetness between mine.

"Well," I say, releasing his lip and letting a slow smile spread across mine, "you can yell at me later, if you want."

But all Aiden seems to want now is our clothes off, our bodies closer, and our mouths otherwise occupied. Between desperate, hungry kisses, we strip each other—a mess of limbs, a few run-ins with the rails of the bunk above us, and one frustrated grunt—from me, unfortunately—when I struggle to push Aiden's jeans from his hips. He smiles against my lips and hunches his way out of the bunk, standing to the side and leaving me naked, cool air from the loss of his body pebbling my skin and drawing my nipples tighter. He says nothing, only tracks his eyes over my body, top to toe, as he pushes his jeans and underwear down. For the few seconds it takes him to step out of them, I return the favor, propping myself up on my elbows to take in every gorgeous, hard inch of him—and when his eyes meet mine, they're bright with something I've never seen there before, a look that's somehow both carefree and anticipatory. The smile that curves his mouth is part playful, part predatory—in the best possible way—and for a second all I can think is, *There,* there *he is.*

But I don't want to dwell on that thought right now, so I reach out a hand to him, pull him by his wrist toward me, a move he has to accommodate with a quick fold of his body to fit in the space above mine, and when his naked skin meets mine, that's *it*—we're done in, more frantic than we were even on the way in here, his knee moving my legs apart, my hips thrusting up to meet his even as he pushes them back down and works his hand between us to touch right where I've been hot and needing him for what feels like days, weeks, months, for-fucking-*ever.* "Jesus, Zo," he breathes out, his fingers deft, tracing the wetness there.

"Later," I say again, and he laughs against my neck, a gentle rumble that sends a new shot of heat between my legs. "I'm not gonna yell at you about *this*," he says, and I laugh too, grabbing for the strip of condoms he tossed beside the bed. My fingers shake as I tear the packet, my head tipping back as he finds a spot between my legs that must've been invented in the last thirty seconds because it has certainly never felt *that* good there.

He watches me while I roll the condom down his length, closes his eyes briefly when I stroke him, and I like that small concession to vulnerability so much that I take advantage, take control. I move his busy hand away from me, move my hips up and guide him toward my entrance, and when he pushes inside me the noise he makes is more arousing than any single word he could have said—a gusting, groaning sigh of relief, a noise like he's set down a thousand pounds of weight, and it makes me *crazy,* that noise. Without thinking I'm pulling his mouth toward mine, tasting that noise, meeting every one of his deep, sure thrusts with my hips. It's fast—I knew it'd be fast, this first time, already I hope not the only time—but he's not impatient. He's moving inside me in a rhythm that's exactly right, banking a fire within me and waiting, waiting, *waiting* to ignite it fully.

My legs clasped tight around his hips, one of his hands on my ass, the other braced above me on the bunk frame, my skin and his already slick with sweat. "Aiden," I say, because I can't wait—I'm too desperate, and he's too good at this, and he answers me with a thrust so deep and perfect and *there*—there's that explosion, that fire he's made me wait for, and we come together, panting and relieved and probably both shocked out of our minds.

Because I can tell already. This fire is going to be hard to put out.

Chapter 10

Aiden

When I wake up the next morning, it's almost like every other morning I've woken up with Zoe in the cabin. Her, up in her bunk on her stomach, arms curled above her head and around her pillow. Me, down in mine, flat on my back, with the kind of morning wood I forgot was possible. The light is low, the cabin quiet except for the sounds of our breathing. My bare arms and chest are chilled where they're exposed to the air, the room always running cooler at night.

But there are differences, too.

Across the way and above me, Zoe's normally silky-straight hair is mussed, a tangle of it resting against her cheek. Underneath the blanket that she's got pulled all the way up past her shoulders, she's not wearing her usual pajamas—loose gray pants, a fitted tank top that she covers with a matching gray hoodie until she gets up in her bunk. Instead, she'd climbed up in her panties and that squirrel t-shirt, her limbs loose and clumsy, her soft smile the last thing I saw before I shut off the light. Separate beds, we'd agreed, both of us deferring to their small size, but probably also deferring to the rules we've set: just sex, nothing else.

Where I'm lying in my bunk, I only have to shift slightly to feel the way the rough sheets set off a tingle against the line of faint scratches that start at my right shoulder blade and trail a few inches down, the mark from the second time Zoe came around my cock. And that morning wood I've got? Right now it doesn't feel so much like the kind of useless insult I've been waking up to for the last two weekends. It feels like my dick is reporting for duty, like it knows that the three times I fucked Zoe last night were warm-ups, that we've got a lot of time and sexual tension to work off, and we might as well get started early.

I close my eyes, take a deep breath, try to settle down. Beneath all the desperation I feel to get inside her again, there's a thread of unease knowing that I haven't had that kind of sex in years, the kind of sex where your whole entire body forgets everything. I'd tried for that kind of sex, especially once I'd known Aaron was in trouble. So much of my headspace was taken up with him—where could I get him detoxed; should I move home; did my parents know what to search for in his room; what was his heart function like; how was his liver holding up—that I'd hoped sex might be a release, an empty-headed break from the constant worry.

But it hadn't been, not really. The feeling of relief would last only about as long as the event itself—but pretty soon after, I'd be worried and guilty again. *You don't deserve any of this,* I'd think, even while I'd made my excuses for why I couldn't stay overnight, explanations for when I'd call again. *You don't deserve this, because your brother is dying, and nothing you've done has stopped it.*

But with Zoe? With Zoe, there'd been nothing but the two of us. Even in this cabin, stuffed with memories I can't look at full in the face, I hadn't thought of anything but her. The smell of her skin. The way her body shuddered underneath mine when I teased the underside of her breast with my tongue. The thready, gasping breath she'd taken when I'd pushed inside her for the first time. When we'd finally worn ourselves out—Zoe collapsed against my chest, my hand fisted in the hair at the nape of her neck—she'd breathed a quiet *Oh my God* against my neck, and I could've fallen asleep right then, not sparing a thought for all the reasons this was probably a terrible idea.

I hear her shift in her bunk and make the soft exhalation that means she's waking up. On autopilot, I swing my legs from the bed, stand on wobbly, fatigued legs, and try not to laugh at the way my dick tents my shorts, so pronounced it almost looks like a gag from a bad movie. I forgot, last night, in our sleepy, delirious tumbles back to our individual beds, to put my clothes for the morning on the bunk above me, so I stumble over to the pile of them on the floor, pulling my jeans on over my shorts with a quiet groan and shoving my feet into my untied boots before I tug on my sweatshirt and head out onto the stoop to wait, same as I do every morning.

It's foggy this morning, but there's sun waiting behind it—it's the kind of soft, misty swirl that feels like nature's cleaning crew has shown up to freshen the air before the day begins. It's even colder than yesterday, when we'd gone out to the zip line, and my body hurts with wanting to go back inside, to pull her out of her bed and put her into mine. But I've got no idea where we'll go from here. In the half-light of the day I've got no idea if she's waking up and thinking it was all a mistake, that we've crossed a line that's too far away from pretend. When I'd gotten back from the infirmary last night—Jesus Christ, I broke into a building so I could fuck her—I'd thought she might've changed her mind, a flash of hesitation in her eyes before she'd made me her offer. *We only do this here.*

Inside I hear the rush of the plumbing, the toilet flushing, and a few seconds later I hear that she's started the shower. She'll be quick about it; she always is, so I don't have to wait out here too long. But maybe I ought to walk this off, not make it weird when we see each other the first time. If last night's the only night we have like that, I'll make it work. We'll go back to the way things were before. Maybe this urge I feel to be with her (and, let's be honest, this boner I have) will wear off naturally. One night of the best sex of my life but I've got to keep focused. I've got to make sure this camp is my first priority.

Behind me, just as I've stepped off the stoop, the door opens.

She's there, her hair still messy and dry, a pillow crease across her cheek, a towel wrapped loosely around her body. "Oh, jeez, it's *cold,*" she says first, hunching her shoulders. But then she looks down at me and smiles. "Coming?" she says, turning back inside, leaving the door open so I can see her drop the towel before heading toward the shower.

I'm up those steps so fast, pulling off my sweatshirt before I'm all the way back inside, and I hear her laugh as she steps behind the curtain. I'm desperate to get in there, but I make a stop by my bunk to grab a condom, and then I brush my teeth faster than I ever have in my life, glad she can't see me clumsily shoving down my pants, one handed. It's a wonder I'm not short of breath when I actually step behind the curtain.

And it's a good thing too, because Zoe's body—holy fuck. It's enough to make my heart feel like it's stopping. I'd seen her, of course, last night, but it'd been mostly dark, and it sure as shit hadn't been with water pouring all over her. Those long, toned legs, that high, plump ass and trim waist. The way she moves that body with full confidence, smooth and strong, owning every inch of it. I've always loved women, loved their bodies, but I don't think any one of them has ever affected me like she has, like she's got one fist wrapped around my dick and another one shoved right through my chest, too close to everything inside me that still feels kicked around and roughed up.

"Good morning," she says, stepping back so I can get closer, partway under the dinky showerhead. I slap the condom down onto the windowsill, hoping she doesn't tag me for being too presumptuous. Hoping I *haven't* been too presumptuous.

"You sore?" I ask her. Which sounds pretty presumptuous. I should've taken a walk; it's too early for me to attempt conversation. "I mean, good morning."

She smiles. "You know I have done it before. It's not like you planted the flag there."

"I didn't say—"

"I'm not sore," she interrupts, leaning her head back under the water, raising her arms to push her hair back from her forehead. I feel like every pint of blood in my body is racing directly to my dick. In about thirty seconds I'll probably reenact a different version of our first meeting and pass out on this shower floor. I set my hands on her hips, and she makes a little *hmm* under her breath before she speaks again. "I feel good."

"I feel good too." I duck my head, feel the hot water rain over the back of it while I dip my mouth lower, lick a drop of water from her shoulder, feel the press of her nipples against my skin. The relief I feel to be doing this—touching her again—is all out of proportion to how I should feel about an arrangement like this, two people in a strange situation, fucking the tension off and drawing clear lines in the sand. "Could feel better," I say, my voice gruff, my hips pressing forward. I need to keep this...I don't know what. Light. Simple. Her body and mine. *This is sex, nothing else.*

But then she surprises me, straightening her spine from where she'd been arched back into the water, setting her hands on my chest, trailing them down as she drops to her knees, her mouth opening against my hip. For a second my mind is blank with the promise of it; I'm all anticipation. *This* is simple. Her mouth, my dick. I don't even have to look her in the eye.

But just as quick my body rejects it. I bend so I can set my palms underneath her elbows, pull her up. "No," I say to her, and her brow furrows. I don't know how to explain it to her, this feeling. She knows by now I'm shit at talking things out, but it's one thing to be rough at conversation; it's another to say the wrong thing when you're naked with someone, about to do something that's intimate no matter what boundaries you've drawn. I'd said it to her last night, out by the fire—this can't be about anything she owes me. And I don't know if Zoe gets off on what she was about to do. But I know myself, and I know if I let her do this, I'll feel it the wrong way. "Let's just—" I begin, backing her against the cold tile of the wall. When she gasps, I reach up and wrench the showerhead down so it still pours over us, so she's warm and wet. She stretches into me, wrapping her arms around my neck and tilting her face up so I don't have to finish my thought, so I can kiss her and touch her and feel her grow more restless under my mouth and hands. She raises her knee to my hip, presses it there in invitation, and there it is again—that perfect blankness in my mind, nothing but her and me, nothing but this thing we can give to each other.

* * * *

We're late to breakfast.

The Dwyers have already taken off, so it's quieter than usual when we come in, and everyone—all gathered around the same table—looks up at our arrival.

"Uh," Zoe says quietly, beside me. "Are we wearing sandwich boards or something?"

"What?"

"Like, 'WE HAD SEX' sandwich boards?"

Weirdly, I look down at my chest, and Zoe cracks out a laugh. "Quiet, you," I say, raising a hand awkwardly in greeting as we walk toward the table.

"I think someone broke into the infirmary," says Paul, and I choke on a surprised cough. Zoe claps my back while I clear my throat, once, then again.

"I need to—" I begin, and then clear my throat again. Zoe slaps me just a little harder on the shoulder. "Paul, that was me. I'm sorry. Uh, after the bonfire, we—" I break off, having no idea how to finish this sentence. *Wanted to have tons of sex but I didn't have condoms?* I don't even know if he'd notice there were a few gone. I'd never even known about this stash until I'd become a counselor. Paul and Lorraine knew that the older kids didn't always follow the rules about staying out of cabins belonging to the opposite sex, and during our training they'd had a nurse come in to give a long, embarrassing talk about safe sex that was more detailed than anything any of us had heard in public school.

"I burned myself," Zoe says. "While I was doing the"—she crooks out an elbow, makes a fist and a funny circular motion with it—"the stirring thing? To help put the fire out."

"Oh!" exclaims Lorraine, looking back and forth between Zoe's hands, her face concerned. Right away Zoe looks like she's realized her mistake, and her face flushes.

"The burn's on her stomach," I say, ignoring Zoe's eyes on me. Lorraine looks stumped by this, but I rush out a clarification. "She leaned over and caught the tip of a smoldering branch."

"Yes," Zoe says. "Just the tip. It was—hot." Oh, fuck. I have never wanted to laugh this hard in my life. But I keep my face straight.

"I wanted to make sure I got a good-size bandage," I say. "I'm sorry. I thought I'd gotten in without damaging the lock."

Paul looks up at me, all forgiveness. "That's all right, son," he says. "I only noticed because you must've forgotten to close up the lock latch all the way when you'd left." I can believe it. By that point, my hands had been shaking with need. "You know, Lorraine, we should've given Aiden a key anyway. He's the medical professional around here. We only know basic first aid, and don't keep a nurse here when we don't have campers. Where'd you learn to pick a lock like that?"

At this, I do laugh. Zoe and I settle at the table, Lorraine handing us each a plate so we can dig into the egg casserole that's in the center of the table. "Actually, I learned it here. You guys used to have a pretty easy lock on the storage unit and one time a group of us picked it so we could play a midnight game of badminton." I pause at Lorraine's doubting expression. "Okay, more than one time."

Tom chuckles, sips his coffee, keeping his eye on Little Tommy, who's toddling his way around the table beside us, his shirt wet with drool. "I tried a few against-the-rules things when I was here too," Sheree says. "One summer Jenny Gregson and I stacked logs up on the side of our cabin so we could climb up onto our roof and look at the stars. It's a wonder we didn't break our necks."

Lorraine shakes her head, putting a hand to her brow as if the mere thought of this stresses her out. "It amazes me the stuff we missed," she says, her expression growing more serious. "Last year, we had two campers who'd smuggled in a small flat-screen and two gaming consoles, a bunch of those... What do you call 'em, Paul?"

"Adapters," Paul says. "Extension cords."

"We don't let our kids have those," Walt says, and I'm assuming he means the games and not the extension cords, but since the Coburg children seemed pretty shocked last weekend by how a tire swing works, I wouldn't be surprised by either.

Still, Lorraine and Paul had always been strict about electronics at camp, even before everything had reached the kind of peak plugged-in state the world's in now. No TVs, only emergency weather radios. No phones in our cabins. No handheld games.

"Anyways, they'd wait until their counselor came and did the final lights-out check, and then they'd set up all these things on that single outlet in their cabin," she says, then purses her lips and shakes her head again.

"We had a small electrical fire," says Paul, patting her arm. "Everyone was fine. Those boys lost all the equipment they had, though."

"And then there were the kids with the—" She shudders a little before she continues, "The *marijuana*." Rachel lets out a dramatic gasp, like Lorraine's just revealed a sex trafficking ring. Obviously I've got complicated feelings about drugs, but there'd been more than one counselor who'd managed to get a joint into camp back during my days here. I'd never thought twice about it until now, seeing Lorraine looking like she might cry.

Sheree clucks her tongue in sympathy. "Oh, Lorraine," she says, putting an arm around her and giving her a brief, sideways hug. "I know how you feel. I worry about my kids at my school night and day. The world is changing so fast."

"I think we've realized that we're not as able to keep up anymore. We hired two assistant camp managers last summer, but when you run a camp, *you've* got to be the one willing to get up at all hours of the night. You've got to be the one convincing those kids you're always watching," Lorraine says. I feel a pulse of tension go up my neck, settle across my shoulders. Even if I can get Lorraine and Paul to see this camp not as a place mostly for kids—even if I can get them to picture a bunch of addicts out here, good people who need another shot—I know the weakest link in my plan is Lorraine's *you*. I'd own this campground, so of course I'd have a stake. But it'd be counseling professionals running the thing, not me. I wouldn't be living and breathing it, not like Lorraine and Paul. I don't think I *could*. The worrying I did over Aaron—I couldn't relive even a diluted version of that, spread out over however many people might be treated here. From the beginning of this plan, I'd known I'd want to keep my distance. The guy you report to, not the guy in the trenches.

"Been tough getting used to that," says Paul, his expression more melancholy than anything I've ever seen. "Don't have the energy we used to, and the kids—they see us as...well...*old*."

"They've probably never seen you do a cannonball," Zoe says from beside me, forking her eggs, and then she immediately claps a hand over her mouth, her eyes wide as saucers. There's a beat of silence while Paul looks over at her, a second of confusion before he bursts out in his booming laugh, always a surprise when you get used to his quiet way of speaking.

"Oh, Zoe. I am sorry about that. I wondered if that was you," he says. "Didn't have my glasses on!"

Lorraine covers her face with her hands, shakes her head. "Paul, I told you to skip the fall swim."

"Well, sweetheart, it's a tradition, you know, and the guys would've been disappointed—"

"You traumatized poor Zoe," says Lorraine.

Zoe waves a hand, swallows the bite of eggs she'd nervously shoved in her mouth while Paul laughed. "I've seen worse," she says, and then she makes this squeak noise in her throat, maybe the beginnings of that *meep!* she described on Friday. "I don't mean worse. I mean, it was fine, everyone's—everybody looked fine? It's not like I was doing an assessment. Basically I didn't even see anything—"

"Woo, honey," Sheree says, laughing. "You ought to quit now."

Zoe's shoulders slump, and I put an arm around her, pulling her toward me and shaking her playfully, while everyone except Walt and Rachel—who look like their milk's turned—laughs. There's a shock of something familiar that runs through my body, and I almost jolt with it, this need to chase down what I recognize. It's like when you catch the smell of something delicious cooking in the air, something you haven't had in forever. That half second where your memory syncs up with your senses and you realize, *Oh, right, cinnamon rolls.*

I drop my arm from around Zoe's shoulders when I've realized it.

It's *family.* That's what it feels like. I'd almost forgotten.

* * * *

"You're awful quiet," Zoe says, when we've pulled out of the campground. We'd packed up in silence, Zoe moving slower than usual, and I'd wondered if she'd been thinking the same thing as me—should we, one more time, before we go back to real life? But in the end, I was stuck back at that breakfast table, too in my head about everything Lorraine and Paul had said, and when I'd zipped up my bag and set it by the door, she'd seemed to take the hint—moving more quickly, making a joke about how she thought her boots finally fit her, or maybe they'd just beaten her toes into submission. I'd wanted to kiss her for that, for pressing on—but I didn't know how. Didn't know how to initiate affection with her that wasn't a prelude to something else.

"Just tired." I reach forward to turn the heater vents her way, like she likes. I can feel her watching me, working me out. It's the best and worst thing about her, the way she watches.

"They won't like that you don't plan to run the camp," she says.

It's the worst. It's the worst fucking thing.

"I know that," I grind out, my voice sounding harsher than I intend it to. I know before she even starts talking that she won't quit, either. We're past that—we were past that before the sex. The more time she's spent with me, the less she holds back.

"The business plan for the other Wilderness/Wellness locations has a position for a camp manager. No special credentials for that, really. It's separate from the counseling functions. You don't want to do that?"

I rub a palm over my head, let out a gusty sigh. "Not really."

"Because you want to stay working as a paramedic?"

"Zo, come on." *Let me off the hook,* I'm saying.

"You can't give that answer to Lorraine and Paul. And they're going to ask the question. It's going to be their most important question. You want to buy this campground and hand it over to someone they've never even seen."

My answer is a roll of my shoulders, a tightening of my hands on the steering wheel.

"You can't just throw money at this. Believe me."

It's that quick that I get angry, and I'm grateful to be driving, to know I have to keep half my attention on some other task. "Are you kidding me with that?" I ask her. "Your actual *job* was throwing money at this. I'm just the guy who had to catch all that money, and you know what? I can't fucking *wait* to be rid of it. You know what the check I got said? The one that came from your firm?"

"No," she says, her voice firm. She's got a spine of steel, Zoe does.

"*Aaron O'Leary Settlement.* Right in the fucking memo line."

She takes a deep breath through her nose, like she's got to recover from that piece of information, even though it can't be new to her. "But if you're just trying to—get *rid* of it…"

"Let me ask you something, Zo," I say, my voice low, angry. "How've you been doing, spending all that money you've got?"

I see her, out of the corner of my eye, rub her palms up and down the thighs of her jeans, see her jaw firm briefly before she answers. "I told you, I'm taking some time."

"Yeah, well. I don't fucking feel like taking some time. Because your money and mine, those are two different things. You had a lucky night. You got drunk and bought a lottery ticket and beat the odds. My brother didn't. He died like a bunch of other poor fuckers who get hooked on something, and every single dollar of this money feels like it's for a hit he took, a bad decision he made. The best thing—the only fucking thing I can think to do with it that won't make me sick is this camp."

It's maybe the most I've ever said to Zoe all at once, probably more than I've said to anyone in the last six months. *She'll quit now, after that,* I think. *She won't fight me.*

And for all of two minutes, she doesn't. She sits silently, her eyes straight ahead, and as my words echo in the car around me, I feel all that quick-fire anger flame out. Now all I feel is tired, and confused, and sorry. Sorry for going so hard at her when all she wanted was to help.

"Hey," I say, soft now.

"Don't apologize," she says, sharply. "You're right that I had a lucky night, and you're absolutely right that I didn't deserve it." I open my mouth, ready to dispute that—who said anything about deserving it?—but she barrels on before I can stop her. "But I'm taking time so I don't screw up again."

What "again"? She reaches up and drags her fingers over her brow, a brief, casual touch that I notice more now that I know how her skin feels under my own fingertips. "Look, I don't know what it's like for you," she says. "But for me, it's easy to make mistakes when big things change. When my dad died, I—I made big mistakes, mistakes that lasted a long time. And winning this money—well, it'd be easy to make mistakes with this too. I've got a second chance here, and I want to do it right." She stops, clears her throat, reaches out to adjust one of the heater vents away from her. It's the barest, briefest pause, not enough time for me to even ask all the questions I have about what she's said: *What mistakes? How long did they last? What does it mean to you, to do it right?* "I'm sure you do want to get rid of this money. All I'm asking is whether you've really thought about it. About the particulars."

"You've seen all the work I've done." But as soon as I've said it, I realize I don't so much mean it as an explanation. I think maybe I mean it as a question.

She shrugs her shoulders, all nonchalance, like we haven't exchanged harsh words. Maybe it's the way we started, me and her—the fact that it was hostile from the start means that we don't feel so uncomfortable when things turn tense. "How much work you do on something has nothing to do with whether it's the right idea."

I slide my eyes over to her again, take in the smooth lines of her profile. Anyone else would see her and think she's entirely unbothered. But already I know better. I know *her* better. I know she won't answer if I ask her anything else, about her mistakes, her work, her money, anything. I know she's given me all she's willing to, and my chest feels tight with something like—frustration. Longing.

But that's bullshit. Me and Zoe, we're not the same. The *camp* is what I'm holding on to, what I've been holding on to for all these months, and hell if I'm going to get talked out of it now. I've wanted this so bad I've been willing to lie to people I care about. I've been willing to get involved with a woman who'd been on the wrong side of my brother's death. That I'm sleeping with her now makes no difference.

Zoe is temporary. This camp is my family's—my brother's—legacy.

"I want this to work," I say.

She leans her head back onto the seat and turns her face my way. For what feels like a long time, she doesn't say anything. She only watches me, and I wish I could get in that head of hers, hear the gears that grind, the ones that make her so good at figuring things out. "Then I want it to work for you," she says, finally.

It's enough, this truce, enough for two people who've committed to a short-term arrangement, who don't have to ask each other the big questions. But after this weekend, it's different between us, however casual we're keeping the sex. I reach out across the bench seat, take her hand in mine. She doesn't have the ring on. Every week, when we get in the car to go home, she slides it off, puts it back in the box, then back into the glove box. I twine my fingers with hers, feel that bare finger between two of mine, ignore the answering disquiet that goes through me at the sensation. I give her palm a light squeeze.

She turns her face back toward the windshield, but she doesn't pull away.

Chapter 11

Zoe

When Kit opens the door to me on Monday night, she looks me up and down, raises an eyebrow, and says, "What's happening here?"

I move past her into the foyer, setting my briefcase on an old, weathered trunk that's probably another gift from Ben's father, so complete is his gratitude to Kit for bringing his son home. "This is nice," I say, sliding out of my shoes and setting them tidily next to the trunk. I'm nervous, unexpectedly so, a flush of embarrassment all along the neckline of my blouse.

"Don't change the subject. You look like you came from court."

"I didn't," I say, quickly. "Is Greer here?"

"Here!" she calls, drifting into the living room, an apron around her waist and a frosting knife in one hand. When she sees me she stops, her eyes widening. "Seems a bit formal for our plans, Z."

Tomorrow is Ben's welcome back party, and our plans tonight involve final prep: all the food we can put together in Kit's still-half-constructed kitchen, maybe an obnoxious sign or two that we'll hang in Henry Tucker's house, where the party will be. It's not ideal, a Tuesday evening party, especially since Kit hardly ever takes a day off and Greer's missing a night class to be there. But Kit says she wants the party on the very day of Ben's arrival, and I get the feeling that there's another kindness behind it too—of the three of us, I'm the only one not available on the weekends right now, and so Tuesday it is.

I look back and forth between my friends, who're now looking at me like I'm a wayward teen coming home past curfew. No way are we getting back to frosting cake and cutting cheese cubes before I spill it.

"I went on a job interview," I say, all nonchalance, as if I haven't spent the better portion of the day trying to wrap my brain around what's happened in the last few hours.

Last night I'd gotten home from camp rattled, exhausted more by my argument with Aiden than by the mostly sleepless night we'd spent all over each other. Lying in my bed, my mind racing through the weekend, I'd kept thinking about it: if he doesn't go all in with the campground, if he doesn't commit to run it himself, he won't get it. And at the same time: if he *does* go all in, if he agrees to run the camp himself, he might not be happy doing the job. Already his brother's death has caused upheaval—his grief, the settlement, his move here, his parents' move away. And now a career change too?

It's not good.

But what else isn't good is my obsessing over it, and by the time I dragged myself out of bed in the morning I'd known it was time for me to back off, to stop putting so much of my effort into something that belongs to Aiden. That's not what I am to him, and the mental energy I'd been putting into his quest for the campground is all too familiar.

So I'd decided to change gears. Had decided to *do* something.

However well I've faked casual, Kit and Greer aren't buying, both of them wearing twin expressions of shock—a synchronized jaw drop that would be comical if it didn't sting a little. It's my fault, I know, that it'd gotten to the point where it probably seemed I'd never do anything useful again—but *still*.

"I guess it's not really a job," I clarify, moving into the living room, Kit right behind me. I sit down on her slouchy canvas couch, reaching out for a water glass that's on the table and taking a steadying sip. Our places are each other's places—that's how it's always been, and reminding myself of this long-established familiarity gives me courage. "I might do some work for Legal Aid, downtown. On a volunteer basis."

I feel, rather than see, Kit and Greer exchange a glance before they both sit, Kit next to me on the couch and Greer in Kit's newly reupholstered armchair, another Tucker's Salvage find. "Z," Kit says, nudging my knee, "we want to know about this."

I tap a newly polished nail against the side of the glass. "You guys know I've been a bit directionless. I figured I ought to do something with myself for once."

Kit purses her lips in this way she has, an expression of displeasure at my flippancy. The revelation that I'd been so miserable at Willis-Hanawalt had been a shock to my friends. I'd never said a word to them about how unhappy I was there, particularly in that last year. All my work—the long hours, the unexpected, always urgent calls, the constant checking of my email—they'd taken it as I'd performed it: a necessary nuisance of work I was good at, work that I enjoyed and was paid damned well for. When I'd finally told them, relieved after cleaning out my office, about the Opryxa cases, about how horrible things had been and how guilty I'd felt, they'd been concerned, understanding. But I thought, too, that there'd been a little crack in our friendship. It wasn't that they judged me for the work I'd been doing.

It was that they'd learned I'd been putting on a show for so long.

I don't want that crack there, or at least I don't want it to get bigger, so I push past my feelings and start talking. I tell them about Marisela, who directs the volunteer services division. I tell them about the email I'd sent her early this morning, though I leave out feeling spurred on by my feelings over Aiden. I tell them that I'd been cautious but sincere—*I'm interested in the work you do at your offices*—and that I'd been genuinely surprised when she'd called me at 9:06 this morning, talking fast and enthusiastic about the possibility of my joining "the team." I tell them about the office itself, where I'd gone this afternoon for an initial meeting that had turned into a two-hour conversation—it's small but clean, smelling a little like stale coffee but with all new furniture, a recent donation from a firm that requires pro bono hours from its associates.

"At first I'd be doing this—well, it's a hotline, I guess. People call in with questions about stuff like power of attorney or no-fault divorces or whatever, and leave a message with an intake assistant, usually college students or people early on in law school. And then I'd be responsible for spending a few hours calling back, doing consultation that way." I'd watched Marisela do two today, one on debt relief and one on a foreclosure assist, and had felt my fingers twitch with something I hadn't felt in months. I was *eager*. Eager to try it for myself. Eager to *work*.

"Zoe," Greer says, "this is wonderful. I'm so—I'm so *glad*."

The earnest relief in her voice makes my face heat again, and I wave a dismissive hand. "It was only an interview. She said she'd call in about a week." Now that the adrenaline's worn off, I feel a nudge of discomfort even thinking about it. What if she doesn't call? Or what if she does, and then I realize I've done the wrong thing again, made the wrong move just by trying to go forward?

LUCK OF THE DRAW

"It's probably a terrible idea," I say lightly. "I'd probably stare at the volunteer law students all day and wonder if I should start Botox injections."

"No," says Kit, unexpectedly forceful. "You need to cut this out, downplaying everything you do."

I offer up this—I don't know what. Sort of a snort-laugh, thick with sarcasm, and Kit stands again, abruptly. Greer shifts to the edge of her chair, her eyes darting back and forth between me and Kit.

"Stop it, Zoe. Stop making a joke out of everything. We're allowed to be worried. You're doing this thing, practically getting on the rack every weekend for Aiden, coming home like you've been infected by his quiet. Now you're finally doing something for yourself—"

"Finally?" I scoff. "All I've *done* is things for myself. You thought I was joking that night we won, my little spa treatments and strippers joke, but seriously, what have I done except please myself?"

Kit opens her mouth to object, but Greer speaks first. "You're figuring things out. Planning for your trip." She says that last part with a slight inflection, a question in it.

I roll my eyes. "Greer, we all know I'm not planning for any trip." I turn my attention back to Kit. "And I'm not *getting on the rack* for Aiden," I tell her, my voice surprisingly loud. "He's been through a lot, and it's not my fault, but I'm part of that story, whether I like it or not. Helping him is the *one* thing in my life that's made me feel like I'm not just a...I don't know. A wart on the ass of humanity, basically." I snap my mouth shut, realizing I've let slip a little too much.

"That's the one thing?" Greer says, and in the softness of her voice I hear something that makes me wince.

"That's not what I mean," I say, but there's no conviction in it, not really. I love them—I love Kit and Greer like family, and it's true that some days over the last few months, my plans with them are the only reason I get out of bed in the morning. But there's this creeping doubt I have, deep down. Maybe Kit and Greer don't know the real me, the ugly, unkind me who's made so many wrong moves, big and small.

Kit looks down at me, and I shift to untuck my blouse from my skirt, avoiding her anger and her sympathy. I'm not sure which is worse. But when she speaks, her voice is gentler, softer. "I know he's been through a lot. I know he's grieving. But you don't deserve to feel like this. If this is how he makes you—"

"He doesn't," I say, and I mean it. He makes me feel like—like I'm tough enough to answer for myself. He asks me the questions my friends have been too kind to ask: whether I feel bad about the job I did, whether

I'll ever go back to being a lawyer, why I'm so afraid to do something with the money. "He's part of the reason I did this," I say, surprising myself.

"How do you mean?" asks Greer.

I think about his hand in mine on Sunday, the harsh words we'd exchanged about the camp and his plans for it. Despite my worries about getting too involved, it isn't just me who pushes him. He pushes me too, and it feels *good*, that pushing, or at least it feels *right*. Necessary. But I don't know how to explain it to them. I don't know how to explain that fighting with him makes me feel as if I'm finally getting somewhere. "I guess it's the camp," I say. "I'm so out of my routine there, you know? So when I get back, I think I might finally be able to make a change."

We're all quiet for a minute, the sound of an old clock on Kit's mantel ticking, and I start fidgeting with a loose thread on my skirt.

"Oh, boy," Greer says, quietly. "You slept with him." My head jerks up, my skin flushing anew. While Kit and I were fighting, Greer was *paying attention*. She always does.

"You *what*?" shouts Kit, and damn. These two—I guess they really *do* know me well, if this is how easily they read me. There is not one single shred of hope I have for trying to get out of this conversation.

I shrug, borrowing a gesture from Aiden.

"You see," Kit says, turning to Greer. "This is *exactly* what I mean." Greer flushes guiltily, sending an apologetic glance my way. But the truth is, I know they've been talking about me. I know it by the way they've been talking *to* me, ever since this camp thing started—pointed questions, furrowed brows back and forth between them, worry over whether I'm getting too involved in this. Kit sits down again, gives me a look that means business. "Let's hear it."

"*Wait*," Greer says, standing up and scurrying into the kitchen. I hear the frosting knife clatter into the sink, and when she comes back, she's holding an open bottle of wine. Kit takes the glass of water from me, dumps it on the spider plant on the sofa table behind us, and Greer tips a serving of wine in before Kit hands it back to me. "Okay," Greer says. "*Do* go on."

This routine we've performed is comical enough to lighten the mood. Some of the starch has gone out of Kit and I feel less like I've got to sit here and plead my case. I curl up, tucking my feet to the side, which leans me closer to her, and already it feels better.

"You don't want to hear more about Legal Aid?" I say, batting my eyes dramatically.

"I kind of want to hear if he has chest hair."

"Greer, jeez," says Kit, but she's laughing.

"He looks like he would. Have it, I mean. He looks…you know. Manly."

"He does have chest hair," I say. "Exactly the right amount. Just enough so you can feel it on your—"

"All right," says Kit. "Don't make it weird."

I laugh, take a sip of wine. "Really, you guys. It's fine. We're attracted to each other, and we made a deal. This is something we'll have between us, while we're at camp. It's not going to go anywhere," I say, repeating words I'd determinedly repeated to myself in the dead of night last night.

"Oh, *right*," says Kit.

"What's that mean?" I ask her. "Let's face it, it's not all that different from how my previous relationships have gone." Sex, plain and simple. Stress relief, a break from reality. I hadn't had time for anything else, hadn't allowed myself anything else, in years.

"You're forgetting that we saw you with him."

"Please," I say, waving a hand through the air. "That was forever ago. I barely knew him then."

"It wasn't even a month ago," says Greer, because she's been exceptionally helpful tonight.

"You look at each other like..." Kit begins, tapping the side of her temple. "Protons and electrons," she finishes, and I groan. "I can do better. Like neodymium…"

"How do you ever get laid?" I say.

"Plenty." She smiles. "Plenty more after tomorrow."

"It did seem like there was something there, between the two of you," says Greer. "You should have seen him look at you while you threw darts."

"It was like you were titanium and he was—"

"Kit, God. Don't try again." I laugh. "It's just chemistry. It'll burn off." *It has to.*

"Invite him to the party," says Kit, interrupting my thoughts.

"Uh. What?"

"Now *that's* a good idea," says Greer.

"No, Kit. I'm trying to keep my distance. Keep it at camp."

"You can keep your distance," she says. "You can stand in the corner. We'll talk to him."

"Ask him to leave a couple of buttons undone," says Greer.

Kit snorts a surprised laugh, but then her face grows serious again. "I don't want you hurt. I'm worried about this." Between the three of us, it's Greer who usually strikes people as the anxious one. But it's Kit who worries, who doesn't much like change to the equilibrium.

"You guys, I'm fine. He and I are fine, together. It's not complicated." But I still think of his hand in mine. Our fingers tangled together, and worse, my thoughts tangled up in his problems.

"So it's not a big deal if he comes, then," says Greer. "He can invite his friends too. I liked them."

I open my mouth to object, but Kit interrupts me. "Zoe," she says, standing again. "I guess I'm not really asking. I have his number too. You call him, or I'll call him. This is important to us."

I look over at Greer, who gives a nod of encouragement. "It'd be better if we got to know him," she says.

"Fine," I say, sounding sullen, but beneath it I feel a familiar warmth, comfort. What I did to deserve these two, I'll never know. But maybe that's the point of us—that I don't have to think too hard about whether I deserve them. They never make me feel like I don't. They never make me feel anything but loved. What distance we have between us is what I put there—my fear, my guilt. For a second, I think about telling them about my vase, but then I think better of it. It'll just ruin the evening—it'll make them worry more. Instead I stand up, take another fortifying sip of wine before setting the glass down.

"Kit-Kat," I say, squeezing her shoulder as I walk back toward her stairs. "I'm going to go borrow one of your nerd t-shirts, and then you're putting me to work."

* * * *

Greer reminds me once more, when we're walking out to our cars after leaving Kit's. We stand on the sidewalk for a minute, Greer passing a file folder to me for a set of documents she's asking me to review, another part of her post-lottery project. She thanks me profusely, then puts her arms around me for a hug, her favorite goodbye—she really squeezes too, skinny-armed Greer. When she pulls back she says, "You're going to call him, right?"

I sigh, roll my eyes. "I *guess*," I say, working up the kind of teenage exasperation that makes me feel like I've earned their look from earlier. Greer smiles up at me, pats my arm. "Check your email," she says. "I sent you a video of a dog playing with one of those springy doorstoppers."

"You're the best," I tell her, ducking into my car.

It doesn't take me long to get home, but once I'm inside I realize the lateness of the hour—almost midnight—is a benefit. I text him a simple

You up? that I'm guessing he won't see until morning. By then it'll be even later notice, even less of a chance he'll be able to come, even less of a chance of us taking this into territory that's well behind the rules of our arrangement.

But when my phone rings, barely thirty seconds later, I feel a secret thrill of delight.

"You all right?" he says when I answer.

"Oh," I answer, embarrassed. In his voice I hear a thread of concern, and I wonder how many times he's had bad phone calls at night, how lightly he sleeps to always be able to hear them. "There's nothing wrong—you didn't need to call back right away. Were you sleeping?"

"I'm on duty." In the background, I hear Charlie's laugh, the low reverb of Ahmed's voice. I feel desperate to see what it's like where Aiden is, to see where he spends so much time. Does he look the same there as he does at the campground, fully in his element? An unpleasant thought strikes me: What did *I* look like, today, at that Legal Aid office? Too slick in my pencil skirt and silk blouse, my four-inch pumps with the glossy red sole?

"I'm sorry," I say. "To bother you."

"You're not bothering me. Don't be sorry." It's simple, what he's said, but there's some latent heaviness too, some echo of our last conversation in the truck.

"It's funny, isn't it? We apologize to each other a lot."

There's a long pause on the other end, a door shutting, and the line gets quieter, the background noise gone. "I wouldn't say it's funny."

"Me neither." I take a deep breath through my nose. Before I get anything out about the party, Aiden surprises me.

"The Coburgs dropped out."

"What?" My voice has that edge of excitement, as though I'm talking to a close friend and about to get some piece of gossip that's bound to be good. A strange sort of bonding, but nevertheless I *feel* it.

"Yeah, I was going to call you tomorrow. Lorraine told me a few hours ago. They drove out to the campground this morning and told her and Paul they'd changed their minds. Said it was enough for them to worry about their own kids."

"Oh," I say, maybe a little disappointment in my voice. That wasn't very gossipy at all.

"Rachel told Lorraine that the camp—uh. That it had lost sight of its principles."

"Eek. I'll bet Lorraine was pissed."

"She doesn't much get mad." I can picture the shrug he uses to accompany this. Whenever he does it, his mouth turns down at the corners as his shoulders come up, like they're connected. "I think she might've been a little relieved. Out of all of us, they seemed the least into it."

All of us, I repeat silently to myself, breathing through the thrill of that inclusion. "So," I say, keeping my voice casual, free of the eager curiosity that's tapping me on the shoulder. "We're not going this weekend?"

There's a pause on the other end, some hitch where I guess Aiden decides how to play this change. "Lorraine still wants everyone up there. Says we can help clean up from Friday's wedding, have a more laid-back weekend." I let out a quiet breath of relief. *It's only the sex I'd miss,* I tell myself. "But if you want to pass, I'll think of something to say why you're not there."

"I don't want to pass." I grimace at the quickness of my response.

"Good." In his voice I hear something I feel all the way down to those glossy red soles. I know what he's thinking, know about what's good between us. Suddenly I'm hyperaware of everything I have on underneath my clothes—the thigh-high stockings, the nude thong and matching lace-trimmed bra, everything designed to fit exactly right beneath workwear, so different from anything I wear at the campground. I wonder if he would like it, if I should pack something like this for the weekend. *Ridiculous,* I scold myself. *It's not a lovers' getaway.* I step out of my shoes, feel nothing but the cold, hard wood floor beneath me.

"My friend Kit's invited you to a party," I blurt. "Tomorrow. If you have to work, that's fine."

"I'm off tomorrow, once I'm home from this shift. What kind of party?"

"It's a welcome back party, for her boyfriend. He's moving here. Ahmed and Charlie are welcome too."

I hear him take a deep breath, and I know the move that accompanies that too. I know he's probably rubbed his hand over his hair, back to front, and I know that within a minute, he'll reach up and see whether he's mussed it too much. I should've told Kit this was a bad idea. Aiden barely socializes with the people he chooses to have in his life. Why would he want to come to this?

"All right," he says, and I realize I must've had my mouth open, ready to take it back, because now it snaps shut with a click. "Should I pick you up?"

I almost laugh, almost offer up a quick *Oh God no,* a reminder to myself more than to him that this isn't a date. It *can't* be a date. It's bad enough we're not keeping it at camp, that I'd stayed up all night worrying over him last night, that I'm on the phone with him at 12:15 in the morning with a blush of pleasure on my cheeks. This is beyond not keeping my distance.

I manage to control my reaction enough to tell him that it's better if we meet there, that I'll have to get there early to set up. Once I've given him the address for Henry's, though, once it's time to hang up, we're both quiet for a few seconds. If this were a night in our cabin, we'd likely be asleep by now—there's not much to do once we're in for the night, and until last Saturday, when we'd broken every rule we'd never officially set, we'd mostly been lights out by ten. If this were a night in our cabin, I'd be in my bunk, hearing the sound of the woods outside, hearing the sound of Aiden's steady breathing and every time he shifts in his sleep.

"Been thinking about you, Zo," he says, in that low voice, and I have to bite my lip from letting my sigh of relief and arousal out into the phone.

"Same," I manage, but in my effort to sound unaffected I sound kind of—business-y. Aiden chuckles on the other end, gentle and knowing.

I hear an alarm trip in the background. "Gotta go," he says. "See you tomorrow."

I'm not sure he hears me say goodbye.

When I slide into bed that night, I may not be worrying anymore, may not be obsessing over whether Aiden's doing the right thing. But it's still his voice, dark and rough, I imagine hearing in my ear.

Chapter 12

Aiden

The office I set up in my parents' house—*my* house, I keep having to remind myself—is in my old bedroom, the one I slept in until I left for college, the one I slept in every time I'd come home for a break. As close as we were, Aaron and I never shared a room. From almost the time we were brought home from the hospital, Aaron needed special dehumidifiers, fans, nighttime nebulizer treatments that made my mom anxious and bleary eyed. When I'd moved back here, I'd done some pretty inconvenient gymnastics to justify avoiding Aaron's room. It'd been the most natural choice for an office—his last year, he'd had his own place, a shitty apartment on the east end, and he'd moved most of his furniture over there, even his old twin bed, which my parents had eventually donated to charity along with everything else.

But I'd been unable to face it. I keep the door closed, avoid looking at it when I pass by to get to this office. Come Christmas, I'll have to think of a new plan; if my parents come home, I'll need to get a bed in there so we all have a place to sleep.

I press my palms to my eyes, shake my head in an effort to clear it from distraction. My laptop's gone to sleep again, because I'm stuck, stuck trying to tell this story about Aaron and my plans for the camp, the story that's supposed to accompany my tour presentation. It's four thirty in the afternoon, a time when my brain is sluggish anyway, and I'd only managed an hour of sleep after my post-shift shower. But I've been opening the same document since Sunday evening when I'd gotten back from Stanton Valley, and so I know I can't blame my sluggish brain and erratic sleep schedule for the block.

I just don't know how to tell this story.

I run the tip of my index finger across the mouse pad, see the screen come to life, bright white and mostly blank, a blinking cursor at the end of the one sentence I've managed to keep: *My brother was more than just his addiction.*

It's more important than ever, I've decided, to get this right. My assertion to Zoe—*I want this to work*—had been echoing in my mind since I dropped her off, and sometime halfway through my sleepless night I'd made a decision. If I want it to work, the story's just the beginning. It's like Zoe said: I've got to be all in. When I'd gotten her text last night, I'd called her back, thinking: *I'm going to tell her.* But somewhere along the line I'd realized I want to tell her in person, when I can read her best, when her voice isn't separate from her body.

I think I can read almost everything from Zoe's body.

From the tinny speakers on my laptop comes a blurting ring, and I snap to attention as if I've been caught out by a teacher, doing homework for another class when I should be paying attention. I click the dialog box that's popped up and wait for my mother's face to fill the screen.

"Hey, Mom."

"Hi, honey." She looks good these days, or at least better than she did. At the new condo in Florida, she's got a small garden plot out back, which she fills with pots of succulents that bloom with bright, desert-like flowers she likes to photograph. She's got color in her cheeks, and her hair seems thicker, a brighter, cleaner white than it was when she'd left here. "How was work last night?"

"Not too bad. Only a few calls." She looks better, is doing better, but the fact that she knows my work schedule so completely is one of the many remnants of Aaron's addiction in her life. Growing up I'd felt lucky to be one of those kids who didn't constantly have to check in at home, who had the trust of my parents to go where I wanted so long as I made curfew, kept up with my chores. But now, my mom asks me to email her my work schedule every week. She knows which day I usually go to the grocery. I know that at least once before, she's called the neighbor to ask whether it seems like I'm having trouble keeping up with the property.

"You're working too hard, this plus what you're doing on the weekends."

I swallow, look at my own face on the screen, rather than hers. I wonder if it has a guilty look about it. "I'm all right," I say, trying not to sound impatient.

I catch her purse her lips, her physical effort not to press me about the camp. Not long after I'd made my plans with Zoe, I'd told my mom it'd be better if she backed off about it, that I'd fill her in when the six weeks were up, that it helped me focus not to talk about it too much. But she's as desperate as I am to feel like that money's doing some good out there, that we've managed to do more with Aaron's settlement than shipping my parents to a place that doesn't have any bad memories.

"Did you see the email I sent you on Monday?" she asks, her voice hopeful.

"Yeah," I say, shifting in my chair. "It's like I said, Mom. Those groups aren't really my thing."

A few months back my mom started going to group grief counseling sessions. Since then, it seems as though she's kept her own pain in enough check to try watching over mine too. She sends me articles about addicts' brain chemistry, about twin loss, about meetings in the area for people who are grieving.

None of it appeals.

"I'm doing good," I add, and I realize that it's not even entirely a lie. When I wake up in the mornings, I don't feel so disoriented anymore. For a while there, it felt like every time I'd open my eyes, I'd have to provide myself with a recap in order to prepare myself for the shock of another day in this life. *You're back home. Your parents moved away. Aaron is dead.* But now I wake up to reality, and I get on with the day. Sometimes—Fridays, mostly—I even look forward to it. "I'm going out with some friends tonight."

Her face brightens immediately. "Really? What friends? Do I know them?"

A hot prickle of shame blooms on my neck, at the backs of my arms. *Yeah, Mom,* I imagine saying, *It's the lawyer. The blonde, the one you said was made of stone. The one who slid a packet of papers across the table at you, the one who looked you straight in the eye when she asked you to sign.* "No," I say. "No one you know."

"Well, I'm so glad you're getting out there." Jesus. She sounds so much like my mom again. So much like the woman who used to cheer our most minuscule achievements at the breakfast table. I feel an answering tug of hope inside me. "Is Pop around?"

But it's too much to hope for. Her face falls, though she tries to hide it. "He's not up for talking much today, Aiden."

I know what that means. He's either sleeping or crying, or staring at the television, unseeing. I turn my head from the screen, pretend to look out the window. "I'd better get going. Lots to do before I head out tonight."

She smiles through the screen, nodding proudly. "Have a good time. You deserve to have a great time."

When we log off, I stare again at the nearly blank page on my screen, Mom's words echoing around me. What would she think, knowing that the promise of a good time tonight lives entirely in Zoe Ferris? It's not even about the possibility of sleeping with her again—we only do that in the cabin, away from all this. It's that *Zoe* is a good time, even when she's not, even when she's pissing me off or calling me on my shit, there's something about her that gets me right out of myself.

I reach a hand out, shut off the monitor, and watch the screen fade to black. Maybe I'll be able to tell the story tomorrow.

* * * *

Never is the difference between me and Ahmed more clear than when we go to a party for someone neither of us knows. When we walk up to Henry Tucker's house, Ahmed is loose and easy, telling me about some buddy of his who grew up nearby, asking whether I've ever been to the salvage yard Tucker apparently owns. I barely hear any of it, because I've gone tense all over, silent and sweaty underneath my button-up. In the past three and a half weeks I've done more socializing than I have in the entire year and a half since Aaron died, and while this afternoon I'd been congratulating myself about getting a little better, I find that now, in the face of the damn thing, I'm rattled by the thought of a houseful of people I hardly know.

It's Kit who I see first, petite and smiling near the front door, but I don't miss the way that smile changes when her dark eyes fall on me. She's kind but wary, same as she was the first time I met her at Betty's, and back then, it hadn't much bothered me. If I thought anything about it at all, it was probably some kind of surprise at Zoe having such loyal, protective friends. But now, I feel a fresh wave of nerves as I look down at her, five feet two of *You'd better not fuck with my friend*. It doesn't matter what Zoe and I have agreed on in the dark, our mouths melded together and our hands all over each other. I'm here at this party, with her friends, and that doesn't feel like just sex. It feels like I'm trying to make a good impression.

"Ahmed, good to see you again," she says, ushering him farther in, and laughing as she accepts the giant hug he gives her, a move he pulls off more naturally than I ever could. "Aiden, thanks for coming," she says, choosing a more measured handshake.

"Sure, thanks for the invite. Looks like you've put together a nice welcome." The small house is crowded, full of laughing conversation.

"Yeah, it turned out well. Your friend Charlie's not coming?"

"She's in D.C.," I say. "Went up to see her wife."

"Oh, I'm glad for her," she says, smiling. Kit seems like a nice person, a genuine person, which somehow makes it all the worse that she's got a more guarded opinion about me.

"Hi," comes a voice from beside me, and there she is, those gold-brown eyes looking at me expectantly, and I forget all about Kit only seeming half-glad to see me. *Zoe* looks glad. Glad and also fucking gorgeous. Her hair's pulled back, but already some of those silky-straight strands have fallen around her face, and her cheeks are flushed from the warm room, the crush of people. Her dress looks to me like a long men's shirt, dark blue, but she's got it belted at the waist, a pair of boots that come up to her knees, and in between those and the hem of the dress is the skin that I felt against my hips last weekend, the skin I stroked while I moved inside her.

"Hey," I say to her. I barely notice that Ahmed's already moved into the living room, shaking hands and looking like he's been here dozens of times before.

"I wanted to introduce you to Ben," she says, turning her eyes up to a tall, smiling guy I hadn't even registered as a presence. "This party is for him."

"Hey, man," I say, practically tearing my eyeballs from her. "Good to meet you."

"Yeah, you too." He shakes my hand firmly before wrapping an arm around Kit, pulling her close to his side.

"Welcome home. Bet you're glad to be back."

"You have no idea." But he's not looking at me when he says it. He's looking down at Kit, his eyes soft on her in a way that makes me slide my gaze over to Zoe, who seems to have developed a real interest in scrutinizing the contents of her plastic cup. When Ben looks back up at me, though, something's shifted in his expression. "I know you've got Z doing this camp thing with you," he says, abruptly, and Zoe's head snaps up. "Ben," she says, her voice low in warning.

"She's got a lot of people who love her," says Ben, not taking his eyes off me. *This fucking guy,* I'm thinking, but at the same time I already like him, like his directness. His care for Zoe.

Zoe laughs, an edge of nervousness to it. "It's probably like, four people, grand total," she says. "Three if I don't count my mother, and today she called and asked me if I'd mind her throwing out my christening gown, so I'm pretty sure she—"

"Zo," I say, and as soon as it comes out of my mouth I know I've done that shit on purpose. *This is what I call her,* I'm saying. I curl a hand around her elbow and squeeze gently, a brief touch that's friendlier than how I feel right now, which is—I don't know what. Possessive. A little angry. Half of me wants to be touching her like Ben touches Kit—like she's mine, like I do it every day. The other half of me is pissed that I want to, and that I can't. We don't do that here; we decided. Here, I'm the guy she's invited because of courtesy, or maybe because of her friends' curiosity. "It's all right," I tell her, before I look up at Ben and give him a short nod. "I know she does."

Ben's got a calm, friendly face, something open about his expression that I don't know if I've ever seen in myself in the mirror. Still, though—he looks at me long enough that the silence feels noticeable, a few seconds shy of truly uncomfortable. "Can I get you a beer?"

The look on Zoe's face when he asks is pure relief, so plain and honest that I touch her again, my palm at her shoulder, a brief, calming circle that Ben and Kit both notice. It's the kind of touch that doesn't have anything to do with "this camp thing," and for a second it feels like Zoe and I are the only two people in the room.

It's only a quick moment of peace and quiet, though, because the place is full up, more people coming in behind me, and Zoe gets pulled into conversation after conversation. For a while, I stay with her, nursing a beer and letting her introduce me to each group of people she says hello to. "This is my friend Aiden," she says. "He saved me from a face full of driveway a month ago." It's so simple, the way she puts it, and aside from the face full of driveway part, I wish I had met her in circumstances so simple. I shake hands, nod, answer what questions I'm asked, and feel as if I'm stretching muscles I haven't used in months.

I know I'm meeting Ben's father even before Zoe tells me his name. The guy looks like Ben coming out of a time machine, and he's got the same easy smile.

"O'Leary," he repeats, when Zoe introduces me, a searching look as he shakes my hand. "Your mother's Kathleen?"

"Uh, yeah," I say, taken aback.

"I sold her a Gorham brush and mirror set about ten years ago, I think...1959, silver detail like you wouldn't believe."

Beside me, Zoe drops back, joins another conversation that's in progress behind us, and I know that's on purpose. It's the same at camp: any mention of my family, and she goes quiet. "Must be quite a memory you've got."

"Almost forgot to put on underwear today," he says, laughing. "I only remember the stuff that doesn't matter."

"I think she bought that set for my cousin's sixteenth birthday. So it matters to someone, anyway."

Henry smiles, claps me on the shoulder. "I like you," he says, and I feel a choking, painful longing for my own dad, whose shoulder-clapping was pretty much the only brand of affection he had on offer, but he didn't spare it. "Your mom still around town?"

"She and my pop moved to Florida a few months back."

Henry nods, looks around the room to where Ben stands, now laughing with Ahmed. Fast friends, those two, and I try not to feel an illogical sense of jealousy about Med's easy nature, his ability to do with Zoe's friends what I can't. "Good to have my kid back in town," he says, more to himself than to me. This sentiment kicks me right where it hurts too. When I'd decided to move here, I'd wondered fleetingly if my parents might change their minds about Florida and stick around. I was back, after all, their only surviving son, and that had to mean something. But the truth is, our family doesn't make sense without Aaron. *I* don't make sense without Aaron. I'm just a remainder, a great big shadow left by the bomb blast of his death, and neither of my parents look at me the way Henry looks at Ben.

Suddenly this party feels like a colossal mistake, a reminder of why Zoe and I need to keep it at camp, and a reminder of why I've kept things so close since I've been home. I'm not suited for any of this right now—I feel like I'm in a room of salt pillars, rubbing all my open wounds up against them as I go. With as much friendliness as I can manage, I disentangle myself from the conversation with Henry, take advantage of Zoe's distraction and duck into the kitchen where I can rinse out my beer bottle. I'll tell Ahmed the night's over for me. He can stay if he wants, Uber it home, whatever. But me, I've got to get out of here.

"Hello," says a soft voice from behind me, and it's just—fuck. I don't feel like talking to anyone. But when I turn I'm staring down into the big blue eyes of Zoe's friend Greer, who's holding a plate of appetizers out to me like she's on server duty. "I thought you might want some food."

Jesus Christ. I do not want some food. I want to get the fuck out of here. But something stops me, some hope that I can make a good impression. I take the plate and manage a polite thank-you. It's quieter back here, a bit distant from the crowd, and it feels like she's cornered me on purpose. I take a bite of a stuffed mushroom, not really hungry but eager to have something to do with my hands, my mouth. In some ways, Greer seems tougher than Kit is—there's no caution or suspicion in her eyes, but instead something deep and knowing, ready to see right through any of your bullshit.

As soon as I swallow she speaks, timing it perfectly so I can't weasel out of responding without being obvious about it.

"We miss Zoe around here on the weekends," she says, leaning against the counter, skipping all the preliminaries. What she needs to know about me, Zoe's probably already told her. "We have routines, the three of us."

"Brunch," I say, wiping my mouth with the small napkin she'd tucked under my plate. "She told me."

Greer nods, seeming pleased that I'd know, or maybe that I'd remember. "She—well. She's sort of our center point. The one we take our cues from, in some ways. Everything's quieter without her."

Ain't that the truth is the first thing that comes to mind, because everything *is* quieter without her. Even when she's right next to me, if she's not talking, it somehow feels like the loudest quiet I've ever heard. "Three more weeks," I say, but I don't know if I'm really talking to her or to myself.

Greer looks up at me, a small wrinkle in her brow as she tilts her head slightly. "Sometimes I wonder if she'll still be a little quieter, once the time's up."

Before I have time to think it through—to wonder if this is just an observation or a warning or maybe some kind of revelation about Zoe's feelings toward me, I hear Zoe call out Greer's name from the other room. I look over my shoulder to see her weaving her way toward the kitchen. "Are you trying to see Aiden's chest hair?" she calls, loud enough that a few people nearby laugh.

Greer's face has gone all pink beneath her freckles, and she rushes out a quick, "Oh, she's joking about—some…thing I said one time?"

Zoe sidles up beside me, nudges my shoulder with her own. "Just on my way out back," she says, nodding her head toward the door. "We need to bring in another cooler. Greer, Sharon's looking for you." She levels her friend with a look, something secret communicated between them. Greer's curving smile looks gentle, approving—and I feel a strange thread of guilt. Here I am, with the people who mean the most to Zoe, people who mean more to her than I ever will. And I can't even admit her existence to my own mother.

"Thanks for the food," I tell Greer before she heads off, and she gives me a casual wave, as though she fully expects to see me again sometime.

Once we clear the door, I feel a clutching relief, not just at the big inhale of fresh air I take, but at being alone with Zoe for the first time tonight. "Hot in there," I say.

She nods, fanning her face, looking as grateful for the break as I am. "It's exhausting."

"That's on account of you working so hard, I'm guessing," I say, ignoring the skeptical look she casts my way. But she *was* working hard in there, circulating and delivering drinks and making introductions, and I'll bet she's the one who noticed about the cooler. It's like Greer said—she's the fixed point in the room, the one everyone tends to orbit around, and this party's not even for her.

I tilt my head back to look at the dark, clear sky above. At camp, you'd be able to see the stars by now, I'm guessing, and I let that thought settle over me, think about how my everyday view stands to change now. "I decided I'm going to take on the management role," I say, surprising myself, and surprising her, I guess, because I see in my peripheral vision the way her head snaps my way. "You were right."

"I didn't say—" she begins, at the same time I say, "I want to do right by Paul and Lorraine. And my brother."

And whatever she was going to say, she stops, and there's a long silence, heavy with something unspoken. I lower my head, look over at her, see where she's got the inside of her cheek caught between her teeth. *Tell me,* I'm thinking. *Tell me what that look on your face is all about.* But all she says is, "That's great. You'll be great."

"Yeah. Thanks." But it feels hollow, this exchange, and suddenly whatever's inside that party feels preferable to the loaded moment out here.

I hear her take a deep breath, and then she raises her chin too, the long column of her throat pale in the dim light from the porch. "I've got a decision to make too, I think. I had this interview. To do some volunteering."

"Yeah?"

"Yeah." She tells me about it, never looking my way—legal advising, she says, for people who can't afford it. At every turn, I hear what she's doing, stuffing her language full of conditionals even as she fills me in: *if I get it. I've never really done most of the kinds of cases they get. I'm not sure it's the right time. I've never been that good with people.*

"You're good with people," I say, at that last one.

She laughs, that sharp edge of sarcasm elbowing me right in the ribs, and I keep quiet. It seems like she feels the silence more, and I don't mind it, not right now. It bothers me, this thing with Zoe, that she's talking herself out of this gig. She'd be good—I meant what I said that night at the bonfire. She's smart as fuck, a hell of a lawyer, no matter what it cost my family personally.

An idea takes shape in my mind as I look up at the stars, as I think about the weekend ahead at camp.

I can feel her look over at me, and after a minute I lower my head, catch her with eyes narrowed in suspicion. She knows my body like I know hers now. For a second it looks like she might say something, her full lips parting before closing again, pursing slightly in a way that sends a pulse of heat to my cock. She doesn't try again, only heads over to the large blue cooler set on the concrete patio. I move quicker, bending down to pick it up.

"Okay, Lancelot, you can back off," she says, nudging me. "I can pick up a cooler."

"It's heavy. Let me get it." My voice is tinged with frustration, mostly because she's bent over in that dress thing she's wearing, and now I feel half-done-for, aroused and impatient and full of the need to get inside her again.

She pinches the back of my hand, *hard*, jarring me out of myself, and when I flinch it away, she grabs one handle of the cooler so now we're sharing the weight, her side hanging lower than mine. She gives me a look like she's captured the freaking flag, and I press down the laugh that's suddenly sitting right behind my breastbone.

"Jesus fucking Christ," I say, no edge in it. I feel that familiar bubble of amusement alongside my desire. "You're so stubborn."

Her mouth opens in exaggerated shock. "*I'm* stubborn? I'd slap you for that, but I'd probably break my hand on that hard head of yours." She huffs out an exasperated sigh, tugs on the cooler. "I can't believe you'd call me stubborn, when you—"

"Don't," I say, tugging on my end. "Don't bring up the thing about driving."

"It's like you think I *can't* drive."

"I know you can drive. I just *prefer* to drive."

"Because you're stubborn!"

"Zo," I say, keeping my voice calm, which gets her all the more riled up. "What do you ask Hammond every time we have breakfast at the lodge? Every. Fucking. Time?"

Even in the dim light from the porch lamp, I can see the way her face flushes. "That's not the same."

"Every time, you ask him if he wants eggs."

"Aiden, it's *rude* about the cereal. If Lorraine makes eggs, he shouldn't ask for cereal!" She blows a strand of hair away from her face, tugging again at the cooler, hard enough that her breasts move beneath the fabric of her shirt, dress, whatever the hell that thing is. Jesus, she's hot. If we were having this fight in the cabin, I'd have it up around her waist by now.

"But Lorraine doesn't care. Which means you shouldn't care. *You're* the stubborn one."

"I am not—"

"Will you just let me take the fucking cooler?"

"Oh my God. I lift weights three days a week, Aiden. It's not even heavy. It's not like your dick is going to shrink if I—"

"Is everything okay out there?"

Zoe and I both freeze, straightening up like we actually have been caught with her dress up around her waist. For a second, our eyes widen comically at each other, and I can tell Zoe's trying not to laugh.

"Everything's fine, Kit," she says.

"Were you yelling at her?" Kit says to me, her eyes narrowed.

Zoe snorts. "I think we both know it's me doing all the yelling. We're having a—" She breaks off, looks over at me again, her mouth curving upward into something wicked. "Aiden doesn't think women should drive."

Kit looks at me like I've just belched at her dinner table.

"I don't think that," I say, quickly.

"Probably he doesn't think we should have the vote."

I bark out a laugh, before I can stop it. "Zo," I say, "stop. Please." The look on Zoe's face—it's a mixture of amusement and triumph, and I know the triumph isn't about embarrassing me in front of her friends. It's about the laugh she's gotten out of me.

Kit is looking back and forth between us, something speculative in her expression. Right then, Zoe drops her end of the cooler, leaving me to scramble before it hits the concrete patio, ice and drinks clattering together inside the thick plastic. I hear her satisfied chuckle. "Time for toasts?" she asks Kit.

"Yeah," Kit says, her eyes resting on me again, briefly, a smile playing on her lips before she looks back at Zoe. "Help me pour some champagne?"

"Sure," Zoe says, and walks up the steps. Before she crosses into the house, she looks over her shoulder at me and winks.

And it's right then I know: we're breaking that only-in-the-cabin rule tonight.

Chapter 13

Zoe

There's something familiar about this: me, recently deposited on the hideous-but-comfortable pink velveteen chair in Aiden's living room, wobbly legged and faintly sweaty, waiting for him to bring me a glass of water.

The differences, of course, are key. I've been deposited here because Aiden and I did not manage to make it to his bedroom, because I came in his front door and he closed it behind me, pressed me right up against it and kissed me like he hadn't seen me in days and days. Soon enough he'd stripped me of all my layers, tugging a condom from his pocket while I'd shoved his pants down. The wobbly legs and the sweat are dual earned—my legs wrapped around his waist while he took me, sure, but I'd also come here straight from a hot yoga class, red-faced and salty-skinned, and Aiden didn't seem to mind one bit. He may have even liked it, judging by the groan he'd let out as soon as he'd put his tongue against my skin, licking up my neck like I was the best thing he'd ever tasted.

When he comes back in the room, carrying a big glass dripping with icy condensation, he's flushed from exertion too, his jeans still unzipped, hanging loose around his waist so I can see his black boxer briefs—so I can see, surprisingly, that he looks like he could go again.

"You need a permit for that thing," I say, taking the glass from him and hiding my smile behind a greedy drink.

He laughs, the sound low and easy, and I think of that first day I sat in this chair—how tentative, awkward, messed up it all was. "You say the nicest things." He leans down, putting a hand on each of the chair's arms, watching me drink. When I lower the glass, he presses his lips to mine, a hard stamp, and turns the chair, swiveling it toward the center of the living room.

"Fancy," I say when he backs up, taking a seat on the couch that's now across from me.

And this is it—this is the other newness we're still navigating—what do we do now, in the aftermath of these interludes we've had every day since Ben's party. That night, I'd driven over here, equal parts excited and nervous, worried I'd misread the signals. But even before I'd shut off the ignition of my car, he'd opened his door, leaned against the jamb, and watched me with a slight grin on his face. I'd smiled back, turned off the car, and lifted my hips, shimmying my underwear down my thighs, over my boots. By the time I was dropping them in my bag, he was opening my door, nearly dragging me out of my seat in the most perfect, desperate way. Afterward, I'd risen from his bed, unmoored in the hugeness of it compared to our twin bunks at the campground, and said I needed to get home to wash my hair.

That he didn't laugh or argue suggested that I'd made the right call.

And anyways, I *do* use a special shampoo.

I hadn't needed to bother with an excuse yesterday, as we'd only managed a single hot, fast quickie, right on that couch Aiden's sitting on, in the two-hour break Aiden had before a second shift. The memory of that makes me flush anew, and I press the icy glass to the side of my face.

Aiden snorts, as if he knows exactly what I'm thinking.

Tonight's different, though. It's Friday, and we don't go to camp until tomorrow. He doesn't have to work, and I'm still largely plans-less, spending too much time per day checking my email to see whether Marisela's gotten in touch, even though I'm not supposed to hear until next week, and even though I still don't know what I'll do about it, whether going back to the law in any form is the right thing, no matter how eager I'd felt on Monday.

I've felt eager before. I'd felt eager with Christopher, back when I'd learned he was in trouble, when I realized I could fix it. I'd felt eager when I'd started at Willis-Hanawalt, when I'd felt like I was finally going to reclaim the legacy my dad had wanted for me. Obviously my eager meter is busted.

Aiden's loose limbed, a little heavy lidded over there on the couch, his eyes on me without any particular signal for me to leave or stay. I want to ask him how it's been going, his presentation, now that he's decided to take on the camp manager role. If I'm honest, I want to ask him a series of about ten hard-hitting questions that might get him to rethink the whole thing, and that's when I remember I'd better get the hell out of here, because I'm meant to be *keeping my distance*, no matter that Aiden and I have broken the only-at-camp rule.

I stand, setting my glass on a coaster, stretching as I head down the hallway toward the house's only bathroom, so I can clean up a bit before I go. It's a good reminder, this hallway. Aiden's bedroom door is wide open, his bed tidy, but he keeps the door to his home office partially closed, keeps another door along the hall shut—Aaron's old room, I'm sure—all the way. If there's a more potent metaphor for the two of us and what we're doing together, I don't know what it could possibly be.

When I come out, my phone's ringing, muffled by the sound of my purse, which Aiden's holding out to me. "Didn't wanting to go rustling through there."

"Thanks," I say, reaching a hand in and peeking at the screen before I even have it all the way out, my stomach fluttering when I see the name there.

I answer before I have time to think better of it, before I register that now I'm going to have this conversation in front of Aiden.

"Zoe?" comes Marisela's voice on the other end, so wholly cheerful that I already know what she's going to say.

"This is Zoe," I reply, holding up a finger to Aiden while I back slowly toward the kitchen, putting some distance between this and him.

"I'm sorry it's taken me a few days to get back to you. I practically wanted to put you on calls on Monday, but you know how it is."

"Oh," I say first, but correct with a quick, "oh, sure. I know how it is. Paperwork and all that."

"Exactly!" And then she's off to the races. She'd love to have me join the team; I could start next week, maybe six hours a week or so at first; if I sign on I'll need to bring a copy of my driver's license, my diploma; if I don't mind she'll send over some documents I can look over while I decide.

I'm nodding, the occasional *uh-huh* thrown in, so aware of warring impulses: first to shake my fist in the sky in victory and tell her I'll be there Monday, second to drop this phone like a hot potato and run like hell from everything she's offering. But I do neither. I stay careful. I don't commit to anything. I tell her to send the documents, tell her I'm excited to look them over. I tell her I'll be in touch as soon as I can.

When we hang up, Marisela's final *I really hope I can convince you* ringing in my ear, Aiden's leaning against the doorway, looking at me. "You got it," he says, his voice even, but his eyes light, a hitch at one side of his mouth that feels about ten times more exciting than the damn phone call. I am in all kinds of trouble with him, and I know it.

"I did."

"Get your sweatshirt on," he says. "We'll go to your friend Betty's place and celebrate."

What.

I look after him, slack jawed, while he moves back into the living room, grabs his jacket off a peg on the wall. "I didn't say I was taking it."

He shrugs into his jacket. "Didn't say you were. Still, you got a gig. Worth a beer, at least."

I think back to that night at Betty's, Kit telling me about Aiden not going out with his crew for months, and now he's basically—I don't know what. Taking me on a date? What are we going to do, make a pro/con list about me taking a potential first step back into my legal career? I don't even want to do that with Kit and Greer, let alone Aiden. In my mind is a picture of my condo—all its clean, white-gray stillness. I should feel something like longing, thinking about all the quiet, careful ruminating I could be doing there while I turn Marisela's offer over in my mind.

Aiden turns to look back at me, his eyes scanning my face while I'm just *stuck*, stuck again, stuck forever. "Zo," he says, his voice half-weary, half-amused. "I just fucked you against this door and came so hard that I'm pretty sure I saw stars. I'm running on about half as much sleep as usual, and that's down to what we've been doing too. Let's get some food and play a game of darts. We don't even have to talk about your new job."

"It's not a job," I say, moodily, but everything he's said is what I need to get unstuck, to start me moving toward the door, to my sweatshirt. It doesn't have to *mean* anything, that I don't so much want to go back home now. We're still keeping our distance, whether we go to Betty's together or not. "I'll take my own car," I tell him, as I zip it up.

"Whatever you say."

* * * *

"No," I say, and then repeat it for good measure. "No, this is not what I agreed to."

Aiden's answer is a low grunt as he tightens the straps of the harness around my thighs, stepping back to look me over. He nods to himself, as if this is all perfectly normal, A-OK, another regular Sunday morning.

It is none of those things, even aside from the fact that I'm strapped into a harness.

I might've known an ambush was coming, might've known there was a reason this weekend's been so easy and pleasant. On the way here on Saturday morning, Aiden had pulled over in Coleville—So you'll stop making calf eyes every time we drive through, he'd said—and walked us to a cafe with gingham curtains and the best hot chocolate I've ever tasted. We'd drank it while we'd walked down Coleville's main street, aimless, unpressured conversation and the kind of taut, fun arguing that frames almost all our interactions, the only thing other than sex that had taken my mind off Marisela's offer.

At the campground that afternoon, he was as loose as I'd ever seen him, his body moving in some new, relaxed way as he'd helped fold up chairs from the wedding. Later, I'd watched him work with Paul to remove a temporary dance floor that had been snapped together over the flat clearing on the lodge's east side, and he'd been all easy calm, laughing once so loud that I'd heard it from where I stood on the porch of the lodge, uncoiling strands of tiny lights from the railings. He'd caught my eye and smiled, as though we had a hundred secrets between us.

It's all the sex, I'd told myself. *I've uncoiled him.*

But no. No, he'd been uncoiling *me*, on purpose, so much so that last night, after pizza delivery to the lodge and a late, laugh-filled game of euchre with Paul, Lorraine, Sheree, Tom, and Val—Hammond having taken over putting the girls to bed—I'd barely noticed when Paul had tipped his chin to Aiden and said, "Still nine thirty tomorrow morning, then?" Aiden had nodded, and now that I think of it, Sheree had hidden a smile behind one of her hands.

Now I realize they're great betrayers, every one of them, because here I am, strapped into a harness and about three seconds away from a profanity-filled diatribe about how *shit* the entire concept of team building is, anyway.

It's different here at the farthest edge of the camp, the trees more sparse and the ground red-clay dusty and flat. We'd only skirted along it during our tour a few weeks back, and then, Paul and Lorraine had told us that a lot of the more advanced team-building exercises took place over here. The only thing I'd noticed at the time was what looked like a couple of shorter than usual telephone poles and wires. Now—*now* I'm finding out Aiden wants me to climb up one of them.

I swallow a lump of dread, staring up at it. This isn't like the zip line, which wasn't even all that high off the ground and which only required horizontal movement. This is so—*vertical.*

"Perfect day for it," Paul says, coming over to check Aiden's work on my harness. "No clouds, not too cold. Sun's been warming the pamper pole for a good couple hours now."

"The what pole now?" I say.

"The *pamper* pole." He pats the one closest to him, like this is something I should have heard of. It is nothing I have heard of, let me tell you what. I don't see anything on this pole that would pamper me.

"I'm about to rock this," says Sheree, beside me, swinging her arms back and forth as though she's loosening up for competition. "I used to be the fastest kid at camp on this pole."

"Now, Sheree," Paul says, shaking his head. "Remember, we don't use the pole for competition. This is about challenging ourselves, not each other."

Jeez, these self-affirmations. I love this guy, but he's so earnest it makes my teeth hurt sometimes. Plus, despite or maybe because of my fear, the pole jokes are stacking up in my brain like cars on the highway. I think Aiden senses it, because he moves beside me and places his big, calloused hand on the nape of my neck, strokes his fingers on the skin there. I shiver, forgetting for a minute all about my jokes, but then I shift away, angry at him for ambushing me with this.

Paul curls his fingers around one of the little metal U shapes stuck in the side, explains to me that these are the hand- and footholds I'll use to climb to the top of the pole. And I'm not just supposed to climb it. I'm supposed to climb it, stand on the tippy-top, and then jump off, trying to hit a rubber ball that's hanging from one of the wires.

"Paul," I say, hoping he doesn't catch the nerves in my voice. "The thing is, I'm not much of a climber. I'm very careful about moisturizing, is the thing. Touch my hands— they're like satin!" I look up to Aiden, pleadingly. He can't possibly, truly want me to do this. If I die we'll never have any more of all that amazing sex we've been having. But he's not speaking up on my behalf; this was his idea, after all. "Got a surprise for you," he'd whispered in my ear this morning, his mouth right against me as he leaned over my top bunk, not even needing to stretch to do it, and my toes had curled in pleasure.

Because I am an idiot.

"I'm sure you've got nice hands," says Paul. "I've got gloves if you want to wear them."

"You know what I like about you, Paul? It's how you're always so prepared."

He gives me a look I've come to recognize on him, a mixture of amusement and confusion that suggests he's not quite sure what to make of me.

"I'm up first," says Sheree, bouncing on the balls of her feet while Tom beams at her in pride. Easy for him, he's got Little Tommy strapped to his chest and also a diagnosed heart arrhythmia. No one's going to make him go up. "You can watch me, Zoe."

Ten minutes later and I'm wringing my hands, my eyes on Sheree's rising form, the space I'm keeping between me and Aiden pointed, deliberate. Little Tommy is making wet, happy gurgling noises while Tom uses his own hands to guide his son's chubby little ones into a rhythmic clap. "Go, Mama, go!" he says, over and over, hoping Little Tommy might repeat after him.

"Aiden," I say, as quietly as I can so that he'll still hear me, "I don't think I should go. I might faint again."

"The fainting was a one-off," he says, echoing what I've said to him so many times. I barely manage a *hmph* of disagreement, boring holes into the side of his face with my eyes. "Watch Sheree," he adds. "She's good."

I do watch, especially as she nears the very top. It's not so much the climb that gets to me. It's this part right here, this part that I know I need to pay attention to if I've got a hope in hell of getting up there and not making an ass of myself. But it's hard to see, from this distance, by what magic she makes it up, even though Paul's doing his best to narrate it for me—*Notice the way she moves slowly to a crouch, watch how patient she is before she attempts to stand.*

She does it beautifully, her arms extended out in front of her at first, parallel with her bent knees, before she slowly spreads them out to her sides, pushing up to her full height. She looks simultaneously small and larger than life up there, and it seems like an eternity that she stands, balancing herself, her legs tight together, her body as still and patient as the pole itself. She looks as if she could wait up there all day, as if it doesn't bother her at all to be there, anticipating that leap.

When she jumps, I slap a hand over my eyes, let slip a gasp of surprise and terror, my heart in my throat. It's that moment, that *leap*, that terrifies me.

But all I hear is her proud shout, Tommy's shriek of delight, Paul and Aiden's applause.

I pull at the straps of my harness. I know I could get out of this. I know I could look Aiden in the face and tell him no again—and he'd listen. But I'm in this harness, everything this weekend has been so good, and I have the strangest sense I'll disappoint him, and Paul, and most of all, *worst* of all, myself.

While Paul's helping to lower Sheree, Aiden moves in front of me, sets his big hands on my shoulders, and then he waits. Waits until I look up, meet his eyes. "Took me three tries to get up there, the first summer I did this. Kept stopping at the halfway point."

"I won't do that," I say, sure of it already. It's not the climb.

"I know," he answers, and I feel a jolt of something so affectionate, so desperate—something inside of myself that's jumping out toward him in sudden, simple gratitude for his confidence, for the way he sees me, for what he sees already about this. It's scary, the way Aiden and I know each other, when we've spent all this time trying not to.

"It's being at the top," I say. "What if I get up there and can't do the jump?"

He shrugs. "Dunno, Zo. Guess you'll have to figure how easy it is to climb back down."

* * * *

It's pretty easy, at first.

I almost enjoy the part where I'm getting familiar with the movement, the crab-like crawl I have to adopt to get from one handhold to the next. There's a comfort in feeling my muscles work like they're supposed to, in being strong from the strength training I do, in being flexible from yoga. Even my breaths are careful, focused—in through my nose, sharp and noisy out of my mouth. All that physical work, all that gym time—one non-worthless thing I've done with my hazy, unstructured existence, I guess.

But then I look down, and my mind stutters with the incongruity of it—me up here, and everyone else below. Where I'm going, there's no wide, steady platform waiting, there's no cheerful companion to send me across a zip line, where there'll be someone waiting on the other side. The higher I go, the more alone I get. My stomach clenches with fear, and I refocus, resolving not to look down again.

"Hey," says Aiden, calling up to me. His voice is close enough still that he doesn't quite have to yell, and this soothes me slightly. "You doing all right up there, Satin Hands?"

Dick, I think, but my mouth curves in a smile. "Can it, Boy Scout," I mumble back, too afraid that if I speak louder I'll come right off this thing.

"You know that's not how we do it here, Aiden," says Paul, his voice sounding farther away. "You've got to *encourage* her."

"Oh, I am," I hear Aiden say, and without thinking I cast my eyes back to him, see him smiling up, arms crossed over his broad chest.

"Don't distract me," I say, some of the nerves falling away from me like loose rocks on a cliff face. "I'm making this pole my bitch. Sorry, Paul!"

"That's all right," he says, chuckling.

I loosen my grip on one of the staples, watch my hand tremble as I pull it away, my other hand and my thighs around the pole tightening instinctively while I reach up.

"Relax your legs," Aiden says. "You don't have to hold on so tight."

You didn't mind it before, I think, remembering the way I'd clutched my thighs around him last night once we'd gotten back to our cabin, fighting to get closer to him even as he'd thrust his weight into me. "Surprised I have any strength left in these babies," I call to him, seeking his face again, and I laugh when he registers my meaning, his brow lowering. Up close I'll bet there's a little flush on his neck, just under his stubble.

I get up another length—next hand, right foot, left foot.

"You're doing great," yells Sheree, clapping. "You look like you belong on that pole!"

"That—I don't know if that's a compliment, Sheree!"

"I heard it," she says. "I heard it as soon as it came out of my mouth. Sorry!"

"You're halfway," says Paul, his voice calm as always, but I notice now that everyone sounds even farther away, and this brings a new sheen of sweat across my back.

"Don't think about what you'll do when you get there," calls Aiden, and I get a secret thrill that he knows what I'm thinking. Though, what else does anyone think about when they're on this damn thing? Probably it doesn't take a genius.

"Can I think about what I'll do when I get down?" I say, ignoring the shaky quality to my voice. "FYI, it involves one of these carabiners and your testicles!" That was probably a bridge too far for Paul and Tom, but I hear Sheree's crack of laughter.

"Can't wait, baby," he calls back, and *oh.* That *stupid* nickname. He's such an *ass.* Such a pompous, offending ass.

I like him so *much.*

I close my eyes, briefly, take a steadying breath, and keep going. There's a point at which it starts to feel good again, the climb. Tiring, but a reminder of my strength. Despite my earlier longing for the horizontal comfort of the zip line, something about the vertical progress is satisfying in its own way, the feeling that I'm not running from something but that I'm climbing out of it. Below me, Sheree and Tom and Paul are cheering me, clapping and calling out words of encouragement. Aiden is quiet, but when I look down, I see he's moved just slightly away from the group, to the other side of the pole, his head back to watch me. He's too far away for me to see much about his facial expression, but I can see in the lines of his body that he's focused. He's rooting for me as much as everyone else.

And I want to stand on the top and jump, I do. But when I reach the last set of staples, I freeze. Suddenly I can't think how—even though I watched Sheree do it, even though Paul's words are ringing in my head—I can't think how to get my feet up there. I reach up to rub my palm over the top of the pole, and it's—it's so *small*, that space, no room for error. I won't be able to stand there. My legs feel so tired now, shaky and clumsy. Isn't it something I've made it this far? Doesn't that count for something? I could let go now. I've still done the climb, after all, and that's more than Aiden did at first.

I rest the front of my helmet against the pole and close my eyes, my body tightening up again, my breathing shallow from a combination of exertion and anxiety.

"Zo!" Aiden calls up to me, and I don't move, can't move. My hands itch to release the staples, to fall back into the bouncing security of the harness, to let my limbs go slack. "Don't you quit," he shouts, and I wish he were right here next to me, talking into my ear like he does when he's inside me. I wish I could hear it like his gruff whisper, the voice that's only for me.

To call back to him—even to say, *I can't*, or *I want to come down*—feels too hard at the moment. I do what feels most manageable, which is to open my eyes, and even as I do it I'm expecting it to be a mistake, seeing everyone from such a great height and knowing fully where I am in relation to them. But all I see is Aiden, far below me, his arms still crossed over his chest. I feel something, when I look at him, some...I don't know what. An exchange, I guess, something physical in his body that seems to charge my own. I *can't* see his eyes, of course I can't. But somehow I can. Somehow I can see him looking at me, challenging me, *pushing* me. It's funny, how I once wanted to shrink under that stare. Funny how the first time he looked at me, really looked at me, I literally fell at his feet—sick, shamed, overwhelmed. But right now he's looking at me and all I want to do is get bigger, get out of my cramped huddle against this pole and stand, rise to my full height, stretch out my arms, and reach that damned ball.

So that's what I do. I take one last look at him, wonder if I imagine him nod his head at me, and then focus. Not on the pole itself, not on the jump, not on the ball. I focus on my own body, on how I can set my hands on either side, on how I can raise one foot, and then the other, between them. I focus on how it feels to crouch there, everything about me compact. If I bunch up my muscles too much, I tip a fraction to one side. If I hold on too tight, everything feels like it's shaking—my body, the pole, the very *air*.

It isn't perfect. It's not Sheree's slow, balanced stand, her five full seconds of poise before she jumped. It's a little rushed, my arms coming out recklessly to the side as I press my quads up, the hardest, most intense squat I've ever done. But I don't slip. I don't make the leap because of momentum or a slip of my shoe or lost balance. I make the leap because I decide to.

I feel the ball slap against both my palms, maybe a little clumsily. I hear the shouts of victory from below. I'm smiling, leaning back in my harness and letting it spin as it lowers, looking up into the blue sky and feeling lighter than I have in months—in years, maybe. I feel fucking *great*. I feel like I could climb that pole again.

I feel the furthest thing from stuck. Spinning there, I know what I'll do about Marisela, about Legal Aid. This is it. This is the beginning of me getting unstuck.

Strong, warm arms come around my legs, and I know they're not Paul's. I know it's Aiden come to get me, but he makes no move to unsnap my harness. He pulls me down his body so we're chest to chest, all the snaps and carabiners pressing between us. His smile is bigger than I've ever seen it, but I only get it for the briefest second, because he tucks my body into his so we're as cheek to cheek as my helmet allows, and says, right into my ear, "I knew you wouldn't quit."

My answering smile feels huge, too big for my face, and my arms squeeze him with all the strength I didn't think I had left. When he pulls away I try to school my expression, to look a little less like I'm a child bursting with glee, but before I manage it he leans in, presses his lips against my smiling mouth—a hard, firm kiss that catches me on the teeth at first until I shape my mouth to kiss him back. And it's so good, that kiss—quick but intense, one of his arms banded around my lower back, the other coming up so he can unsnap the closure underneath my chin.

It's the first kiss he's ever given me in front of other people. And it's not for show.

"You did so good," he says, and kisses me again.

"Okay!" says Paul from somewhere behind us, not quite embarrassed but maybe on the edge of it, and I realize I've got one leg hitched around Aiden's hip. I can't blame the harness for it—I'm just pressing close to him, getting to where I know him best, where we say everything best. "That was a wonderful job, Zoe," Paul says, "just wonderful! How do you feel?"

"I feel awesome," I say, my too-big smile back. Sheree and Tom congratulate me as Aiden and Paul help me out of the harness, and I can't stop looking up at the pole, at the height I scaled, the dive I made. I can't stop thinking about the press of Aiden's lips against mine, the way it felt to have his arms around me after coming down.

If I had a gratitude jar, I'd put this day in there.

I'd fill it with slips, all for this day's memories.

Chapter 14

Aiden

I remember all the people I've had die on the job.

My first was in my second year running: a pulmonary embolism, dead before we even got him on the rig. My second, a car crash, two victims. My third, an MI, husband in the rig with us, watching his wife breathe her last. Twenty-three in all, over my ten years running, first as an EMT and later as a medic. It seems morbid, maybe, to keep a count, but I guess I think it'd be more morbid *not* to, to have it become commonplace, to not remember.

But I'd give anything, anything at all, to forget the last hour.

The call had come in at 5:06 a.m. Female, twenty-five, possible overdose. *Lights and sirens,* the dispatcher had said, which meant we needed to hustle. I'd done overdoses since Aaron; they were too commonplace to avoid. But they still made me sweat a little harder, made my hands a little unsteadier.

You want to tell yourself, I guess, that you'll be going somewhere seedy, somewhere where there's cooking spoons on the dresser, hollow-eyed spectators who scatter under the lights of the rig like cockroaches. You want to tell yourself that there's a type, because that helps you make sense of things. But there isn't, so I wasn't surprised to be headed to a nice neighborhood. I wasn't surprised to pull up to the large, perfectly maintained Tudor, professional landscaping, fancy lights lining the walk. I wasn't surprised by any of the details I learned over those next frantic twenty minutes: Sidney, her name was. Living with her parents, sleeping in her childhood bedroom. A bad back injury while playing on her college soccer team. Addiction to prescription opioid painkillers. Just home from rehab yesterday.

Unconscious.

Unresponsive.

In the rig, her parents following us to the hospital, Ahmed and I had done everything. Intubation. Twelve lead to monitor heart function. IV line to pump her full of Narcan, sodium bicarbonate. Ahmed doing CPR when she'd lost her pulse, me putting pads on for the AED. Epinephrine, trying to get a shockable rhythm. Over and over again, until it started to feel awful, like we were just rag-dolling her around, Charlie in the front, calling ahead to the hospital. *One more time,* I'd thought, more epinephrine in her line, and I'd opened my mouth to say her name, to shock her back—*Sidney!*—but instead I'd said his name, quick, automatic, and utterly humiliating.

Aaron.

Across from me, Ahmed had stiffened, and I'd corrected. "I'm fine," I'd said quickly. "I'm fine."

No change by the time we'd gotten to the hospital, and Ahmed and Charlie had taken over, covering the transfer and paperwork. It takes longer than you'd think, the hanging around, the paperwork. Long enough to find out the doctors couldn't do any better than we had done. Long enough to find out Sidney was gone.

I'm quiet on the ride back to the station; we all are. But while Charlie and Ahmed manage at least a few duty-related exchanges—meds we'll have to replenish, paperwork we'll have to file—I say nothing, a black, twisting pain in my throat that's nearly choking me. When we pull up, it's two minutes until our shift is over, and the next crew is in the bay, sipping coffee, laughing and talking. It's normal—it's so fucking *normal*, and I feel frozen in this seat. I feel like if I move, it'll just be to destroy this truck with my bare hands. It suddenly seems so wrong to ever use this vehicle again. It should be buried, set on fire, put out to sea, *something.*

When Charlie and Ahmed get out, I see Charlie shake her head, a slight turn, but the expression on her face must convey something, because the new crew adjusts, turns solemn, one of them looking my way in sympathy. That's all I need to extract myself, to get moving. Med stops me, a big hand on my shoulder. "Take off, man. Charlie and I will close out."

"I'm all right."

"I know," he answers, giving my shoulder a firm slap of recognition. "No shame in needing some time, though."

"Yeah," I manage. "Thanks."

I don't look at him, or at Charlie, or at anyone else as I grab my things from my locker and head out. But in my car, I feel as lost as I did in the rig, unsure where I should go next. It's seven in the morning, and before the call we'd all gotten a few good hours of interrupted sleep, and I doubt I could get any shut-eye even if we hadn't. Even now, when I blink, I see her open eyes, the green cast to her skin. I can so easily rearrange her features. Make them into Aaron's. She was slight, like he was. Fine bones underneath thin skin.

I drive without seeing, the kind of autopilot where you get home and think, *How did I get here?*, where you remember none of the traffic lights you stopped at, none of the intersections you passed through. Except I haven't gone home. I've gone to Zoe's. I'm parked right outside her building, the place where I've waited for her, or where she's waited for me, every time we've left for Stanton Valley.

There is not one person who I should want to be around less after I've watched a woman die from the same thing that killed my brother. But *should* means nothing to me right now. It's only been two and a half days since I dropped her off here, after our weekend, and it feels like a lifetime. If I'm honest it felt like a lifetime even before this morning. When I'd dropped her off on Sunday, I'd lingered at this same spot, not wanting to be apart from her after a weekend that had been damned near perfect, after the days before where we'd spent stolen time at my place. There's something new between us now, though neither of us had been able to say it, and she'd slid from my car like she does every Sunday. I don't think I'd stopped thinking of her since, not until these last frantic couple of hours, where my head had been full with trying to put color back in Sidney's sunken, wasting skin.

So right now, all I want is to see Zoe's smooth, bright skin, her hair in the sun when it gleams and changes color. I want her smile, her sharp, clear voice. I am too wrung out to care about why.

I'm greeted in the lobby by a black-suited doorman who sits behind a high, granite-topped desk, a headset in his ear. He greets me with a grating, cheerful, "May I help you?" I didn't even know this place had a doorman, didn't think much past getting in the door. Now I wonder what will happen if I have this guy call up, if Zoe will not, in fact—despite how things are between us now—want to see me at seven o'clock on a random Wednesday morning, no phone call first. But I don't think about turning back. My seeing her feels as necessary as my next breath.

"I'm here to see a resident. Zoe Ferris."

He nods, asks my name, and types something onto his laptop, and in a few seconds he's speaking quietly into his headset while I try to make myself look calm and disinterested, like I don't feel as if I could tear this place to pieces just to get what I need. I catch sight of myself in a mirror across the lobby, wincing at the state of my uniform, the dark circles under my eyes.

"You can go on up, sir," the doorman says. I hear a buzzy click that must open the glass doors behind him, leading into a bay of elevators. I head toward them, then pause and turn back, embarrassed. "I don't know her apartment number."

If he thinks it's odd, he doesn't reveal it, telling me where to go. In the elevator, I keep my hands tucked into my pockets, my head down, not wanting to see anyone or anything until I get to her. And when the doors ping and open, she's there, standing right in front of them, dressed like I haven't seen her since that first day—sleek, fitted dress, this one black, a green cardigan buttoned over top. Her hair is pulled back in a low ponytail, her lips glossy pink. For a second, I think I must visibly deflate at seeing her this way. *What I wanted,* I think, *was* my *Zoe.*

"Aiden?" she says, her brow furrowed. I pause so long that she has to hold a hand out to stop the doors from reclosing, so I step out, expecting to make this quick. I notice, for the first time, that she's not wearing shoes.

"Sorry," I manage to grind out. "I don't know why I came. I should've figured—fuck." It dawns on me what Zoe must be doing, dressed like that. "Fuck, is this your first day? I'm an asshole." Behind everything I'm feeling is a whisper of satisfaction that she's doing it, that she took the leap, same as she did this weekend, when I was so proud of her that I felt like I'd burst.

"It's not my first day," she says, quickly, sharply, that voice I wanted to hear. "I was making breakfast."

"Dressed like that?"

She looks down at herself, then back up at me. "Aiden," she says again, her tone serious. "Tell me what happened."

"Bad night at work." It's all I can stand saying about it, at least right now. "Only thing I could think was—I don't know. Just came here."

Her face flushes, and she looks—she looks so *alive*. I focus on her face, ignoring the prickle of unease I feel at seeing her in her professional clothes, a sense memory of something ugly between us. "Come have breakfast with me," she says.

"I probably shouldn't. I didn't think this through. I need a shower."

"You've got clothes in your car?"

"Yeah."

"Okay. Go get them. You can shower here. The code for the front is star 1631. I'll leave my door unlocked. We'll have eggs and toast. Would you like coffee or tea?"

Thank God for her professionalism, for that starched-up way she looks. My body feels like it's loosened a little as she's given me these instructions. "Coffee," I say, and proceed to follow every one.

* * * *

When I step out of Zoe's bathroom after my shower, I feel normal enough, less fuzzy headed and shocked, to take in my surroundings. Zoe's place isn't big, but it's expensive looking, wide-open space for the kitchen, dining room, and living area, almost everything in shades of white or pale gray, a dark wood floor beneath. If I weren't in here myself, if I hadn't just washed my hair with a shampoo that smells like her, I wouldn't even believe someone lives here. There are no family photos, no stacks of mail or tangled cords sticking out from the plugs, no pairs of shoes resting by the door. On the marble island she has a glass bowl filled with lemons, the only spot of color in the place except for her. She holds the phone to her ear with one hand, speaking quietly; the other she uses to pour coffee from a French press into a white mug. When she looks up and sees me, she offers a small smile, nods for me to sit at the island.

She ends her call and shuts off her phone, setting it out of the way on the counter.

"I'm sorry if I messed up your morning."

"You didn't. I got an early start today. I don't need to be anywhere for a little while." She turns away, busies herself with plates and silverware that she sets in front of me. She opens the oven and peeks in, same with the broiler drawer underneath, and within minutes she's served me a huge portion of eggs, fat slices of toast alongside it, a small white dish of butter set onto my plate, already perfectly softened.

And then, Zoe just—*talks*. She's not much of a cook, she says, but her dad used to make big breakfasts. That's why she likes going for brunch with her friends, but she's pretty good at the basics, eggs and toast like what we're eating now. Once, she tells me, during a particularly rough stretch of weeks at her job, she'd fallen asleep at the breakfast bar where we're sitting while she waited for her frittata to cook, and she'd had a small fire that she'd had to pay a hefty fine to the condo board for. She's on that board, and they're in the middle of a complicated vote about new equipment to purchase for the fitness center. She likes it here, mostly, though when Kit bought her place she thought about a house. Then again—she says, having the conversation entirely with herself—Kit's house is a little shabby, under construction all the time, and sometimes she comes home from there and has to take a bath to relax. "I like simplicity," she says, gesturing around her with her fork. "In case you couldn't tell."

In the pauses she takes to sip her coffee, or to take a bite of her food, I realize that I too am relaxing, bit by bit. Zoe has filled up all the space in my head with this chatter, these details that don't matter really but somehow *do*, the little things about her life that get me out of that rig, that stop me thinking about death and failure and being just a few minutes too late. She talks all through the meal, and she talks when we stand to clear our plates, when I rinse them and she slides them into the dishwasher, when she takes a white towel from the edge of the sink and wipes her smooth, perfect hands with it.

The truth is, I want to fall at her feet, to press my face right against her middle and cling to her in great, aching gratitude for the way she's chased away the worst of this morning. But that's not who we've been to each other, not so far. We've touched each other in all kinds of ways—for show, for sex, and last weekend, for celebration—but not really for comfort. So I settle for a gruff, inadequate, "Thank you."

She shrugs, refolding the towel and placing it back in its spot. When she looks at me, she's calm, assessing, completely untroubled by my strange presence here, or at least she's doing a damn fine performance. "Want to walk me to work?" she asks, and then quickly corrects, "To volunteering, I mean?"

What I should say is no. On that walk I'll have to engage in some kind of conversation, and really, I don't think I could. What I can handle is what we've just had—me, quiet, and her keeping the wolves at bay. But she doesn't stick around for my answer, slipping away into her bedroom, returning after a minute with her hiking boots on, a pair of high heels hooked on two fingers of her right hand. "Look at me," she says. "I've become one of *those* people."

And then she smiles at me, and I suspect I couldn't say no if I tried. If talking is what it takes for me to stay close to her, even for just a few minutes more, I'll fucking talk.

* * * *

"You're nervous?" I ask her, when we're about a block from her place. It's cold, probably too cold for a walk. I'd offered to drive her instead once we'd cleared the front door of her building, though I'd hoped she'd say no.

The cold felt good, bracing, and anyway if I drove her that'd be less time for me to take her in. "The walk will do me some good," she'd said, and kicked one of her booted feet out in front of her. "Plus I don't want anyone to miss this amazing outfit I'm wearing. This dress is Alexander Wang. I think the boots really make it sing." I'd silently put Alexander Wang on my Google list and said a prayer of thanks she'd passed on my offer.

She's quiet for a minute beside me, swinging the black tote where she'd tucked her heels, her breath puffing in white clouds in front of her. "I'm not nervous. I did a couple of hours, yesterday afternoon. It was—good. Strange good, but good."

We stop at a crosswalk, Zoe's shoulders up and back, her chin held high. She's got sunglasses on, big ones, and even in the boots I can see the way she'd look, going to work every day. The two other guys who wait alongside us are both in suits, and I can see one sneaking a glance at her out the side of his eyes. I resist the urge to make him eat his briefcase.

"How strange?" I say, once we're moving again. My hands are tucked into my pockets, Zoe's wrapped in leather gloves that match her camel-colored coat, belted tight at her waist. I wonder what it'd feel like to walk with her hand in mine, and then make a fist in my pockets instead of grimacing at how ridiculous this thought is. It must be the hiking boots; they're scrambling my brain. This isn't camp, this isn't my truck, and this isn't my house. It's none of the places we do this thing between us.

She makes humming noise in the back of her throat, and Jesus, I have to remind myself that this isn't bed, either. "I did one callback yesterday, my first one. It was a client whose father just got diagnosed with Alzheimer's."

"Ah." We've got a few regulars at Sunset Terrace with Alzheimer's. Even with good care they're sometimes a liability to themselves, with us getting called in for self-inflicted injuries that require our help.

"Anyways, I had to do some work before I called back. I had to refresh myself on a few things, durable versus springing power of attorney, how you name more than one agent, that kind of thing. That was a branch of the law I hadn't done much of when—well, you know."

"Sure," I say, and wait for some answering plane of distance to open up between us at the mention of her last job. But it doesn't come. That plane doesn't even exist anymore most days. I'm still thinking about holding her hand, after all.

"But I did well, or at least according to Marisela I did well—she runs the place—and I think I really helped this woman. When we got off the phone, she sounded like she knew what she wanted to do."

"That sounds good. Doesn't sound strange at all."

We split, steering around a woman walking a small white dog that's barking persistently at a leaf skittering across the sidewalk. She waits until the sound won't drown her out to speak again. "But then when I looked down at the log list, where all the calls are waiting, there was—there was a *ton* of stuff. Debt relief, foreclosure assistance, two more power of attorney requests, an identity theft case. And you know what I felt, looking at all that?"

I look over at her and she breaks stride for a few seconds, looking up at the sky and taking a deep breath before breathing out: "I felt *excited*." Then she marches forward, and I hustle to catch up to her. This time, I ignore every reasonable cell in my brain and take her hand in mine, keeping my head down and my eyes on our feet, which move hypnotically in step.

"Seems like it's been good for you, starting this," I say, to cover the strangeness of this moment, of us walking down the city street as if we're a couple, as if it's Take Your Boyfriend to Work Day.

"But—I just wonder, is it that way for you?" she asks, and I think my hand may jerk in hers, because now I know where she's going with this. "It's weird, knowing that every single thing on that log list is causing someone on the other end a lot of stress and hardship, while I'm—I don't know. I'm almost *grateful* to have them call back. I'm glad to have the chance to solve a problem. I ought to make another—" she cuts herself off, shakes her head before continuing. "Do you feel that way? You see people at their worst moments, you know? Do you ever feel glad to be there, glad you can fix them?"

I swallow back what feels a whole fucking lot like tears, and I'm glad it's so cold out here, in case I need some weather event to pass my stinging eyes off on. "I can't always," I say, and she stops. A woman behind her clucks in annoyance, brushing past us with a murmured, "People are trying to *walk* here."

She tugs my hand, pulling me so we're tight against one of the granite pillars that flanks a bank entrance, out of the way of pedestrians. She takes her hand from mine and pushes up her sunglasses, looking up at me. "Is that what happened, then?"

I offer a quick nod. "Overdose."

I wait for her to say something soft, pitying—maybe an *Oh, Aiden*, with breathy sympathy and sad eyes. Maybe she'll do like Ahmed, a gentler version of his shoulder pat. I'm braced for it, I guess, knowing that when she does, it'll break the spell of this morning. I didn't want her pity. I only wanted *her*, only wanted to be around her.

But she doesn't say anything, not for maybe a full minute. She just watches me, her eyes searching back and forth between mine, her lips set in a firm line, that strong set of her jaw slightly upturned. "Who was it?" she asks, finally, and it's not at all what I expected, but it's the right thing, the exact right thing.

I look away, look at the sun gleaming off one of the windows of an office building across the way. We must be pretty close to wherever her new office is, I figure. "I can't say much," I tell her, knowing it won't hurt her feelings. Zoe knows all about HIPAA, patient privacy, my legal obligations as a provider. But I can tell her the things that are sticking with me: how young the patient looked to me. How her face looked pained, no matter what drugs she was taking to manage pain in the first place. How narrow her wrists had been. How she'd reminded me of my brother, and how I'd fucked up and said so, in the rig.

It only takes me a couple of minutes to say what I can say, but it still feels like I've set down some of the weight I've been carrying. I watch Zoe's gloved hand while I talk, the one clutched around her bag. When I'm finished, she doesn't say anything at all, and that's the right thing too. It's like the two of us have agreed to a moment of silence for what's happened. We've agreed that there's nothing at all to say.

But when we start walking again, it's Zoe who talks first. "What's the status of your story?"

"Uh. What?"

Her glasses are down over her eyes again, her posture still straight and elegant as we walk.

"Your story," she repeats. "The presentation. Basically it's three days away," she says, and she obviously doesn't have one shred of regret for busting my balls about it; that's clear as day. What's more surprising is that I'm pretty sure I'm enjoying it.

"Right, three days." I clear my throat. "It's rough," I tell her, because that's the truth. I've been working on it every day since that party Kit threw, and it's gotten easier since I've made one major change that's required a good deal more logistics but a lot less staring at the computer with a sick feeling in my stomach. But it's not all that polished, not yet. It's going to need a lot of work to look as refined as what Val had done, or as authentic as what Sheree and Tom had put up.

"Aiden," she says, stopping again, and this time, when another irritated pedestrian clucks in displeasure, she offers a curt, "Oh, cut the shit," at his back. I'll bet he feels that verbal slap all day. Then she looks at me again, lifting a hand to further block the sun that's shining right on her. "Do you still, really, want to do this? The camp?"

I take a deep breath, look down the street, wait until the noise of a city bus passes. "This is for my brother."

"It's going to be every day, Aiden. Every day, you'll have people at that camp who are suffering. Who you may not be able to save. You've got to be prepared for that."

I swallow, thick and uncomfortable. I don't know if you ever get prepared for that. I think I must understand that better than she does. "I'm all in," I tell her. "I've got to be all in." I look back at her, wish she'd lift those glasses up again, so I could look in her eyes and see what she's telling me with them. But she doesn't make a move. She stays still, those tiny parentheses at the corners of her mouth.

"Okay," she says, finally. "Tonight we're going to get drunk and do a puzzle."

I blink after her, confused, as she starts walking again. "That sounds..." I trail off, not knowing how to finish that sentence. It sounds fucking weird; that's how it sounds.

"Here's the thing, Aiden," she says, her voice in that bossy, no-bullshit register she's got. "One way or another, you're giving that tour on Saturday, and you'll hate yourself from here to eternity if you don't get it right. You know it, and I know it."

"Right," I say, oddly buoyed again. I feel like I'm a boxer on the ropes, getting shouted out by my cornerman while he slathers Vaseline all over my fresh cuts.

"So you've had a lousy morning, and you need some sleep and a night off thinking about everything that's horrible." She stops, and one building ahead I see the sign for Legal Aid. She turns to me, putting her sunglasses up again and looking me straight in the eye. "So go home, get some sleep, and come back here at four to pick me up, because"—she breaks off and gives a dramatic sniffle—"because I'm not doing this walk again. And we're going to go get sandwiches or burritos or a pizza and some beer, and then we're going to do this 'doors of the world' puzzle I have, which will be nearly impossible even if we're sober. And then tomorrow morning, you and me, we're driving to Stanton Valley a day early, and we're going to do the presentation there. We're going to walk the tour, figure out the story. Okay?"

I don't miss that she's said *we're*, and I know she doesn't miss the smile that's tugging at the corner of my mouth, a smile that would've felt impossible a few hours ago. Even now I shouldn't *want* to smile, thinking of taking that walk, figuring out the presentation, smoothing out the rough edges that are all over it right now, despite the work I've been doing. "All right," I say.

"Fine," she answers, and it's a little funny, how clipped she's said it, like she's won an argument we weren't even having. "I'm going now." She turns to walk away, but stops and rushes back, shoving her bag at me before she leans down and starts undoing the laces of her boots. "Holy shit, I almost went in there in these boots!" she says, more to herself than to me, and I smile, watching her balance on one foot while she tugs a heel out of the bag. When she's done, she grabs her bag back and gives me the boots. "Don't lose these," she says, as if I'm planning to just casually drop one between here and my car. Her cheeks are even pinker now, the cold plus bending over, and probably the lecture she just gave me.

And I think, despite what she said before, she might be a little nervous about going in there, about this leap she's still taking.

"Zo," I call to her, when she's started to walk away again. I must look like an idiot, standing here holding a woman's hiking boots in the middle of the sidewalk, but I find I don't really care. When she turns around I tell her, "It does feel like that for me, a lot of the time. To solve someone's problem. I don't think that's anything to feel bad about at all."

When she smiles at me, I hold those damned boots a little tighter, and then turn to make the long walk back to her building, already counting the hours until 4:00 p.m.

Chapter 15

Zoe

In the end, we don't get drunk and do a puzzle. Aiden falls asleep on my couch after one beer and I sit next to him, resisting what feels like a perverted urge to curl myself against him, all his warm heat and solid strength, even when he started this day so defeated. From where I am, I can see the guilt vase, which I'd tucked onto a windowsill when Aiden had been showering this morning. Somewhere in there is the slip for Aiden's parents, the slip that would've included him too, if I'd known about him then.

But there may be something you can do, he'd said to me, back on that first day, when I'd been ready to walk away from him and concede that the entire guilt vase project had been a vanity project that I hadn't thought through, a half-drunk, all-weak attempt at getting unstuck. Now it's not even two months later and I'm on my couch again, not alone this time, just starting to feel alive and like myself. It's the first time I've felt I had a way forward since I walked out of Willis-Hanawalt on that last day, all my lottery promises swimming, indistinct, in my mind. It's not the guilt vase that's done it, though of course there's been good to come out of my new friendship with Janet, my mentorship of Dan, and my way, way better manners in coffee shops and parking lots.

It's been Aiden. No, it's been *me* and Aiden, something about me and him together.

So how can I not help him with this, with his story, with this presentation, with everything he says he wants for the camp? How can I not give him the one thing he's asked me for?

I'll be adding slips, I guess, slips for Paul and Lorraine, for telling them this lie that gets to be less of a lie with each passing day, since I don't fake anything with Aiden lately. And I'll be adding a slip for Aiden too, though I don't think he'd see it that way. But I don't think it's right for him, the camp—not this way, not in the way that means he uproots his life and starts all over again. I think he'll miss his work, which even on bad days gives him a sense of purpose and control. I think he'll miss Charlie and Ahmed, who he talks about with indulgent, grateful affection, more so now than when I first met him. I think he doesn't really *want* to manage a campground as a full-time job. I think he's doing it because it's what it takes to win, because it's what he's promised himself and his family he'll do.

And I think—I *know*—that promises like that can wear on you, especially when you're grieving. It's the same way my job wore on me—living out my father's hopes for me, being the person I thought he'd want me to be. *Becoming* that person so much that I hardly knew who I was without my job.

But how, *how* can I not help him? How can I not give him what he's asked me for? How can I not give his family that?

I must fall asleep eventually, but when I wake up in the morning I'm in my bed, under the covers, and Aiden's beside me, lying on top of them—flat on his back, hands clasped loosely over his middle. It's the closest we've ever come to sleeping next to each other, and I wish, with an almost physical ache, that I hadn't slept through the feeling of him carrying me in here and laying me down.

I slip out of bed, move as quietly as I can into the bathroom, and when I come back, Aiden's sitting up, feet on the floor, scraping a hand through his messy hair. "All right that I stayed?"

"Don't be ridiculous," I say, watching the little notch at the corner of his mouth that tells me he's on the verge of a smile. I did that for him, have done that for him, and I—I want to *keep* doing it, no matter the seed of doubt I have. I tell myself that this isn't the same as it was with Christopher, me jamming myself into someone else's problems to avoid my own. I'm dealing with my own. I'm moving on, and it's okay for me to help him too, so long as I keep hold of myself.

"I got coverage for my shift today," he says, his voice still gravelly with sleep, the first time I've heard it that way outside of camp. He lifts his phone in the air, waving it a little. "Ahmed emailed."

"Good. You need a day off."

"Off of one thing, at least. You still want to go today?"

I take a deep breath through my nose, slow enough, I hope, so he doesn't see my chest rise. "I'm in," I say, and turn away to pack my bag.

* * * *

"Sixty-eight minutes." I tap my thumb against my phone screen to stop the timer from turning. When I look up at Aiden, he's got his hands set low on his hips, an expression of frustration in his eyes.

"Goddammit," he says, on a gusty sigh. "Where am I going to take eight fucking minutes off?"

"Relax. Let's think about this." I sit down on one of the benches of the outdoor classroom, Aiden's copy of the presentation binder spread open in my lap. It feels better than expected to sit down, like all the muscles in my legs are doing a hallelujah chorus, and I'm pretty sure I make a small groan of relief.

It's Friday afternoon, only a couple of hours before we expect Hammond and Val and Sheree and Tom to show up for the weekend. This is probably our last run-through of it, Aiden's presentation, and I can't say it's been an easy go of it. Aiden and I are both tired, and the presentation itself isn't easy to do over and over, no matter how much we've focused on not making it too heavy.

I look down at the tour map, at the typed notes Aiden handed me yesterday when we'd arrived. I'd been surprised, I guess, to see what he'd done for the presentation. For the last couple of weeks, he'd told me, since Ben's party, he's been collecting testimonials from patients who've been through the programs elsewhere, the ones in Colorado, New Mexico, California, Maine. Some by email, some by phone, one—on Tuesday, right about when I was doing my first call at Legal Aid—by video chat. They'd been easy to get, he'd said, because the program owners already know about Aiden, already know he's looking to bring a facility here. They're ready to get moving on a lease, so they give him what he needs, and what he needs—what I told him he needs—is a story. Or, in this case, *stories*.

It's not that it isn't good. It *is* good. It's moving, it's painful, it's hopeful. Lorraine will definitely cry, and I won't be surprised if others do too. Over the last day and a half I've helped him smooth it out, tie the stories he's got more strongly to whatever location we're at on the tour—how equine therapy worked for one of the patients when we're at the stables site, how shared living spaces function for patients coming to rehab out of methadone clinics while we're at one of the cabin sites. I do what I can do, to give him what he says he wants.

It's just that it's got nothing to do with Aaron. Aiden doesn't even say his name, not once.

I shift on the benches, tap my finger against my lip while I think. "Cut the second stop at the cabins?" I suggest, and look up at him.

"Maybe. But I've got to explain how the population would be separated, how we could use the different cabin groupings for—"

"You can do that all at one stop," I tell him, holding out the binder and pen, gesturing for him to change the route so we can shave off the time. He takes a seat next to me, but before he sets to work on the map, he puts an hand on my knee, squeezes gently. "Let's quit after this," he says. "You're tired."

"I'm fine."

He shakes my knee, a smile pulling at the corner of his mouth. "I'll check you for ticks."

I give an involuntary shudder. "Gross. If that's meant to be a double entendre, you ought to know right now that you're terrible at it."

He chuckles, bends his head to his task, and I dig deep for the relief and pride I usually feel when I manage to crack open that hard shell of his. But he's right. I'm tired, and a little wary too, nervous and concerned and it's hitting me, all at once, that we're almost done with this, that the presentation is the last major hurdle, and then one more week and this will be done—*we'll* be done. I look toward the lodge and see Lorraine out on the porch, deadheading a pot of mums that are fighting the increasingly cool weather. Under Aiden's plan, the lodge will have to expanded considerably for counseling services offices. He's got a schematic in his binder that shows half of that wraparound porch removed, a whole new wing that would eliminate the space Paul and Lorraine had used, just last weekend, for a wedding dance floor.

I told him to take out that schematic. Maybe they don't need to know about that, for now.

When he's done, we both wave at Lorraine and set out hiking our way back to our cabin. We stay mostly quiet, and when I look over at Aiden, I can see that he's running through it again in his mind. I think maybe once I catch his lips moving, practicing it out, and my heart tugs in admiration, in something else I don't want to put a name to.

Once we're inside our cabin, I decide a hot shower is in order, maybe a nap if I can swing it before we have to meet the group. Aiden passes on the offer to join me, the binder already set out on the desk, ready for him to review again. I purse my lips in an effort not to say anything, to warn him not to overdo it so he doesn't sound robotic tomorrow, and head into the shower. I turn the water as hot as it will go, stand under it way too long, arranging my body in the way I know now is best for avoiding that stage-five-clinger shower curtain. It's a little funny, how used to it I am now. I know the water's harder here, so my soap takes longer to lather. I've even gotten weirdly used to my bunk, to waking up close to the ceiling. I've got this stretch I do when I'm climbing out of it in the mornings, arching my back while I keep my hands wrapped around the top rail, my whole body lengthening in relief.

When I come out to the main room, though, I see I won't be doing that stretch tomorrow.

Aiden's taken apart my bunk, has found a way to detach it from the one below, setting the two beside each other and shoving them together, the once-bare bunk beneath mine made up with clean sheets and a blanket of its own. When I look over at where he sits in the chair, I can see the skin underneath his stubble flushed slightly pink, whether from embarrassment or exertion or some combination of the two. "Felt like we could use a real bed," he says, shrugging.

"Right," I say, a little stiffly, ignoring the feeling of his eyes on me while I walk to the dresser, pull out fresh clothes.

"That all right with you? I can put them back." He's already up, moving over toward the beds, but I stop him.

"No, it's okay," I say, crossing to him, putting my arms around him while I'm still in my towel, probably making his whole front damp. This is so different, this weekend, this affection, this—tenderness. It's been different for a while, but him showing up to my place has changed everything, and I don't know what kind of complication sharing a bed is going to do to me. Or maybe I do know, but I don't want to think about it too hard just now, with those two bunks looming. I lean back from him, adjust my towel, and shrug casually. "It'll be nice," I say, forcing my voice into its light, teasing register. "Very civilized."

He tips his head, some faint curiosity that passes through his expression before he smooths it out, turns back toward the desk. "Very," he says quietly, and we don't talk much after that.

* * * *

I think about that bed too much through dinner, but if there's a silver lining to Aiden's obsessive preparation for his presentation it's that he decides to do one more round after dinner, and so I settle into it on my own, pillows stacked up and my ereader on my lap, as near as I can get to my nighttime routine at home.

He comes in late, after eleven, bringing the smell of crushed leaves and cold night air with him, his movements careful and quiet. "I'm awake," I call to him, waving my book in the air, its screen lighting me up with the faintest glow. I can see him, though, in the light from the entryway, and he looks better—a little tired, but more relaxed too, a different person from what I saw yesterday morning.

"It went okay?" I ask.

"Yeah," he says, turning toward one of the sinks, toeing off his boots while he puts toothpaste on his toothbrush. I'm glad he's not going to shower—he'll still smell like the outside when he comes in. "I think it'll work." Then, like he's worried he's jinxed it, he shoves his toothbrush in his mouth, scrubbing vigorously to shut himself up. It's a few minutes before he finishes washing up his face and hands. I notice, this time, that he doesn't forget and shut off the light, and my standard protesting reminder dies on my lips. When he comes into the living space, he undresses quickly, draping his clothes over the desk chair before pulling on a pair of mesh athletic shorts and crawling in beside me.

There's a moment—a tightening of the air between us, where I think— *What now?* It's late, the day so long, and both of us are tired. The kind of sweaty, half-frustrated sex we have doesn't seem fitting tonight, me with my pajamas and my book. I shut off the screen and set it down on the floor, tucking it slightly underneath the bed, wondering if maybe I should get up, go to the bunk that's usually Aiden's, sleep apart again.

The whir of my thoughts is stopped by his arm snaking around my waist, pulling me toward him, and I do what feels most natural, curling onto my side so he can tuck in behind me, his chin resting on the top of my head, the whole front of his body pressed against the whole back of mine. But my spine is stiff, that ramrod posture I used to have at work. Aiden tightens his arm around me and says, gruffly, "Don't overthink it," and somehow, it's enough. I don't want to overthink it. I just want to be warm and sleepy like this, with him.

I'm drifting off when I feel Aiden's body twitch and stiffen beside me, a grunt of discomfort escaping. He lifts the arm he has wrapped around my waist, twists his torso away from me, another small grunt. "I'm sorry," he says, when I stir, turning toward him. "Sorry," he repeats, and reaches his arm up, crooks his elbow awkwardly as he tries to reach and scratch at a spot on his back.

"S'okay," I murmur, moving so I can put my own arms around him, and I scratch right above the spot he tries to reach, and he makes the most gorgeous, satisfied noise, a growly bear delight that makes me smile.

"Oh, God. Keep doing that. Harder. A little to the left."

I press my smile into his chest, loving the way his body shivers in pleasure, the way his muscles bunch underneath my fingers.

"More," he pleads, shifting so my hands go to where he wants them. "Feels so good."

"You're like an old man," I say, laughing now, all that awkwardness gone. "Or a bear. You should go outside and rub yourself up against a tree, be with your comrades."

"Trees don't have nails like yours," he says, releasing another groan.

"Did you get into something? Poison ivy, or…I don't know what. Other itchy-type plants?"

He chuckles, a rumble in his chest that I feel against my breasts. "No. Just sometimes get itchy at night when it turns cold. I think your soap yesterday made it worse."

"That soap is made with cocoa butter," I say, annoyed, and he breathes out another soft laugh.

I run my nails up and down his back, pulling him so he rolls partway on top of me. He resettles, hunching down and resting his cheek against my chest. The scruff on his cheek and jaw abrades my skin, but I don't mind. I keep my hands moving over the muscled planes of him, as far as I can reach in this new position, and Aiden sighs against me, his warm breath tickling underneath the edge of my camisole, blowing against my left nipple, which peaks in response. He notices, lifts his head enough to kiss me there, gently, no intention to it, before resting against me once more. And it's the perfect kiss, the perfect feeling, somehow. It feels like we're not in a hurry, like there'll be time and time again to get back to him inside me.

And all of a sudden I feel tears well up behind my closed eyes, my throat constricting slightly. I almost recoil at the shock of it, my mind immediately racing to account for the oddity: *The last couple days have been stressful. You're overtired.*

But deep down, I know it's something else. This moment, and this man, and these two twin beds shoved together in this cold, spartan cabin—it's the most intimate experience of my life. It's the feeling I chased in those stupid, careless months after my dad died and I'd felt so alone. Of all the things I've done for Aiden over the last few weeks, it's this thing—this small service that makes him snuffle and wriggle in boyish delight—that makes me feel as close to him as I've ever been to anyone.

I swallow reflexively against the tears, and Aiden props himself up, rising over me, his brow furrowed. "What's wrong?" he asks, and I can't do anything at first but clamp my lips shut, shake my head in a wordless *nothing* while I wait for this storm to pass.

"Zo," he says, one hand stroking the hair back from my forehead, the gesture so new that a fresh clutch of emotion seizes my throat. "Don't look like that." It's so abrupt, so commanding, and I smile a little, a few tears that I'd held in springing out of the corners of my eyes. It's that knife-edge feeling I get with Aiden, all the time, mixed-up emotions he brings right to the surface in me. Anger and lust. Frustration and sympathy. Fear and freedom.

Lonely...and still, somehow, in love.

"I was married once," I blurt, the only thing I can think to say that will keep me from thinking about what I've just admitted to myself about how I feel for Aiden. I've said it because I want him to be shocked. Because I want to push him away.

But other than the stilling of his hand, he doesn't move at all, and I am desperate to fill in the silence. "I'd just turned twenty," I tell him, and I expect, any second, for him to roll over onto his back, to have to tell him the rest of this without his eyes right above mine and without the heat of his body so close. He doesn't do any of that, though—he's turned to stone up there, but surprisingly, it doesn't feel hostile. It's just what Aiden does when he's turned his full attention to something.

I don't tell it quite the way I did, years ago, to Kit and Greer. Here, it's messy, not chronological. I start in various places, have to circle back and fill in the blanks, though Aiden asks nothing as I talk. *He was much older. It only lasted a few months. His name was Christopher. I met him after my dad died. It was a bad time for me. I gave him my inheritance, to save his business, this shitty little bar where I learned to beat you at darts.* It strikes me how little time it takes to tell it, the basic story always the same: I was grieving, and I didn't know what to do. I was young. I'd inherited money I didn't want. I made a mistake, lost most of the legacy my father left to me. Then I cleaned up my act and I started over.

When I'm done, Aiden's stillness and silence start to feel uncomfortable, recriminating. I offer a meaningless, "So," and roll onto my side again, away from him, the movement awkward—my hair catching under his arm, one of his legs heavy over mine at first.

"How much older," he says, softly, hard to hear over the movement of my body and the rustle of the sheets. He repeats it when I pause before answering.

"He was thirty-eight."

This strange intimacy we've forged means I can *feel* him thinking, even though we barely touch now, just the faint brush of the hair on his legs against my smooth ones. I lie there, my eyes open, staring across the room, my gaze level with the exposed pipes beneath one of the sinks.

"You were too young," he says, finally.

"I know," I snap back. Maybe I expected his censure, but it still hurts to hear it.

He sets a big hand on the curve of my shoulder, stroking down to my elbow, which he cups in a tender, unfamiliar gesture. "Zo," he says, his voice soft, the way it was in those first minutes after I'd fainted in his driveway, how I imagine he talks to the sick and scared people he picks up to put in his ambulance. "I mean this guy, he shouldn't have married you. He should've known better than to marry someone your age."

Kit and Greer said this too, when I'd told them—making Christopher the predator, absolving me of responsibility. But I'm defensive of my own guilt, of the shit I deserve to eat for that time in my life. "I asked him. I gave him the money of my own free will. He was—is—a good person." I mean, I guess he is. I've never spoken to him again, not after the divorce.

He strokes his hand back up to my shoulder, tugs lightly so I roll onto my back. "So are you," he says, simply.

I close my eyes, not realizing until he's said it how much I want to hear it, from him more than anyone else. "Your brother," I whisper, so he doesn't forget—or maybe so *I* don't forget—why this isn't permanent.

"You're not responsible for what happened to my brother. You know that." He leans down, rests his forehead against mine. "I know that too."

"I am sorry. You've never wanted to hear it from me, but I am."

He's quiet again, and I try not to let the disappointment pierce me. Aiden will never give me anything of Aaron. He won't even give this camp anything of Aaron.

"We should sleep," I say, just to say something, and anyway, it's true—we've had a long couple of days, and tomorrow's so important. When Aiden rolls onto his back so that we're now awkwardly side by side, untouching again, I know he's agreeing implicitly, and my face feels hot with embarrassment at having taken the night in this direction—spoiling the easy familiarity of backscratching and teasing. I begin to shift into a more comfortable position, but before I can move, Aiden moves back on top of me, his skin hot and tight, like his muscles have all bunched up underneath.

"Did you love him?"

I almost repeat the question, to stall. After all that, I want to give him the long answer, the answer that makes me look better—*I thought I did, but I was young, and grieving, and I got love mixed up with movement, with doing something.* But I shear it of these platitudes. They don't really matter, in the end. "No," I say.

He kisses me then, his tongue licking into my mouth, and before long it's heated—his hand under my camisole, cupping one of my breasts, one of his legs pushing between mine, nudging them apart. I wrap my arms around him, using those nails he likes so much to dig into his back, until he grunts in pain, or pleasure, or both. I'm as desperate as he is, arching my back off the bed to get closer to him, tensing in frustration when he pushes my hips back down. He curls his fingers around the waistband of my pants and underwear, tugging them down over my hips to my knees, where I kick them off the rest of the way. I reach my hands into his shorts, squeeze his ass, force his erection against me, and he leans down, sucks at my neck. I register dimly that it will leave a mark, and all I can think is, *More of that, leave more of those, make sure I feel this tomorrow.*

I bend my wrists so I can press his waistband away from his body and get his shorts off, but he plants his knees and reaches around to stop me, lifting my hands from him and pulling off my top, then circling each of my wrists in his hands. He tugs them up, setting them on either side of my head, and lets go, kneeling between my legs and looking down at me, his stare telling me, somehow, what he wants me to do. I slide the backs of my hands up until I feel the cold steel of the bed frame and I curl my fingers around it. He nods, one quick duck of his chin, and the movement thrills me, my hands gripping tighter until there's a sound—a tiny clink against the metal bed frame that indicates I forgot to take off the ring tonight. I know Aiden hears it. I see his mouth tighten, but I don't have time to wonder what that means.

Because then—then Aiden starts to take me apart.

He starts at my mouth, kissing me slow and deep—long, drugging kisses that he only interrupts when I take one of my hands from the rails to touch him. "No," he says, thrusting his hips against mine, once, and I do what he says. He moves down, teasing the underside of my right breast with his fingers, setting his lips and tongue to my left, and he stays and stays, switching between them, touching and licking and sucking them each until they ache, until I'm straining to bring my legs together, to rub them against each other if he won't come to me. This is what he wants, I realize, to make me crazy like this, to see how close he can get me to coming just from the hot press of his mouth against my nipple, the pulling, pressing bluntness of his fingertips—and to my surprise, he *is* getting me close, closer than I thought possible from just this simple act that I've always thought of as a little foreplay, or a little extra incentive during the main event. "Aiden," I whisper, "*please.*"

It comes out like a whimper, and his hand is gone from my breast, splayed low on my abdomen so that his fingertips fan out, his thumb crooking down over where I'm wet, where I need him—and then he presses, exactly enough, right there, and I need nothing else, no rubbing or grinding. I just *come*, from all the anticipation he's wrought in me, and it's long, shuddering, not slow to start but slow to spread all through my limbs, even into my hands, which are gripping the bed so tightly that I can feel his ring pressing hard into my skin.

I wait, breathing hard, for him to strip, to get a condom and get inside me. But he does none of that. He pushes himself lower, not far before he encounters the other end of the metal frame, and he grunts in frustration, barely hesitating before he hooks his arms beneath my knees and lifts, moving me so I lie diagonally across both mattresses. And then he lowers himself, kneeling on the floor, and presses his mouth against me, open and searching. I'm so wet that I tilt my hips back, a shy reflex. "No," he repeats, bringing me back to him, and it's what I need to be able to enjoy this—his commitment to it, his moans of pleasure. When one of his hands leaves my hip, I know where it's gone; I know he's gripping himself, as turned on as I am. I close my eyes, picturing it, the hand he used to touch me closed over his cock, and I feel another orgasm building—and that's what he wants. I can *feel* him wanting it, coaxing it from me, and when it comes, when I cry out, one of my heels pressing into the mattress, our pushed together beds splitting apart a little, Aiden groans in relief, licking me softly until the pulses stop.

He stands, stripping his shorts and grabbing a condom, and when he's covered himself he climbs back onto the bed, putting his back against the wall. It can't be comfortable—the bar from the bunk has to be cutting him right across the spine—but his jaw is set, his eyes on me as he pats one hand on his thigh. "Here," he says, drawing me onto his lap even as I'm climbing on, settling myself over him, ready to give him whatever he needs, whatever he wants so that he can feel as good and wrung out as I feel right now.

I'm drawn tight from what we've already done, and I hold my breath as I lower myself, letting it out slowly only when he's stretched me enough to get halfway there. He catches my exhale, kissing me, his hands in my hair, and before I know what's happened I'm right against him, as joined as we can be, our hips moving together. He's got to be wound up, ready to come any second. I can feel it in the way he holds himself, and I know how to make it happen, another new intimacy I'm realizing that's between Aiden and me, how well I know his body. If I stroke my hips down, clench the muscles inside...

But he seems to know what I'm planning, and he stops kissing me, cups my jaw, and leans forward so he can whisper in my ear. "One more," he says, part question and part plea, punctuating it with a graze of teeth over my earlobe.

I shake my head slightly, shuddering at the feel of his stubble on my neck. "I can't," I breathe out, tipping my head forward, resting it heavily on his shoulder, sweat on my brow meeting the slick skin that wraps tightly over his muscles.

"Need it," he says, slowing his hips, letting me set the pace, and when I slide over him slowly, I feel the first stirrings of something new building within, so surprising that I gasp, my breath thin. "I need you," he says, and with those three words the tension within me ratchets up. I find a new rhythm, one that gets me even closer.

"*Oh*," I breathe out, and he pulses inside me, his fingertips digging into my waist harder now. "Aiden, I—" I bite down on my lip, finishing the thought in my head, saying it over and over to myself silently as I come, short and explosive—*I love you, I love you, I love you.* But even the words in my mind are drowned out, eventually, by Aiden's release, the rough sawing of his breath, and mine too.

I expect a quick uncoupling. It's so hot now between us, our skin sticking together, and I haven't forgotten about what that bar must be doing to Aiden's back. But before I can make a move off of him, Aiden gathers me close, his arms tightening around my waist, his face pressed against my chest. *Say something,* I think, to myself or to him; I don't know which.

But he doesn't, and after a minute of him holding me, I lean away, gently pulling off of him while he holds the condom. When he moves off the bed, heading toward the bathroom, I see the red stripe left across his back. I imagine touching it and memorizing the indentation that's left there.

Because I know it'll be gone in the morning.

Chapter 16

Aiden

I wake up in the crack.

Overnight I've pressed close to Zoe, my chest against her back, my arm around her waist, but that means I'm sleeping right where the beds are pushed together, where either my weight or our activities last night have disrupted things, and my hip and shoulder are sinking by degrees, my head cocked awkwardly to get real estate on Zoe's pillow.

Slowly, so I don't disturb her, I roll onto my back and move over, missing the warmth of her body and the rich, slightly musky smell of her skin. I turn my head toward her, watch the rise and fall of her body as she breathes in the deep, even pattern of a heavy sleep. At the back of her head, her hair is tousled, some of the fine strands sticking straight up, quivering slightly from the air blowing out of the vent above us.

Zoe, married? I think, as I watch her lying there. My reaction to it—to the initial revelation, and everything she had said after—had been quick, almost violent in its strength, a feeling in my body that sounded like *no.* I'm not a barbarian; I don't have any claim on Zoe's past or future, but something about the bleak way she'd said it, and the strange, directionless way she'd talked about her past, had made me feel agitated and angry. Who was this fucking guy, fully an adult, marrying a twenty-year-old woman, still in college, dealing with the sudden death of a parent? What kind of dirtbag would take a woman's inheritance like that? And what was Zoe like back then? Was she like she is now, controlled and sophisticated but with flashes of this irreverent, bold humor? Was she as good at reading people then? Did she chat this guy right out of his bad moods, make him forget everything that made his life feel unmanageable? Did he feel like his soul was being wrenched from his body when he was inside of her?

Fuck, it's an awful thought, one I hate myself for even considering. Disrespectful to her, and torturous to me.

I sit up then, swing my legs over the side of the bed. The floor is cold, and outside the sky is gray, the first day we've been here that fall hasn't shown up in all its glory. I'd like to fix the beds, push them back tight together and crawl back in there with her, wake her up and get inside of her again, sleep all day next to her. But that's ridiculous, because this is it—presentation day. This is the day where I show up for what I've been working toward all these months. Whether it's gray out there or not, whether I have a warm woman beside me or not, I'm in this.

Behind me, Zoe shifts, makes a soft, sleepy noise as she turns over. I look back at her, feel a thrill of satisfaction as her palm coasts over the sheet beside her—feeling for me. I press my hand over hers, letting her know I'm here, and her eyes flutter open. Even in the dim early-morning light, I can see the gold of them, how bright they are. Sunlight against changing trees.

I am so fucking gone over this woman, it is ridiculous. Terrifying.

"Hi," she says, and then she smiles up at me, and—*is* it terrifying? Isn't it okay that I get to feel something for a smart, funny, gorgeous woman, a woman who makes me feel less like I'm on an island all by myself, just gathering supplies to stay alive until...until what, I don't know.

"Hey," I say, leaning down to kiss her on the cheek. This affection— it's new for us, and I'm surprised at how good it feels. It's on the tip of my tongue to say something else to her, something that'll make clear that maybe I've got more in me than soft gestures for her, that maybe there's some way she and I can work this out beyond the campground.

But when I open my mouth to speak, it's all business. "I've got to get showered. I want to get out there early, go through it one more time."

She nods, props herself up on one elbow. "Want me there?" she asks, and I think, *I always want you there. I want you everywhere.*

After today, the hardest part of this will be over—I'll have done all I can. It'll be up to Paul and Lorraine. After that, I can think of what it'll be like for Zoe and me. Whether there's some way we can make this work in another context, whether what passed between us last night might mean there's something for us beyond all this.

I'm smiling down at her, probably goofy looking as all hell, but then the sharp ring of my phone pierces the air. "Hang on," I say, squeezing her hand once before standing and crossing to the desk. It's my parents' number and right away I know it's not good. Even if they had in mind to talk to me outside of our usual scheduled twice-a-week calls, it's 6:30 in the morning on a Sunday, no sane time to call anyone for casual conversation. "Mom?" I say when I pick up, noticing out of the corner of my eye the way Zoe sinks back down onto her side, her expression hidden from me now.

There's a pause, silence on the other line, and so I say it again, more forcefully, more anxiously this time.

"It's me," says a gruff, raspy voice, a voice I haven't heard in what feels like months.

Oh, Jesus, I think, sick with dread. "Has something happened to Mom?"

"No. I was calling to—ah, well. To ask if you remembered something."

I sit heavily on the too-small chair, hearing it creak beneath me. Hell, my knees felt weak there for a minute, thinking of what news I was about to get. I'm relieved, but not overly so—it's still too strange that it's my dad calling, not my mom, who initiates all our family conversation these days.

"Sure, Pop," I say.

"You remember when your mother and I took you kids to Disney World?"

I smile with the memory: the worst family vacation ever. Aaron and I had been nine, had been begging to go for at least the previous two years. We'd driven down in Pop's old station wagon, loud with various rattles and whirs, the air conditioner broken and the gas tank guzzling up so much fuel that we had to stop all the time. My dad had been grouchy, my mom had been falsely cheerful, and pretty much the second we'd crossed into the state of Florida we seemed to encounter all manner of new allergic triggers for Aaron. He had terrible hives, his breathing was raspy and uneven, and his eyes were so watery and swollen that he could barely see, which mattered less once Mom had upped his dose of Benadryl and he'd fall asleep for hours. He'd been too sick to go to the park for the first two days, and so we'd holed up in our dingy hotel room, playing cards and watching cable. And when we finally got to the park? I don't think any one of us had ever felt that kind of heat in our lives, rising up from the pavement like something directly from hell, the lines long and the people loud and rude, all the souvenirs costing more than we could afford. We made it through three hours, all of us trying so hard to enjoy ourselves, until Aaron had stood, a melted Dole Whip in his small hand, and said, "This is awful. I hate everything about this place," and all four of us had laughed and laughed.

"I remember." I've set one elbow on my thigh, have lowered my head to cradle it in my hand. It hurts to think about this—it physically hurts, those aches in my joints returning with a vengeance.

"There's this one picture I found," he says, and I can hear from his voice he's been crying, again. Before Aaron died, I'd never seen my dad cry, not ever. He'd been almost comically stoic, even when Aaron was having his lowest times, when he was in and out of rehab, jail. But now he cries a lot, as though he was saving his whole lifetime supply of tears for this. "It's you and your brother coming off Space Mountain. I think your mother took it."

"Don't know if I've ever seen it." I'm so conscious of Zoe in the room. She has not moved.

"You're holding his hand," Pop says, and holy fuck. I have to clench my hand into a fist now, keeping it pressed against my forehead. I can feel Aaron's small hand in mine, hot and clammy. I couldn't speak if I tried.

"That's all, really," he says. "Just found this picture."

"Okay, Pop." I listen close to hear if my mother's there, rustling around in the background, but it's quiet. "Where'd you come by the pictures?" I ask, frustrated, angry. If he's this low, this raw all the time, my mother should be keeping this shit away from him. Packing it away so he can never see it, not until he's ready.

It's not fair that I'm thinking that, that I'm putting it on her. She's the one reading all the books, going to all the support groups, after all. She'd know better than me what's right for my dad. But I can't see sense about this, and I know it. I only want him to stop hurting.

Across the room, Zoe sits up, picks up her discarded pajamas and pulls them on, her head bowed as she stands and wanders into the bathroom.

"Just thought I'd have a look today," he says. "Wishing you good luck, and all that."

"Thanks, Pop. Maybe you ought to put Mom on." Probably it was her idea for him to call me, anyways. No way has he been keeping track of when I'd be giving this presentation.

"She's out."

If it's possible, my stress level rises another notch. I hate to think of him there, alone, probably surrounded by a photo album that's page after page of gut punches. What makes it worse, I guess, is that I can't even really picture it. I've never been to the condo, don't have a sense of its layout from the pictures my mom sometimes sends. I've never sat on the new furniture they have down there, have never taken in their new view. I can't picture what my dad's looking at, other than at this three-by-five memory of his two sons, back when we were all right. When we were whole. "She coming home soon?"

He clears his throat. "I'm sure she'll call you. Give you her own pep talk."

The chair beneath me squeaks out its indignation at my size, at my shifting in discomfort. I don't have a good feeling about this, him there alone. "Sure," I say.

"You always helped your brother. Like in this picture. You were so important to him."

I stand then, face the window, my back toward the room. So if Zoe comes in, she can't see the way my chin tightens up in suppressed anguish. He means something good with this—he means to remind me I'd been good to Aaron and that what happened to him later wasn't because of me. But I can't hear that. Can't hear anything but the ways I didn't help him, the ways I wasn't important enough. I wasn't important enough for him to save himself.

"All right, Pop. I'd better get out there."

We hang up and I take a deep breath, steady myself against the tremor of grief he's just set off with nothing more than a few quiet words of well-wishing. In my mind, I start rattling off the opening lines of my presentation, something concrete to grab onto. The day stretches out in front of me like a huge, yawning void. If I get this right today, my whole future changes. Everything about my life will be different.

Again.

"Are your parents okay?"

When I turn to face her, she's leaning in the wide doorway into the bathroom, her hairline wet from washing her face, her skin scrubbed pink and clean. Her voice is quieter than usual, and I know it's because of what she's asking. She's tiptoed around the subject of my parents since that first day we met, and I guess that's smart of her. The question is innocent, but it's the same thing she asked that day, pressing her way into my life on her quest for forgiveness, and I'm so keyed up from that exchange with my dad, from my nerves about the presentation, that I can only hear her guilt. Ten minutes ago I could barely think of anything but how I might manage to keep her, but right now, in this moment, she feels like part of the problem, not the solution.

"They're fine. I ought to get ready." I move toward the dresser, start pulling out clothes for the day.

"Aiden," she says, a statement all on its own, and I still, briefly. "You don't have to do it."

I don't do anything but stare at her, stripped of every single thing she came to me with when I first met her. Her dress, her heels, her perfect makeup and hair. She's beautiful. Beautiful, and as terrifying as ever.

"I will go with you right now and we can tell Paul and Lorraine the truth about us, about this. You can tell them it's not the right time for you to do this."

It's my last out, and she is serving it up to me like a gift. I don't have any doubt about what she'd do if we went down to that lodge and stood in front of Paul and Lorraine. She'd try to tell them both it was her fault, this whole fake engagement. I wouldn't let her, but she'd try. It'd be awful, telling Paul and Lorraine. It'd be awful, calling my parents and telling them I'd given up on the camp. It'd be awful, starting over with that pile of blood money, or watching it get bigger in some cold, stale bank account, statements delivered to me every month while I try to wait this out, wait until it's not so painful.

It'd be awful, thinking I'd let my brother down.

Still, for one brief, hopeful second, I think about what it'd be like to leave here with her beside me, both of us untangled from this lie, this *life*.

Too brief, though, and too hopeful.

I know where my loyalty lies. I know the promises I've made.

"No," I tell her. "I can't."

* * * *

If she's angry at me, she hides it well.

I'd skipped the group lunch, done another run-through, which means I've done it so many times I'll be dreaming of it for days. I'd done the same when I'd been doing my training for the paramedic exam—I'd fall asleep at night and see myself wandering around a grocery store or shopping mall, unable to leave until I'd identified for every cashier the arrhythmias in an EKG, always my toughest challenge. Back then, there hadn't been half as much riding on getting it right, so I figure the dreams this time around will be worse.

When I'd finally shown up at the lodge, Zoe had been there, in her regular seat at the table where we always eat for group meals, looking as calm and casual as she had on that first day we were here. "Hi," she'd said, waving me over, smiling brightly. "Val was just sharing some ideas for honeymoon locations." She'd been as calm as she wasn't on that first day, when talk of weddings had made us both skittish and awkward.

By the time Val and Sheree had given their instructions to the camp staffer who'd be staying behind with the kids—this particular presentation an obvious nonstarter for the youth set—I'd been sweaty with nerves, and Zoe had stood by my side, patted my lower back twice, softly. "Ninety minutes," she'd said. "Less than ninety minutes, and this whole thing will be over."

That had been—haunting, I guess. More haunting than comforting.

But now we're in it, fully in it—Zoe beside me the whole time, all my practice paying off, I think. I've not stumbled over the details once. I've answered every question.

"If you take a look at page twelve of your packets," I say now, my voice feeling a bit strained from all the talking, "you'll see that most patients come to the Wilderness/Wellness program on physician referral." I pause, waiting a well-rehearsed few beats for my audience to read over page twelve, half the page showing stats for the types of referrals, the other half with brief but convincing quotations from doctors in the state of Virginia who have sent patients to the other centers.

I watch as Lorraine lifts her reading glasses from where they hang around her neck, nodding as she reads. It's hard to tell, really, what Lorraine and Paul have been thinking through this. Not much of what I've said here invites a lot of laughter, and for the most part, everyone's been quiet and serious throughout. That worries me, but Zoe told me yesterday that this is what I should expect, that whether I talk about Aaron or not, no one who's listening is going to be lighthearted when they know they're hearing this pitch from someone who's been personally affected. "People aren't going to say much," she'd said. "But that's not really a bad thing."

When Lorraine looks up, I begin again. We'd timed the stuff about physician referrals to this stop in particular, the infirmary, so that I can talk about the two full-time nurses that would be on staff, the medical director that would work on-site a minimum of three days a week. This is different, I tell them, from the clinical psych staff that's kept on staff— Wilderness/Wellness tries to keep those functions separate, so that patients don't necessarily see their treatment here as highly medicalized. I talk, too, about the major insurance companies that cover sixty-day stays, the treatment financing that's offered through a third-party vendor for people who don't have insurance. I dislike this part, the money stuff. It feels ugly, particularly after Aaron's failed rehab efforts, and the money those efforts cost our family. One night, not long after my parents had received the settlement check, I'd worked out how many days I could've paid for Aaron at Wilderness/Wellness, if I'd only had that kind of cash.

It'd been a lot of days.

I ask for questions, same as I have at every stop, and this time Paul raises his hand. "What kind of changes would you need to make to a building like this?" he asks, gesturing to the infirmary.

"Pretty big ones here." The infirmary's basically a modular house, factory built, three small windows, unreliable plumbing. "We'd look to expand the space, open it up. As you can imagine, many of the patients are cautious about hospital-like spaces, so natural light is key."

Paul nods. "Probably need better security too, huh?"

"Yeah, I—" I break off when I notice his teasing smile, his small gesture toward that lock I picked. "Oh. Right, yes."

Beside me, where she's been for all of this tour, Zoe breathes out a quiet laugh, and before I've even thought of it, I've reached out, set my hand on the nape of her neck, my thumb moving lightly over the soft skin there while I try not to think too hard about the memory of our first night together. Still, for a second, it feels like everything from this morning, from this whole presentation, has faded away. What would we have told Paul and Lorraine, after all, if we'd gone to them this morning, told them *the truth about us*? Because right now, it feels like nothing about me and her is a lie.

"Shall we go on back toward the lodge?" she says, gesturing an arm out for everyone to pass. If I'm the info guy during this thing, she's the friendly, supportive guide. She passed out the packets, reminded people where to go next, checked her watch to keep us on schedule. We drop back while everyone moves on to the next stop, our last. "How do you think it's going?" she asks, quietly.

"Was going to ask you the same thing."

She smiles at me briefly, steps over a root that's sticking up in the trail, which she knows by heart is there now. "You're doing well. Getting lots of questions."

"Zo," I say, slowing my steps a bit, letting the group get that much farther ahead. "This morning—"

"Let's just finish this," she says, cutting me off. It's not harsh, the way she says it. But she's right, there's no use getting into it now, not when we're so close. There'll be plenty of time after to talk about everything that's happened between us over the last few days.

The plan is for everyone to take a seat in the outdoor classroom for this last stop, and Zoe leads the way, taking her own seat before patting the one beside her for Lorraine. Lorraine, in turn, pats Zoe's knee when she sits, smiling at her in the kind of affection she gives out easily to her campers and friends, and Zoe's face flushes in a kind of shy, surprised pleasure, an expression I haven't seen on her much. Not for the first time do I let my mind try picturing her here in a more long-term way. Ever since I'd decided that I'd do the camp manager role here, I keep thinking of it. No matter how many summers I'd spent here as a kid, it's like the adult version of me now can't see myself at this place without her. At first I'd thought it was because I'd lost that kid version of me when Aaron died—that I couldn't see myself here without *him*.

But no. That's not it at all.

I swallow nervously, shift on my feet one last time as Hammond finally takes a place next to Val. This is the part where I give a wrap-up, where I talk about each one of the patients I mentioned along the trail and where they are now. *Phillip, nineteen, in technical school for heating and cooling systems, twenty-three months clean. Brandi, twenty-two, a hairstylist, thirty-eight months clean. Kellan, twenty-seven, one of the first patients to move through the Colorado program, married and a father of one daughter, a college graduate, six years clean.* I've got seven total I'm supposed to mention here, plus the stats on stability rates five years after completing the program. I'm supposed to talk about why programs like this are the future of drug treatment. I'm supposed to talk about the combination of cognitive behavioral therapy and wilderness therapy.

A strong close. That's what Zoe had called it, back when I went through it with her the first time, though maybe her voice had been a bit stiff.

But for some reason, so close to the end, I stumble. I confuse Phillip with Kellan, and I get flustered enough about it that I go back over it and do it again, conscious of the slight, wincing secondhand embarrassment from my audience. I clear my throat. "Sorry," I say, resisting the urge to wipe a sweaty palm across my jeans. "Been a long couple of days." Before I begin again, I catch Zoe's eye, and she raises an eyebrow, gestures up to the podium. *Want me to do it?* she mouths, and I give a subtle shake of my head. "So probably it's clear," I say to the group, "that a lot of people have had success with this." That's not really a part of my script, that awkward transition, but at least I get going again.

It's not a strong close, that's for fucking sure. It's like all the practice has caught up with me, and the words I'm saying seem disconnected from their meaning, so that when they come out, I'm sort of observing, with one part of my brain, how strange they sound. I'm not so much looking at my audience as I am looking *around* them, no real eye contact, and somewhere in the back of my mind, a thought nags at me: *You don't want this to be over.*

But then, finally, it is.

Zoe had told me not to expect applause, that there wasn't some kids-in-costume flourish here, that it might feel more like a whimper than a bang. But it's still jarring, the quiet—the way everyone's staring down at their materials, I guess a little unsure about what questions to ask. As we'd planned, Zoe gets up and walks to the front, stands beside me. We didn't talk about what she does next, which is to slide her fingers between mine, squeezing our palms together. Still, she sticks to her script. "Aiden and I thought it'd be a good idea to head back into the lodge now, take any questions you have in there. This is a tough subject, we know, so take a few minutes."

We wait together for everyone to go ahead of us, following slowly behind. "I fucked up the end," I murmur to her, only slightly embarrassed. Mostly I'm relieved to have a second alone with her.

"It was fine. It felt real." I look over at her, her chin tilted down as she walks up the lodge steps, and I squeeze her hand to get her to look at me.

"Almost there," I tell her, and she nods, solemn. Too quiet.

Inside, we stay like that, side by side. I'm eager to get off my feet, but it feels good to be in here, away from the bite of the cold air, and within a few minutes, everyone seems to warm up a bit. Hammond goes up to check on the kids, but everyone else sticks around, and there's praise and questions and Paul and Lorraine seem interested, maybe even a little proud. I relax by degrees with Zoe next to me, her hand in mine, and off script, I do better with the questions—I'm not so focused on how long my answers take or how they'll affect the timing of a tour stop.

Almost there, I repeat to myself silently, even as I'm listening to Val—always obsessed with demographics—ask me about whether there's an age limit on patients. But when I open my mouth to answer her, something catches my eye across the room, the front door of the lodge opening slowly—a weak arm, probably, up against a very heavy door.

With the light behind her, it takes me a minute to register.

But that's her.

My mother's here.

Chapter 17

Zoe

She's taller than I remember.

It doesn't make sense, of course, that it's the first thing I think when I see Kathleen O'Leary standing there. The first thing I think should probably be something like *abandon ship*, but instead I stand stock still beside Aiden, my hand still in his, my skin flushing in a hot shock of surprise and shame. It's possible—probable, even, that I murmur a quiet "Oh, *no.*"

Beside me, Aiden jerks in surprise, and I feel his hand heat, briefly, before he pulls it away from mine, my first indication of how wrong everything is about to go. "*Fuck,*" he murmurs, for my ears only, or maybe not for my ears at all, but I've heard it.

"Kathleen?" says Lorraine, her voice a happy question before she moves toward the door, calling, "Oh, Kathleen!"

She's not seen me yet, or if she has, she hasn't yet registered who I am. That much is clear, because right now she's smiling, her arms out to Lorraine, and then to Paul, who's also crossed the room to her, adding to Lorraine's exclamations of surprise. It's a meeting of old friends, I guess—maybe the O'Learys and Dillards weren't close, but if Aaron and Aiden spent over a decade of summers here, clearly there's a history, and I can see it in the way they embrace and then stand back from each other, cataloging what must be years of changes.

It's not that she's taller, I realize, still staring. It's that she's healthier looking. Her hair is a shiny white, her face lightly tanned, her back straighter than it was when I watched her walk from conference room four. For a ridiculous, stupid, suspended-reality moment, I look toward Aiden, open my mouth to say something like, *Hey, your mom looks great,* but already he, too, is moving away from me, his stride slow and his shoulders set firm. I slide my eyes to the door, wondering: *Would he want me to slip out?*

"That's your future mother-in-law?" says Val, interrupting my half-baked thoughts of escape, and I suppress a wince, unsure of how to answer now. Will Mrs. O'Leary play along? Does Aiden have some way to tell her, I think, as I watch him lean down to kiss her cheek, that I'm here, that there's something he hasn't told her yet, but he'll explain it all later?

But that's not what he's telling her. From here I can hear Mrs. O'Leary say, "Oh, he's fine, honey," because what Aiden must've have been asking her about, in this brief, critical moment, is his father, about that call from this morning, the one that had me making one last, desperate attempt to stop this. At this precise moment, it is painful, physically painful, to know that it didn't work. If I had pushed harder—if I'd told Paul and Lorraine myself, maybe—I could've stopped this, what's about to happen. Aiden would've been angry, of course, but it wouldn't have turned out *this* way. "I wanted to be here for you today," I hear her say. "But I guess I missed the whole thing!"

"Yeah," I answer Val, finally, quietly, and she *tsks* in some commiserating annoyance. "God, it's just the same with Hammond. He's completely a sucker for his mother, I swear. You know she called me Valerie for an entire year? My real name is *Valentine.* I told her that the first time I met her." I think I manage a smile; I think I manage to shift my eyes to her and nod, acknowledging her story. But my insides feel like the center of a tornado. Every single thing around me is spinning entirely out of control, breaking apart, and I'm a great column of whirring noise.

I feel it the second she notices me. She's seen me, past Aiden's shoulder, and I've never seen a face do what hers does then, such an abrupt transformation from happiness to—I don't know what. It's not anger, not sadness, not cruelty or vengeance. It's...*blank.* Like I am not even worth the very worst of her emotions.

I think I might, in spite of myself, take a slight step back. "In-laws," Val says, staying by my side in a gesture of loyalty that I find strangely comforting, no matter how fleeting it's likely to be. "I swear, they're just *jealous.*"

"Zoe, my goodness!" calls Lorraine. "Come on over here." But it's not even really necessary—she and Paul are already ushering Mrs. O'Leary farther in, Aiden beside her, his face full of dread and panic. We lock eyes for a brief, painful second, and I can feel it, what's in that look. *This is the end.*

"Mrs. O'Leary," I say, when she's standing in front of me, my voice steady and clear. It's the voice she would've heard come out of my mouth before, and I add a professional nod. Oddly, this feels like the thing I *should* do for her—it's kinder, in some way, not to upset her expectations. Still, I can't do old Zoe as completely as I might like, what with my thermal shirt and my messy ponytail, my dirty hiking boots, now well worn-in from weeks of walking this land alongside Aiden.

She barely looks at me, turning her eyes instead toward her son. "Aiden?" she asks, and in her furrowed brow I see the only relic of his face in her, the only way they look even a little related.

"Mom, if you could—"

"Don't be telling me you kept her a secret from your own mother too," says Lorraine, laughing. "When he called us and said he'd be bringing a fiancée, we could hardly—"

Mrs. O'Leary's eyes snap back to mine, and I feel myself flush all the way to my hairline, feel my stomach drop to my feet when she shifts them down my arm, to my left hand, and her mouth purses and twists in what must be shock—though not, I hope, recognition. I can't imagine how she'd feel if I'm wearing a ring of hers, or of a member of her family.

Aiden clears his throat. "I need to explain something," he says, and what's awful is that everyone's sort of gathered around now, or at least they've come closer. Tom and Sheree have taken a seat at a nearby table, and I can tell they're pretending not to watch, pretending to concentrate on Little Tommy pushing a toy train across the wood floors. Val's not even bothering with such etiquette—she's looking at us like something good is coming.

"You're with this person?" Mrs. O'Leary says, and that's all I need to know about where this is going to end. *This person.* I almost want to laugh at having been so reduced, so fully categorized into nothingness. Mrs. O'Leary's voice, after all, is only the audible expression of what I'd thought about myself for so long, back when I was so stuck—that I *did* nothing, *was* nothing. "Do you know who she is?"

"Wait, who is she?" says Lorraine, and Mrs. O'Leary briefly looks to Aiden again, a pause where she must realize that there's something here Aiden has not told anyone, some complexity that she can't account for.

He opens his mouth to speak, but I interrupt him. "I'm an attorney who worked on the settlement case for Aaron." Sharp, like I'm putting a knife through this whole thing, slicing myself off from everyone else in this room. It's a bit of wishful thinking, doing it this way—to hope I could be extricated so easily from the community we've built over the last five weeks, no matter what brought us all here.

Aiden looks over at me, his face a mask of shock. Today has been so difficult for him already. I can see, behind his eyes, how overwhelmed he is, how painful it is to see his mother, and to have to tell her this, this inevitable truth about what I'm doing here. It's like his circuit board is overloaded.

"Is—is that how you met?" says Paul, tentative and confused, and this is fucking *miserable*; one of us has to end this, to let everyone in this room know the wrong we've done, and at least give them some clarity.

"I asked Zoe to be here with me," Aiden says, before I can open my mouth to do it for the both of us. "She came to see me several weeks ago to—" He stops, clears his throat again, looks over at me. He doesn't want to say what I came to see him for—to apologize—and I don't know if he's doing that out of kindness, out of respect for my privacy, or because he doesn't think his mother will believe it. He begins again. "She came to see me, and I—saw an opportunity."

He shifts as soon as he's said it, moves his weight to a different side of his body, a physical effort to figure out how to do this, or redo it. Me, I'm still frozen, maybe even more so now, because of course what he's said is true—I *was* an opportunity, guilt-ridden and willing to do whatever he'd asked of me, and, whether I realized it then or not, curious about him. Eager to know him.

But it still tears my heart right in half.

"An opportunity for *what*?" Mrs. O'Leary says, her first flash of anger.

"Several weeks ago?" repeats Lorraine, looking back and forth between us, and I can see what she's trying to do. She's trying to find a way to make it possible that Aiden and I have not lied, that we're somehow really, truly engaged after a matter of *several weeks.*

Slowly, so I don't draw attention to myself, I bring my hands together. I slide Aiden's ring off my hand and for a few seconds I hold it tightly in my fist, feeling it press into my palm.

And then Aiden tells the truth.

* * * *

Here are the three strokes of luck I have that afternoon, after Aiden tells his mother, and Paul and Lorraine, and everyone else, that our engagement was just for show:

One, I have my phone with me, tucked into the back pocket of my jeans.

Two, in the chaos following, which includes Hammond coming downstairs with all three very excited, very rowdy girls, Aiden doesn't notice right away when I slip out the lodge's front door.

Three, Aiden doesn't notice, but Sheree does, and she offers to drive me anywhere I want to go. She takes me to the little bakery in Coleville, the one where Aiden bought me a hot chocolate. She stays with me while I call Greer, then she insists on giving me five dollars so I can get myself something to drink while I wait. Before she goes, she asks if I want to pray with her. I say no thanks but she still hugs me goodbye, as if she hasn't just found out about me, about the lie I've been telling her and everyone else from the second we all stepped on that campground. I give her the ring I'd stashed in my pocket, and she agrees to make sure Aiden gets it.

If there's a fourth stroke of luck, it may be that I don't cry until I'm in Greer's car, but I like to think of that coming not from luck, but from a lot of hard-earned practice.

"You want to sit for a while?" she asks, and I shake my head.

"Just drive," I manage, swiping at my face.

"You don't have any things with you?"

"My fr—the woman who brought me here said she'd get my pack from Aiden."

"Okay," she says, and for the next ninety miles she drives, and waits. Greer is more comfortable with silence than anyone I know, and she knows I won't talk until the tears stop.

So it's a pretty quiet drive.

When I notice that we've pulled off an exit ramp toward Kit's place, I stiffen in my seat. "Greer," I say. "No."

At the next red light she turns to me, her blue eyes so big and clear. "I already called her. We do these things together."

"She knew from the beginning it was a bad idea. Self-immolation, she said."

"She's not going to crow over you, Zoe. She loves you."

I swallow back a fresh wave of tears, close my eyes, and lean my head back on the seat. That we're even having this conversation—that I'm afraid to face one of my best friends in the world—is another profound, painful reminder of the mistakes I've made these last couple of months, letting this thing with Aiden drive any kind of wedge between us. If Kit tells me she told me so, she'll be right.

When we pull up to the curb, she's on the front porch, her arms crossed over her chest and her brow furrowed beneath the rim of her glasses, and before Greer's even switched off her engine, she's down the steps and out her small gate, reaching for my door even as I'm opening it. "Are you okay?" she says, her eyes cataloging my puffy eyes, my tear-streaked face. It's possible, I realize, that this is the first time she or Greer has seen me cry, so long as we're not counting laugh-crying, which I've done a lot with these two.

They hustle me up the front steps and into the house as if I'm some damaged starlet, bailed out from a dumb, reckless mistake, hounded by the press. As soon as we cross the threshold I see Ben's boots inside the foyer, and feel a sudden shock of embarrassment, enough to stop me dead in my tracks. It's bad enough that Kit and Greer are going to see this.

"Maybe we should stay on the porch," I manage.

"It's too cold out there, hon," says Kit, and the kindness in her voice almost breaks me again.

"Z," says Ben, coming into the foyer. He's got a giant bag of peanut M&M's in his hand—my favorite—that he holds out to me. "If he hurt you, I'll fuck him up."

Kit rolls her eyes, but I can tells she's a little proud too, and a lot grateful. I offer a weak smile and take the candy. Sweet, genuine Ben. I was so hard on him, back when we first met, grilling him at Betty's like he was a danger to my friend. He loves me because Kit loves me, but I think he *likes* me, too. He reaches out, gives me a brief hug before he slips up the steps.

It's just the three of us then, and I breathe my first sigh of relief in hours.

* * * *

"He said—you were an opportunity?" says Greer, sounding surprised.

I've told them the whole thing now, though it's taken a while, because I've done a bit more crying and because Greer and Kit seem so rattled by it that they keep offering me things: the candy, water, alcohol, a sandwich, a blanket, and—at one particularly desperate point, I guess—a hot towel, like we're on a first-class flight to Patheticville.

I shrug. "I was."

"He's an asshole," says Kit. "He wouldn't have made it past the first week without you."

That doesn't have the desired effect, probably. Probably Kit wants me to start feeling indignant, remembering all the shit I shoveled for him that first week at the campground, my bag of breakfast food and my smiling, eager friendliness with Paul and Lorraine and everyone else who'd been there. But there's no indignation there, not yet, and probably not ever. To me, memories of that first week feel oddly tender and simple, such a contrast to the intense complexity of the last few days, and to the messy, chaotic unraveling of it all tonight.

"Maybe that would've been better for him, though," I say. "If he wouldn't have made it past the first week. If I hadn't said yes."

"Zoe," says Greer, her voice firmer than usual. "Please don't blame yourself for this too."

Kit looks over at her, surprised that Greer's beat her to it. "Yeah," she says, looking back at me. "Don't."

I take a deep breath, flatten the bag of still-unopened M&M's on my thigh, feeling the bumps of candy against my palm. "It's not the right thing for him, this camp. It's not what he really wants, not for himself."

"This is the face I make," Kit says, gesturing vaguely at her head, "when I am trying really hard to give a shit."

"Kit, I know—I *know* what he said, and I know it wasn't pretty." *An opportunity.* I hear it echo in my head again—still true, and still painful. "But he's so—he's so *sad*. And he feels so guilty, and he's been trying to—" I break off, meet her eyes. She's sympathetic toward him, I know she is. But what she feels for me is always going to be bigger than any feelings she can muster toward him. "I love him," I tell her, and I watch her eyes widen in shock. "I know it's over, but still."

I let that sit in the air between us, this big thing I kept from them—that I kept from myself, I know, for longer than I'm willing to admit. With sudden, painful clarity I realize how much I would've enjoyed telling them more—how much fun it would've been to tell them about the way Aiden and I had fought and laughed, the way we'd pushed each other, the way being with each other had been easy and hard, all at the same time. And now that it's over, it feels like I won't ever really get the chance.

They're both quiet for a minute, the only sound in the room the crinkle of plastic from my candy-bag fidgeting, and eventually Greer stops that by taking it from me and opening it. I'm pretty sure the handful she takes is stress-eating related.

I take a deep breath, steady myself. "You know that night we bought the ticket, and we all said what we'd buy with the money?" I ask, finally.

"You said you wanted an adventure," says Greer.

I nod, my head feeling heavy, congested with tears I still haven't shed. "What I really thought, that night, was that I wanted to be forgiven. I wanted to feel better about the things that I've done. The stuff I did at my job, the stuff I did after my dad died—I don't know. The person I'd become." From where I sit in Kit's armchair, I look out the front window, across the street. A porch light illuminates the neighbors' fat dachshund digging a hole in one of the flower beds, covering its belly in dirt.

"You're a great person," says Greer. "You've always been a great person."

I give her a small smile in thanks, not even really taking her words in. "I wanted forgiveness from Aiden, from his family," I say. "And I guess I got an adventure instead."

"Zoe," says Kit, "the camp does not have to be your—"

"*He* was the adventure," I say. "A stupid, reckless adventure that I should've known better than to go on. And now—the way it's all turned out—it's another sin to add to the pile."

"Don't say that," says Greer, and Kit and I both slide our eyes toward her. "Yeah, everything unraveled in the end, and he—he could've handled things better, once his mom showed up. But whatever happened—you were different, these last few weeks."

"Different how?" I say, because I guess I'm a glutton for punishment. I guess I didn't get enough in that lodge, Aiden's mother looking at me like I was nothing.

Greer shifts on the couch, worried, maybe, that she's gone down this path. "After we won, you were definitely different. You weren't wound so tight, I guess, once you left your job. But it still seemed like you were...I don't know. It seemed like you were *trying* so hard." I suppress a wince at this, knowing just what she means. I *had* been trying so hard. Laughing too loud, making a joke of everything, my books about around-the-world trips, my fucking guilt jar. Trying to find something to *do* with myself. "But the past couple of weeks?" she says. "I've never seen you like that. I thought I knew your laugh, your smile. But I don't think I really did, not until lately. So it wasn't stupid. No matter how it turned out, it gave you something."

There's a long pause, while Kit and I take in what Greer's said. It's how it always is with Greer. It's almost like you have to get used to her for the first time when she really commits to saying something. "What she said," says Kit.

"You thought it was a terrible idea, from the start," I say to Kit. "You never liked this whole thing."

Kit takes a deep breath, adjusts her glasses. "I think I was a little jealous."

"What?"

"You've always known the right things to say to us. The things that would get us out of our own heads, or that would get us to take risks. You're our bullshit detector, our conscience. I knew you were struggling with your work, and I knew you were struggling after you quit, too. But

I—I couldn't seem to find the right thing to say or do, to get you out of it. I think maybe it bothered me that would be him, or his camp, or whatever, that managed it."

"Oh," I say, because I can't say anything else, because here come the waterworks again. Not as fast or furious this time, but enough that I feel the tears track down my cheeks.

From her spot on the couch, Greer grabs my hand and tugs, hard, until I'm forced to stand and stumble over toward where she and Kit are sitting. Soon enough, I'm between them, right in the join of the couch cushions, their bodies pressed against mine, keeping me from sinking. "I'm sorry for that," says Kit. "I'm sorry I didn't know how to help."

"Me too," says Greer.

"Hey, don't," I tell them, reaching my hands out, setting one on Greer's arm, one on Kit's knee, pretzeling us all up in a way that reminds me of what I still have, what I'll always have with these two. What I almost messed up. "I'm sorry I didn't ask. I'm sorry I wasn't more honest. I'm sorry I didn't talk to you more about—I don't know. Everything, I guess. My job, and how I felt about it. The way I felt after we won. I think I—I like being the tough one for you guys. I got used to playing that role. Maybe too much."

"Idea," says Kit, raising a finger in the air. "No more apologizing between us? We're okay. And you're going to be okay."

I sigh out a breath of relief. *No more apologizing.* What a concept. "Good idea," I say.

We're quiet then, aside from my sniffling, a sound that I would normally find humiliating coming out of my own self, but I can't muster any shame. I still feel so unbelievably, hugely sad. I'm still thinking, in spite of myself, about what Aiden's doing now, about whether Sheree has given him the ring back, about how it'll go with his mother, about what more he's said to Paul and Lorraine. When I'd left Willis-Hanawalt all those months ago, what had surprised me most was how little I'd thought of it after, in terms of the day to day. How few things about it I'd missed.

It won't be like that, not with this. I can feel it waiting for me like a physical presence, the *missing* I'm going to do. The campground, the people I met there, and Aiden.

Aiden, most of all.

But I have this, I tell myself, steeling my body for the long weeks to come, feeling the warmth and kindness of my friends next to me.

"*Great* idea," says Greer. And then after a pause, she pats my hand where it rests on her arm. "And anyways, let's be honest. It's me that's the tough one."

I laugh, for the first time in what feels like forever, lift my hands to wipe the tears from my face. For once, I'm okay being weak, at least for a little while.

Chapter 18

Aiden

Having my parents back in the house is strange, disconcerting. When I'd first come back here, I'd thought it'd surely been a mistake to move in, to live in the place where we'd all been as a family. It's a small place, all one floor, but it'd felt huge and soundless to me, and I'd find myself repeating these routines of my parents' that I didn't even know I'd internalized—before bed, checking all the locks in a certain order, like Pop always did. In the morning, opening the back door to let extra light into the kitchen, like Mom did.

Now that they're both here—my dad flying up just two days after Mom and I returned from Stanton Valley, a special request, I'm guessing, in the aftermath of my fuckup—I find that they've remembered all those routines, taking them over for me while I move through the house, quiet and devastated, angry and defeated.

I'm not going to get the campground.

That much was clear, of course, after the presentation itself, the way Paul and Lorraine had looked back and forth between me, Zoe, and my mother. For Zoe and my mom they'd at least seemed to have sympathy. But for me? Disappointment, through and through, and I'd thought nothing could be worse until Paul had called me yesterday evening, one week since the most disastrous, humiliating revelation of my life.

"We both want you to know that it isn't about your plan for the camp," he'd said, his voice so much more gentle than I deserved. "And it isn't about your not...you know. About your not having a family. We both want you to know that we're sorry if we gave you that impression—"

I'd cut him off, barely able to stand him offering any sort of apology to me. "You didn't," I'd said. "This was all my doing."

He'd told me that they'd talked it through a lot, that the campground had meant so much to them, almost their whole lives. That while they hoped I'd find a place for the Wilderness/Wellness camp, they weren't sure if I was ready for something like this. "I bought that land when I was twenty-three years old," Paul had said, the pride in his voice unmistakable. "I bought it for her, to give her something she would love, and we've loved this place like it's something that came from us, together. It's important to us that the next owners have a similar ethic in mind."

I'd heard that like a bomb blast—so loud that it'd deafened me to everything the rest of the day except for my own thoughts. Wasn't it love that had inspired me to go after the camp? My love for my lost brother, my best friend, the other half of me that I couldn't save? I'd worked it over in my mind, again and again, but I'd kept coming back to the same thing.

I hadn't done it for love.

I'd done it for guilt. For grief and pain and the determination that I could fix something after so many years of not being able to fix the very worst thing in my life. I'd brought Zoe in on it, and it didn't matter what I felt for her now. What mattered was what I'd felt for her then, how I'd brought her there under false pretenses. How I'd used her. *Convenient,* I remember telling Charlie and Ahmed. *Willing. Available.* After all that had changed between us, after everything she'd invested all on her own in helping me, I'd basically called her a means to an end in front of people she'd come to like and respect. It makes me sick to think of it. It had, actually, made me physically sick, that afternoon at the lodge. Once I'd realized she'd gone, I'd run out onto the porch, had seen Sheree's car driving away, and dry-heaved in panic over the railing.

"You don't want anything?" my mom says from across the table, where she's been sitting for the last twenty minutes, silently working at the word jumble in the paper and occasionally looking up at me in concern. I pretend not to notice, to be interested in the front page, but I haven't turned the page for as long as we've sat here, same as I haven't touched the bowl of oatmeal she set at my elbow.

"Not hungry."

"You've got a long shift ahead. You should eat."

I wonder if Zoe's been eating, I think, picturing her in the seat I'm in now, tidily eating a peanut butter and jelly sandwich while I glowered at her, every feeling I had toward her then the wrong one. I stand up, the bowl in one hand. "I'll get something on the way in," I lie. "You think Pop'll want this?"

"Maybe," she says. Pop's outside, raking leaves, still ten times quieter than he used to be but even I can see that something's different about him. Maybe it's the house, getting back into the routines of his old life. "Aiden, sit down here with me for a bit."

"I've got to get going."

And I really, really do. Right now work's the only thing holding me together, the only place I feel useful. But even work's not easy—Ahmed and Charlie know that things have gone wrong, and the only thing I can say about that is that neither of them have bothered to say that they told me so. Instead they pick up a lot of my slack, doing all the extra, anal-retentive chores I usually take care of—inventory and fridge clean-out and equipment testing. And they tread lightly, particularly after Tuesday's shift, when Ahmed told me that the night before, he'd run into Kit and Greer coming out of Betty's. No sign of Zoe, he'd said, though they'd had takeout bags with them. I'd felt my chest compress under the weight of all the questions I had no fucking right to ask.

But then we'd got a call, Mrs. Gilchrist again in another new nightgown, and I'd been spared from even trying.

"Just for a bit," she says. "You look tired."

Seems like there's been no point in sleeping, either, really. Every time I close my eyes, I see her. Even when I'm foggy headed and bone tired, I see her, that gray-faced shame I'd seen in her when my mother had said, *You're with this person?* I'd said nothing—nothing at all—to defend her.

I slide back down into my chair, too tired to bother arguing. I'm in this house like a ghost, not even in my own body. It's not even the phantom-self feeling I used to get, right after Aaron was gone. It's worse, if that's possible, as if I've compounded the loss.

It feels as if there's no self there at all, no part of me that I can rally to care about what's coming.

My mom takes a deep breath, pushes her word jumble away. "I know you're disappointed about the camp."

I keep my eyes down on the table, my hands clasped loosely across my stomach, waiting for this to be over. There is not one thing worth explaining to my mother about my disappointment, about how little of it has to do with that fucking camp.

"But you'll find another location, Aiden. I know you will. You made a mistake, getting that woman involved, and I'm sure that was a big part of the problem, and—"

"Mom," I say, for the first time realizing that I do, in fact, remember how it feels to care. I run my hand up the back of my neck, over my hair, inhale through my nose before I speak again. "I did make a mistake. But Zoe is not even one single shred of a part of that mistake. What she did, how you know her—that is not her." I pause, take a big breath through my nose before blowing it out on a frustrated sigh. "Or—you know what? It is her. It's part of her, same as the part of her that wanted to fix it, and if I hadn't fucked everything up she'd have had a chance to say her apologies to you and Pop and get on with her life. It's me that was the problem."

"Well, I doubt that," she says, defensively.

"Don't," I snap. "Don't doubt it. Don't make me into the perfect son here, Mom. I have never deserved it less than I do right this second."

"Honey, all of us, even Paul and Lorraine, we understand what you were trying to do for your brother."

I push back from the table, taking up the bowl again and dumping it into the sink, relishing the clank it makes. "I wasn't doing it for him," I say, turning and leaning back against the counter so I can see the surprise register on her face. "I was doing it for myself, to feel better about what a shit job I did when he was alive. To make it okay that I couldn't save him."

Mom is silent, her mouth slightly open, her eyes darting to the back door, where my dad still rakes. She doesn't want him to hear this, but oddly enough, I get the feeling he could take it.

"The only good that came of it was her," I say, quietly. "I'm sure you don't believe it. But with her—I felt like myself again, for a while."

"Aiden," she says, her voice disbelieving. "Do you...*love* this woman?"

Involuntarily, I laugh—it's a dark, ugly thing, short and scornful. "Yeah, Mom," I say, like it's the most obvious thing in the world, because, at least to me, it *is*—now it is, at the worst possible time, now that I've lost her. I press the heels of my hands to my eyes before I let them drop back, curling them around the edge of the counter behind me. "It hurts how I love her." I can feel how I've steeled my middle to say it. That's where it hurts, right in the center of me.

"Hurts all the time?" she asks, quietly.

I think about being with Zoe, at the campsite. The way I'd loved to watch her, right from the beginning—the way I'd loved it, even when I thought I was hating it. The way she made me laugh—out-loud prayers and peanut-sized ticks and Cocktoberfest and marshmallow stuck in her hair, every time she called me on my shit or served me up a steaming hot plate of *you're-being-an-asshole*, every time she called me Boy Scout. "No," I say. "Hurts since she's gone."

"Well," she says, and then repeats it. I wish I could say there was some understanding there, some way I've gotten her to change her mind. But I can't tell what she's thinking, can't tell if she'd ever have room for forgiving Zoe, and that's a damn shame. It's what Zoe had wanted from me, more than anything, that first day, and I wish I could go back and give it to her.

"If you knew her," I say, because it feels like I have to say it, some last thing I can do for Zoe even though I've lost her. "You'd see her the way I do. She's funny as hell and ten times smarter than me on her worst day. She's loyal and she works harder than anyone I've ever met. On herself, on whatever her friends need, on whatever I needed from her."

She doesn't say anything, looking down at her hands and then back out to the yard. I don't have time to stick around for what she may or may not have to say in response. I say a quick goodbye, grab my keys and phone, and head out.

I doubt I've convinced her, but I guess it doesn't matter.

* * * *

When I get home that night, my dad's in the pink chair, swiveled to face the flat-screen, one of the few possessions I'd brought back from Colorado, though I haven't watched it much. Seeing him there brings a fresh sting of pain to my chest, the way he's so passive. He's barely acknowledged my coming in. "Hey, Pop," I say, clapping his shoulder as I pass by him on my way to the kitchen, same as he used to do to me. It's late, past 11:00 p.m., so I know Mom's been in bed for at least an hour, and she's left a container of food for me on the counter, a sticky note stuck to the plastic cover with instructions on how to microwave it, like she's forgotten that I'm a grown-ass man, living on my own for over a decade. It's nice, of course, how thoughtful she is, but holy shit, I wish I was alone here. I don't feel like being taken care of, not right now, and especially not by my mother, not after our tense exchange from this morning.

Still, a man's got to eat, especially after almost thirteen hours on duty, so I heat up the plate.

I bring it out to the living room, set it on the coffee table in front of me while I lower my aching, sorry ass to the couch. I've got the next two days off, a good thing for my body, I suppose, though I don't relish the thought of negotiating this house with both my parents in it for forty-eight hours, and they've said nothing about when they plan to leave. On-screen is some kind of police procedural, a big, broad-shouldered bald guy in a leather jacket and a badge showing on his hip lecturing a room full of rookies about contaminated evidence. My dad looks completely enraptured.

"You like this show?" I say, and he grunts an acknowledgment.

Normally I'd let that go, but something about that noise he makes is so familiar to me. I know it's because I've made the same one a hundred times, clammed up and barely engaged and trying not to let loose all the shit I'm really thinking, and the only person who's never let me get away with it is Zoe. "What's it about?" I ask, and shove in another forkful of—fuck, I don't even know what this is, some kind of hamburger-potato mash that'll probably keep me up with heartburn. I chew slowly, waiting for his answer.

I feel my dad look over my way, but I keep my eyes on the plate, not wanting to push him. "This cop's gone bad," he says. "Everyone thinks he's great, but he's got some kind of situation with a hooker and a bunch of illegal guns."

"Nice," I say, which makes no fucking sense, but at least we've had some semblance of a conversation.

I finish off my food, take a big gulp of water, and sit back, watch with him for a while. I don't much like this kind of show, but something about it ends up being pretty soothing—the cop's gone bad in general but in specific he's about to bust some asshole who beats on his kids, and I guess that's something. When the credits roll, my dad looks at his watch, taps his finger lightly over a button on the remote, not changing channels or shutting it off, just—contemplating, I guess. "You know, I think he loves that hooker," he says, out of the blue.

"Probably don't call her a hooker, Pop. I don't know if people say that anymore."

He shrugs. "I know you think I watch too much TV."

I look over at him, surprised. This isn't what we do, me and my dad. We don't talk about the stuff that there's good reason not to acknowledge. "I didn't say anything."

He mutes the TV, clears his throat. "Guess you probably don't see it so much, but I watch less than I used to. I like this show and another one, one your mother's got me into about a lady park ranger."

"Pop," I say, shaking my head, the first real smile I've felt in days twitching at my mouth. I'd pay good money, all my fucking money, to see Zoe's face when my pop said "lady park ranger."

To see her face at all, I guess, if I'm being honest.

"I'm doing a lot better than I was, you know," he says, and he reaches up, wipes his eyes. *Fuck,* he's crying again, and I drop my eyes back to the now-empty plate. "I go to those meetings sometimes, the ones your mother likes. And I got someone I see down there in Florida, someone who helps me with things. Take a lot of walks with your mother."

"That's good." I swallow twice, then clear my throat. That choking feeling again, and I push the plate even farther away from me, wishing I hadn't eaten.

"All different ways people get over things," he says, pushing up out of his chair and tossing the remote at me. It lands with a slap on my chest, then falls to my lap. "You'd better figure out yours."

He looks down at me for a second, one brief nod of his chin—a poor substitute for affection, but I'll take it. I watch him walk toward the front door, unlocking and locking the deadbolt, then leaning his shoulder against the door until it makes this little *click* of approval. I watch him move down the hall, hear him do the same at the back door. The routine completed, he heads back to bed, his footfalls quiet on the carpet.

For what feels like a long time, I don't even move. I stare right at that muted television, not registering anything that's on the screen. I'd thought I was getting over it, I guess, or maybe I thought there was no getting over it, and so I hadn't really tried. The camp wasn't trying, not really—the camp was just me running, running to something else so I wouldn't have to stop and look around me, to really catalog everything I'd lost. And so look what I'd done, look how I'd fucked everything up, the very same thing Zoe had warned me about all those weeks ago, driving back from the campground after the first weekend I'd been with her, been inside of her. She'd told me it was easy to make mistakes. She'd told me about her own.

She'd tried, so far as I would let her, to stop me.

There's that pain in my middle again, breath-stealing. I'd done wrong by her, not just because I brought her in on this mess with the camp, a mess she'd agreed to for her own reasons. I'd done wrong because of *this* mess, the mess that's inside of me ever since I got that call, the last call for Aaron. The call I'd known was coming, somewhere deep down inside me. I'd known it was coming years before it actually came. I've been fucked up and grieving, too scared to face it, too willing to let her take the lead in getting me out of my own head.

I shut off the TV, set the remote next to my abandoned plate, and stand, my eyes running over every piece of furniture, every lamp, the old carpet, the curtains my mother made back when Aiden and I were in ninth grade.

It's like being in a museum.

I walk out of the living room, down the hall to where I had my office set up, where I've blown up an inflatable mattress so my parents can sleep in my—*their*—room. I stare down at it, this sad-as-fuck bed, twin size, basically a life raft, smaller and less comfortable than my camp bunk. I hear my dad moving around in the bathroom, brushing his teeth. When he's done, he does this little cough, and it sounds so much like Aaron that I bend down, yank the edge of the mattress, sheets and all, toward me. At first I'm just trying to cover the noise, but pretty soon it's clear to me what I mean to do with this air bed, and I don't even care that my dad sees me pull it out into the hallway, his brow barely wrinkling before he gives me another nod of acknowledgment and turns toward his room, closing the door behind him.

It's awkward, doing this—I'll have to go back for the pillows, and the fitted sheet pops off, bunching everything else with it. But I drag it across the hall, reaching out behind me with one hand to open the door to Aaron's room, pulling it all the way in until I can lay it right down there in the center. It's sad in here; that's all there is to it. On the walls you can see faint outlines from where pictures used to hang. If I open the closet door, I'll see a badly drawn Yakko from Aaron's probably too-long *Animaniacs* phase. If I close my eyes, I think I can still catch the smell of him—not his deodorant or cologne or the cigarette smoke that used to cling to him there at the end, but *him*, skin I knew as well as my own, skin that *was* my own.

Yeah. It's fucking sad.

But I think it's time I lived in it for a while.

Chapter 19

Zoe

The truth is, it feels sort of good to be alone.

I'm home after another full day of work at Legal Aid, where I've spent almost every day for the last two weeks, calling people on that log list like it's a literal lifeline. They're not short calls, and they're not always wrapped up after a single conversation. I did four calls last week with a Mrs. Adelaide Martin, an eighty-six-year-old widow who'd had her identity stolen and who'd never used the internet in her life. By the fourth call, she'd started calling me *darling* and invited me to play bridge on Saturday with her friends at Sunset Terrace.

I'm probably going to go. Adelaide seems like good people.

But doing the calls, working with Marisela and the other full-time staff, getting to know some of the volunteers who come in, usually around the time I'm leaving for the day—it's a reminder, I guess, of the time I used to need after work to unwind, not talk, let my mind quiet down. And there's been little time for that, because Kit and Greer have been on full-time Zoe watch, dinners here or at one of their places, an extra spinning class or two, manufactured reasons why one or both of them needs to come over. "Ben's sanding the floor in the guest bedroom," Kit had said one day last week when she'd come over with an overnight bag and an absolutely unconvincing expression of desperation. "It makes my eyes itchy." No way would Ben want Kit sleeping elsewhere after so short a time, and Kit's eyes looked just fine to me, but she'd come in and we'd watched three episodes of a home renovation show, during which Kit made loud complaints about how much "perfectly good stuff" the hosts kept throwing away from the houses. The very next night it'd been Greer, swearing that her older sister—also her roommate—had a very important third date, and she wanted to give them some privacy. I'd helped her study for a sociology exam, but I'm pretty sure she was faking her efforts to recall key details about toxic masculinity and intersectional feminism. In fact I'm pretty sure she'd taken that exam already, but I'd played along.

They're worried, which is fair enough. It was only a couple of months ago, after all, that I'd been putting up Kit while she'd been split up from Ben, and during those few weeks Greer and I had done everything short of asking for biometric stress tests to judge her mental health. But at this point I'm getting the sense of how overwhelming all that attention can be. Even my mother seems worried; when we video-chatted last night she asked if I was forgetting under-eye cream, which is basically a DEFCON 1 level of concern coming from her. Of course she also asked if I'd mind celebrating Christmas in February this year so that she could go on a cruise with her new boyfriend, so I guess there's still a limit to her maternal instincts.

But tonight I've managed to convince everyone to give me a little space, and their willingness to let this pass gives me hope that I'm getting better.

Still, I'm no dummy. I know that I'm no good with unstructured time—see, obviously, the last several months of my life—so I've made a plan, at least for this evening.

The guilt vase is still on my dining room table, empty now. I'd dumped the slips a couple of nights after the campground debacle, not angrily or sadly or hastily. Just—quietly. I'd looked at each one before I'd dropped it in the recycling bin, knowing, of course, that I wouldn't forget any of them. *I'm* the vase, that's the thing. That's the truth about making mistakes, about making the wrong choices. You live with them, and if you're lucky you get enough perspective to see where you went astray. You figure out what you can do to repair the damage, and you figure out how to do better going forward.

And no one would say I'm not lucky.

Still, it takes me a little while to rally myself to my task—too much time lingering over my dinner, too high of a word count responding to a simple message about condo board business, too-careful research into the next round of cooking classes Janet and I will start in a couple of weeks.

Finally, I remind myself that this is a modest task. A small, unselfish, honest gesture, the kind of thing I should've have done all those weeks ago. The kind of thing that's not about my guilt, but about someone else's feelings.

I pick up the phone and dial.

"Hi, Lorraine," I say, when she answers.

"Oh, Zoe," she says, or…sighs, I guess, the sound in her voice a combination of relief and sadness.

"I hope it's okay that I'm calling."

"Of course it's okay. I was hoping you'd call."

I take a deep breath through my nose, let it out slowly before I speak again. "I just needed to tell you, Lorraine, both you and Paul, how sorry I am about being dishonest. There's no excuse for my part in this. You made me feel so welcome, and I loved every minute of my time in Stanton Valley. And I—well. I apologize sincerely."

"Not every minute," she says.

"What?"

"We both know you didn't love every minute. That first weekend you worked so hard I felt like I ought to write you a check at the end, and that's back when I thought you were in it for real."

It lands heavily, despite her light tone, for all kinds of reasons—she's right, of course, and I don't deserve to have it sugarcoated. But it's so complicated. It *was* so complicated, even on that first weekend. I *was* in it for real, even then, even though I hadn't known then what Aiden would mean to me, what I'd come to feel for him. "I guess that's true," I say, standing from my seat at the dining room table so I can pace around, work off some nerves, while we do this. "But even then I liked it. I liked you, and Paul." I pause, unsure of how much to say next. I don't know how much she knows about Aiden and me now—I'd left the lodge before anyone had asked whether we'd ever even managed to become friends over the course of our ruse. "I liked everyone, really."

"Hammond could use some improvement," she says, and we both laugh a little, before the line between us goes quiet again. I pass into the kitchen, grab the sponge off the rim of my sink, and scrub at a nonexistent spot on the counter.

"Lorraine, I *am* sorry."

"Oh, honey. I know you are. And I'd be lying if I said I wasn't upset at the both of you for what you did. It really threw me and Paul for a loop. I don't think it was any secret from you that we've always felt real strong toward Aiden, and this has been a disappointment."

I take a deep breath, take in that disappointment. Own my part in it. I put the sponge back.

"But," she says, her voice gentle, "I really appreciate you calling me, and saying what you said. That means a lot."

How simple it is, I think, to do this with Lorraine. How grateful I am for that. How lucky I am to know her. "I'd like to come there, sometime, and tell you and Paul in person, but I didn't want to just show up unannounced." I've learned my lesson about that. "I know I sort of ran off there at the end. I'm sorry for that too."

Lorraine makes a funny clucking noise, tongue snapping against teeth. "I can't say I blame you for it. Quite an afternoon, wasn't it?"

I close my eyes at the thought of it. I've done my best, over the last couple of weeks, not to conjure it all up in my head—Aiden's face especially, arrested in dread and fear and something like anger. Instead, when I think of him, I make valiant, rarely successful efforts to remember the best moments I had with him with a sort of distant placidity. This is the healthy thing to do, I tell myself, the thing that shows I'm *over* it—if I can just look back fondly on it all, appreciate it for the moments that were good, I'll feel less hollow. Eventually, I tell myself, I'll be able to see it all for what it was, what I *promised* myself it would be: a fling, great sex with a nice guy, all of it with an expiration date. It'd only come sooner than what I'd expected, and that's okay. That happens.

"Well, you know," I say, searching for a bit of that mature, thoughtful distance now, "I'm sure it made it easier for Aiden and his mom to have me out of the picture, so maybe it wasn't all bad."

"Uh-huh," says Lorraine, clearly unconvinced. In the brief quiet after, I want to ask her what's happened with the campground—whether she and Paul made their decision and announced it last week, as they'd originally planned, or whether Aiden's and my mess had ruined that too. But I don't think I'm entitled to ask after that information. If she volunteers it, okay—but if not, it's not my place to know.

"Have you heard from him?" she asks, interrupting my thoughts.

"Not really." I don't want to explain to Lorraine that I ignored three calls from him, all made on that night I'd left, that I'd waited, half in hope, half in fear, for him to call again in the days after.

He didn't.

"Have you?" I ask, doing my best to sound as if I'm just asking after the weather.

"Paul spoke to him last week." I want to know about that call so bad that I pick up the sponge again, just to have something to squeeze in my hand.

"Ah." I can't manage anything else.

"You were so convincing," Lorraine says then, surprising me, and I slump back against the counter, waiting for what she'll say next, knowing it won't be easy. I should have figured it wouldn't be so quick. "I guess

I'd be more angry at that, Zoe, if I thought it was possible for the both of you to fake it so well."

My eyes well up with shamed tears, and I tilt the phone away from my face so she won't hear my accompanying sniffle.

"Obviously I don't know you all that well," she says into the quiet I've left there. "But I think I know him, and boy did he look at you with something fierce in his eyes." *Like protons and electrons,* I think, remembering the way Kit had teased me that night, back when I'd told her all about keeping my distance.

It's embarrassing how much I wish that what Lorraine has said is true—that Aiden watched me, *wanted* me, as fiercely as he'd wanted that campground. As fiercely as he'd wanted to do something for his family.

But any hope of that had vanished when I'd seen Kathleen O'Leary that day. When I'd remembered, again, what mattered most to him, and what would and should always matter most to him.

His family. And I would never—*could* never—be a part of that.

"Well," I say, lamely, "it's complicated, I guess."

"I guess," she repeats, just as dully.

"Anyways," I say, hoping she doesn't comment on how rapidly and flippantly I've changed the tone. "I really appreciate you taking my call. And if you'd talk to Paul about my coming sometime—"

"Of course I will."

"Thank you."

"But Zoe, even if you come sometime—and we'd love to have you—I hope you're able to put this behind you. To move on."

"Ha," I say, the blandest possible laugh. "That has historically not been my strong suit, Lorraine."

"Well," she says, her voice back to the way it always is—hopeful, encouraging, kind. "Maybe it will be this time."

* * * *

You are qualified to file for a no-fault divorce if you—

"Zoe," says Marisela, and I startle in place in the storage room, the stack of pamphlets I'm looking down at rustling in my hand.

"Yes," I say, straightening my posture. "Sorry. I was going to refill the information display case out front. Seems we always run out of the divorce ones first."

Marisela cocks her head at me, a tiny line she has between her eyebrows furrowing. "We don't really need you to do stuff like that around here. Focus on the calls." She says it kindly, and I clear my throat, tapping the stack against the shelf to straighten them. Add Marisela to the list of people who've worried, especially when I showed up here extra early this morning, a bit restless, I guess, after my call with Lorraine.

I *do* need to move on. I know it.

"I'm done with the log list," I say.

"Wow," says Marisela, genuinely impressed. I'd bask in it a little more, especially since first thing this morning the clinic posted a job ad for a full-time legal services attorney, and Marisela's already encouraged me to apply—first with a sticky note stuck right in the center of the desk where I sit, then in an email with the job announcement attached, and then in person when I'd refilled my coffee. "Specializing in employment disputes and cases against health insurers," she'd said, nudging me. "Someone with your corporate experience would be excellent."

But as much as I want to apply, as much good as I think I could do—would I be doing it for the right reasons? Would I just be trying to assuage my own guilt, again? After all, it's not like my work here is purely unselfish. Legal Aid is helping me move on, professionally speaking, making me feel good about being a lawyer again.

And most of the time, while I'm here, I also manage to avoid thinking about how I'm not moving on, personally speaking. *Most* of the time.

I take a deep breath, looking down at the pamphlets again.

You are qualified to file for a no-fault divorce if you have not shared any residence with your spouse for over six months—

"The phones are already ringing," I say, casually. "I'm sure I'll have more to handle soon."

"Actually, you've got someone here waiting."

I set down the pamphlets, a tingling unease in my fingertips. Somehow, I just *know*. "A walk-in?" I say, as casual as I can manage.

Marisela shrugs. "I guess. Aiden O'Leary? He says he knows you."

I look at her, and there must be something pleading in my eyes. She seems to shift something in her posture, becoming sturdier, taller, more determined. "I'll get him out of here. Don't come out."

"Oh," I say, embarrassed, and roused by the protective instinct I still apparently have for him. "No—it's really okay. He's my—" *This separation must be continuous,* the pamphlet says. "He's a former client. Or his family were former clients, sort of."

"Okay," she says, but I get the feeling I'm not going out there without Marisela right at my back. I look down at my dress, a black-and-gray tweed that is, once again, about ten times more formal than anything anyone else here wears, but I cling to the old habit, and I'm grateful for the distance it'll surely put between me and him.

With the intention that your separation will be permanent, I read, picking up the pamphlets again and carrying them with me out into the office's main space, feigning busyness. I'll make this quick. Whatever he came here to say, I'll make it quick. Maybe this will help, actually. Maybe it will help me move on.

When I look up, he's there, just inside the front door, worn jeans and a navy t-shirt underneath an army-green utility jacket, the one he used to wear at camp sometimes. I know just how it smells, that jacket. Like cold air and woodsmoke and him. He looks so simultaneously familiar and out of place that I feel my heart tear anew.

"Here she is," says Marisela, a little loud in my ear, seeing as how she's standing with her shoulder practically pressed against mine. Somehow, she's made these three words sound menacing as all hell, and I look over at her, impressed and surprised. Marisela would probably shred someone in court, and later, when my head and heart aren't full of the man standing a few feet away from me, I'm going to ask her about that.

"Thank you," he says, and *oh.* I missed the sound of his voice. I blink down at my pamphlets before looking up again.

"We can talk over here," I say, gesturing toward the desk where I do most of my callbacks. Distant professionalism: I wear it like it's a favorite pair of shoes.

Marisela doesn't go back to her office, instead taking a place where the office intern usually sits. A few desks away, Marisela's assistant Kori is on the phone, either listening to messages and recording notes on her pad or eavesdropping and doodling. I don't really care, either way—I'm glad to have the company. Aiden's so terminally private that I doubt he'll have anything to say worth their hearing, and I feel my breathing slow. *This will be fine,* I tell myself. *Separation will be permanent.*

I take a seat across from him, glad for the desk between us, my hands clasped on the cheap blotter where I sometimes scribble quick notes during callbacks. I open my mouth to say something, a bland *Nice to see you* or a more curt *What can I do for you.*

But before I can, he utters a single syllable on a sigh of relief that turns my insides to buzzy snowflakes, swirling all around. "Zo."

My knuckles turn white. "What can I do for you?"

He clears his throat, sits forward a little in the chair—too small for him, like almost all furniture is. I'd thought about that, the other night, at my condo. At how big he'd looked sitting on my breakfast stool, that awful morning he'd come to me. Like a colossus on a tiny pedestal, one that would break under his weight. "I need to say some things to you. And if you don't want me to say them here, that's all right. You tell me where and when."

I look over at Kori first, who snaps her eyes back down to her pad. Definitely doodling. Marisela's not even pretending to be busy; she's got her arms crossed and is leaning back in that chair and looking at the back of Aiden's head. If I felt braver, I'd tell him we should step out. Go out for coffee, take a walk, meet somewhere for a quiet, civilized debrief.

But I don't feel brave. I feel like I've cried a lot of tears in the last two weeks; I feel like I've missed him more than I can say. I feel like I don't trust myself alone with him, don't trust that I wouldn't make a fool of myself, that I wouldn't ask for just one sniff of that jacket. *Separation will be permanent.* "Here's fine."

He nods, a new determination settling over his features, taking a deep breath before he speaks. "I wanted to tell you this story," he says, and a ripple of something—something electric and arresting—travels up my spine. "You said, back when this thing started, you said I needed to tell a story if I wanted the camp."

"Right," I say, swallowing. I'm looking at a little space over his shoulder, a long-ago trick from my days in mediation. If you do it right, it seems like you're looking the client in the eye.

"Since Aaron died," he begins, and my eyes snap to his, where our gazes tangle for a brief, painful second. He breaks off, lowers his head, his elbows resting on his knees. He's close enough that even in the soft clamor of the office I can hear him swallow too frequently, a click in his throat. He's breathing sharply, inhaling through his nose, and what I realize, with a jolt of panic, is that he's crying, or at least he's trying not to cry.

"Let me start over," he says. "Just let me start this over."

"Okay." My voice is small, unsteady, the only sound my own tight throat will allow. I wait, holding my breath, for him to collect himself, for his shoulders to rise.

"When Aaron was alive, I was never alone. Ever. Even when I moved away, even when he was at his sickest, I was never alone, not really. I never believed in all that mystical twin shit, especially because of the way—" He breaks off again, rubs a hand over his hair, back to front, that now-familiar gesture. "Because of how different Aaron and I were. People used to think I was older than him, because I was so much bigger, that I'd got held back a grade or two. But then when he died, I got it. I've never been so alone in my life."

"I'm so sorry," I say, because I am. I may be done apologizing for Aaron's death, for the job I did. But I will never stop being sorry that Aiden has this pain, no matter what's happened with us.

He shakes his head, a firm, focused *no*. "You're the hero of this story," he says, fierce and plain, the clearest he's spoken since he sat down. "You were my rescue boat, Zo."

"Your—what?"

"My rescue boat. I was on this island, all by myself, and you came to rescue me."

"Aiden, I'm not sure—"

"The island is where I've been since he died. Or maybe it's where I always was, but I used to have him there with me. He died and he took half of me with him, I guess, and damn if I didn't know what to do. Damn if I didn't feel like I'd die on that island too."

I flatten my hands on the blotter, purse my lips and lean forward, any movement to remind him we're in public, that there are people listening. The Aiden I know would never want anyone to hear this. But he barrels on, talking right over my propriety, maybe even getting a little louder.

"I thought it was the camp that was going to be the making of me, or the—the remaking of me? The way I'd get put back together. But the minute I met you, Zo, I should've seen it was you. You came to rescue me and I should have known it a long time ago. I never laughed so much as I did with you, never in my life, and you're probably not going to believe that, seeing as how I kept it as hidden as I kept everything else with you. But I laughed all the time, on the inside."

My heart is beating so fast and my skin feels so flushed—I'm overwhelmed for myself, concerned for him, unsure of how I should respond to something so public, so different. His hair is a mess, and up close I can see that his t-shirt is on inside out. I lean forward, try to see if I can smell alcohol on him, even though I've never seen him drink more than a single beer at a time. I just—I don't know what to *do*.

I cling to the only thing I can in the moment. "Did you—have you heard anything about the camp?"

He ignores me. "That day you came to see me, that was the day I got off that island. That's the day my story got going again. You weren't an opportunity I saw. That's the worst thing I've ever said in my life, and you don't know how much I wish I could take that back. You were the beginning of everything for me. And I know you've got every reason not to be with me. I panicked that day at the lodge. I couldn't see past my own grief and guilt, couldn't see what you'd known all along about me and that camp. And I know I'm fucked up. I know I'm grouchy and antisocial and I'm guessing your friends don't think anything good about me at all. But I wanted to come here, and tell you that I love you."

He's said it loud enough that Kori gasps a little, and I'm pretty sure Marisela is giving heart eyes to the back of his head while she scoots her chair a little to the side, trying to get a better look at him. I notice these things because I don't know what to do with what he's just said. I've spent the last two weeks in hell, missing him, hating him, loving him.

Hating myself for loving him.

"I think I've loved you since you fainted in my driveway. Since you handed me my ass at darts. I should've told you that a hundred times before now. I should have followed you right out of that lodge, should have known I only had one shot to get off that island with you and I fucking blew it, and I will regret it every day of my life, Zo, I promise you that."

"Aiden, please, this is—" *This is too much, too hard,* I want to say. I will never move on from this.

"I know I messed up our ending. For the story, I mean. I don't expect anything from you. You've done more for me than I've ever deserved. But if you call me, Zo, if you ever call me, or need me, I'll come. I owe you everything, and I will love you even if you never let me see your face again. You are the best person, my favorite person, the only person I needed to prove that there was still something good for me in this life after Aaron."

He stands then, the chair scraping across the floor, and looks down at me, not like he's just told me he loves me but more like he's about to do ten paces before a duel. If I were in my right mind I'd be able to laugh at how comically, out-of-place aggressive he looks in contrast to all the perfect, soft, beautiful things he has just said.

But I'm not in my right mind. I'm in my shocked, overtired, on-the-verge-of-tears mind. I love him back—of course I love him back—but I'm hurt right down to the center of myself and I am terrified of everything. I don't even move.

He leans across the desk and down, presses a firm kiss to the top of my head, so I'm looking right at the notch in his throat that smells so good, where I've pressed my nose to him a dozen times, and my eyes sting with the tears I'm holding back.

He doesn't see them, because he doesn't look again. He just turns and leaves the way he came, all his words clanging around the room behind him.

Chapter 20

Aiden

"I don't know, man," says Ahmed, wiping the back of his hand across his brow. "I wouldn't have gone to where she works."

"Oh, you don't know," says Charlie. "You've asked Betty on a date at her work once a week since October."

"She's gonna come around," Ahmed says, leaning down to roll up another length of carpet. "I think she likes my beard."

"I think she likes more ironic facial hair. One of her bartenders has a mustache that curls at the ends," Charlie answers, but she's teasing. I'm pretty sure Ahmed's right, actually, and Betty will come around. The guy's damned charming, after all.

We're at my place, the three of us and my pop, tearing out the carpet in the living room. Yesterday I'd done the hallway, and over the next couple of days I'll get after the bedrooms too. My mom's back in the kitchen, working steadily through the cabinets, a big donation box set on the table, ridding the space of extra small appliances and utensils, all the stuff she left here but that I never really use.

It was my idea, that morning after I'd woken up on the floor in Aaron's room, cold and stiff jointed, to get to work on this house, cleaning it up, updating it as best I can. Can't say yet what I'm doing it for—whether I'll sell it and start over in a place of my own, or make this place into something new. Either way, it's been a good distraction, and especially good over the last two days, while I've done exactly what Ahmed's doing right now—ruminating over whether I made a mistake, going to Zoe.

"What I'm saying is," he adds, grabbing for a roll of duct tape and sitting on the roll of carpet he's just finished with, "you should've done something bigger. Skywriting a big ol' *I'm sorry* over her place or something."

Charlie takes the tape from him, picks at the corner until she frees a new length. "Disagree. Big gestures are empty. You've got to do the simple things." She's smiling as she helps Ahmed tape up the carpet, and I guess that's got to do with her and Autumn, with the way they've been fixing things between them over the last month. These days Charlie carries around a pocket-sized schedule Autumn made for her, one that's got blocked-out times for video calls, a small box-chart where Charlie can cross off the days until their next visit. It's not like I'm trying to look closely at it, but there's a lot of pink hearts on the thing.

I try not to be jealous.

"Doing all right over there, Pop?" I ask, looking to where my father's stood from his place pulling staples from the hardwood. I can see he's thinking about making an escape to the kitchen.

"Your friends talk a lot," he says, as if he thinks he's being quiet enough that the people less than ten feet away from him won't hear.

"Rude," says Charlie, but she laughs as she watches him retreat, and he waves a hand behind him. Despite his complaints, it seems maybe like my pop likes the noise, at least for a little while, or maybe—*maybe*—he just likes being around me.

Three times since that night he told me, in his own way, to get my shit together, we've gone to one of those group meetings my mother told me about. We sit in the back, not much talking from the O'Leary contingent, but no one seems to mind. The first time, I'd barely been able to sit still, shifting in my seat, crossing and uncrossing my arms, rolling my shoulders, restless with listening to others in the room being so open, so raw and tearful and sometimes angry. At one point, during that first meeting, I'd looked over at Pop, eager to commiserate, eager for a shared *How are these people doing this* look, but he'd been perfectly still. Not comfortable, I guess—I don't think anyone would be comfortable with grief like this. But he sure as shit wasn't hiding from it.

So I wasn't, either.

It was the third meeting that gave me the idea to go to Zoe. I'd been tired, coming off a night shift, only time for a quick shower and change before I'd picked up Pop to go. We'd come in late, and I didn't mind a bit, skipping the Styrofoam-cup coffee and awkward small talk that preceded the first two I'd attended.

There'd been a woman there, maybe in her forties, tall and calm looking, dressed in a navy pantsuit and heels like the ones I'd seen Zoe wear—thin, sharp like a weapon, almost scarily tall. When she'd raised her hand to share, she'd done it as though she'd been preparing for it, and maybe she had. She'd lost her daughter two years ago—seventeen, a car wreck, one late Friday night. Not even a year later, she and her husband had divorced, like lots of couples who lose kids. That was okay, she'd said, maybe not okay but understandable, because things hadn't been all that great even before. But the problem was, some guy at her work asked her out last week, and she'd said yes. Then she'd lost it, had spent an hour sobbing in a bathroom stall before finally taking the rest of the day off. "I said yes before I even thought about it," she'd said. "I forgot that I'm not a woman who goes on dates. I haven't gone on dates for eighteen years."

"Are you going to go?" one of the other group members had asked, and without thinking about it I'd sent him a sharp look for his curiosity. Jesus, it was so *intrusive*. All of this was so intrusive.

But no one else seemed to think so, not even her. She'd only shrugged and said, "I don't know. Should I?" and then it seemed like everyone had an opinion: *It all depends if you're ready; It's too soon if it makes you have that response; Sometimes you have to get out there; I'll bet your ex hasn't waited to start dating; Do you feel like you'd be betraying your daughter's memory?* And I'd been near enough to shouting at everyone, to asking them what business it was of theirs, before it'd hit me like a brick over the head: she's *making* it their business. She was brave—that's what I realized while I watched her listen back, while I listened to her give tentative answers that she wasn't sure about. Sometimes she'd say one thing, and then walk it back, a big mess of jumbled thoughts that wasn't at all like how she looked. She was brave, figuring out how to live her life, in all this shitty aftermath. Figuring out how to see what was still left around her.

And I was such a fucking coward.

Somewhere in the middle of it, I'd stood from my seat, not thinking, and the guy at the front of the room, the one who runs these things, had looked at me and said, "Did you want to share something today?"

"Next time," I'd said, and looked down at Pop, who was already putting his arms back into his coat. I *did* want to share something, but only with her, first.

I'd dropped Pop off back at home, had tried to prepare myself, on the way to Legal Aid, for seeing her in the flesh again. I *had* seen her, once, since that day at the campground, but only by accident. I'd opened the camera app on my phone to snap a photo of the serial number on a box of latex gloves I needed to reorder for the squad inventory, and there she'd been, a freeze-frame of her stern face at the end of that video, the one she'd taken at my house the morning she'd fainted in my driveway. My finger had hovered over the screen, desperate to see her mouth move, to hear her say my name.

But I didn't do it. I'd closed the app, had torn off the corner of the box of gloves instead and marched it back to the office with me, my phone burning a hole in my pocket. Her face burning a hole in my heart.

So maybe I wasn't as prepared as I should have been. Maybe I should've thought it through. Not skywriting, but damn. A little polish wouldn't have hurt. Fuck, my t-shirt had been inside out, I'd realized, once I'd gotten back into the truck, my hands shaking. I'd probably looked like a hobo.

"Maybe you ought to call her again," says Ahmed, interrupting my thoughts.

A part of me bristles, an old habit dying hard. But I'm trying to remember that woman, letting everyone weigh in on her possible date. "I told her I don't expect anything from her," I say. "I meant it."

There's a beat of silence, probably while Charlie and Ahmed exchange one of their looks about me, but it's an easy silence, and we each go back to our tasks, Ahmed and Charlie starting to work on cutting up a new section, me taking up the staple removal my dad abandoned. I take deep breaths while I work, try to let loose the tension that's so heavy in my gut. This might be it. This might be the life I have from now on, and I've got to get right with that. It's a good life, building a team with Ahmed and Charlie. Making things right with my family. Figuring out what to do with Aaron's money, something that I've accepted will take some time.

It'll never be as good as it could have been, if I'd managed to keep her, but I've got to live with that. With what I did to her, and with what we did to each other, starting out the way we did.

After a while, my mom wanders in, looking over our progress, her gaze lingering on me longer, faint but obvious concern in her eyes. "How about a break? I could make you guys something."

I almost laugh as I stand, brushing carpet fibers off my knees. It would have annoyed me a week ago, this caring enthusiasm, but now I take it for what it is. She's just enjoying this, people in this house, and I expect it's something she missed long before Aaron died. Once he'd gotten sick, really sick, my parents had stopped socializing much, had stopped opening their door to neighbors and friends who had always, always come around a lot when we were growing up. Right now, she's acting like it's snack time during a playdate, and I guess that's all right for as long as she's here.

"Oh," I hear her say, a little confused, and when I look up at her, she's watching out the open front door, the one we've been tossing rolls of carpet out of all morning.

I hear a car door slam, and I think my heart stops for a beat. I look at my mom first, because I'm too chickenshit to look out the door, to get disappointed. Just for a second, I want to live in the reality that it's her out there.

Mom turns her face to me, gives me a steady look. "Aiden," she says, her face serious and kind. "There is nothing from me you need to worry about." *It's her,* I'm thinking, and the thought is pounding so loud that I almost don't hear what she says next. The truth is, it wouldn't matter even if I didn't hear her. I'm almost halfway out the door already.

But I'm still glad I catch it. "If you love her," she says, "I'm sure I'll love her too."

* * * *

I almost don't believe it at first, really seeing her out there.

She's come from her office, I'd bet, or else she's just come here to do business. She's got that coat on, the camel-colored one, from the day I walked her to work. Beneath it, her legs in black tights, long and shapely in her heels.

I do what I did all those weeks ago when I saw her car pull up to my driveway. I step out onto my porch, take the two steps down, and eye her, as cautious as I was that first day. This time, I'm not afraid of what she's come to start. I'm afraid of what she's come to finish.

I take a deep breath, walk toward where she stands, stock still, by her car, and I think that was her plan all along. We're doing this, right in this driveway, right where it started, and that doesn't bode well for me, I guess. But whatever she's got to say to me, I'll take it. I've earned it.

I tuck my hands in my pockets, take in her face. Two days ago, she was so surprised to see me. She'd barely said anything at all, her skin pale and her eyes tired. Still beautiful, but not quite herself. Today, it's different—color in her cheeks. Her lips pink, glossy. Her posture ramrod straight. Whatever she's about to say, she's thought good and hard about it.

"Your story needs work."

In my pockets, my hands twitch, knuckles bumping the fabric. I clear my throat, but when I speak, my voice is still rough, thick with the same emotion that had been there in her office. "Should've practiced more," I say. "Got nervous."

She nods, looks out toward the street, as though she's cataloging all the houses along the way. I'll bet she can see more of it on a day like today, everything more visible now that the leaves are almost all fallen from the trees. I try to be grateful for this pause, long enough for me to gaze at her profile. It feels like I've loved to watch her for the longest time.

"I know you're sorry about what happened at the lodge," she says, bringing those gold eyes back to mine. "And I know it was...a hard day for you. A confusing day. I wish it hadn't happened like that."

Her eyes move to my throat, to the heavy swallow that must bob my neck. I'm nervous; I'm so fucking nervous to have her here. She holds my fate in her hands, and I think I must be looking at her the same way she looked at me all those weeks ago, when the day was too hot and she was too overwhelmed, coming to me with something that must have been so hard to say.

Her expression softens, giving me all the sympathy I didn't give her that day. "But I love you too," she says. "Obviously."

Holy shit, I think, my mind stuttering over what she's said. *She's going to forgive me.* She's not even done speaking before I take a step toward her, my chest flooded with hope. But she holds a hand up, her sharp-edged jaw set, and it stops me in my tracks. My shoulders tense with all that deadlocked feeling. We stand close, maybe an arm's length between us, but right now it feels like a gulf, and I have to steel myself, tighten up everything in my middle to keep from putting my arms around her, pulling her toward me and keeping her from saying what I'm afraid she'll say.

"In this story you're telling," she says, keeping her eyes on me, "we rescue each other. That day I came here, you rescued me, too, and not just because I damseled-in-distress all over your driveway." She lifts her chin, looking strong and unflappable, so unlike a damsel in distress that it'd be funny if my heart weren't in my throat. "It was wrong of me to come here that day—"

"Zo—" I begin, but she shakes her head, purses her lips. I may well break my back teeth from the way I clamp them down, wanting to stop this, but she let me say my piece, and I've got to do the same.

"And I knew it was, almost as soon as I pulled up. I knew I was looking for a quick fix for...for the things I'd been feeling about my work and my past and my...myself, really." She stops, clears her throat. "But even still, you gave me something I didn't even know I was looking for, and you got me unstuck from the life I'd been living. You don't know how grateful I'll always be for that. For helping me see that sometimes you start something for a selfish reason, but you can continue it—you can finish it for another kind of reason. A good, kind, unselfish reason. And for helping me see that…that I have to move on." That composed expression breaks then, and her eyes track down. She twists the tip of one shoe, just a little, against the driveway's rocky surface.

When our eyes meet again, I wonder if she can see what's in mine.

Defeat.

She's come here for closure, in spite of the feelings between us. She's ending it. A thank-you and goodbye, good luck, have a nice life, and I can't even say I blame her.

Forgiveness is never easy, after all.

But then she takes another step toward me, sets a hand on my forearm. Her hand is cold against my warm skin, and goosebumps rise in the wake of the path she takes to my wrist. She tugs, softly, so that I pull my hand from my pocket.

And then she links her fingers with mine.

My eyes close with the feeling of it. It's relief or fear, hope or anguish. I don't know which, won't know until she gives me an answer, something I can hold on to. When I open my eyes again, I'm looking almost right into hers. We're so matched when she wears those heels. "Remember that night at the bonfire?" she asks, and I nod, a tip of my chin down. I look at our joined hands, unmoving, just like I did that night. I'm trying to make this driveway and that dirt clearing collapse in this moment, to forget about all the shit that happened in between. "You said it couldn't be about anything but what we want from each other. You and me, Aiden, we've got to be done with debts. With what we owe each other."

I raise my chin and look at her again. Is this what she means? That there's just too much of that between us for it ever to work?

"Zo," I say again, after a too-long pause. My voice is almost a whisper, a fact that'd embarrass me if I gave even one single damn about my pride in this moment. "I told you that night, you are smart as fuck. Whatever you're telling me here, you're going to have to spell it out. I miss you so much I can't think straight."

She laughs, breathy and quiet, and there it is again, that rush of hope. "I'm saying I want to be with you. Not because I owe you. Not because you owe me. Just—just because."

It's lightning fast, my hand jerking away from hers, the other one coming out of my pocket, and then I'm catching her up, my arms around her waist, her feet off the ground so I can hold her tight and high against me, so I can press my face in the soft curve of her neck, so I can release the gusty sigh of relief and—yeah, fuck it—the quiet, pained sob that says everything about how much I've missed her. How much I want her, how much I need her.

When I put her down it's to cup her face between my hands, to set my mouth against hers, soft and searching, the first kiss we never really had. And it feels so good, so natural, nothing I've got to rehearse or practice for. I feel her hands on my sides, stroking my skin through my t-shirt, and my hips pitch forward, just a little, wanting to press her back, into the door of her car if I have to, just so I can get closer. My whole body is electric with relief and gratitude.

She pulls back from me before I'm ready, and I must let out a noise of dissatisfaction, one that makes her mouth curve in a smile, her lips pink and swollen. "Wait," she says, lifting a hand to my chest, setting her palm over my thudding heart. "The camp?" she asks.

"You know that wasn't for me, Zo," I say. "They knew it too."

She nods, pats me where her hand rests. "I talked to Lorraine, but I didn't want to ask her. You're okay, though?"

Okay? Holy hell, I could pick her car up and throw it in the street if she asked me to—I'm that jacked up, that happy. But I know what she means, or at least I think I do, some of the fog in my head clearing now that she's here. "I'm all right," I say. "Going to a support group. Getting my shit together. You got me unstuck too."

She smiles, leans forward and kisses me again, like a quick reward between two people who do this all the time. "Sorry it took me a couple of days. I had to think about it. Talk to my friends." She shrugs. "That's how I am, I guess."

"I would've waited longer, Zo. I meant what I said. I would've come, whenever. Wherever."

That earns me another smile, this one shy, not much like the Zoe I know, but that's the thing about her and me. We're going to see a lot of different sides to each other now, now that we're doing this for real.

"I applied for a job too," she says. "I think I'm going to be good at it."

"I'm sure you are," I say, touching my thumb to that smile, loving the feel of her lips against my skin. "I can't wait to hear."

Her mouth flattens into something more serious then, those gold-brown eyes meeting mine. "We've got so much work to do, you and me." Then she tips into me, setting her forehead against my jaw, and I hear the deep breath she takes, the way she inhales me. "Your parents. My friends. The money. Everything."

It won't be easy, the way we've started. Behind me, in that house, are two people Zoe has to get to know in a whole new way. It doesn't matter what my mom said, before I came out here. It doesn't matter that she'll be on her best behavior, will treat her as nice as I didn't on that first day Zoe came. It'll still be hard, those memories. It'll take time.

I pull her close again, my arms wrapping around her now, her hand pressed on my chest between us. "We'll be all right," I tell her, and I mean it. I'll *make* it all right. I've worked so hard, since Aaron, every day a new drudgery, a new challenge to get through while I ran from my grief, but none of it made me feel good. None of it made me feel excited, like I was going toward something. I can't wait to work that hard for me and Zoe, for our life together. "Turns out, we make a good team."

She laughs, short puffs of breath against my neck that make the base of my spine tickle. I feel her face shift as she looks over my shoulder, toward the house. "Not so much an island anymore," she whispers, and I crane my neck to look behind me, to see my mom and pop in the house, looking out the storm door at us, Ahmed's big body behind them. I don't see Charlie, not at first, but she's there too, pushing Ahmed off to the side so she can see past him. No, not so much an island, and it took her to get me to see it.

I turn back toward Zoe, and her cheeks are flushed in embarrassment at our audience. "Come in," I say, a teasing smile spreading across my face. "I'll make you a sandwich."

"In a minute," she says, and for that minute we're quiet, holding each other, folding into each other in relief. She feels so good that I feel familiar pressure build in my chest, around my throat, behind my eyes, though it's not so terrifying now. This'll be new to her too, this cracked-open version of me, but she won't mind. She's the one who's been trying to get in there, after all, chipping away at that hard shell. I tip my mouth so it's next to her ear, the same way I know makes her shiver. "I can't believe I deserve you, Zo," I tell her, quiet words for her only in this little cocoon of privacy we've made out here in the open air. "But I'm going to treat you so good."

She leans back, one of her cool hands on my neck, the other still over my heart, her smile widening as she looks at me. "Take it from me, Boy Scout," she says, patting my chest gently again. "Sometimes, we get a lot more than we deserve."

Epilogue

Zoe

Two years later

"Sorry, sorry, sorry!" I call, bursting through the door, dropping my purse on the table, kicking off my shoes in the entry, not bothering to set them aside. I strip off my coat, sort of smooshing it, rather than actually hanging it, on the wall where Aiden installed a coatrack last year when he moved in. I count it a win that I don't hear it slide to the floor when I hustle away toward the bedroom. As I pass through the living room, I notice my empty mug of tea from last night, my laptop closed and sitting on one of the couch cushions, my favorite throw blanket bundled in the spot where I'd sat last night, working on a brief while Aiden sat beside me, studying for a test he took early this morning.

I only wince for a second.

I've gotten more used to it now, more easy with myself and this space, over the last couple of years. I'm busy, that's part of it—not so bound to routines anymore, and relishing some of the chaos of my job rather than trying to recover from it. But part of it is sharing this space with Aiden, finding my peace with him rather than in quiet, sleek, pristine rooms. It's not always tidy in here when I get home, but it's always *restful*, knowing he's here or that he will be.

Well, it's *almost* always restful.

Our bedroom looks a bit chaotic at the moment, a big open duffel on the bed, a stack of mostly unfolded clothes beside it, my half-formed efforts at packing this morning before I had to get to the office. Aiden's boots and mine are beside each other on the ground, a lot of miles on them now. The sight's not unfamiliar, and not just because Aiden and I started out going on weekend trips together, back when we were faking it. We've taken a lot of trips, me and him—at first, to places that were important for getting to know each other better, more honestly. To Florida, first, where we spent part of the Christmas holiday after the initial, somewhat strained efforts between me and the O'Learys when Aiden and I got back together. Outside of Barden, things had been—well, not easy, but easi*er* between us, and as Aiden had promised, his parents had started to see me differently, especially when it turned out that Robert and I both had a lot to say about a show with a park ranger. Last year I'd started receiving a package from them once a month, addressed only to me. It's always something jarred and homemade—pickles, jam, cherry syrup, orange marmalade. Two months ago, the package had included a recipe, and Aiden had smiled and smiled before sticking it to the fridge.

We'd gone to California too, in part to see my mother, but also so I could show Aiden where I'd grown up, where my father's office had been, where I'd gone to school. I'd even shown him Christopher's bar, part of my history, though he'd been grim faced and silent as we'd driven by. My mother, of course, loved him—she loves men, gorgeous ones especially—and Aiden had tolerated her fawning attentions, though in the hotel at night, curled around each other in bed, he'd asked, endearingly frustrated, "Why doesn't she ever ask any questions about you?"

There'd been other trips: Colorado, to see friends from his previous job, and to teach me how to snowboard (not a successful endeavor, but I did like the snow pants). Vermont, last fall, where we'd taken an alarming number of pictures of turning leaves, laughing at night as we sorted through them (*They all look the same!*). Six months ago, our biggest trip, to Italy, Aiden's first time out of the country and also probably the last time he ever tries to convince me to go topless on a beach.

Adventures, big and small, for the two of us.

He comes out of the bathroom then, dressed but his hair still wet from the shower, and I make a weak effort to ignore the heat that gathers low in my stomach, between my legs, at the sight of him. "How'd it go?" I ask.

He nods, gives me a small smile, and leans in to give me a kiss—a natural, quick intimacy that still makes me feel warm and safe all over. It's like this now with me and Aiden, our lives joined in all the ways that matter, except the most official ones. I'm reluctant about that, for the obvious reasons, for mistakes I've made before, but lately—lately, I think: *Maybe it's time.*

"All right, I think," is all he says, but I'm guessing that means he aced it. He actually *is* a bit shy, Aiden; that's what I've learned since I've been with him. What I used to think was dislike for me was—well, maybe partially dislike for me, once upon a time. But also shyness.

He's been working to get certified as a paramedic instructor, a new challenge he's excited about to add to everything else he's doing. I'd be worried about his schedule, but it's funny—we're more alike than we'd thought, initially. We both like to stay busy, both enjoy the challenge of hard work. I've worked harder in the last year than I have in all the years I spent at Willis-Hanawalt, and all of it, even the tough parts, feel so *good.*

This weekend, some of the hardest work, some of the work we've shared between us, pays off.

"I'll be ready in five minutes," I say. "I'm sorry I'm late. I had this—"

He quiets me, putting his lips against my neck, pressing there softly before he says, "It's okay. We're not in a hurry."

I shiver, close my eyes briefly to regain focus.

"Nervous?" I ask. He'll do a speech at this, the dedication, and he doesn't much like speeches. This one, I know almost nothing about, but I know he's been working at it, late nights using my laptop, a little file in the corner of my desktop that's titled *For Aaron.*

He only shakes his head.

I sort through the stack of clothes, shove a few things next to his in the duffel, grab my bag of toiletries from the bathroom. He leans in the doorway, watches me with a dangerous smile while I unzip my dress at the side, shimmy it down just for the gleam he gets in his eyes. "Bet you can't wait to see me in flannel again," I tease, rolling down my stockings with exaggerated slowness. Across the room, his eyes turn sharp, predatory.

"Zo," he says, his voice low, "I'm sorry, but we're going to be a little late."

* * * *

Aiden

The campground went to Val.

No one pretends like it's a joint affair, like Hammond's got anything to do with it, but that's just fine, I think. When I see Val and her three girls there, Hammond on the periphery, I think it's still what Paul meant, back when he called me that day. This camp is like something that came from them, a future for their girls—older now, but still all giggling innocence, more interested in Zoe and her shiny hair and lip gloss than they are in me. We've gotten to know them more over the last couple of years, the group from the Stanton Valley Campground competition forming a little society of our own, meeting here every once in a while for hikes, for cards, for catching up.

That's partly because there'd been genuine affection, even after what Zoe and I had done, especially after we'd made our apologies. But it's also because Val realized quickly that her summer sleepaway camp for girls might benefit from year-round programming, and soon enough Stanton Valley had become a joint project, Sheree and Tom working with Val to plan outdoor excursions for her school and his community groups in the fall, Lorraine and Tom holding retreats for over-fifties in the springtime. Wilderness/Wellness, of course, needs a single-use space, and they've moved on here in Virginia, finding a spot about an hour west of here. A portion of Aaron's money has been invested in the start-up.

But a portion of it has gone here too, to the acreage Zoe and I bought from Val and dedicated as a memorial forest, just over seventy acres that we've named after Aaron and that'll be managed by a local land trust, used to teach summer campers about conservation and sustainability. Yesterday, our first morning here, I'd done the dedication, revealing the small sign Zoe and I had picked out a couple of months ago and making the speech I'd started writing over two years ago. *My brother was more than just his addiction,* it had started, and then I'd told them all that much more—how much he'd loved this camp, first of all. Being outside, no matter the hassles it caused him, healthwise. He liked the world, my brother, no matter how tough it always was on him.

It'd taken me a long time, lots of those damned group therapy meetings, to be strong enough to do that, and afterward, Zoe had hugged me tight and told me how proud she was. But she knows as well as I do that this, like everything else about the foundation we've started in my brother's honor, is owed in part to her, to the work we did together to research and get it started. It's a scholarship program, mostly, helping to fund rehabilitation and aftercare for addicts.

And if I'd thought Zoe was fierce before—well. Seeing her tackle her work at Legal Aid while she works with me on the foundation has given me a new perspective. She likes it out there—being challenged, solving problems, kicking ass. Lately, she and Marisela have been making noise about going out on their own, hanging out a shingle and shoring up funding to take their legal services work independent.

So maybe that's why, on Sunday morning—a morning I'd hoped to spend sleeping in with her, pressed up close in the shoved-together bunks I'd arranged as soon as we'd arrived—she'd woken up early and nudged me awake, first with her sharp elbows and then, more effectively, with soft, tickling kisses along my abdomen. "I'm going to do the pole today," she'd whispered, once I'd murmured enough to be counted awake.

"You're damn right you are," I'd said, catching her hips and pulling her closer.

"I think you spent too much time around Hammond yesterday," she'd said, wriggling away, leaving me hard and aching.

We don't get all that many lazy Sunday mornings, me and Zoe. She's still got brunch, and every month or so it turns into a whole group affair—loud, sometimes hours-long meals, the kind of thing I once would've hated. But brunch has a lot of Zoe's laughter, a lot of her teasing me, teasing her friends. It has her hand on my knee or on my back, some constant connection she keeps with me. And it's got people I like too—I get Ahmed and Charlie to come when they can, but also every one of Zoe's friends is a friend of mine, a family we've built between the two of us.

I grumble all the way on our hike out to the pole, a comical role reversal that Zoe doesn't hesitate to remind me of. "Look at me, doing this hike, Boy Scout." She turns to walk backward, grinning. "You're dragging ass like it's your first time out here."

"I'm dragging ass because it's eight in the morning and you gave me a hard-on."

She gives an exaggerated pout, then places a finger over her mouth, shushing me.

Good thing too, because when we get to the clearing, Paul and Lorraine are already there, Val and Sheree too, all the kids nearby, laughing and drawing pictures in the red clay with sticks.

"I'm going first," Zoe says, rushing to Paul for help getting harnessed in. Sheree comes up beside me, pats my shoulder. "Look at her now," she says, shaking her head in surprise. "She's tough, that one."

"That she is."

"Well done yesterday, Aiden," says Val, flanking my other side. "I still think it would've been better with the microphone," she adds, in true Val form, and I catch Sheree's good-natured smirk in my peripheral. I think Sheree was relieved, honestly, not to get the camp. As much as she loves it here, I don't know if she ever truly wanted to leave her school and her

home, and anyways, Val's as smart as Zoe knew all along, a good person
to take this camp into the future.

I'm quiet, watching Zoe harness up, watching while she crouches down
to say something to one of the twins, who laughs and puts her little hands
on Zoe's cheeks. I got no problem saying it takes my breath away, watching
her, knowing she's mine to love, and it's still, no matter what I've done in
the last couple of years, the thing that makes me most proud in my life.
If Aaron were here, he'd love her too, and I'm proud I can think about
that without feeling the big, black emptiness I used to feel. I still get that
phantom-limb feeling, but somehow it's become its own kind of comfort,
knowing he'll never really leave me.

Before she turns to climb, Zoe gives me a goofy thumbs-up, blows me a
kiss. I make my face mock serious in challenge. I watch her go up, and with
each handhold she takes it seems like my chest gets a little tighter—pride,
sure, but also anticipation and gratitude and lust and love and every other
thing Zoe makes me feel. Two years with her and I'm back in the world in
ways I never even thought of when Aaron was still alive—traveling and
making friends and hell, starting to be a teacher in the next couple months,
so long as that test I took on Friday went as well as I thought. Two years
with me and she goes to sleep at night excited about the next day, okay
with herself and what she's doing.

And that's when I think it. *Know* it.

It's not really relaxing, what I'm thinking—it's not like a peace settles
over me. It's a change of plan, after all, something big I'm going to spring
on the woman I love when she's reaching the top of a high, lean pole, no
matter that she's strapped in, perfectly safe.

"Zo!" I shout up at her, knowing she won't fall. She's at the top, steady
now, as good as Sheree ever was, arms loose at her sides. I may be far
away, but I know her body so well, know when there's no tension in it.
She tips her chin down, finds me beneath her, my arms crossed over my
chest, my feet planted apart. As loose as her body is up there, mine is
tense and coiled, as alert now as I am out on the job. But this is it, this
is the moment, no matter what I'd planned for later: the fire I was going
to light for when she got home from work, the dark purple irises—her
favorite—I was going to buy to stuff that damned vase full of, the one I
know started this whole thing. I was going to ask Kit and Greer to hide
back in our bedroom so they could scream and hop in delight once I'd
asked her, same as they did when I went to them one night two months
ago and asked them for help picking out a ring. To be honest, I'd asked

for their permission first, but then for help with the ring, help they'd given with thrilled, clapping enthusiasm.

But this is it.

I take a deep breath, no way she can see that, but if she's like me she might feel it, might feel a bit of what I'm feeling down here—sure as hell but also nervous as fuck.

"Marry me," I call out, loud and steady. Beside me Paul claps his hands together once, and in my peripheral I see Lorraine lean into him. I'm not taking my eyes off Zoe up there, but I'll bet Lorraine's smile is a mile wide.

"Oh, *Aiden*," says Val, a note of disappointment in her voice. "This is really all wrong. When Hammond proposed, he—"

"You cannot be serious with this, Val," says Sheree, laughing. "This is the most romantic thing I've ever seen."

Zoe hasn't moved up there. She's standing at the top of the pole as if she's an extension of it, as if she's just grown up to her full height. She wouldn't want me to say so, but I like this about it most of all. Being on my knee in front of Zoe for this wouldn't be down far enough for what I'm asking her, for how grateful I'll be if she says yes. We're done with debts, done with owing each other, but that doesn't mean I'll ever get used to the idea that I deserve her.

"I'd want to keep my name," she shouts down, and Sheree laughs.

"Fine by me," I say, trying to keep down the smile I feel breaking through.

"I'm not making a scrapbook, Val!"

"I give up," Val mutters, but she directs her next comment to me. "Of course I'd give you a discount on the lodge as a reception space."

If there's more chatter I don't hear it. I'm not going to hear anything until she answers me. Even from this far away I know her eyes are locked on mine; I can see that smile spreading across her face. I can feel her loving me all the way from up there, and she doesn't need to say anything at all.

Because Zoe—beautiful, smart, kind, complicated Zoe, *my* Zoe, my future *wife* Zoe—she stretches her arms out, and with a shout of happiness, she takes the leap down to me.

Acknowledgments

As always, an immediate and profuse thank you to readers for taking a chance on a new author and a new series. I absolutely fell in love with Zoe and Aiden while I wrote their story—they have stayed with me for months and months—and I hope you shared in some of that love while you were reading.

One lesson Zoe learns in this book is that sometimes you have to lean on the people you love the most and show them the parts of yourself you like the least. This lesson was also one I had to learn, and while I wrote Zoe and Aiden's book I relied on many friends—old and new, in-person and online, writers and non-writers alike—to help get me through insecurity and writer's block and all the other strange, relentless ups and downs of writing a book. A special thanks to dearest friends Amy, Jackie, and Elizabeth, and my mom, who all keep me honest and who remind me I've almost always been where I am before, and have come out on the other side.

Heaps of thanks to the romance writing community more generally, which generously welcomed me to the fold over the course of the period during which I drafted this book. I am especially grateful to Ainslie Paton, Olivia Dade, Adele Buck, Jen DeLuca, Elisabeth Lane, Adriana Anders, and Katharine Ashe, as well as to every single incredible participant in #RWChat and to the ladies of HBIC Nation. An extra special thanks to Eloisa James, who has always been unfailingly generous and kind to me, no matter what sort of dumb question I asked her.

What kind of luck I've got to be able to work with the extraordinary Esi Sogah, I'll never completely understand—but I'll take it. Esi, you are the most fun and the most sharp and you send the best gifs, and everyone who reads this book should know that it is one million percent better because of Esi's influence. My agent Taylor Haggerty is similarly amazing and magic-making. Thank you to the entire team at Kensington/Lyrical, especially Lauren Jernigan and Michelle Addo; thanks to April LeHoullier for a keen copyediting eye and to Tammy Seidick for another heart-eyes cover.

To my husband—I mean, it *is* annoying that you manage to be as smart, handsome, kind, and funny as you are. But I love you forever anyways and I could never write a good hero without you there to remind me what one is truly like.

Also by Kate Clayborn

Keep reading for a sneak peek at Greer's story
Coming soon!

And don't miss
BEGINNER'S LUCK

Available now from
Lyrical Shine
Wherever ebooks are sold

Prologue

Greer

When I first see him there, I think I must still be dreaming.

I'd woken up at three-thirteen a.m.—unlucky, that—the sharp planes of his face still fresh in my mind, my skin still flushed, the sheets tangled around my legs, and I'd nearly gasped in embarrassment over it. Dreaming about *him*, of all people, a man I'd only met hours ago. A man so handsome I could barely look him in the eye without flushing. A man who wore all his vast experience in the rangy, confident movements of his body. A man whose friendly, innocent hug at the end of the night had felt like electricity to me, like being shocked awake after a long, unnatural slumber.

A man who also happens to be my best friend Kit's brother.

Alex Averin.

Now he pauses as he steps across the threshold of Boneshaker's, my favorite coffee shop not two blocks from Kit's house, where he's supposed to be staying for the weekend—where, I've decided, I'll avoid until he leaves, since I'd basically gone acutely nonverbal in his presence. Between me and Zoe and Kit, my two closest friends, I've always been the quiet one, but last night I'd brought shyness to new heights, barely managing three full sentences over the course of dinner and dessert. I'd watched as Kit had beamed over him, proud of everything about her brother, and proud of everything that she was getting to show and tell him about her life here: her job, her newly-purchased house, even her budding friendship with Ben Tucker, a guy who I could already tell was more than half in love with her. And I'd watched as Zoe—cool and funny and unflappable—had traded stories with Alex of travel to Europe, to South America, even to Australia, where they'd both, apparently, visited the same koala refuge.

I'd just *watched*.

Watching. My speciality. For years, the only habit I was healthy enough to cultivate.

I return to that specialty now—so familiar, like I'm a wayward, crooked drawer that's been pushed back into its track and now can slide easily into place, flush with its surroundings, barely noticeable. I turn my body in my chair slightly so that I'm not directly facing the door, arranging my book in a way that makes it possible for me to seem like I'm reading, though I'm still one hundred percent tracking him. As he moves toward the counter, the heads of all three women at a table beside me turn to watch him, one of them actually letting her mouth fall open a little.

I can't say I blame her. He's beautiful, that's the thing—not just handsome, not just a strong jaw and a tall, fit leanness, broad shoulders and narrow hips, not just thick, jet-black hair that's gorgeously messy, exactly as it was in my dream, exactly as I'd *made* it in my dream. He's actually *beautiful*—smooth olive skin underneath his heavy stubble, and high, cut cheekbones that transform into something softer and kinder when he smiles. Full lips, white teeth, his right-side incisor a little crooked. Clear, bright green eyes that you can see across a room, framed with long, black lashes that leave a shadow on his skin when he lowers them.

From where I sit I watch him order, watch his mouth move: *coffee, black*. He pays in cash, shoves a dollar in the tip jar and the barista looks like she wants to propose marriage. He smiles at her and I try to telegraph her a message: *Oh, I know. It* hurts *when he smiles like that.*

He moves down the counter to wait for his coffee and I swivel again in my seat, curving my shoulders and looking down to my book again, hoping he doesn't see me. Without the cover of Kit and Zoe, my awkwardness will seem worse—either panicked silence or a blurting non-sequitur, and I don't think I could face his quizzical brow, his gentle smile of pitying encouragement, the same one he offered up last night across the table after I'd stumbled over answering a question as simple as *Where did you grow up?*

In my dream, though...he looked at me with total concentration. With desire.

I shake my head, force my eyes to focus, training them back at the top of the page of my textbook, so I can start reading all over again, since I'm sure I've lost every bit of information I read over in the minutes before he walked in.

"Hey," comes a quiet, deep, already familiar voice from above me, and for a second I keep my eyes down, hope I've somehow developed actual powers of invisibility, rather than just your standard wallflower syndrome.

But I can feel him there, watching me, those thick black brows probably arranging themselves into the most charming little furrow. *This again*, he's probably thinking.

When I turn to face him, to look up to meet those sea-glass eyes, my elbow knocks my textbook from the table, and Alex reaches a hand out, catching it easily at the spine, not even disrupting the steaming coffee he's holding in his left hand. I think I let out a small groan of frustration, or of exasperation—I'm sure at any moment, after seeing that display of his reflexes, either the barista or the open-mouthed latte-drinker will just toss her panties across the room at him.

"Cultural Anthropology," he says, looking down at the book he's just rescued, his lips tipping up wryly, some ironic recognition. This renowned photojournalist who's traveled the entire world, has seen it and so many of its cultures through his own eyes—who's shaped, through his lens, the way other people see it—holding my little college textbook, my little lottery-induced dream of a college degree. It must seem—

"I always wanted to take a class like this," he says, smiling down at me, and for a second I think about throwing *my* panties at him.

It feels like a good two and a half minutes of me simply *blinking* at him, adjusting to the handsome-glare his face gives off, but in actuality I'm pretty sure it's only a few startled seconds before I manage a weak, "It's a good class."

He nods, gestures to the seat across from me. "Mind if I sit?"

"Oh," I say, pulling my papers toward me, clearing space for him on the table. "Sure." Inside my head there's a tattoo of a thought: *Don't think about the dream.*

"Thanks," he says, sinking into his chair. "Didn't get much sleep last night." *Don't think about it*, I tell myself again, hopelessly.

"Did you and Kit have a late night?" I feel ludicrously pleased at how normal and casual I've managed to sound. Now that the shock has worn off—or I guess now that my eyes have adjusted to his presence—I feel a bit more settled, ready to converse like a normal person.

"Sort of," he says, and when he shifts in his seat I notice something for the first time. He has a bag with him—a sun-bleached canvas rucksack, one of its straps duct-taped, and as my eyes settle on it he reaches a hand down, tries to tuck it more tightly under the table.

"Are you—are you *leaving* already?" The disbelief in my voice—it seems to lash him like a whip. He snaps his head to the side to look out the window, inhaling sharply through his nose. "You're supposed to stay for the whole *weekend*," I add. Kit's been preparing for Alex's visit for days, ever since his quick, unexpected call to let her know he'd be in town—a call she'd greeted with such genuine excitement and hope that I'd immediately felt a prickle of unease. Never good luck, I'd thought, to look forward to something that much.

He looks back at me then, and I'm tempted to lower my eyes.

But Kit—Kit must be so *disappointed.*

"I got called in for a job," he says, and it could be true. Alex shoots for *The New York Times*, for the AP, once, even, for *National Geographic*, photographs that Zoe and I *ooh*-ed and *aah*-ed over when Kit had shown them to us last year. But because I'm good—I'm so, so good at seeing every single thing, at *watching*—I notice it. I notice the way the corner of his mouth, right there on the left side, twitches. Barely a split second of movement, a pull of his lips that'd be entirely hidden from the casual observer.

"You're lying." I stare right into those eyes, those sea-glass eyes I'd avoided looking at last night, and I hope mine are burning right into his. I hope I've put into them all the accusation I mean to level at him. Kit's heart is probably broken—all her plans for him this weekend, all the things she meant to show him about her new home. All the time she's been waiting for him to come.

I remember: I can do more than just watch. When it comes to the people I love, I can do anything. "You can't do this to her," I say. "You can't leave."

The look he gives me—it's nothing like what I saw in his face last night, nothing like the gentle, indulgent smiles he gave to Kit, nothing like the low, laughing surprise he'd had for Zoe's bold sense of humor. Nothing even like the open curiosity in his eyes when he'd seen me for the first time.

It looks like anger.

"I can," he says, and his voice is forceful. Unapologetic. So, so *confident.*

There's a thick silence between us, the sounds of the café tinkling and vague. But I hear his voice like an echo.

I can.

It sounds so—it sounds so *true*. There isn't anything stopping Alex—he's healthy, he's successful, he's made his own way in the world. Someone— his sister, me, anyone, probably—may tell him *you can't*, but he doesn't have to listen.

He could get up and leave right now. He could pick up his rucksack and take his coffee with him, walk out this coffee shop's doors. There'll be a trail of women's undergarments in his wake.

Instead he shifts in his seat, puts his elbows on the table, and holds his to-go cup between his hands. The movement puts him closer to me, the steam from his coffee wafting between us, warming the space between our bodies. For a split second I'm back in that dream, and I drop my eyes to the table. There's a stray penny, tail-side up, beside his right forearm.

"Out there," he says, nodding toward the door, his voice softer now, a still-rough texture to it that now doesn't sound quite so unapologetic. "Out there is the thing I waited for my whole life."

I press my lips together, roll them inward, a habit I seem to have picked up since I started my college classes. Trying not to over-participate, trying not to get a reputation as the eager adult degree student while the slackers in the back roll their eyes at me, hoping for an early release from class.

Alex's eyes dip to my mouth, and suddenly I don't care so much about seeming eager. I use a fingernail to tap out the curiosity I feel building in my shoulders, my elbows, my wrists. I hear the *plink, plink* of it against the ceramic. "What's that?" I ask, my voice hardly above a whisper.

And then he smiles. He smiles like he—like he somehow *knows*, like he heard me make that wish six months ago, the night Kit and Zoe and I had all joked about our possible lottery win, a win that became a shocking, I'm-still-not-over-it reality. The night I'd told my friends that all I'd want was an education.

"Freedom," he says, and he could not have cut me deeper if he'd held a hot knife against my body.

My secret wish, the one I'd made silently that same night our numbers came up, the one I'm working so hard to make come true—with my winnings, with my college classes, with every small effort I make to be stronger, healthier, more independent.

Without ever leaving the sixty-five square miles of this city.

I lean back in my seat, lengthening the distance between us. I let the moment stretch a beat too long, my eyes on my mug, my book, the penny. Strangely, even though we don't know each other well—at all, really—I can feel him waiting for me to argue, to push back. And when I finally meet his eyes, that's what I see there.

Expectation. Anticipation.

Maybe not quite what I saw in my dream, but maybe not all that different, either.

But Alex isn't who I thought he was, not if he'll leave Kit this way. And his freedom isn't the same as mine, not if it looks like this—a beat-up bag, a faraway look, no limitations, no attachments, no debts, no thought to who or what you leave behind.

I let go of that electric, curious heat he makes me feel. I replace it with all the disappointment I feel on behalf of my friend. I pull my book closer to me.

"I'd better get back to studying," I say, keeping my gaze level, uninterested, aloof—the corollary gift of my shyness for moments like these.

He doesn't wait long. Maybe a few seconds of taut silence before he stands again and hoists his bag over one shoulder, his cup of coffee still steaming in his hand. Oblivious, clearly, to the way so many eyes in the café are newly drawn to him.

"Greer," he says, tipping his chin down in some old-fashioned gesture of acknowledgment that—despite my new opinion of him—feels like a brand on my skin. His smile is different now: smaller, sadder. "Maybe I'll meet you again sometime."

And then he's gone, ducking out the same door he came in, and I don't see him again. Not for almost two whole years.

Not even in my dreams.

Beginner's Luck

When three friends impulsively buy a lottery ticket, they never suspect the many ways their lives will change—or that for each of them, love will be the biggest win of all.

Kit Averin is anything but a gambler. A scientist with a quiet, steady job at a university, Kit's focus has always been maintaining the acceptable status quo. A sudden windfall doesn't change that, with one exception: the fixer-upper she plans to buy, her first and only real home. It's more than enough to keep her busy, until an unsettlingly handsome, charming, and determined corporate recruiter shows up in her lab—and manages to work his way into her heart . . .

Ben Tucker is surprised to find that the scientist he wants for Beaumont Materials is a young woman—and a beautiful, sharp-witted one at that. Talking her into a big-money position with his firm is harder than he expects, but he's willing to put in the time, especially when sticking around for the summer gives him a chance to reconnect with his dad. But the longer he stays, the more questions he has about his own future—and who might be in it.

What begins as a chilly rebuff soon heats up into an attraction neither Kit nor Ben can deny—and finding themselves lucky in love might just be priceless . . .

About the Author

Kate Clayborn lives in Virginia, where she's lucky enough to spend her days reading and talking about all kinds of great books. At home she's either writing, thinking about writing, or—during long walks around her fabulous neighborhood—making her handsome husband and sweet-faced dog listen to her talk about writing.

Kate loves to hear from and connect with readers—follow her on Twitter, on Instagram, and on Facebook. Visit her at www.kateclayborn.com to sign up for her newsletter.

CPSIA information can be obtained
at www.ICGtesting.com
Printed in the USA
LVHW03s0005200618
581338LV00001B/56/P